The
Dark
Lake

The Dark Lake

Sarah Bailey

GC

GRAND CENTRAL
PUBLISHING

NEW YORK   BOSTON

Grand Central Publishing
Hachette Book Group
1290 Avenue of the Americas, New York, NY 10104
grandcentralpublishing.com
twitter.com/grandcentralpub

Originally published in 2017 by Allen & Unwin in Australia
First U.S. hardcover Edition: October 2017

Grand Central Publishing is a division of Hachette Book Group, Inc. The Grand Central Publishing name and logo is a trademark of Hachette Book Group, Inc.

The publisher is not responsible for websites (or their content) that are not owned by the publisher.

The Hachette Speakers Bureau provides a wide range of authors for speaking events. To find out more, go to www.hachettespeakersbureau.com or call (866) 376-6591.

Library of Congress Cataloging-in-Publication Data has been applied for.

ISBNs: 978-1-5387-5990-5 (hardcover), 978-1-4789-2258-2 (audiobook, downloadable), 978-1-5387-5991-2 (ebook)

Printed in the United States of America

LSC-C

10 9 8 7 6 5 4 3 2 1

For my sons, Oxford and Linus,
who have somehow managed to make the world
feel both bigger and smaller,
at exactly the same time.

These violent delights have violent ends
And in their triumph die, like fire and powder,
Which as they kiss consume.

William Shakespeare, *Romeo and Juliet*,
Act II: Scene VI

now

When I think back to that summer something comes loose in my head. It's like a marble is bouncing around in there, like my brain is a pinball machine. I try not to let it roll around for too long. If I do, I end up going funny behind the eyes and in my throat and I can't do normal things like order coffee or tie Ben's shoelaces. I know I should try to forget. Move on. It's what I would tell someone else in my situation to do. Probably I should move away, leave Smithson, but starting over has never been a strength of mine. I have trouble letting go.

During the day it's not so bad. I'll be in the middle of doing something and then my mind wanders to her and the little ball ricochets through my head and I stop talking in the middle of a sentence, or I forget to press the accelerator when the lights go green. Still, I can usually shake it away and keep going with whatever I was doing without anyone noticing.

It's amazing what you can keep buried when you want to.

But sometimes, late at night, I let myself think about what happened. Really think. I remember the throbbing heat. I remember the madness in my head and the fear that pulsed in my chest. And I remember Rosalind, of course. Always Rosalind. I lie flat on my back and she appears on my bedroom ceiling, playing across it like a lightless slide show. I click through the images: her in grade one with her socks pulled up high; her walking down Ayres Road toward the bus stop, backpack bobbing; her smoking a cigarette on the edges of the school oval; her drunk at Cathy Roper's party, eyes heavy with dark liner.

Her at our debutante ball, dressed in white.

Her kissing him.

Her lying on the autopsy table with her body splayed open.

I can't even tell anymore whether the pictures are from my memories or ones I came across during the case. After a while, everything starts to blur together. A few times I've got it all mixed up and Ben ends up on my bedroom ceiling, sliced open on the autopsy table. When that happens, I get up, turn on the hallway lights and go into his room to check on him.

Once it was all over I promised to make a fresh start. To stop letting the past weigh me down. But it's been hard. Harder than I thought it would be. So much happened that summer. It lives on inside me somehow, writhing around like a living beast.

It's weird, but in a way it's sort of like I miss her.

I miss a lot of people.

One memory I do have that I know is real is from our final year of high school English. It was warm and the windows were open on both sides of the classroom. I can still feel the breeze that ruffled across us as Mrs. Frisk roamed around the room firing questions at us. We were studying Shakespeare, *Romeo and Juliet*. This class was different from the English classes in earlier years. If you made it this far, you were serious. Even the boys would generally pay attention. No one sniggered at the love scenes like they had a few years earlier.

Rose always sat up the front, her back ruler-straight from years of ballet, her thick caramel hair spilling down it like a wave. I always sat near the door on the other side of the room. I could look at her from there. Watch her perfect movements.

"What do you think Shakespeare is getting at when he declares that 'these violent delights have violent ends'?" Mrs. Frisk's forehead beaded with sweat as she stalked around the edges of the room, stepping in and out of sun puddles.

"Well, it's foreboding, isn't it?" offered Kevin Whitby. "You know they're doomed from the start. Shakespeare wants you to know that. He loved a good warning to set the scene. These days he'd be writing shit-hot anti-drug ads."

Soft laughter bubbled up from the class.

"It's a warning, sure, but I don't think he's saying they should stop."

Everyone paused, caught in the honey of Rose's voice. Even Mrs. Frisk stopped pacing.

Rose leaned forward over her notebook. "I mean, Shakespeare goes on to say, 'And in their triumph dies, like fire and powder. Which as they kiss consume.' So he's basically saying everything has consequences. He's not necessarily saying it's not worth it. I think he's suggesting that sometimes things are worth doing anyway."

Mrs. Frisk nodded enthusiastically. "Rose makes an important point. Shakespeare was big on consequences. All of his plays circle around characters who weigh up the odds and choose to behave in a certain way based on their assessments."

"They didn't make great choices for the most part," said Kevin. "They all had pretty bad judgment."

"I disagree." Rose looked at Kevin in a way that was hard to categorize as either friendly or annoyed. "Romeo and Juliet were all-in right from the start, even though they knew it probably wasn't going to end well." She smiled at Mrs. Frisk. "I think that kind of conviction is admirable. Plus, it's possible that the happiness they felt in their short time together outweighed any other happiness they'd have felt if they lived their whole lives apart." She shrugged delicately. "But who knows. Those are just my thoughts."

I think about that day often. The fresh fragrant air pouring through the windows as we debated the story of the two young lovers. Rose lit by the sun, her beautiful face giving nothing away. Her elegant hands diligently making notes, her writing perfect compared to my own crude scrawl. Even back then, she was a mystery that I wanted to solve.

There were a few minutes when I was alone with her in the autopsy room. I felt wild. Absent. Before I could stop myself I was leaning close to her, telling her everything. The words draining out of me as she lay there. Her long damp hair hanging off the back of the steel table. Glassy eyes fixed blindly on the ceiling. She was still so beautiful, even in death.

Our secrets circled madly around the bright white room that morning. Rocking back and forth on my heels as I stood next to her, I knew how far in I was again, how comprehensively her death could undo me. I looked at Rosalind Ryan properly for the last time before breathing deeply, readying myself, letting her pull me back into her world, and I sank down, further and further, until I was completely, utterly under.

Chapter One

Saturday, December 12, 7:18 a.m.

Connor Marsh jogs steadily around the east side of Sonny Lake. He throws a quick glance at his watch. He is making great time and it feels good being out of the house and running in the fresh air. The kids were crazy this morning; they'd woken at six and were still bouncing off the walls when he left the house an hour later. The place is way too small for two little kids, especially boys, he thinks. And Mia was in such a foul mood. He can't believe that she had a go at him about the fishing trip next weekend. He hasn't been away in ages and has been taking the boys to footy or soccer every Saturday morning for over two years now. Connor grimaces, frustrated at how unreasonable she can be.

His feet pound along the dusty track, making an even beat. *One, two, one, two.* Connor often finds himself counting when he is trying not to think too much about running. His legs burn more than they used to and his ankle hasn't been the same since he fell off the ladder at work a few years back. Still, he is fitter than most guys his age. And he has a full head of hair. Lots to be grateful for.

The day starts to wake in earnest. Connor catches glimpses of the sun through the messy tips of the gums. Another scorcher is on the way. Birds trill from their lookouts and the wispy haze of sleep across the lake is starting to clear. Connor sighs. He's taking the kids to a fifth birthday party at ten, followed by a seven-year-old's birthday party this afternoon. Weekends sure are different these days. He would give almost anything to crack open a beer and watch the cricket in peace.

Connor steps heavily on a stick. It flicks up and scratches along his shin.

"Shit." He stumbles before regaining his balance. The cut stings as it breaks into a thin red line. He slows his jogging, panting. He won't bother doing another lap now; he needs to head back home anyway to help get the kids ready for their party marathon. Walking, he places his hands on his hips as his heartbeat calms, breathing jaggedly from his mouth.

A duck flies low across the water, wings outstretched. Rubbish dots the edges of the lake. Chip packets and Coke bottles are held hostage by the rocks and submerged branches. The heat has caused the lake to creep away from its banks. Tree roots are exposed like electric wires. Connor's eyes scan the water. He really should come running here more often; get back into a routine. He can remember training here for athletics years ago, doing laps around the track before school, the burn in his thighs. He notices the gaping eye of the stormwater drain, pitch black against the glare as it disappears into the clay wall of the lake. A little further along, Connor notices something caught at the water's edge; it appears to be made from some kind of fabric. He squints and realizes he is looking at hair swirling out past a line of reeds. His feet lock to the ground. It looks like human hair, a woman's blonde hair. His heartbeat picks up again. His limbs feel hollow. Two steps forward confirm it is indeed a woman face down in the lake. Bare white arms are visible every time the water ripples and long-stemmed red roses bob across the top of her watery grave.

A cluster of swans watches Connor from under the old wooden bridge. One of the birds lets out a low, haunting cry.

He drops to his knees and worries for a moment that he will be sick. His breathing slows and then quickens again. He looks back at the body and then jerks his gaze away. Barely thinking, he dials triple zero and thrusts his phone against his ear.

Chapter Two

Saturday, December 12, 7:51 a.m.

I stand in the shower with my head against the wall as blood oozes out of me. I had guessed I was about six weeks along but hadn't been sure exactly. I wonder if my denial has made this happen; my complete lack of acceptance. My sheer desperation for it not to be real. The blood mixes with the water before it disappears down the drain and I squeeze my eyes shut and wish I was a little girl again, tucked up in bed, my mother's soft pout of a kiss pressing against my forehead.

God, I miss her.

Scott left early this morning to beat the traffic. He's secured a couple of weeks' concreting work on a large housing development just north of Paxton, a town about thirty k's east of Smithson. Ben is at my dad's; he slept there last night because of our early starts. Dad will be getting jumped on about now. Ben is always so cuddly in the mornings.

I can hear my phone ringing but I don't move. The cool tiles feel firm and reassuring against my skin as I spread my palms out on either side of my face. Trying to focus. Trying to feel normal. After a few minutes I lift my head. My vision takes a while to adjust. My guts ache, the pain settling in low and deep.

I'm exhausted. I feel separate to my body. To my mind.

I know I should probably go to the hospital but I also know that I probably won't.

The bathroom is misty with steam. The bleeding seems to have slowed. I wash myself carefully and turn off the tap. The pipes shudder through the walls. I step out of the shower and pull a dark gray towel around me. I look at the mirror but I am just a blur in the fog. In the bedroom, I throw the covers across the bed and kick a slipper underneath it, stopping for a moment and leaning forward to catch my breath as sharp pain runs through me again. I dress quickly, lining my pants with a pad before pulling on black jeans, a plain gray t-shirt, low black boots. The temperature is climbing steadily and the leftover heat from yesterday still lingers unpleasantly in the house. I pour a glass of water and throw back a couple of Advil. Then, staring at the wall, I think about the day of loose ends in front of me: paperwork, a few reports to follow up, a cold case Jonesy has asked me to review. I picture my small desk in the middle of the station's main room and wish that I had an office. My mobile rings again as I am towel-drying my hair: it's Felix, and I look at his name on my phone and think a million things.

"Yep, hi." I keep my voice light. "I'm on my way. I'm just about to walk out the door."

"Go straight to the lake, Gem," he says, and I love the way his accent curls around my name.

I try to understand what he's saying. "Why? What's happened?"

"A body's been found. It's a teacher from Smithson. A Rosalind Ryan."

The room turns upside down. I sit heavily on the bed as I clutch at my throat, forcing myself to breathe. Felix keeps talking, oblivious. "She used to be a student there too, apparently. Your age. You probably knew her."

Set in between a burst of mountain ranges, Smithson is a little oasis of greenery in the middle of endless fawn-colored acres of Aussie farmland. Smithson is known for "catching the rain" that runs from the mountains, which is ironic as it's the surrounding farms that actually need it. It's changed a lot over the past decade. Carling Enterprises, a major cannery business, built a manufacturing plant on the outskirts of the town in the late nineties, just as I was finishing school. The large silver structure already looks grossly out of date but is nevertheless a hive of activity. It milks the surrounding area dry, sucking the fruit from the trees and yanking the vegetables from the ground, and in return spits out over ten million cans of tinned fruit and vegetables every year. This productivity has slowly but steadily grown Smithson from a modest population of just under fifteen thousand to one of almost thirty thousand. Factory workers, truck drivers, engineers, food scientists, marketing people: new faces are everywhere. Suddenly, Smithson, the Noah's Ark town that had always proudly boasted two of everything, multiplied. There are five bakeries now, and that's just in the town center. Someone told me that Carling does this all over the world: bases itself in regional areas where the land is cheap and permits are easy to come by, and implants its business into a community, completely changing the landscape and the culture. In fairness, Smithson probably needed a bit of a kick in the arse, but it can be unsettling watching the giant trucks descend on our little world, the roads groaning under their weight, the smoke streaming out behind them.

To the east of the town center is a large lake surrounded by dense bushland and a popular community park. Sonny Lake is really Smithson Lake but no one ever calls it that. I don't know why, but it's been Sonny Lake as long as I can remember. Even the road signs read *This Way to Sonny Lake*. My parents were married there in a very bohemian ceremony back in the seventies. I've got a photo of Mum from that day on my bedside table. It was taken just after she and Dad said their vows. There are daisies in her hair and a glass of punch in her hand. She looks about twelve.

The lake backs onto the main high school. When I was in primary school I used to come down here with Mum to feed the ducks and to hunt for four-leaf clovers in the grass. In my high school days, the lake was where we came to smoke cigarettes, drink stolen alcohol and kiss boys. The old gazebo on the little bridge across the water provided the perfect place for a ghostly séance, and the ancient wooden tower in a nearby clearing was a great vantage point from which to see if someone was coming. Once you climbed its creaky, winding staircase, you reached a lookout where you could see the entire lake, the main highway and all the way to the high school. It was also a great place to hide. Before he died, Jacob and I had spent hours up there talking and kissing and more. I close my eyes briefly, picturing his young face. He feels so far away now.

I try to avoid coming here.

Sonny Lake is already swarming with cops who are fencing off nosy passers-by. The lake is a popular hangout in the summer and, around two years ago, the council built one of those modern, soft-edged playgrounds at the north of the park to complement the rickety old one that remains to the west, but I've never thought to bring Ben; there are way too many memories lurking around for a Sunday afternoon play date.

Several people in jogging gear huddle nearby, talking quietly to each other as I walk past. Then I spot him. Detective Sergeant Felix McKinnon, my partner. My insides bubble gently and as always I marvel at the effect he has on me. His brow is furrowed as he bends down to talk to one of the forensic guys who is brushing at the ground just off the path. I see a white tarp a little further down in the reeds. Casey, our photographer, is snapping away to the left of it.

I allow myself to process the fact that Rosalind Ryan is dead. I suddenly feel startled to find myself a fully grown adult. I remember how her summer school dress molded to her womanly figure. I remember the way my own uniform brushed below my knees, how I tried to pin it at the waist and the hem to look more like hers. I breathe deeply and exhale slowly. Walking down toward the lake, I set my face to blank. I try to block out the well-worn images of Rosalind that are fighting to settle in my vision. I try to block out everything. The sun is cracking through the last of the clouds and beats down like fire. The air is sharp. Dry. We are going to have to move quickly. We need to get her out of here.

"Hey," I say.

"Hi." Felix smiles up at me, squinting into the sun. "You okay?"

My vision blurs with patches of white. "Yep." I shrug his question away. I gesture to the white tarp. "What are you thinking?"

"Hard to say. We ID'd her from a coin purse in her jacket that had a school library card in it. There's nothing else on her except for her keys, which were also in her jacket. No phone or bag that we've been able to find yet." He wipes at his forehead, already beaded with sweat. "Fuck it's hot." Felix is still trying to get used to the relentless heat that invades Smithson every Christmas. "She was in the water when the guy found her but Anna doesn't think she drowned. She thinks she was strangled. But there's also a nasty injury on her head. No visible stab or gunshot wounds. We'll know more when we move her, obviously." He staggers to his feet. A few gray hairs glint above his ears. The skin around his eyes wrinkles as his gaze meets mine. I look away before I can't.

"So did you know her? Remember her from school?" he asks.

I nod and look out across the lake. Two ducks bob along side by side, the beautiful markings on their faces like stage masks.

"She's not the kind of person you forget."

"Yeah, I figured. Were you friends though?"

"It was high school! We were all friends until we weren't. You know what it's like when you're that age."

He raises his eyebrows and looks as if he's about to say something else, so I cut him off before he can. "Felix, is this our case?"

He's still looking at me curiously but says, "I think so. I was in when the call came through and Jonesy asked me to call you. Matthews might kick up a stink but yeah, I reckon it's ours."

A familiar current pulls through me. A new case. My head clicks into gear as I try to start firming up the possibilities. But it's Rosalind Ryan lying dead over there in the water, I think. It's *her*. My usually reliable brain is stuck on an image of her face and it glitches over and over like a buggy computer screen. The click of Casey's camera forms a steady beat behind us and the sound bores into my ears. I deliberately take a few deep breaths before I say, "Good. I really want to work this one. Look—" I finally turn to meet Felix's eye "—I knew her a bit from school but it's not an issue. Honestly." I try to ignore the throbbing in my abdomen. "So who found her?"

"That guy over there with Jimmy. He went to Smithson High too, but I think he's older than you. He's pretty shaken up. His wife is coming to get him soon. Name's Marsh."

I look at the well-built man clad in running garb sitting on a park bench with Jimmy, one of our constables. I think the man is Phillip Marsh's older brother. I don't think we've ever spoken.

"I'll go and talk to him."

"Okay. Don't be too long—we need to take a look at her before we get out of here."

I make my way over to our witness, trying to remember his name. Spencer? Cooper? Something like that. "Hello."

Jimmy and the man look up at me.

"I'm Detective Sergeant Gemma Woodstock."

Jimmy smiles at me briefly. "This is Connor Marsh. He found the body of the young lady this morning. He was running laps."

"Hi, Connor," I say.

"To be honest I was only going to do one. One lap. I'm not as fit as I used to be." Connor doesn't look at me as he speaks. His eyes are fixed on a stick near his feet. He is nudging it back and forth between them.

"Tell me about when you first saw the body," I say.

He kicks at the stick again. "God, it was so weird. You know?" He looks up at me again and there's a flash of recognition in his eyes. I'm pretty sure that after I finished school and started going to the gym behind the library I'd see him there lifting weights. He squints and turns his gaze to the lake. "I was running. Just down there, along the bend." He points down to a curve in the path about twenty meters from Rosalind's body. "I wasn't thinking. Well, you know what I mean: I wasn't thinking about anything in particular. I was just running. I decided not to do another lap and started to slow down and then I saw her in the water." He breathes out heavily. "I didn't know what she was at first. Thought it was probably rubbish or something. And then I sort of realized what I was looking at in a weird moment. I totally freaked out." Connor pushes his hair back from his eyes and says, "I heard one of the cops say she's a teacher at the school."

I hold his gaze but I say nothing and keep my expression neutral.

"I know the one. She went there too, like us. She was really pretty." Connor looks at me. "Probably in your year, I reckon."

Jimmy's head snaps toward me. I ignore him.

"Connor, did you notice anyone else this morning? Anyone hanging around? Anything at all that you can remember might be helpful."

He is looking at the ground again. I notice the top of a tattoo snaking out of his ankle sock. It looks like the Smithson Saints Football Club emblem. "I don't think I saw anyone. Maybe there was a girl in her car when I first pulled up in the car park. Talking on her phone. I think I remember that."

"Anything else?" I press.

"I don't think so. Well, not really. I think I ran past someone walking their dog at some point. A guy, I think. An older guy maybe. Sorry, it was pretty early and I wasn't paying attention."

"That's okay. If you recall anything else just let us know."

"Do the flowers mean anything?"

"The flowers?"

Connor nods. "Yeah, there were flowers around her in the water. Looked like roses."

I exchange a look with Jimmy. He shrugs subtly. "We can't speculate at this stage. We'll obviously be investigating everything." I speak smoothly but my blood has turned white-hot.

"Can I go soon? My wife is coming to get me but she'll have the kids with her, so I think I should wait near the car park." He glances down toward the crime scene and shivers despite the heat. "Not here."

"That's fine, mate, I'll come with you."

Jimmy's calmness is always reassuring. He'd make a great voiceover artist selling life insurance or something.

"Hey, Connor, one more thing," I say as they get up. "You didn't touch the body, did you?"

"No way. I didn't even go very close. To be honest, I'm not good with stuff like that."

"A good way to be, mate, a good way to be," Jimmy says, leading Connor away.

Rocking onto the balls of my feet, I survey the scene again. A couple of young girls wearing neon running shoes and black lycra are clutching at each other, their faces ashen. They're probably Smithson students, I think, grimacing. There are a few mothers cautiously pushing their children on the swings and half-heartedly helping them to navigate the slide as they fix their eyes squarely on the activity near the edge of the lake. I can hear the low hum of a chopper approaching. Bloody reporters. We need to keep moving.

Felix sees me coming and breaks away from the techs, raising his eyebrows in a question.

"The guy's clear," I tell Felix. "Saw nothing, knows nothing. We'll pull him in later today or tomorrow to get it all logged and double-check with his wife for an alibi, but I doubt he can help us."

"I didn't think so," says Felix. "Well, c'mon, let's talk to Anna and get this done so we can get moving."

"I was going to suggest that exact thing."

We smile briefly at each other as we walk along the rocks to where the reeds start. I see the dark entrance to the stormwater drain and can't help feeling that someone could be watching us from in there.

"Hey," I say to Felix, shaking the paranoia away, "what's with the flowers? Connor Marsh said her body was covered in them."

"Yeah," he says, turning his head so I can hear him. "Long-stemmed red roses were floating all around her in the water. Fucking creepy."

I picture it, thinking for a brief moment how perfect she would have looked covered in roses under different circumstances, and keep following Felix. Suddenly I experience a jolt of emotion so strong, I think I will fall into the water. This can't be real. I focus on remaining upright, my eyes fixed on the back of Felix's head, and breathe deeply.

Gray water laps gently at the brown dirt under my boots and then I see it: a foot, pale and ethereal, floating out from beneath the tarp. I remember watching Rose on the podium at the end of the local pool on a swimming sports day, her dainty feet squared together as she bent down low, snapping her goggles on, ready to jump into the water.

"Hey, Gem!" Anna's head appears from the other side of the tarp.

"Hi, Anna," I say, shielding my face from the sun and stepping over a dirty plastic bag, crab-walking along the edge toward her.

Anna is standing knee-deep in the lake in her waterproof scrubs. She looks like an astronaut. I can tell she is hot; her face is red and her fringe sticks to her forehead in messy little lines.

"Right," she says, when we are close enough. "Well, guys, you know the drill. We have a deceased female, twenty-eight years of age. Her birthday would've been on Christmas Day, actually, according to her ID, which is a Smithson Secondary College teacher's library card. She's been dead for at least five hours, but it could be up to eight; the water makes it hard to tell. I'll be able to be more accurate later. Like I said to McKinnon earlier, I think she was dead before she hit the water. There's a large wound on the side of her head. I'd guess she was struck with a rock or something with rough edges but this should be clear when we do the autopsy. There might be dirt or gravel that confirms the weapon. I'd say she was strangled too, based on the marks on her neck, and obviously I'll want to run tox as well. I'm thinking lovers' tiff. Or a random attack, especially if her wallet is missing." Anna pushes damp hair away from her eyes. "Either way, this isn't pretty. It looks like she's been assaulted too: her underwear is missing and there is some bruising around her thighs and upper arms. Again, I'll know more when we get her back to base. But I can rule out suicide and accidental death for you. This is a homicide."

I look at Felix. He is staring down at Rosalind, seemingly deep in thought.

Anna gestures for the forensic team to come and get Rose's body. The reporters have arrived and are roaming up and down the police line like hungry lions. I see the black puff of a microphone bobbing along above the small crowd. The glint of a camera lens. The flick of sleek, TV-ready hair.

Great, the last thing I need today is a run-in with pocket-rocket reporter Candy Fyfe.

Anna puts her hands on her hips. "Okay, guys, I'm done here. We've taken all the shots and bagged everything. Nothing that I think will be helpful. Mind you, there's bloody rubbish everywhere. Water never helps."

"Yep, much better if everyone was killed in the middle of a wide open sports field on a still day," says Roger cheerily. Roger is one of our longest-serving forensics. He's been with the Smithson police force for almost forty years and has a perpetually sunny attitude regardless of the situation. I often picture him at home, happily telling his wife about his cases: "Yes, the dead girl was strangled, it seems, murdered in cold blood. Pass the salt, please, darling."

Roger and Fred, our other forensic guy, pull up the tarp and place the stretcher carefully underneath Rose's left side. Above us is the belly of a low-flying helicopter, and I come around the right side to block the view of her body. Rose is pulled onto the white surface. Her face is exactly as I remember it. A Disney princess beauty: her even features waiting patiently for a prince's kiss. When I heard a few years ago that she'd returned to Smithson and was a teacher at the school, I was disappointed. I wanted better for her than that. Her hair hangs to the side, and Fred picks it up and pulls it along her face so that it rests across her shoulder and down the side of her arm. He looks at her as if she is a sleeping child. I remember that Fred's wife had their first baby a few months ago and I wonder what is going through his mind.

Rosalind's toenails are painted a vivid blue and there are silver rings on her fingers. Her brows and lashes are dark against her pale skin. I remember trying to re-create those eyebrows in my bedroom. Even though my coloring was much darker than hers, it had never looked right.

Fred and Roger close the body bag around her. The marks on her neck are almost black. Her dark chocolate eyes stare unflinching into the burning sun. The harsh buzz of the zip and then she is gone.

"Right, well, I'll see you all soon, I'm sure." Anna's already checking her phone as she walks off toward the car park.

We instruct the field team to begin the search.

"Start with the area around the lake," I tell Charlie, our field lead. "Then move into the playground and the bushland. And get rid of all these people. It's a bloody nightmare."

Several uniforms start instructing people on the outskirts of the police tape to leave. I watch as a teenage boy casually holds out his phone and takes a photo of Rosalind's body being bundled into an ambulance before sprinting off toward the town center.

We're already running out of time to get in front of this thing.

I turn back to the lake. The water gives nothing away.

Once everything is set in motion, we get into my car and head back to the station. Felix is listening to voicemails. He reaches over and gives my hand a slow squeeze. A deep shiver plays through me. I pull my hand away and flick on the radio to drown out the buzz in my ears. The ache has settled deep in my groin where my belt is pressing and I shift my weight, trying to placate it. I can't tell how much I'm still bleeding and want desperately to get to the bathroom at work. I want to be alone.

I brake suddenly, seeing a red light just in time. Felix throws me a look but I keep my gaze on the road. *Rosalind Ryan is dead. Rosalind Ryan is dead*, I think, over and over. And then I think that somehow I always knew that something like this would happen.

Chapter Three

"Are you sure you're fine to work this one, Woodstock?" says Jonesy. There is coffee spittle in his mustache. His belly protrudes past his pants and he rubs at it distractedly. "McKinnon tells me you knew the dead girl."

We are standing in one of the little offices off the main room of the police station. Ken Jones, our chief superintendent, has obviously decided that Rosalind's murder warrants his presence. I can't remember the last time I saw him down here on a weekend.

I recall flashes of Rosalind's face in the schoolyard. Glimpses of her creamy skin in the school change room, her large eyes glowing back at me knowingly. Years later, I slowed my car to watch her walking in front of me, arms heavy with shopping, her long skirt swishing above her feet. Her grainy face in my high school yearbook faded from the rub of my fingers.

Her staring back at me in class, daring me to look away.

I know every inch of her face.

I clear my throat. "Yes, sir. I knew her a bit but it's not a problem. Honestly. We weren't friends and I haven't really seen her since we were in school. Ages ago."

My heart is flying; I hate lying to Jonesy but how else can I put it? It is impossible to explain Rosalind to him in any other way.

"Well, good. 'Cause I want you to throw everything at this. Both you and McKinnon. Get tight on this one. It's going to be big." He takes a noisy slurp of his takeaway coffee. "Do what you need to do today, sort out her family, and then get some sleep so you can hit the ground running tomorrow."

"Yes, sir, of course."

"You're up to it after last week?"

"Yes, sir."

"Good. Terrible, all that was."

I adjust my bag; the strap is digging sharply into my shoulder. I think back to last Sunday night, to opening the peeling bathroom door and finding the desperate, beaten-down young woman who had decided it would be better to drown her baby son in the bath and then slit her wrists as she held his dead body, rather than spend another night in fear of her violent ex-boyfriend. "Isn't it all pretty terrible these days?"

"Certainly feels like it sometimes. Well, anyway, let's get this show on the road." Jonesy pats me hard on the back as his phone starts to ring. "Ah, here's the bloody maintenance man. The air-con in the main room has carked it again," he says and walks away, scrambling to get his ringing phone out of his pocket. The *Pink Panther* riff is abruptly cut off as he starts barking orders.

I stare at the large painting hanging on the wall next to the water cooler: a blurry blue-gray sky set atop green mountains. I think about Rosalind, dead inside the body bag. My insides are wound tight like a spring, my organs suddenly too large for my body. I tap my foot and wish Felix would hurry. I don't want to be alone with my thoughts right now.

He appears around the corner holding two coffees. He sees me and smiles. "Here. You probably need this."

"Thanks." I take the coffee from him even though the thought of drinking it is making my stomach churn.

"I just spoke to Charlie. They've found her car in the top car park. The one in between the school and the lake."

"Charlie called you?" I say.

"Yeah. Just now."

"I thought you were talking to your wife."

Felix shoots me a withering look. "I was, Gem. And then Charlie called me. Want to see my call log?" His accent wraps sweetly around the word "*log*" and I want to kiss him.

"Don't be silly."

"Her car's not a primary crime scene, apparently. Anna's gone back to do a once-over but it's locked and seems fine. We can go have a look before they move it, if we want."

"Okay. Good."

"So, since her car was in the lake's top car park, maybe she knew she was going to end up at the lake last night?" he says.

I think about this. "From memory, the car park at the school is tiny. The teachers would use that lake car park all the time because it's only a five-minute walk away. So she might have just always parked there."

"Maybe it's changed since you went there," says Felix.

"I don't think so. I drive past there sometimes and it looks pretty much the same." I know I'm talking quickly. I stop to breathe.

Felix cuffs me amicably on the shoulder but then lets his eyes linger on mine. A flutter runs through me. "Are you really okay, Gem? It must be weird going to school with her and then seeing her like this."

"Seriously, I'm fine. It's just a bit of a shock, I guess."

"Okay, right, you two." Jonesy is off the phone. "C'mon, let's get this thing moving. Get Matthews and Kingston as well. I want them across this, just in case."

I roll my eyes but Felix walks off to grab the others. Gerry Matthews and Mac Kingston, both in their late forties, are detective sergeants too but wear their superiority like a badge. They have no time for me and the feeling is mutual.

Once the five of us are crammed into Jonesy's messy office, we work through what we know.

"Deceased twenty-eight-year-old female. Rosalind Elizabeth Ryan. English teacher at Smithson Secondary College. It appears she lived alone in a small place on the highway. The body was discovered this morning at Sonny Lake, just before seven-thirty a.m. She was bashed and strangled, and there's suspected sexual assault." Felix reels off this information as if it is a classified ad and I can almost pretend I don't know her. That I can't see her lifeless limbs floating in the water.

"And who found her?" asks Jonesy. "Some jogger you said, Woodstock? Have we cleared him?"

"Yes, sir, I think he's clear. He knew her very vaguely but we'll obviously get a lot of that with her growing up here and being a teacher at Smithson." My voice sounds odd, like I'm talking from the next room.

"Okay, get his statement sorted and put that to bed. What else? Time of death?"

"Anna thinks late last night or early this morning," I tell them.

"Any ideas on what she was doing down at the lake?"

Matthews clears his throat. "There was a big production on at the school last night. A stage play, I guess. My wife went. I just spoke to her. She said that at the end our dead girl was up on stage getting flowers and doing a thank-you speech. Apparently the play was very good."

I remember Rose on stage in our final year of school, absolutely captivating as Medea. Her wild eyes like daggers as she looked out over the audience, bemoaning her plight.

"She was always really into acting," I say.

"Woodstock knew her back in school," Jonesy explains to the others.

I avoid making eye contact.

"Right," Jonesy continues, "well, the school needs to be a secondary crime scene, pronto. Seems like she never made it home. Seal it off and start working over it. And check out her place too."

"I've already had a team seal it off," I say, ignoring the look that Kingston gives Matthews.

"Good," says Jonesy. "You and McKinnon check it out once the forensics have gone through it. Interview whoever you need to. Who's going to do the family?"

"I'm happy to…"

"No." Jonesy waves Matthews' offer away. "I want McKinnon and Woodstock to do the family." He looks me in the eye. "The father is a bigwig in business, so tread carefully. Apparently he's very friendly with Mayor Cordon. I want the formal ID done asap. People are talking so we need to confirm the identity today. Autopsy tomorrow; Anna knows already. Once all that's sorted, I want you to get a grip on what happened at the school last night. Who, what, where, the usual. Reporters are already clogging up the phones. I can't believe your mate Candy Cane hasn't called me yet, Woodstock, but it's only a matter of time."

"She's not my mate, sir."

"She's a pain in the arse, that's what she is, but nonetheless she and the rest of the rat pack will be all over this. It's a great story and just in time for Christmas. Bloody fucking nightmare." He pushes at his sparse hair and rubs his eyes. He seems surprised to find us all still there when he looks up. A few beats go by until he roars, "Well, go on then—move it!"

We scatter.

I found my feet when I became a cop. After years of teetering on the brink, wildly close to the edge, the force pulled me back to safety; I walked tall again. Dad said my uniform made me look strong. I think that I simply stopped looking at the ground when I wore it. In the beginning my days were reactive: traffic accidents, petty theft, lost property, broken windows. Over time they became more proactive: tracking known offenders, looking for patterns, getting inside their heads, attempting to predict and prevent their next move. We had a lot of grads from the city come and do stints with us. Typically, young cops need to do their time in the regional areas but it's not reciprocal; I haven't done more than a few weeks in the city, not since my training. Smithson and its surrounds are all I've ever really known.

A good four-hour drive from Sydney, it's hot here in the summer and freezing in the winter, but I soon discovered that crime isn't seasonal. Along with the wholesome country air comes a lot of booze, a lot of boredom and a whole lot of violence. Felix, fresh from the streets of London, assured me that the police skills we apply here are the same, it's just the scale that is different. I'm sure that's not true—I think he just didn't want me to feel like I was missing out—but either way, I know that everyone would agree that I'm good at this. It suits me.

From the beginning I liked the hunt. The endless puzzles to figure out. The permission to focus on one thing and shut out everything else. It's a profession sympathetic to selfishness. I found it relaxing after years of blaring noise to legitimately claim tunnel vision, to dive wholeheartedly into something, to have an excuse not to talk to people, to justify my mysteriousness.

Being a female cop in Smithson did come with its challenges, but in a way I reveled in those too. They gave me something hard and real to buck up against. A living, breathing obstacle that I could conquer; a stark contrast to the murky nothingness that was the deep well of my grief. The soundtrack of leers and put-downs that followed me around only made me more determined, more focused.

Jonesy had a soft spot for me from the start. His initial fascination at a woman being able to navigate the testosterone-soaked locker room extended to him being impressed every time I fronted up, calm and capable, to a nasty road accident, a messy suicide or a violent conflict. To his credit, he seemed determined to avoid typecasting me, often deliberately sending the others to break bad news to family members rather than assuming they needed my soft touch. I'd heard him talking on the phone a few months into my appointment, declaring to someone that I was "as tough as old tin." It wasn't a father figure I lacked, and he never overstepped the fence I had carefully built around myself, but I did get a bonus uncle in Jonesy, and I can't say I minded. The guys in the station *were* brutal and his backing was not so overt as to make things worse for me; rather, he became a subtle and powerful—albeit bumbling—ally, and I yearned to make him proud of me.

It had been a long time since pride had seemed important; the grief that swarmed around Dad and me did not allow a normal parent–child relationship. Our focus was almost solely on survival. Dad never relaxed enough to enjoy parenting me most of the time; there were moments of nervous joy but generally he was too busy looking over our shoulders for looming danger. Having lived only with Dad since I was thirteen, I initially found the proximity of so many other people, particularly so many men, overwhelming. Their scent hung over the station; their constant hunger unsettled me. Their jokes were crude and cruel. I set my jaw and swallowed my frustration and, occasionally, my fear. I had very little on my side. Not only was I female but I was also young, keen and sharp: a dangerous combination.

About a month into my first year, I attended a robbery at one of the local garages with Keith Blight, a worn-out old boy who saw no place in the police force for women. He thought I'd be better off taking my feelings and my handbag straight to the nearest beauty parlor. The mechanic had managed to detain the thief, a scrawny, acne-scarred backpacker who spat on the ground approximately every sixty seconds. We arrived and I pulled out my handcuffs only to have the ferrety criminal smirk at me and then exchange a knowing look with Blight, who seemed equally amused. They both thought I was a joke. A kid cop and a girl to boot. I said nothing, knowing that any protest, any reaction at all, would simply be deemed emotional, giving them exactly what they expected from me. My face burned as I pushed the backpacker's oily head down and shoved him into the police car. Anger raged through me, threatening to erupt into a scream.

And then, a few months later, the Robbie case came along and changed everything.

Chapter Four

Saturday, December 12, 1:46 p.m.

Smithson in general is fairly leafy and George Ryan's house is undoubtedly in the leafiest part of town. Smithson has always had a wealthy area to keep the rest of us in our place; it's just that before the Carling plant was built, it used to be the retail franchise owners, a handful of bank managers and the former owners of successful family farms who lived at the base of the rolling hills on the edge of town, on the opposite side from Sonny Lake. Now it's more likely that Carling's top-tier executives are neighbors both at home and at the office.

"Nice place." Felix ducks down to look up through the windshield at the full length of Rosalind's old house.

"Yeah."

"I imagine this house was party central back in the day?"

"Unfortunately not. Rosalind kept to herself. Well, sort of." I try to explain. "She was popular but she was very private. I don't know if anyone really went to her house."

"Why not?"

"I'm not sure. She was unusual."

"Well, hopefully she's got easier to work out since then."

"Yeah," I say again, though I doubt it.

I look up at the house too. I know her bedroom used to be on the second level to the left: I would occasionally catch her silhouette in the window as I watched from the other side of the street.

I shake myself back into the present and push my phone onto silent.

"Okey-dokey," says Felix. "Let's do this, then, shall we?"

We get out of the car and slam the doors heavily behind us. I don't mind if George Ryan knows someone is coming, though of course nothing will ease him into the shock he is about to get. Unless he already knows, I think darkly.

Telling family and friends about a murdered loved one is never easy. Parents are usually the worst, their grief so pure and unchecked. They tend to immediately recast the dead adult offspring back to their childhood version. Distraught mothers often relive the moment they first held their infants, and shape their arms into an empty cradle, even if the birth was sixty years earlier. On the other hand, children of the newly dead are often bravely stoic, realizing their new responsibility and position at the top of the food chain. Plus, they are busy with a myriad of distracting, grown-up jobs: legal tasks, funerals to arrange, relatives to inform. Siblings are distraught, of course, but there is often a strange ingrained competitiveness that has them imagining the roles reversed. They picture themselves as the dead child and compare hypothetical grief and reactions. Even in death, the ability to pull rank can be strong.

Informing the family of a murder is particularly difficult because our best chance at a solve is maintaining a completely open mind. We must have the ability to see past a broken stare. To look beyond pale-faced agony and the wringing of hands. Murderers are people too, and in many instances the grief they show for a victim is real, despite having caused it.

George Ryan is listed as Rosalind's next of kin. I'm pretty sure she also has three older brothers.

"I can only remember one of them," I tell Felix, as we walk to the door. The driveway is lined with a cloud of wattle and the sun bounces off it, making a ferocious yellow blaze. "He seemed kind of cocky. I think the others were a bit older than us."

"No mother?" asks Felix.

"I don't know," I say. "Not that I can remember."

The front door flies open just as I am about to press the doorbell.

"Hello?" A short, clean-shaven man with neatly combed hair and a complexion starved of sunshine stands in front of us. A rush of air-con swirls out from behind him. His small eyes dart back and forth between us.

"Hello. Sorry to arrive unannounced but we need to speak to George Ryan."

The man bobs his head up and down. "Oh. He's only just out of bed. He's not feeling one hundred percent."

"Well, I'm afraid we'll still need to speak with him. I'm Detective Sergeant Woodstock. This is Detective Sergeant McKinnon."

A haze of understanding falls over the man's stare. "You'd better come in then. I'm Marcus. George's son." He steps aside, gesturing for us to enter. On our left is a polished wooden stairway. To the right, a high-ceilinged hallway displays a heavy-looking oil painting.

"Is Mr. Ryan unwell?" Felix asks, as we follow Marcus toward the back of the house.

"He had surgery yesterday," Marcus informs us. "But he's recovering well."

Felix and I exchange looks. We are probably about to bring his recovery to a grinding halt.

"This way, please," says Marcus. "Everyone is in here. My brothers are here too."

He leads us into a large open room at the rear of the house.

Three men sit on a giant cream couch along the right wall of the room. Their eyes are glued to the cricket, which is playing soundlessly in high definition on one of the biggest televisions I have ever seen. The ceiling peaks directly above them and windows are cut into its sides, casting blades of light onto the floor near their feet. Photographs crowd the mantelpiece. On one end there is a large frame featuring a striking raven-haired woman with glittering blue eyes. From the kitchen I hear a radio tuned in to the cricket match on the TV.

Outside, a sparkling lap pool glitters in the bright sunlight.

"Hello," I say. "I'm Detective Sergeant Woodstock and this is Detective Sergeant McKinnon."

Six eyes look at me blankly.

"Please sit," insists Marcus, coming up behind me and ushering us into chairs. "This is my father, George Ryan. And my brothers, Bryce and Timothy."

If Bryce and Timothy recognize me, they don't show it. Steam curls from the mug that George Ryan is holding. He is the largest of them all: broad across the shoulders and overweight, but in a way that suits his frame. He is very pale. His hands shake as he steadies the tea on his knee. His younger sons flank him. While Marcus looks like he has stepped straight out of the early twentieth century, Timothy and Bryce are quintessential modern Aussies. They are both deeply tanned with loose-necked t-shirts, surf-brand shorts and wiry hair like ivy woven up their muscled legs. Straight white teeth underneath denim blue eyes complete the look.

I look at each of them in turn before speaking to George Ryan. "Unfortunately, we have some very bad news." I take a huge breath and close my eyes briefly before saying, "Your daughter Rosalind was found dead this morning. We believe she was murdered."

A ball connects with a bat on the radio and it sounds like a gunshot. The crowd oohs and aahs, and I watch carefully as the shock hits the Ryans square in the face.

Marcus looks desperately at his father and brothers and then back to me. "What?"

George Ryan shifts into an upright position, clearly in pain. "Rosalind is dead?"

Timothy and Bryce are gobsmacked bookends staring dumbly into their laps.

"Yes. I'm so sorry."

Marcus scurries to the kitchen and snaps the radio off. The silence rushes through the house and I find myself desperate to say something. "We believe Rosalind died late last night or very early this morning. After the play at the school."

"What happened?" George Ryan's booming voice is glorious. Syrupy and thick, it catches in his throat.

Felix leans forward. "We don't know yet, Mr. Ryan, but it is a homicide investigation. Your daughter was attacked. We're terribly sorry, but can we please ask you all a few questions? We really need to know as much as we can. It will help us to find out who did this."

George Ryan lets out a deep sigh, straight from his soul. He grimaces as he pulls himself up to place his mug on the coffee table. I imagine going from the ordeal of surgery to being told that your only daughter has been murdered.

"My little girl is dead?" His face wobbles wildly and his eyes seem unable to focus. He looks to me for confirmation. To check that the awful thing I just said is true.

I nod quickly, considering his reaction.

He pushes his fingers against his eyes and holds them there for a moment. "Ask us anything," he says to the floor.

"I'll get some water," says Marcus, jumping up from his chair again. His eyes are bright with tears and his lip quivers.

"We're fine, honestly."

"No, no, come on, please," he insists. "It's so hot."

I sense Marcus needs to have a task. "Thank you," I say.

"Get me a water too, please, Mark," says George softly, as Marcus walks out of the room. "And bring me my pills."

Felix is firm. "We know this is a huge shock. Maybe let's start with when you all last saw Rosalind. Timothy, what about you?"

Timothy's eyes are huge. He stares at the mute cricket game on TV, his jaw shaking. "Well, I went to the school play last night. It was a really big deal for Rose." His eyes jump from me, to Felix, to the floor. "I didn't get the chance to speak with her though."

Bryce's head snaps up. "I didn't know you went."

George, too, looks at Timothy in surprise.

Timothy shrugs. "I hadn't seen her since Dad's birthday." He turns to me and wipes some tears from his eyes. "Um, Dad's birthday night got a bit intense. I acted like a dick and Rose was upset. I knew the play was important to her so I wanted to go."

"All she talked about was that play," says a bewildered-looking Marcus, returning with a silver tray on which are several glasses of water. "She was very excited about it when I last spoke to her." He hands me a glass. He speaks so softly I have to strain forward to hear him. "I live in Sydney. I'm home early for Christmas because of Dad's operation yesterday. Rose and I usually speak once a fortnight but I've only seen her once since Dad's birthday in October."

I glance at Timothy in time to see an almost imperceptible twitch of his eyes.

I turn back to Marcus. "Did you go to the play too? Seeing as you were here."

"I only just arrived this morning." His voice breaks and he looks away. He wipes his face with his hand. "I was planning to go next weekend."

I shift my gaze along the couch. "What about you, Bryce? When did you last see Rosalind?"

"At Dad's birthday dinner, like the others. So October the seventeenth." His eyes bore into mine. "I haven't even spoken to her since. We don't really talk much. That sounds awful now." He gulps some water. "But it's true. To be honest, I'm not quite sure this has sunk in yet. What did she do?"

"What do you mean?" I say.

"Why did someone attack her? Was she fighting with someone?"

"What makes you say that?" I ask.

Bryce is sheepish, clearly regretting his comment. "I don't know. I guess I just figured she did something that made someone lose it."

"Did she do that a lot? Get people offside?" Felix probes.

Timothy stares at the floor. Bryce opens his mouth and then closes it. Felix arches his eyebrow at him.

"Well, she can be difficult," says Bryce feebly.

"Difficult?" I say, ignoring his use of the present tense.

Bryce looks to Timothy for support. "Yeah. Well, she always speaks her mind, which I guess some people find challenging."

"Had she mentioned any specific run-ins with anyone lately? Arguments?"

Now Bryce is the one to fix his eyes on the floor. Timothy shakes his head slowly.

George Ryan clears his throat, cutting off our conversation. "I just can't imagine how this could have happened. It doesn't make any sense. No one would want to hurt Rose."

"It's very hard to understand something like this, Mr. Ryan," I tell him. "It may never really make sense, but we need you all to help us try to piece things together." I place my glass down and ask, "When did you last see her?"

"At my birthday as well. I've been away a lot since then, you see, trying to get everything ready before...well." He trails off and then seems to remember he was talking. "She did call me on Thursday to wish me well for my operation. We talked about the play. She was very proud of it, you know." He drops his head and shudders through a hopeless, silent sob.

"It was based on *Romeo and Juliet*, is that right?" I'd looked it up on the school website before we came here.

He lifts his head and focuses watery eyes on me. "Yes, yes, she loved all that stuff. She really battled to get it happening. The school didn't want to put on a play this year. There were issues with funding or something, so it got delayed several times. I think she was quite frustrated about that. She was very passionate about it and kept pushing the principal to endorse it. That's just Rosalind all over: determined."

Bryce, Marcus and Timothy don't move. George Ryan pops some pills out of the packet that Marcus gave him, dropping them on his lap before washing them down with the cold water.

He continues, "And all those kids in year twelve got behind her, agreeing to be in the play even though school had finished. They must have really liked her."

I nod, reminded that we need to talk to all of these students as soon as possible. I wonder what will happen with the play now.

The sun has moved across the floor onto my foot. I pull it away into shadow. "So, Marcus, you were in Sydney last night. Timothy, you went to the play. Bryce, what about you?" I ask.

"I was here. I flew into Gowran yesterday afternoon. I saw Dad briefly at the hospital, but he was pretty groggy so I didn't stay long." He seems out of breath.

"What about after dinner?" I press.

"I had a work call and then had some dinner here. I spoke to my girlfriend at some point. She lives between Smithson and Sydney and was already here at a place she rents out, but she wasn't feeling well, so she canceled our plans just after I landed."

Felix turns to Timothy. "Do anything after the play?"

"Just came straight here. Bryce was here. In his room."

Bryce nods in confirmation.

Something is nagging at me. Timothy and Bryce's "Dear Diary" recall is all a bit too neat. But as I study them I see real sorrow in their eyes. I change gears. "Did Rose have a boyfriend?"

"A boyfriend? No, no. No boyfriend," says George.

"Okay, well, what about earlier this year? Was she seeing anyone?"

"No. Nothing like that. She had a few boyfriends in school and uni but nothing serious. She was very into her teaching. Very dedicated. Not running around like half the silly girls are these days."

Timothy and Bryce exchange loaded looks from opposite ends of the couch. Marcus gets to his feet and hovers near my elbow for a few moments. His anxiety is palpable. He clutches at his hands and then clears his throat twice. "Do you want food? I think we have biscuits or maybe some cake."

"How often are you here?" Felix asks him abruptly.

He stammers, "It—it depends. Probably three times a year."

"And you?" Felix says to Bryce.

"Same. Maybe a bit more. My girlfriend is here almost every second week at the moment so I come with her sometimes."

"And you live in Paxton?" Felix says to Timothy.

"I did. I own a place there. Well, half a place, according to the lawyers. I'm in the middle of a divorce so I'm staying here at the moment. I'll get a new place in the new year."

I catch Timothy's gaze and feel the hairs prickling up my legs.

Felix turns to George. "Mr. Ryan, I have to ask, does Rose have other family? Her mother?"

"My wife Olivia is dead. She died a few days after giving birth to Rose. From a hemorrhage."

"I'm sorry to hear that. That must have been incredibly difficult."

"Yes. It was a shock, just like this. And I had small children to worry about then. Truth be told, Olivia was not a well woman before she died. Marcus was always a great help. Especially once Olivia was gone."

Outside a bird swoops suddenly toward the pool and flits across the surface. Inside, the only sound I can hear is the soft whir of the air-conditioner.

"Is there anything you can think of that might be worth telling us about?" I ask. "Something she said? Even something that seems like a little thing?"

Bryce and Timothy exchange looks again but shake their heads. Marcus swallows noisily. George Ryan just stares at his hands.

"Well, thank you. We'll leave you alone." I stand up and gesture at Felix to do the same. "We truly are so sorry. Look after yourselves. You've had a terrible shock. We'll do everything we can to work out what happened to Rosalind."

They all stand except for George. His eyes fix on me, years and sorrow etched into his face. "Yes. Please find out who did this to my daughter."

Marcus walks us to the front door.

"We'll be working through her phone records, her house, what happened on the night she died—everything." Felix shakes Marcus's hand. "We're doing everything we can."

Marcus holds his hand for a few beats.

Felix adds, "One of you will need to come down to the station today to complete the identification. Your father may not be up to it?"

"Oh. Yes, of course. Well, I'll speak to Dad and see whether he wants to . . . or perhaps I'll just go myself. He's probably not really well enough. He's supposed to have strict rest until Monday."

"How about I call you in an hour? You can let me know then," says Felix.

"Yes. All right." His face crumples before he pulls it back into line. "God," he says, almost to himself.

"Marcus, make sure you tell any other family and friends sooner rather than later," I say gently. "This will be all over the news tonight."

He nods, looking lost.

We step outside into the heat.

Felix pauses and turns to face Marcus again. "Did Rosalind keep living here after she finished school?"

Marcus stands in the doorway. I can see glimmers of his father starting to creep onto his face. "Ah, no, she wanted to do the student thing. Plus, I think being the only girl . . . perhaps it was a bit hard for her. I think she felt a bit lost living here. She never really found her place. Anyway, she moved to Sydney, did arts at uni and traveled a bit—you know, normal stuff." He pauses and we wait, both thinking he's going to say something else, but he just stands there blinking at us.

After a few moments Felix smiles sadly. "Well, take care, okay? Like I said, I'll give you a call in a little while. But you call us anytime you need. Or if you think of anything."

Marcus moves his mouth into a tight smile and closes the door gently, his footsteps echoing as he walks down the hall.

"Wow," Felix whistles, as we make our way down the driveway.

"Wow what?"

"I don't know, but they're something."

We get back into the car. "Can you be more specific?"

"Well, I don't know where to start." Felix fastens his seatbelt. "I mean, we've obviously dropped a bombshell on them, but they seem so *weird*. No wonder she got out of there."

"Define 'weird'."

"*That*." Felix makes his eyes bug out and I laugh.

"Timothy looked at me funny," I say. "Like defensive or something."

"He had a weird vibe. They all did. Especially the younger two."

"Well, they were in shock."

Felix dismisses the Ryans' shock with a wave of his hand. "They were strange. Like cardboard cut-outs. And Marcus would have to be the most awkward person on the planet. I want to run background on all of them and get alibis confirmed asap."

"Of course," I agree. "I just don't want to jump to conclusions. Getting news like that throws you. You're allowed to act a bit weird." I start the car and pull away from the curb.

"When can I see you?" Felix says.

"Huh?"

"When can I see you? You know, *properly*?" His voice has a desperate edge and my body stirs in response.

I keep my eyes on the road. I think about this morning in the shower. It feels like it happened a long time ago. I blink the scene away. I wonder if I'm still bleeding. I can hear his breathing next to me. I guide us back toward the station. Felix grabs my thigh hard, digging his fingers in around its curve.

"Monday night," I say, staring straight ahead, my heart beating so loudly I think he can probably hear it.

Chapter Five

Saturday, December 12, 7:03 p.m.

Scott looks up from whatever he is frying on the stovetop as I walk in. He takes in my drawn face and what he calls my "police eyes"; the intensity that is reserved specifically for tracking down evil.

"Bad day?" he says evenly.

I look up to answer him but am distracted by aerial shots of the crime scene at Sonny Lake on the TV. I recognize the top of my head. The footage is interspersed with a recent head shot and a photo of Rosalind dressed in white and smiling prettily at our debutante ball. She looked like an angel that night. I hated my deb dress. I remember Jacob clumsily giving me a corsage on our front porch as Dad self-consciously snapped photos. I spent the entire evening trying to adjust the straps on my dress. In every photo from that night I have a slightly pained look on my face. My foundation was about two shades too dark and my lipstick too brown. If that was my first foray into womanhood I would say I failed spectacularly.

Ben careers around the doorway from the hall and catapults into my legs, wrapping his arms around me. "Mummy!"

"Hey, sweetheart."

"Granddad and I flew a kite!"

"That's great, darling."

"You're on this case?" Scott tips his head toward the TV.

"Yep."

"On the case, on the case," Ben babbles and I shoot a look at Scott.

"Hey, buddy, why don't you go get those stickers Granddad gave you to show Mum?"

I watch Ben's dark curls bob up and down as he runs off along the hallway to fetch his latest favorite thing.

"Did you know her? She went to Smithson, right?"

"Yep. She was in my class. I knew her."

"Jesus." Scott flips off the gas and starts to spoon stir-fry onto two waiting plates and into Ben's Peter Rabbit bowl.

Ben explodes back into the room, clutching his new stickers.

"Look! Look, Mum. See? I have Ninja Turtles! All of them!"

"Wow, darling, that's great. Let's have dinner first and then you can show me properly." I guide him to the table.

We settle in front of the steaming food. Ben eats noisily, making little beeping sounds every time he swallows a carrot. Scott looks down as he eats steadily, one forkful after another. Everything about Scott is precise. If he says he is going to be somewhere at a certain time, he is there. Our bills are paid on time. Our bins are always put out the night before. I often think he would make a good forensic analyst instead of a concreter. He would be at ease with all the order required. Scott prefers things to be linear; to happen in the right order, one after another. Crawl, walk, run. Our being parents without being married drives him crazy.

Ben chatters away about the kite and Ninja Turtles. Scott clears our plates and tidies the kitchen as I am mistaken for monkey bars by our son. I can hear the newsreader recapping the details of Rosalind's death, describing it as the "Smithson school teacher killing."

"Right, kiddo, bedtime for you." Scott tickles Ben on the belly. He squeals with delight.

"Goodnight, baby man," I say, kissing him on the forehead.

He zooms off, still making little electronic sounds as he bounces against the walls.

I grab a beer and sink onto the couch, letting thoughts whirl around my head as I half watch the cricket. Nothing is adding up. By all accounts, Rose was in good spirits last night. The opening night of her school production was a huge hit. It does appear that the aura of mystery she'd carried in high school had extended into adulthood. "She kept to herself" along with "such a beautiful girl" are common themes in the commentary that we and the scrappy bunch of uniforms we've managed to secure so far have gathered from our initial interviews. No one we spoke to knows anything about a boyfriend or a lover, but we haven't made contact with many people yet.

I keep playing the scene with the Ryans over in my mind. There was such a stiffness to their grief. Felix is right—it's odd.

I've uncovered an assault charge against Timothy Ryan: he allegedly punched another guy in a pub brawl about six months ago but the charge was dropped before it ever went to trial. Apparently the victim was his ex-wife's new boyfriend. As a result, Timothy has become the main focus of our investigation. I have some uniforms working through his personal finances and phone records, and we're trying to confirm his alibi.

In the end, Felix went with Marcus to identify Rosalind's body a few hours after we spoke to the Ryans. George wasn't up to it. Marcus didn't say much, but gasped when the sheet was pulled back to reveal his dead sister's face. He nodded quickly and said, "Yes, that's her. Oh my god."

Nothing is cut and dried at this stage. I remind myself that working a case is a marathon, not a sprint, as Jonesy is fond of telling us. Even though he makes it clear he would prefer more sprints.

I flick a quick text to Felix. *Meet me at RR's house tomorrow. 9:30? We can go through it after the forensic guys are done. Then we can do autopsy and get background done before the briefing?*

My phone buzzes almost immediately. *Roger that boss. Very romantic. Dream sweet x*

I knock back the last of my beer. Shrill giggles echo up the hallway from the bathroom. Ben thinks brushing his teeth is hilarious. He is becoming such a little boy now. So confident and so curious. He no longer fits in my arms properly and I'm finding it harder and harder to carry him. I think about him having a sibling; another little Ben. I can see his baby photos on the bookshelf from where I am sitting. I remember breathing in his scent just after he was born, not quite believing that he was mine.

Scott comes back down the hall and I get up to fetch another beer. He pours himself a bourbon and joins me on the couch. He pulls my foot into his lap and strokes it absently. I glance at his profile but he seems intent on the cricket. He needs a shave; his face is dark with patchy bristles. I wonder if he will bring up getting married again. His proposal from a couple of weeks ago still hangs in the air between us. I wish it would disappear. I finish my beer and place the bottle on the coffee table. My eyes glaze as I watch the action on the screen. I slip into sleep for a few moments and wake with a jolt, slightly disoriented.

"You okay?" Scott says.

"Yeah. Just knackered. I better go to bed. We've got a massive day tomorrow."

"It's about to get crazy for you, isn't it?"

I stand up and stretch out my back. It clicks uncomfortably. I picture Rosalind face down in the water. Her bruised neck and vacant stare.

I remember the blood swirling around my toes in the shower this morning.

Felix grabbing my thigh in the car.

The burning pain in George Ryan's eyes.

Scott is still looking at me, his face filled with concern. He runs his finger along the rim of his glass, waiting for me to answer.

"Yes," I say. "It sure is."

Chapter Six

Sunday, December 13, 9:24 a.m.

Rosalind's house is one of eight modest cottages positioned on a nondescript stretch of the Ross Highway. Smithson's public hospital is about five hundred meters up the road and there's a 7-Eleven opposite her driveway. A vacant block of land two doors along on the right has an old mattress propped against the fence and weeds almost a meter high. The dwellings are made from an off-white fibro with peeling cream window frames. A few plants are growing half-heartedly in the common garden beds between the driveways but there are more weeds than anything else. The patchy-looking sawdust scattered in between them looks about a decade old.

Rosalind's place is the neatest. There is a new doormat on her porch and an array of pots around the front entrance with a few flowers reaching out of them. A pair of thongs is set neatly to one side of the door. A bird-bath hangs from the brick window that cuts into the porch and it shifts slightly in the breeze. The drone of the highway traffic rings in our ears as we greet Jimmy and sign the crime scene register.

"Jeez, I guess teaching salaries are even worse than ours," Felix says, slipping booties over his shoes and snapping on latex gloves.

"They probably are," I say, pulling my gloves and booties on, "but considering her family home, this is pretty strange."

"Maybe George is the kind of father who thinks you need to make your own way," Felix suggests.

"Maybe. But he's obviously happy to let Timothy stay with him."

Felix shrugs. "True."

The forensic team deemed Rosalind's house clear yesterday and have taken a few samples to run through the lab. They don't think she returned here after the play, which makes sense given that she was attacked in such close proximity to the school. I'm curious to see her house, to get a glimpse into her private world.

We duck under the line of police tape. I open the front door. Petrol fumes from the highway fill my throat as I step inside.

The house begins in the kitchen. There is a small table with a vase of white daisies in the middle. They are still standing tall, despite the heat, so must only be a few days old. A coffee mug is in the dish rack along with a single plate, a few forks and some spoons. A faded tea towel hangs neatly to the side of the sink. The shelves in the small fridge are scattered with a couple of sauce bottles and a small carton of milk. White wine bottles fill the rack on the fridge door.

Felix picks up the half-empty one and looks at the label. "Nice. This bottle would have cost more than my weekly grocery bill."

I know very little about wine but even I can tell the label is expensive. An almost empty rubbish bin is nestled under the sink. Half-a-dozen empty wine bottles are lined up next to it. Felix confirms that they are all at the upper end of the market. In the freezer is a stack of Tupperware containing some kind of sauce. A bottle of vodka lies next to them.

"She was definitely a drinker who knew her way around wine, but I don't get the feeling she had many guests, do you? They wouldn't fit in here." He gestures to the tiny rooms.

"You think she got blind on her own?" I ask.

"That would be my guess."

I bend down to look through the drawers and cupboards. They are mainly empty, just a couple of worn-looking pots and pans. An old blender covered with a layer of dust. I stand up too quickly and blank for a moment, dizzy. A faint floral scent enters my nostrils.

"It's like she was an old lady or something," says Felix. "With a penchant for outrageously expensive booze."

I nod, running my fingers along the rim of the daisy vase. There are no photos but movie posters are everywhere: in the bedroom, in the lounge and in the spare room. A large old-style cinema poster announcing the debut screening of *The Godfather* is Blu-Tacked to the back of the toilet door. Dramatic scenes seem to close in on us from every angle. Familiar Hollywood faces are everywhere I turn. Magnets dot the fridge, most featuring a quote or a poem.

"She must have been a real movie buff," says Felix, turning in a slow circle to take in all of the posters. "And a bookworm," he adds, noticing the bookshelf in the lounge.

It's the nicest piece of furniture in the house; dark mahogany shelves are built into the wall and run the entire length of the room. Rows and rows of books are crammed into every square inch. There are hundreds of them. I remember how Rosalind seemed to slip into a trance whenever she was reading aloud to the class or acting out a scene. She always seemed so far away. I often wondered what she was thinking.

"Well, she was an English teacher. I guess reading is kind of essential."

"I thought she was a drama teacher?" Felix says, confused.

"I'd say she teaches both," I tell him. "I think they are often paired together. At least, when we went to school they were."

I remember poor Mrs. Frisk yelling at us to use our bodies as tools and then awkwardly watching on through the necessary love scenes in our school plays.

"I bet you would have been good at drama yourself." Felix's eyes dance as he looks at me. The small room suddenly seems smaller.

I wish, not for the first time, that we could go away together. Escape. Sit on a beach and drink cocktails, make huts from driftwood, make fire from sticks and never come back. I want to wrap my body around him forever. But then Ben's little face looms before me and I shake the fantasy away. "Come on," I say, "let's get this done so we can get back to Anna."

I head toward the bathroom, trying to focus. There's an entry from Rosalind's bedroom but a shelving unit has been placed in front of it so I go through the main door off the hallway. I am greeted by a shower over a small bath. The tap drips. Faded gray towels hang from cheap gold hooks on the back of the door and a bathmat riddled with tiny holes is folded on the side of the vanity. I stand in front of the mirror and try to picture Rosalind here every morning, brushing her long blonde hair and putting foundation on her perfect skin, but it doesn't seem to fit somehow.

I pull open the cabinet doors and my face disappears. Inside is like a portal to a different world. Shining bottles of shampoo and body lotion line the bottom shelf. Expensive teeth-whitening products are arranged on the next shelf up alongside what must be thousands of dollars' worth of makeup. L'Oréal, Estée Lauder, Chanel. I don't even know what half of the products are for. I pick up a full contraceptive pill packet and turn it over, wondering whether it means she was seeing somebody. I'd taken mine religiously, but about two months ago had forgotten a day when I worked an early shift and then had got into a routine that was a day out. Then I worked late one night and accidentally skipped another day. A few weeks later I knew immediately that I was pregnant. The aching of my breasts and the slow tumble in my stomach were such visceral reminders of how it had been with Ben.

A few bobby pins are scattered across the middle shelf and a few hair ties are loosely bound around the stem of a designer hairbrush. Despite the expensive products, it still seems impossible that someone as glamorous as Rosalind groomed herself in a bathroom like this.

White chemist packets pepper the top shelf. I reach up and pull them down. Two brands of antidepressants and two Valium prescriptions, dated from September to November.

"What was going on with you?" I whisper.

"What, Gem?"

"She was on meds," I call out.

Felix sticks his head into the bathroom. "Who isn't? Hey, so I can't find a diary or any sex tapes but I did find something weird. Look."

I leave the pills and follow him into the bedroom.

It's a stone. Flat and smoothed by time, it has softened into the shape of a crude love heart. A neat X has been drawn on the back of it with a black marker.

"I found it in her bottom drawer."

I breathe out, thinking. "Anything else interesting in her drawers?"

Felix drops the stone into an evidence bag. Something about that movement reminds me of cracking an egg into a bowl. "Not unless you consider a book of poems and some Bonds undies fascinating."

I swat at him gently and look around the small bedroom, which is so different from what I had pictured for her. The rug on the floor is faded. I recognize the gray bedspread as one that Kmart sold a few years back; I have the same one in blue. My hands are on my hips as I take in the giant artwork hanging above the bed: a stark, haunting painting of a tree. I let my eyes get lost in it.

"This house is so strange. The wine, the movie posters, the art." I gesture to the piece on the wall. "Her makeup is all top-shelf stuff too. But everything else is so basic."

"Yeah, it's pretty weird." Felix is typing a message into his phone. "I'm not really getting a clear read of this woman."

The tiny room is suffocating. I'm struggling to take a proper breath. It's as if my lungs have shrunk. I stamp my foot, suddenly desperate to go outside. Felix jumps slightly.

"C'mon," I say. "Let's have a quick chat to the neighbors. See what they say about her."

We walk to the top of the drive. I take the first cottage, he takes the next, and we alternate like that for the next forty-five minutes. Surprisingly, all seven occupants are home; the investigation gods are clearly smiling down on us. On the flipside, all we learn is that Rose was a perfect neighbor, perhaps a bit shy but always friendly enough.

An itchy young man in number three tells me that Rose had asked him to fix a light fitting a few weeks ago and then left beer on his doorstep the following day. "Didn't expect anything in return. I would have done pretty much anything for that smile of hers. So yeah, I helped her out from time to time. Just odd jobs around the house. She used to sunbathe at the top of the driveway sometimes. I couldn't help but notice. She'd give me a wave. Very friendly." He wipes at his eyes, which are red raw, and scratches his elbow again. "I'm really going to miss her."

An old woman in number five is warier and obviously hasn't been watching the news. "Something's happened to her, hasn't it? I saw the policeman come yesterday with that ribbon you lot use."

"Yes. I'm afraid so."

She purses her lips. "Ah. Beautiful girl like that. It figures."

I don't have the heart to tell her that bad things happen to ugly girls too. It's just that they slip off the front pages a little bit quicker and are less likely to be the subject of *A Current Affair* specials.

"She's dead then?"

"I'm afraid so, Mrs. . . . ?"

"Miss Murphy. Never married." She says this proudly, as if she has escaped a fate worse than death. Then, "Oh dear. That poor girl."

"Yes, it's very sad," I say.

"Well, my fault for not watching the local news, I suppose," she says primly, but her jaw wobbles. "I only ever watch the BBC."

"I'm sorry, Miss Murphy. I know this is hard but I just want to ask you a couple of questions about Ms. Ryan. Did you ever see anyone hanging around her place?"

She clasps her hands formally. "Not really and I'm home all day. I'm always sure to keep an eye on things. I sit in the chair over there near the window."

I look over to a chair rendered shapeless by a mountain of blankets. A fan and a heater are propped about a meter from the chair, aimed at it like spotlights.

"And nothing ever seemed out of the ordinary?" I ask.

"No. I don't think so. She didn't have many visitors, which always seemed strange for a girl like that. A young man did come a few times. Her brother, I think, from the way they were together. And a few weeks back a man came in a posh car. I remember that because it was the same day that Luis died on *The Street*, god bless him, and I stood at the front door to get some fresh air—a bit upset, I was—and I saw the car. They talked outside though. It didn't seem like a romance call, if you know what I mean."

I nod, taking notes. "That's very helpful. Is there anything else?"

"I don't think so. It's actually rather dull around here really."

"Do you remember what her visitors looked like?"

"I think so. The man in the car was flashy. Nice suit, nice smile. Older. Maybe forty? Doing well for himself. The other one was young. Dark hair. Tall. Good-looking, but all slumped over. Terrible posture."

"How old?"

"Well, it's hard to say these days, isn't it? Twenty-five? Or it could be older. Or younger. Honestly, I'm not sure. It's not like I was spying on her."

"Of course not. Well, thank you for your time."

Felix and I meet back outside Rosalind's.

"Anything?" I say to him.

"Nope. Just a bunch of bullshit about how pretty she was. One guy clearly had the hots for her, which normally I'd be all over, except it seems that everyone had the hots for her. You?"

"Some male visitors we need to track down but no real leads. Mainly just a disappointed Miss Marple who's wanting a bit more action than this block delivers."

"Huh," says Felix.

We stand looking at Rosalind's home for a moment, the pots of flowers leading to the plain flyscreen door, the pinwheel in the largest pot doing a lazy turn in the wind.

"Well," I say, "it's usually the way, I guess. Nosy neighbors never come through with the goods. Only in Hitchcock."

"Exactly." Felix looks at me and briefly everything else disappears. I'm so lucky to be able to spend so much time with him, yet it's so horribly unsatisfying. I want to reach out and hold him. Be a normal couple.

Reluctantly I break the moment. "Let's head back. Anna should be ready to start the autopsy by now."

We make our way down the short drive back to the cars. I spot a guy with a camera getting out of a beat-up Holden. I recognize him from the local paper. Smithson is just waking up to Rosalind's death, but no matter what happens it will be in the local news for months. Probably years. I've only been involved in a couple of high-profile cases since I joined the force. I see the guy raise his camera to snap a shot of Felix and me getting into our cars. A familiar shiver runs down my spine as I duck my head out of sight. I've worked on all kinds of mysteries, some that have really got under my skin, some that have got me on the front page of the paper, but certainly none that have ever been as personal as this.

The Robbie case happened by accident. It started as a run-of-the-mill car theft. The girlfriend of the owner reported it and I just happened to be walking through reception when she came in. Young and skinny, she had a voice that hit high notes every third beat as she recounted finding the car missing that morning, how she and her boyfriend heard nothing, how the thief must have known how to get the car started without keys, and how yes, they had insurance, which was lucky.

I listened to all of this with my back turned as I pretended to sort through papers on the bench. Immediately I just knew something was off. Why was this girl coming in to report her boyfriend's missing car—"He's at work, you see, had to catch the bus!"—and how was it that her boyfriend was driving a brand-new Audi when her hair had the distinct tint of supermarket dye and she'd said that she waited tables at Woody's for a job. Her boyfriend, Warren Robbie, was twenty-four and a brickie. Yes, he could come in tomorrow to report the theft if they really needed him to, but they'd figured the cops would want to know immediately. Surely they had a better chance of catching the guy that took the car if they started looking as soon as possible? Surely her statement would be all they really needed?

Dale Morton, the cop on the desk, scribbled down the information and explained that yes, Warren Robbie would need to come in to make a formal statement but that he, Morton, would put the report into the system straight away and see what turned up.

The girl looked deeply concerned at this, twisting her scrawny ponytail around her fingers.

"Often these cars are found burned out in the bush somewhere within forty-eight hours," Morton explained. "Kids just mucking around and having fun. But with a car like that someone may actually want to keep it. Hard car to hide, mind you."

The girl—Stacy Porter, I found out later—smiled at Morton encouragingly, looking up at him through her mascara-coated lashes.

"How long you been with your boyfriend?" he asked her.

"Three years. Almost *too* long. You know what I mean?" Her tinkling laugh chimed through the station but her movements were jerky. This was not a girl who relaxed very often, I surmised. She had the wary look of a beaten dog. "We're really just like good friends now."

"Oh yes, I hear ya. Yep, uh-huh."

A now uncharacteristically diligent Morton took down a few more details and then she left, a cloud of cheap perfume lingering in her wake.

I thought about Stacy and the alleged theft for the rest of the day. I knew in my gut that car wasn't stolen, but that in itself was not so unusual; playing the insurance companies was almost a national pastime. It was the girl. I sensed Stacy's brash front was hiding something far more sinister. I would have bet anything that her boyfriend assaulted her. The smattering of bruises that I'd clocked on her upper arms was a dead giveaway. Again, not so unusual. Unfortunately, over half our cases had an element of domestic abuse, but it seemed risky to send the girlfriend you abused to a cop station. What if she saw it as an opportunity to ask for help?

After Stacy left, I hit the road, dutifully completing my patrol shift at the local shopping center, which was essentially an exercise in tolerance as I listened to Constable Toledo drone on about his in-laws for the best part of the afternoon. Rather than going home after, I headed back to the station to see what I could find out about Warren Robbie. Not much, it seemed. He'd left school just shy of his seventeenth birthday and got his driver's license the day he turned eighteen. He'd held down a job with the same bricklayer ever since and had applied for an ABN a year earlier. He split his time between the original employer and doing jobs for himself. Insurance on the Audi was taken out two months earlier. He'd purchased the car four months before that. In cash, from what I could tell. There were no records of a payment but nothing to suggest he'd have access to that much money either. Certainly his bricklaying salary hadn't paid for the car.

Driving home later, I detoured past the house Robbie rented. A dark wooden cabin on the outskirts of Smithson, about five kilometers from my place, it was set back from the road and surrounded by thick bush. A lonely outside light was on. I sat in the car for almost half an hour, watching the shadows moving through the house.

The next morning, I got in early and deliberately loitered near the front desk. At about eight, Warren Robbie came in. I knew it was him from the ID photos I'd seen the day before but his face was now half covered with a rangy beard and his hair was longer. His left eye was shaded by a large bruise and he wore a long-sleeved jumper despite the temperature outside already passing thirty degrees. Charming and personable, he went through the motions of reporting the theft, joking about having to catch the bus in this heat and politely wondering whether it was okay if he contacted the insurance agency to "get the ball rolling on that stuff."

"Pretty hot out to be wearing a jumper like that," I said from the back of the office.

He looked up, and in the harsh fluorescent light, I could see the soft shine of makeup that had been carefully applied to hide bruises that were clearly far worse than they had initially appeared.

Warren Robbie's mouth pulled into a half-smile. His eyes glittered and, against my will, I found myself looking away. My body shifted into flight mode, my in-built radar deeming him unsafe.

"Guess I'm not that hot yet. Got out of bed and came straight here."

Morton looked back and forth between the two of us, irritated at my comment and seemingly unsure what to do next. *"Anyway,"* he said, glaring at me, "thanks for coming in, Mr. Robbie. I said to the girl—ah, Stacy—that the statement needs to come from you just 'cause all the paperwork is in your name, so if you can sign the stat dec we'll be all set. Just your autograph here, please, and you can be on your way."

Morton laughed awkwardly and Robbie acquiesced, smiling along. He sent a short glare in my direction before leaving.

"Thanks, Dale, my man! Nice doing business with you."

For a couple of days I pushed Robbie and his missing Audi out of my mind. I drove past the dark little house a few times but nothing seemed out of order. About a week after he came to the station a new blue ute appeared in the driveway. There was something about him that my body seemed to physically reject but I had court cases to prepare for, traffic hours to log, and I'd just moved in with Scott, which was taking some getting used to. I'd never shared a room with anyone before and I was surprised every morning to find Scott there. Him moving next to me. His breathing. I was pregnant at the time too, not that I knew it, and my body was responding as if it had been shot by a tranquilizer. But busy as I was, Warren Robbie lurked in my mind like a disease I couldn't quite flush from my system. It wasn't the insurance fraud keeping me up at night. It was the fear in Stacy Porter's eyes when she'd realized that she would have to tell Robbie that he needed to come in himself. It was the quiet evil that I'd sensed in his own dark eyes.

And then, about two weeks later, on an especially hot night, I pulled over a ute with a broken tail-light just outside of Smithson. The windows were down and straight away I knew it was them. The long yellow tail of Stacy's plait hung in parallel with the undone seatbelt. She'd been crying and one side of her face was red but I went through the motions of explaining the issue with the tail-light, writing out the ticket and checking Robbie's license. His presence was overpowering; I'd never felt so repulsed by another person. His anger burned through the air between us and I was unsure how to finish the exchange. I didn't want to let him go. I wanted something on him, something real. I wanted Robbie put away. Permanently. I hadn't wanted anything so badly in a long time. I sensed that he was capable of something truly terrible.

After the tail-light incident I became obsessed. After two weeks of sleepless nights and post-shift drive-bys, I went to Jonesy and told him I had suspicions about Robbie.

"Malc Robbie's boy?" said Jonesy.

"I guess so. I think his dad used to own the petrol station?"

"Sure did. He's dead now. Got himself shot hunting with a mate a few years back, if you can believe it. Some mate. He's got three sons, I think. Warren's the youngest but I don't remember any of them being trouble. A bit rough, perhaps, but hard workers. What's got you going on him, Woodstock?"

"Nothing specific, sir. I guess you'd call it a gut feeling." Jonesy opened his mouth and was, I'm certain, about to tell me just what he thought about gut feelings, so I hurried to add, "But I'm sure that a car he reported stolen was bogus and I think he beats his girlfriend. He had a black eye when he came in too. He's trouble."

Jonesy leaned back heavily in his chair and put his hands behind his head, studying me. I suspected that he thought he looked like a wise old detective, possibly the one from *Batman*, but really his stance just showed off the sweat patches under his arms.

"Woodstock, you're a good cop. You've impressed me so far. You're making the guys on the floor nervous, which I like. I was just telling Lucy the other night that I think you're a great kid." The last part was said gruffly and I felt an unexpected wetness surge in my eyes. "But I'll tell you something for free. Feelings will get you nowhere. This game is all about facts. Get me some facts on the Robbie boy and I'll be right there beside you nailing his arse for whatever he's done, but make sure you focus on doing your day job. There's nothing that some of the boys here would like more than you getting caught up in some wild-goose chase."

"Yes, sir," I said, feeling strangely sated.

"Don't give them the satisfaction, my girl, okay?"

"No, sir, I won't," I replied, meaning it.

Chapter Seven

Sunday, December 13, 11:31 a.m.

Smithson has the only real morgue in a hundred-kilometer radius. Lucky us, we get everything along the scale of death and destruction from around the region. "The Regional Death Capital" as Anna is fond of saying. Felix and I don't always go to the autopsies. Some detectives prefer not to; some claim it muddies their objectivity. Sometimes we take turns and sometimes we're just too thin on the ground. Logistics are as common in death as they are in life. There is relentless scheduling and organizing, slotting in the gory box-ticking around a bit of admin and the weekly pizza night. Felix and I have recently started to let the uniforms go when it's appropriate and we just read the reports afterward, or we have them give us the highlights—there's not always enough death to go round and they need the experience—but there is no way I'm going to miss this one. Mentoring aside, I prefer to be present at autopsies when I can; it sort of feels like it's the least I can do to pay my respects to the victim. I've never told anyone this, but when it is a child I always go. I have this thing about them being lonely and scared and needing some semblance of maternal comfort in that horrible, airless room. However, this is completely different from any post-mortem I've ever been involved in: I feel compelled to see Rosalind again before she is gone forever. I think about the clues lying in wait across her body and I feel an almost magnetic pull toward the suite we all call "the Last Chapter."

After so many days in the stuffy heat of the police station, I thought I'd be grateful for the air-con, but it's turned up too high and goosebumps break out on my arms. Felix and I are perched on the beaten-up sofa in the waiting room drinking takeaway coffees. The springs gave way some time in the late nineties and it's not unlike sitting on a block of cement. I suppose this is not really a place where people need to get comfortable.

Felix looks at me and I can see tiny tan flecks in his dark green eyes. "You okay?"

Before I can answer, his phone is ringing and he shoots me an apologetic look as he stands up, pushing through the heavy door to step outside. Warm air swirls around me. "Hi, honey," I hear him say.

I wander over to the window and look out across the car park. The wind has picked up now and plastic bags are catching and flying in short bursts across the concrete before becoming tangled in bushes. I see Felix pacing back and forth as he talks into his mobile. I spot Anna's car so I know she is here. I take a sip of coffee and almost vomit. I throw the almost full cup in the bin. I imagine the contents spewing out and circling around the rest of the rubbish, just like the dirty lake water had curled around Rosalind's creamy skin. I shake the image away.

"Hey, Gem!" Anna's voice is like a ray of sunshine in the sterile corridor.

She would have to be the girl least likely to slice dead bodies open for a living. On face value, she's more a fifty-sit-ups-before-sunrise-and-tequila-shot-at-dusk type.

We don't get too many murders out here, and they tend to be a result of domestic violence or alcohol fueled tussles. Friends killing friends and husbands killing wives. The longer I am in this job, the more I realize that the lines between love and hate and life and death are blurry. More often than not it's drug overdoses and suicides that have me standing next to Anna as she turns someone inside out.

Anna is extremely competent and widely regarded around the station as one of our best assets. She's still young, only about three years older than I am. It's a miracle that we haven't lost her to the city yet. Jonesy used to think the same thing about me but believes I am less of a flight risk now that I have Ben. Phelps, the previous medical examiner, was a crude character but a brilliant ME. A real Hannibal Lecter type, classical music and all. We often joked at the station that it's lucky his patients were dead or he wouldn't have had any. Fortunately, Anna, his incredibly capable trainee, managed to inherit his skill but not his weirdness.

"Hey, Anna," I reply, smiling through a grimace as I follow her down the hallway to the autopsy suite. The waves of pain are still way worse than I want to admit to myself.

Anna snaps the lights on. The room is cool and airless. "Ah, fuck it," she says.

"What?"

"Left something in the office. Give me a sec." She walks out, leaving me alone with Rosalind. She is lying naked on the metal platform in the middle of the room. Aside from the angry marks around her neck and some slight bruising on her thighs, she is flawless. Her perfect breasts, larger than I had imagined, roll slightly to each side but still point skywards, fulfilling all manner of universal fantasies. Her veins are delicate webs underneath her skin. Her wrists and ankles are almost childlike. Her lashes are dark and fan prettily; little shadows spiking out beyond them. I had wondered what she looked like naked so many times. I never expected this to be the circumstance under which I would find out. I walk over and stand beside her. I look into her eyes and wonder what they saw in their final moments. I whisper things to her that I wouldn't dare say to anyone breathing. Words tumble out and I'm left empty and drained from the sudden release of my secrets. The clock ticks loudly from the wall above my head.

"Right, let's do this." Anna barges back in, snapping on latex gloves.

I step away from Rosalind, my heart racing, skin on alert across my body. I clutch involuntarily at my gut and then quickly drop my hand.

Anna walks around and picks up Rosalind's arm, shifting it away from the edge of the table.

"Should we wait for the others?" I ask.

"I told them eleven forty-five. They're late," Anna replies, pressing a button on her phone to record her analysis. "Deceased female. Rosalind Elizabeth Ryan. Twenty-eight years of age. Found Saturday, twelfth December at around seven-thirty a.m. face down in Sonny Lake in Smithson, New South Wales. Suspected homicide. Trauma to the head and suspected strangulation." She looks at Rose's waxy face. "No suspects at this time."

Felix and Jonesy enter the room. I can feel the heat coming from Felix as he stands next to me. Anna flashes them a quick, businesslike smile.

"And the guy who found her?" asks Anna.

"A local man on a morning jog," I say. "Connor Marsh. We've cleared him."

"Jeez. Just the thing to have you renewing your gym membership." Jonesy laughs at his own joke, widening his stance and leaning heavily against the wall.

Felix's hand scrapes softly against mine. A tingle pulses somewhere between my chest and throat.

"Right, I'm going in." Anna puts on her mask, adjusts her gloves and circles her shoulders as if she's about to throw a punch.

"What a beauty," says Jonesy helpfully. "A bloody waste killing a girl like that."

Anna tackles Rosalind's wounds first, prodding into the ugly redness that is like a blooming flower on her left temple.

I stare at her until my eyes blur, until she becomes a mass of indistinguishable pixels. I think about transferring money into my savings account, my court appearance for a rape case in the new year, stopping to get petrol later, what I'm going to get Dad for his birthday. Anything to stop the piercing sound of Rosalind Ryan's body being sawn open. Whatever air was trapped in there is forced out as her chest plate is cracked open. That's the part that always gets me. It makes no sense but it's like my brain reasons, *Well, no one could survive that, so they really must be dead.*

"What's with the roses that were all over her?" asks Anna.

"We think she was given them at the end of the play. She wrote and directed it. Maybe she still had them with her afterward?"

Anna nods and keeps prodding Rose. "Kind of creepy that she was covered in flowers. Sort of like a real burial."

I nod. Felix and I have talked about the flowers already, figuring they must mean something. An apology, perhaps? An attempt at a proper send-off?

I look at Rose, trying to ignore all the clinical markings and death tools. It is bizarre how death grabs at a body: claws at it, owns it. I must have attended at least fifty post-mortems by now. Each one sticks in my mind for a different reason. The most violent. The weirdest. The most straightforward. The youngest. I still vividly recall watching the autopsy of a three-year-old who had been killed by her stepfather. I held her hand as she lay on the table. Anna and I both cried.

Anna is making comments as she works, detailing her findings and Rosalind's general health. "Non-smoker, I think, but the liver is a bit of a mess. She had dinner before she was killed." She scrunches up her face while she works through the stomach and intestines. "Some kind of dessert too. Maybe strawberries. And definitely alcohol in the hours before she died, judging by the digestion."

Anna moves to the next stage of the examination. More robotic now, she reports her findings like she is reading a textbook. Jonesy peppers the procedure with unnecessary conversation before grabbing me around the shoulders and saying, "Sorry, Woodstock, I keep forgetting she was your mate."

I shrug him away. I'm so used to the autopsy table chitchat now that I barely notice it.

Anna continues, "She definitely struggled. Though it doesn't look like too much. I'd say she was already on the ground trying to scramble away rather than fighting back. This is dirt, not skin." Anna is inspecting Rose's fingernails, bagging the slivers that she has carefully clipped off. "Definitely some recent bruising on her thighs but nothing conclusive." Then Anna starts to examine her genitals, looking for signs of sexual assault.

I deliberately tune out and begin counting the rubbery scratches on the floor.

It isn't until Anna says, "Mm, well, this is interesting," that I snap back to the present.

"What is it?"

We all lean forward.

"Seems your dead girl was pregnant."

Chapter Eight

Sunday, December 13, 3:43 p.m.

I call Scott to tell him I'll be home late. Then I spend the afternoon poring over what I can access of Rosalind's social media accounts, phone records, medical records and financials but because it's a weekend, there's a lot of information that I can't get hold of yet. The field crew is at the school trawling over the grounds looking for any signs of a struggle or a murder scene, but so far they haven't come up with anything. Charlie calls just after 4 p.m. to let us know that a small bag has been located down the back of the oval, deep in some tall grass, with Rosalind's phone, purse and lip balm inside.

"They're all wet," Charlie tells me. "Must have gone into the lake with her to begin with and then I guess the killer ended up dumping them here."

"Did you search the stormwater drain?" I ask him. "The one near where she was found?"

"'Course." Charlie sounds like he's eating an apple. I can picture his big ruddy face covered in freckles as he marvels over the unsavory delights hidden on the grounds of my old high school. "Did that first thing. It was empty apart from water, dead animals and a shitload of graffiti."

"So nothing unusual then?"

He laughs. "Gem, it's a high school—there's heaps of weird shit everywhere but nothing that seems relevant. We're still looking though."

"Thanks, Charlie."

"Well, I'm not going to tell you it's a picnic. It's fucking hot out here. Mossy can't handle it. He's sitting in the shade under a tree fanning his face with a chip packet."

"Tell him he's weak."

"Will do."

A fresh team had gone back to do another search of the lake and the car park this morning but nothing has turned up yet. I get started on Rosalind's phone records.

"Anything?" Felix comes over to my desk just before 5 p.m. and places a milky-looking mug of coffee on the edge. He's nibbling on a muesli bar and I realize I'm starving.

"Not really," I say. "She's not on Facebook, only Instagram. It's just photo after photo of pretty things. Flowers, cute animals, rainbows and quotes. Mainly Shakespeare and dead poets that I remember from high school. It's all very vanilla. But there is a photo of that heart-shaped rock you found. She wrote *LOVE* when she posted it. That was two months ago. The only other thing that's vaguely interesting is an arty shot of a rotting apple and a close-up of red lips. I think they're hers." I hold the phone out.

Felix takes a quick look and raises his eyebrows at the image. We ran the rock for fingerprints but only found hers and a few other blurry half-prints that were no use to us.

"What about family? Friends?" he says, still looking at the lips.

"Zilch. No people in the shots at all. It looks like some of her students follow her, though, which might be worth checking out."

I think of all the family photos on Felix's pin board. I have photos of Ben and my dad all over the house, and Scott has snaps of his brother and parents. Even Phelps, our prickly old ME, used to have a photo of his wife on his desk at the morgue—the two of them at a Halloween party dressed as zombies.

"Just like her house," says Felix. "Did you notice how there were no photos there either?"

"Mm. Yeah, most people display at least a couple of happy snaps. Also, her phone records are the leanest I have ever seen. I need to get the names but there are only about six numbers." I show him the printout. "And she didn't have a landline, only a mobile. The e-mail address linked to her Instagram account has virtually nothing in it."

"Maybe she had a secret e-mail address and accessed it from some-where else," says Felix.

"That's what I'm thinking." I open my drawer and get out a packet of sultanas. Chewing them, I continue, "Someone called her just after ten-thirty on Friday night. Probably around the time the play finished. Maybe just after."

Felix's eyes widen slightly. "Okay, good. And?"

"It's a dead end so far. She missed the call and it was a blocked number. Probably a pre-paid SIM. Local, but that's all we know. So basically I'm getting nowhere."

"And we don't know who her gentlemen callers were either," he adds.

"You're right," I agree. "It would be good to know who the man in the fancy car was."

Felix is looking at a crime scene photo that is poking out of the manila folder on my desk. "She seemed very frugal on one hand—especially when you consider her family home—but then there's the wine and that makeup."

"Yeah."

My thoughts are cloudy. I can't quite work out what's tugging through my consciousness. Rosalind's blood-red lips keep interrupting my thoughts.

"You know," I say, swallowing more sultanas, "her bag was found at the school, tossed into some bushes. So it's most likely that the killer either followed Rose down to the lake or led her there, killed her, dumped her in the water and then took her bag—maybe trying to delay us ID'ing her, or maybe they thought there was money in it, whatever, but it means they made their way back through the school after she was dead. It just feels to me like that points to someone who was watching her all night. Maybe they'd planned to confront her about something after the play finished or maybe they'd arranged to meet and something went wrong. Maybe she had a stalker. I don't know. It's almost certainly got something to do with the school, though, don't you think?"

"It does make sense. We'll hit the school tomorrow," Felix says. "We need to talk to the other teachers, the students, work out who was at the play on Friday and if anyone saw her afterward. We need to get our hands on the CCTV—if there is any. Hopefully we'll get something."

He opens his mouth as if to keep talking, but ends up just smiling at me. "What?"

"Nothing." He looks at me longingly before saying, "I'm going to do some digging into Timothy for a bit. Marcus is clean, by the way—his alibi checks out. He didn't leave Sydney until Saturday morning. And Bryce's girlfriend, Amelia Posen, has confirmed she felt unwell and canceled their plans. She says they spoke on the phone late on Friday evening, which matches the story he gave us though it doesn't exactly let him off the hook. But I still think it's Timothy that's off."

I nod, fighting a wave of tiredness. "I'll look into George Ryan."

He nods and I watch him walk back to his desk. Despite the ache in my gut I want to be able to kiss him; pull him on top of me. Have him inside me. The desire is so overwhelming sometimes that it hurts.

Instead, I start to trawl the net and our records for anything I can find on Rosalind's father. Jonesy was right; George Ryan is a minor celebrity in the business world. Over thirty stories load, referencing him and his companies. Years ago he launched a recruitment company for low- and mid-tier health roles. One of the first in Australia, it had benefitted from the sudden influx of women and migrants into the workforce. He sold it in the late eighties for over a million dollars and then moved into property development. The successful company, simply called RYAN, has an office in Sydney as well as Smithson, and has projects all over regional New South Wales.

I recall Rosalind's poky apartment: the almost empty fridge and the Kmart bedspread. We're going to need to speak to George Ryan again. I tap my pen against the side of the computer, trying to make sense of what Rose's brothers said about her.

Marty Pearson looks up at me from the other side of the desk. "Cut it out with the pen, can you?" he says gruffly.

"Huh? Oh, sorry," I say, putting the pen down. Looking away from the screen is making everything seem slightly too bright. I lean back in my chair to stretch out my spine. Marty gives me his standard disparaging look before he disappears down behind the partition again, shaking his head. If Marty had his way, no one under forty-five would be a cop.

There's a commotion at the front desk, and vague wafts of swearing and crying roll into the main room. Someone has put on the radio in one of the interview rooms and Bon Jovi is softly belting out "Bad Medicine." I return my eyes to the computer screen and read through a few more articles about George Ryan's business ventures. It seems that Marcus was involved in the business for a short stint but there is barely a mention of Timothy and Bryce, or of Rosalind. There are, however, several photos of George and his sons at various local industry nights. There is nothing on Rosalind apart from a local newspaper story about the upcoming school play.

Just as I am about to shut my computer down, I find a small article in the local paper from January 1985 covering the death of Olivia Ryan. In the photo, taken on their wedding day, the woman from the mantelpiece at the Ryans' stares out at me. Her thick dark hair frames her heart-shaped face, and her crystal eyes are reminiscent of Elizabeth Taylor's in her heyday. A tragedy, declares the paper. It seems thirty-three-year-old Olivia suffered a hemorrhage two days after giving birth to her first daughter, Rosalind, and fell unconscious from the blood loss. She died two days later. George Ryan was quoted as saying that he was devastated by the sudden loss of his precious wife and would do everything in his power to look after their three young sons and brand-new baby angel.

Chapter Nine

Monday, December 14, 7:32 a.m.

Jonesy has called us together to officially kickstart the investigation. We had trouble getting resources: a murder/kidnapping took place on Saturday afternoon, a few kilometers out of Paxton, and all spare bodies in the region were allocated to finding the newly motherless seven-year-old girl and her violent father. Fortunately, she was found unharmed late last night in her dad's ute on a long stretch of country highway. Her father was discovered about fifty meters away in bushland, his brains blown to pieces.

Rosalind's death has formed a blanket over Smithson: mixing with the relentless heat, it's a creeping, vapor-like cover that sticks to everything. Voices are low and theories are exchanged in clusters outside the newsagent and the post office. Eyes dart around as if seeking a killer in the shadows. Beautiful piles of flowers form little mountains of love and grief at Rosalind's front door, the lake and the school. It's true what they say, that death unites us, pulls us together, though I see beyond this primal unity and think that perhaps we pull each other closer to check that we are who we say we are. We are all trying to work out what went so horribly wrong.

The energy is frenetic, buzzing with the newness of a bona fide mystery. There is nothing like this feeling, the hard fact that a death must have a story. We detectives must fill in the blanks: we have the ending but not the beginning or the middle. We need to know what happened in reverse. I usually love this stage. The satisfaction of problem-solving makes my soul sing. But this is different. I feel a flatness. And a mild flutter of fear. In many ways I'm scared of going backward through Rosalind's life in case it merges dangerously with my own. My past is something that I've always been happy to leave be.

There are about fifteen uniforms in plainclothes seated at the tables in the Waratah Room, underneath the overworked ceiling fans. Matthews, Kingston and Pearson are also present. The uniforms are mainly from Gowran and Mt. Lyall, though two are from Corburn and two flew in from the city. Eager and desperate for murder experience, I picture them fist-pumping at the first sign of carnage on the nightly news. Jonesy is pacing at the front of the room, stopping sporadically to rock back and forth on his heels. The bottom of his belly winks out and I can tell he wants a cigarette. Large prints of Rosalind—dead and alive—dot the pin board behind him. Several sets of her dark honey eyes stare out across the room. In one of the shots she's dressed in a soft mauve jacket with her hair pulled back, exposing her delicate throat. Her face is arranged into a sad, knowing smile. I fight the strangest urge to smile back.

One of the uniforms is fiddling with the venetian blinds, trying to get them to drop, and the rustling sound is slowly driving me spare. I look down and realize my hands are in fists. I didn't even get to see Ben this morning. He was still asleep when I left; his arm wrapped around his soft-toy fire truck. Scott asked me whether I'd be home for dinner as he handed me a plate of toast. I told him I wasn't sure.

I need a coffee. I start to walk toward the kitchen to make one just as Jonesy slaps his hand down on a desk and yells, "Right!"

I move back to my spot just inside the door; I don't feel relaxed enough to sit down.

"Here." Felix appears, placing a takeaway coffee from Reggie's in my hand. He keeps looking straight ahead. We're very careful at work, but we are partners and this means a certain level of intimacy is expected. Plus, we both have kids and most of the people we work with simply aren't imaginative enough to assume we have time for anything as frivolous as lust.

"Thanks," I whisper, gently glancing my knuckles against his.

Jonesy begins. "Right, by now you all know that Rosalind Ryan, a twenty-eight-year-old female, was found dead in Sonny Lake on Saturday morning. Beaten and strangled. Suspected sexual assault. She was a teacher at the local high school and by all accounts very popular. No witnesses and no clear motive or suspect. No partner that we can tell at this stage and no obvious beef with anyone. The media is already crawling like flies on shit over this"—Jonesy pauses to jerk a thumb at Rosalind's photographs—"for obvious reasons."

He breaks into a mild coughing fit and grabs the ledge of the whiteboard to steady himself. "So we need a solve and fast. Being a teacher, the school parents will start to be pains in the arse too and we don't want this kicking around for months. The mayor called earlier and he's putting the pressure on as well." He hikes his pants up, which only serves to highlight the flabby skin around his waist. "Now, not for a moment do I think that this is a serial, but you know how these things play out. If we don't pin someone for this, then it may as well be the next Jack the Ripper and we're all fucked."

He coughs again. "One other thing. Our victim was pregnant at the time of her death. Approximately ten weeks along, according to Anna. We have no idea whether it's relevant to our case or not but keep it in mind. And for the love of god, keep that information to yourselves." He looks around the room in what I assume is an attempt to appear stern. "Woodstock and McKinnon are leading. We've got you lot for at least a week, maybe more, but let's plan not to need it. Now go. And no overtime. I mean it."

He exits the room, stumbling on a bin and flailing into the wall. His muttered swearing fades as he walks toward his office. There's a smattering of laughter and at least one "dickhead" whispered.

I make my way to the front of the room with Felix close behind.

"Right, guys, this is how the next couple of days look." My voice is strong and clear. Matthews rolls his eyes and I give him a swift glare. "We meet every morning at eight and again at three to check in. If you can't make it, you have a good reason and you ring in your progress to myself or McKinnon—no excuses. One of us will always attend."

There's nodding and a few of the guys get out their phones to log the appointments in.

"We'll review the hotline calls at every check-in, and follow up anything that seems legit. We've done the basics but there's a lot to be getting on with. The primary search is complete. We're not clear about her exact movements on Friday but we know she was at the school in the evening no later than seven. She was there for a play—kids from the school were performing a version of *Romeo and Juliet*. Our victim wrote and directed it, and apparently it was very impressive. And a big deal for the school. We know there were issues in getting it happening, so maybe she put quite a few noses out of joint along the way. We're looking into everything right now so keep your ears open about any tension.

"Sonny Lake is not a direct route to her home, so there was no obvious reason for her to be at the lake after the play. Our guess is that she was either meeting someone there, or she was lured there by someone she trusted. It's possible that someone physically forced her there but that seems unlikely based on the post-mortem. Plus, someone would have noticed if she was grabbed at the school."

Sets of alert, shining eyes flick between me and the photos of Rosalind. I think of how much more beautiful she was than I am and wonder whether they are all thinking the same.

"We've only spoken to the immediate family so far. McKinnon and I will be heading to the school shortly to cover off the principal, colleagues and hopefully some students. I want you guys on this side of the room—" I gesture to my right "—to begin working through the audience from Friday night. Start with the students. Tread carefully with minors. I want parental consent for any formal questioning if they're under eighteen. You know the drill, and if you don't, then get up to speed. Offer counseling whenever you think it's necessary."

I pause, feeling the potent charge of determination in the room crackling over the group. I can smell the raw desire to track down the person who has taken it upon themselves to disrupt the natural world order.

"Where possible, refer any kids to Matthews and Dixon. I'm sure they'll be happy to help." I smile sweetly at Matthews, who is industriously picking at his teeth with his fingernail and ignoring me.

Felix steps forward. "Work smart. Batch trips together so you don't waste time in the car."

I nod. "Okay. So before Thursday we want to have done all the main ones: friends, exes, colleagues, students, extended family, doctors and anyone who comes forward with a statement. We need to cover the guy who found her and anyone who saw her last week and can vouch for her state of mind.

"We need to pull any CCTV footage we can access, and I want every record we can get our hands on. We've made a start but we want everything. Dental, medical, psychological, phone, internet, financials, spiritual, whatever."

One of the uniforms raises his hand slightly. "What are you guys thinking at this stage? Random or personal?"

"Personal," say Felix and I in unison. We glance at each other and then quickly look away. Matthews smirks.

"But nothing is really clear yet," says Felix, more quietly. "So let's just get going."

I'm not ashamed to say that I went after Stacy. It was cruel, but I figured she knew stuff about Robbie that could help me find an angle. She had the facts, as Jonesy had put it. In between my shifts and navigating my new relationship with Scott, I formed a plan. I could tell that Stacy was not overly intelligent, but she was shrewd, and while life with Robbie was originally exciting it had probably now reached a point where she felt trapped and scared; addicted to him, but not happily.

One Saturday morning, I followed her to work at Woody's, a run-down-looking roadhouse between Smithson and Mt. Lyall. I went inside and took a seat by the window, ordering a coffee which, when it came, tasted so much like dish-washing detergent that I could only manage a few sips.

"Stacy," I said, when she came to check if I wanted anything else. In her black skinny jeans and tight black t-shirt, she managed to convey sex and fear at the same time.

She looked up at me, surprised. Light purplish crescents underlined her eyes.

"Yeah?" Her voice was soft in the middle and sharp around the edges, like a home-cooked pie.

"Tell me about Warren Robbie."

"What?" Her eyes shifted back and forth in quick little circuits.

"Does he hurt you?"

"*What?*" Her voice turned to a hiss and she squinted at me.

"Does your boyfriend hurt you?"

"Who are you?"

She didn't remember me from the tail-light incident. "I'm a cop. And I know your boyfriend is bad news and I think you know he is too."

She scoffed at me and rolled her eyes, more confident now. "He might be bad news but he's not scared of cops; he's not scared of anyone."

"Are you scared of him?"

She didn't answer me, just sort of dug her heel into the floor and rolled her eyes again.

"I think you want a better life. You deserve to be treated better. He gets all this money by doing bad things, right? But you don't see any of it, do you?"

Her jaw remained hard, muscles working furiously, grinding her teeth together.

"What next? You end up having kids with this guy?"

Stacy spun around sharply and walked off toward the kitchen, the end of her plait so fine that the elastic band looked huge around the feeble strands of hair.

Stacy came to the station the next day asking for a "girl cop with light brown hair."

I was easy to find.

"Walk?" I suggested.

She nodded. Her hands scrambled together as if she were putting on hand cream. "He's been getting worse lately."

I led her toward the skate park. There, I gestured for her to stand against the concrete wall and I did the same. "Worse how?"

"Just worse." She bit her lip. "Angrier, I guess. He gets so mad sometimes."

"Was it his idea to report the car stolen?" I said it calmly, as if I knew that it hadn't been taken.

"Yeah." She picked at a thread coming loose from her sleeve. "His cousin took it to the city and sold it. You know, win-win." She wiped her fist along her nostrils. "He gets bored and wants to do crazy things. Last night he woke me up to drive him out to Dwyer's paddock so he could shoot some of the cows."

"He shot at someone's cows?"

She nodded. "I told you. He's always doing crazy shit."

"Does he hit you?"

"Sometimes."

"Can you leave? Do you have family around here?"

"No. I ran away from home years ago. We don't talk. But I have a friend that lives in the city. I called her this morning and said I might come to stay soon. She's at uni. I wanted to go to uni too but Robbie says we can't afford stuff like that."

In the end, Stacy did leave. I didn't see her again until the trial. After she'd gone, I watched Robbie whenever I had a spare moment. I drove past the house, I spied on him at his worksites. I followed him to the pub and sat in the corner observing as he threw back beers and leered at women and threw darts with such frightening precision that I found myself swallowing nervously while I sipped my wine. I don't know why I didn't pull him in about the cows or the car. I think I just sensed that something bigger would happen. It had become important to catch him, to show everyone that I could do more than traffic offenses and petty theft.

Two weeks after Stacy left, I watched Robbie drinking beers with several men on his front porch from my dark car. After an hour, I carefully followed when he jumped into his ute and drove to the Saloon Bar, a dive of a place that doubled as a half-hearted strip club. He'd been in high spirits at the house, laughing and animated. By the time he got to the club he was clearly getting drunk. He ordered more drinks, pulling the waitresses close to him as they walked past, whispering in their ears.

Another hour went by and I was about to leave—Scott's missed calls were compounding on my phone—when suddenly, like a spider, Robbie struck out and grabbed a girl, yanking her onto his lap. There was a roughness to his movements, I could see it from meters away, and even though she was laughing, it was obvious she was scared. I gripped the stem of my empty wineglass as he whispered to her. Then suddenly they were on their feet and out the door. By the time I got outside, his ute was squealing out of the car park. With my heart in my throat, I jumped in my car and raced after him. I worried he was very drunk; I'd watched him knock back at least three beers and as many bourbons. I prayed he wouldn't crash and kill the girl, hoped I wouldn't round a bend and be confronted with her dead body, him alive, roaming the scene like a rabid dog.

Instead, I pulled up at the end of his street with my lights off and watched through the trees as he shoved the girl against the wall near the front door. She cried out. He grabbed her face and I realized he was gagging her, covering her mouth so she couldn't scream, and I thought to myself, *My god, he's going to kill her, it's actually happening*, when he rammed her head hard against the wall. I saw it loll back, limp, and then he yanked open the door and they both disappeared inside.

I called for back-up then grabbed my gun and sprang out of the car. Lights came on inside, indicating his path through the house, and I stood just shy of the porch, trying to decide what to do. I knew I shouldn't go in alone—I didn't even know who else was in the house—but I was convinced that he would kill the girl and in the end that was all I could think about. I pushed into the house and followed the sounds, noting a shabby-looking wooden table in the kitchen with bags of white power on it. The air smelled like stale booze and sweat and fear, and I wondered how many girls had been brought here, powerless and terrified.

When I got to the bedroom Robbie was attempting to rape the poor girl, who was out cold. Her bruised lip was like a strawberry in the dim light and a black eye was just starting to show. Her bra was dotted with tiny smiling cartoon suns. I held up my gun and said all the right things and I wanted nothing more in that moment than to shoot him dead, but I held my stare and calmly directed him to get up, pull his pants up, and go and stand against the wall with his hands high.

"You piece of shit," I said to his freckly back.

Robbie grunted and then laughed as he swayed slightly against the wall.

The girl didn't move. After checking for a pulse and finding one, I carefully draped a sheet across her.

The house turned out to hold more of Robbie's secrets than I had ever expected, though I am sure there are many more that we will never know. The drugs in the kitchen were just a taste of the fully operational amphetamine lab we found in the garden shed. Then there were the weapons: four unlicensed shotguns and an antique dagger. We turned up fake IDs and wads of money stashed away under the house. But it was the two bodies we found in an old well in the yard that really changed my fortunes. A runaway, just like Stacy, who had gone missing five years earlier, and an Italian backpacker who had been assumed to have suicided down one of the local gorges due to a carefully placed backpack, had died at the hands of Robbie. Several of his friends were fingered for the weapons and the drugs but only Robbie was linked to the murders. Annie Charleston, the eighteen-year-old student he'd attempted to rape that night, was battered and bruised but recovered in full, at least physically. Her family moved away after the trial. I don't know whether Robbie would have killed her that night, but I know the part of me that had been dormant for a long time came alive as I stood in that room with my arm out, heavy with the weight of the gun, my body burning with the ability to make the badness stop. It felt incredible.

I did my interview with Candy Fyfe, up-and-coming reporter, the next day.

I had woken, feeling sluggish, just after 9 a.m., with Scott hovering nearby offering me water and telling me that even though what I had done was amazing, I really shouldn't have risked my life like that. I nodded, knowing that if given the chance I would do it every day.

When I was sitting across from Candy in her boss's office, her perfect dark skin glowing, she was all sisterhood and girl power, and I know I came across as cold and prickly. She was not a good enemy to make but I felt sick and anxious, increasingly panicked about what the last few weeks of my Robbie obsession had allowed me to ignore.

"How does it feel to have virtually single-handedly taken down a serial killer? I mean, some cops will go through their whole careers never doing what you have done in a couple of years. You're a star!"

She managed to make it sound like I'd put extra cinnamon in some already tasty muffins.

"I'm just glad he was caught. He was dangerous, like a loaded gun."

"A loaded gun. Great, yes." She tapped her pen against her teeth. "That's a good visual. I like to write as if I'm painting, you see."

She smiled at me, her coal-dark eyes piercing. I couldn't stop looking at her large white teeth exploding out from bright orange lips. Sitting next to her I felt flat and pasty, as if all the color had been drained out of me. I wished I could disappear into my gray pants and shapeless long-sleeved t-shirt.

"So are you going to become a celebrity cop now? You could probably write a book or something!"

I looked at her blankly. "No, no. I'm just going to keep doing what I'm paid to do, I guess."

I disappointed Candy that day. I didn't give her that fierce, feisty, girl-power cop thing she wanted. The article she wrote on me was vaguely condescending. She managed to flatter me, calling me a prodigal detective and Smithson police force's best asset, while at the same time suggesting that this had all been a huge stinking pile of luck. Of course, deep down that was what I was worried about too.

Walking back into the station that afternoon, I felt apprehensive. I knew that I had done the right thing, a brave thing even, but I also knew that I had broken unspoken rules. I had gone rogue and it had worked, but in the process I had made everyone else look inferior and lazy. Jonesy beckoned me into his office. He was puppy-dog excited. No one else in the main room seemed to move. I stopped still too, and just stood in the middle of the open office for a second. The water cooler chose that moment to force a large bubble of air to the top of the tank, mirroring my choppy stomach. I felt completely exposed.

Once we were safely behind the glass, Jonesy said, "How'd you know, Woodstock?"

"I told you, sir. I had a feeling."

He whistled. "Well, it's a good thing you did. This changes things for you, Woodstock. Won't be easier, not at all—harder, I'd say—but you can tell them all to get fucked now. A fucking serial killer. I can't believe it." He patted me on the back and swept a disparaging look through his glass wall as if the rest of the force were annoying toddlers who needed their nappies changed.

"Thank you, sir."

"Okay, Woodstock, we'll talk more tomorrow about what this means, but it's good, I guarantee you that much."

"Sir, I need to tell you something," I said, riding a wave of nausea.

"Yes, of course. Don't tell me you have another feeling!"

"No, sir. It's just that I'm pregnant."

Chapter Ten

Monday, December 14, 8:37 a.m.

Josie Pritchard watches Gemma Woodstock peer through the windows of the school library as the man with her takes a phone call. She hasn't seen the Woodstock girl in years, except for that business with the Robbie boy in the papers a while back. It seems completely bizarre that she is a police officer—and a detective, no less! Josie narrows her eyes; Gemma looks much smaller and skinnier than Josie had thought she would. As a teenager she had the kind of figure that one expected would thicken. The charcoal suit she is wearing is doing her no favors though: badly tailored and set oddly across her shoulders. And those shoes! Josie's eighty-year-old mother wouldn't be caught dead in shoes like that. *She hasn't had a mother to guide her,* Josie reprimands herself. Ned Woodstock renovated the Pritchards' laundry a few years back and Josie had wondered how such a clueless man had managed to raise a teenage daughter. It's really no surprise that Gemma looks like a bargain basement mannequin.

The tall, handsome man returns to Gemma's side and they talk briefly before walking toward Nicholson's office. Josie grabs the last of the Tupperware containers from her car and shuts the trunk, then makes her way to the canteen. Huddles of parents are milling around the school today, clearly spooked by this Rosalind Ryan saga. Her own kids are off playing somewhere, curious but seemingly unaffected by the murder, which she loosely breezed over this morning while doling out Weet-Bix, juice and raisin toast.

Poor lost young girl, thinks Josie, clicking her tongue as she cuts across the quadrangle. Rachel, her eldest, was taught English by Rosalind Ryan last year but none of Josie's other kids had been in her classes. Josie didn't know Rosalind well but she had always found her mildly off-putting. Her suggestion, in the parent–teacher interview, that Rachel needed to "slow down" in her essays and *feel* the words, didn't inspire much confidence in Josie.

"I'm not sure she's all there," she said to Brian as they drove home afterward.

"Oh, she's all there all right," Brian responded, laughing and shaking his head. "Damn, if I'd had an English teacher like that I might have actually read a book once in a while."

"Don't be revolting," Josie snapped, turning away from her husband. Typically, he didn't seem interested in discussing the shortfalls of their daughter's teacher.

"She's always daydreaming," Rachel reported of Ms. Ryan when Josie investigated further the next day. "But she's pretty cool. And she's so beautiful."

Josie didn't really know what to make of the young teacher, with her long princess hair and strange old-fashioned clothes, always looking at everyone with that haunted wide-eyed stare. Men seemed to have no sense when it came to her. Those idiotic year twelve boys were constantly embarrassing themselves, slobbering after her like mindless dogs. And there were the problems with Kai Bracks a while back. Even John Nicholson, the boring-as-watching-paint-dry principal, appeared love-struck; he was always staring at her and promoting her silly plays. Rachel ended up doing very well in her exams, though, so the woman could obviously teach. Still, this murder business seemed to suggest something sinister was going on in her life, and Josie can't help feeling a strange sense of satisfaction. She knew something wasn't right with that woman: she tends to have a radar for these things.

"Morning!" Josie pushes into the canteen's back room and hangs her bag on a hook by the door. The room is stifling, the air thick and soupy from the heat of the oven.

"Oh, isn't it terrible about Ms. Ryan!" Amy Parsons trills into a hanky as she grabs at Lucy Holbert's hand. "I can't stop thinking about it. Poor woman."

"Such a shame," agrees Lucy, patting Amy's hand. "Especially after that wonderful play."

Josie settles her heavy form into the spare chair and opens one of the containers. Chewing on an apple bran muffin, she looks at the two women in front of her. "Did you both go to the play on Friday?"

Amy stares at her hands, twirling the remains of the tissue between her fingers. Lucy reaches down to rustle through her bag. Amy nods quickly.

"Hmmmph." Josie swallows the last of the muffin and pushes her irritation away. "I had my sister over for dinner on Friday. I cooked paella, one of Jamie Oliver's thirty-minute meals. Delicious."

"Sounds wonderful," replies Amy.

"I suppose the play won't go ahead now," says Josie. "Shame, I have tickets for this Friday." She doesn't really, but she probably would have gone at some point and made Rachel come with her in exchange for a new top or some makeup.

"It really was very good," says Lucy. "She did an amazing job with those kids. Rodney Mason and Maggie Archer were incredible. They all clearly adored her. You should have seen the roses they gave her at the end. Just beautiful."

The timer starts to beep and all three women jump. Amy and Lucy busy themselves with loading the trays of biscuit mixture into the oven.

Josie reaches for another muffin. As she chews, an unexpected image pops into her mind, of Rosalind Ryan in a stark white coffin, eyes open and seductive like the actress from *American Beauty*, surrounded with bouquets of blood-red roses. She laughs to herself, thinking that John Nicholson would slip quite nicely into the fawning Kevin Spacey role.

Chapter Eleven

Monday, December 14, 8:41 a.m.

Being back at Smithson High is completely disorienting. It's not even called Smithson High anymore, a fact I am reminded of frequently due to someone's eagerness to embrace the rebrand. The words *Smithson Secondary College* scream out at me from the signs directing us toward the various facilities, and there are stickers with the new logo adhered to all the bins. Wisps of the past are everywhere, but at the same time everything looks new. I'm half terrified that I will see a faded version of my former self running past with a group of childhood ghosts laughing and playing. I have only been back here twice since school finished. Once for Jacob's memorial service, which still remains the single most difficult hour of my life, and once to arrest a kid I was chasing who had used the school as a shortcut to get to the lake. This time it's different. This feels slow and bright and real. The heat crackles around us as we walk across the gravel car park, past the old flagpole with the rippling Australian flag and the set of classrooms that everyone used to call "The Sisters."

"Why are they called that?" I remember asking my friend Janet, when we first came to the school. She always knew the answers to things because she had two older brothers.

"Because," she said, rolling her eyes, "all their paint is peeling, like they're taking their clothes off, and they're a different color at the bottom where it looks like skin. So all the boys say they look like slutty sisters with no undies on."

Felix's phone rings. He glances at the screen and says, "I need to get this, it'll be quick."

I nod and he wanders off. I watch a raven try to pull a burger wrapper out of a bin. Across the car park an overweight woman is struggling with something in her trunk.

"Okay, well, that's a bit weird," Felix says, walking back.

"What?" I'm looking up at the old library. The former dark gray has recently been painted a thick rich cream but the same faded poster about the joy of reading is still on show in the window to the left of the door.

"Rose bought that place outright about ten years ago."

"Really?"

"Yep. No loan, just cold hard cash. She lived there for a few months and then rented it out until she moved back in just over four years ago."

I kick at a crushed Coke can. "Well, maybe it's not that weird when you consider who her dad is. I'm guessing he gave her the money for it. I mean, what would the place have cost back then? A hundred grand? One twenty?"

"About one ten actually."

I throw him a wry smile. "*See.*"

"You're like a Smithson property connoisseur, Gem."

I give him a light kick on the shin. "She was nineteen then, so it must have been her dad's money. We should find out if George Ryan gave all of his children a little kickstart like that."

"I still think it's strange that she lived so frugally," says Felix.

"She did have nice wine though," I remind him. "And that makeup. And the artwork."

Another raven eyes us warily before marching over to its mate to join in the bin attack.

"It doesn't make sense, does it? I know her teaching salary wouldn't have been much, but still."

I like the way the light is cutting across Felix's eyes, making them glow green. "I agree it's odd," I say, picturing Rosalind sitting in the front row of our classes, her face pensive but her gaze playful whenever she caught me looking at her. I'd never been able to figure her out.

"Stuff with money is always odd!" Felix says it sunnily but I know that his family has had huge issues with money. His dad gambled away half the family fortune, leaving his mother with almost nothing. Then his wife, a dentist, was sued years ago when they lived in the UK, which led to them selling their house and moving here. I don't know the details but Felix told me that they basically had to start over. He doesn't like to talk about money, which suits me just fine. It's never been a huge part of my life.

"Let's visit George Ryan again," Felix says. "Maybe he can fill in the blanks. Now let's go see the principal."

I nod. A strange shiver of familiarity runs through me as we walk past classrooms. Young faces peer at us from all angles. It's 8:45 a.m. and students are starting to arrive. They've updated the uniform since I left but it's similar. Midnight blue jumper, a gold-and-blue-checked dress. I can remember the itchy pull of the synthetic fabric on my wrists and neck, the breezy freedom of the summer skirt.

"Look," says Felix, pointing.

Stuck to the side of the brick wall outside the main office is a poster promoting Rosalind's play.

"'A modern day reimagining of *Romeo and Juliet*'," he reads. "Didn't Baz Lurhmann already do that?"

I shush him and look at the poster, feeling a deep stab of sadness. It suddenly seems important that Rosalind got to see that first night of her play. Saw that it had all come together and got to stand back and watch the timeless story she loved so much play out. The poster is striking. Two shadowy profiles facing each other with bolts of lightning cutting between them. It strikes me as oddly dark and abstract considering Rosalind's light and sunny Instagram images.

"C'mon, let's go," Felix says impatiently.

A trio of young girls walk toward us dressed in a uniform of denim cut-offs, thongs and singlet tops. They are a tumble of tanned limbs, lip gloss and long straggly hair. Short hair must be out, I think, absently running my hand through my shoulder-length tangles. All three have red eyes and the pinched look of grief.

"Year twelves," I mutter, after they've passed. "They must have decided to meet here even though class is finished for the year."

"Yeah. They all look just like Maisie."

I glance at Felix but his eyes are fixed straight ahead and I'm not quite sure what he is thinking. His daughters are a foreign concept to me; most of the time I can't believe that they are real. He clears his throat and squares his shoulders.

I straighten too. John Nicholson is coming out of the main office, looking flustered, in a navy shirt and cream pants. His hair is thinner than I remember and his eyes sag a little to the sides. He still has the anxious gait that would have suited a woman far more than a man. His head bobs from side to side, and then he sees us and manages to seem relieved and terrified at once.

"Gemma. Well. It's been years. Well."

He looks at me and an awkward silence falls over us.

"Well, anyway…" He trails off. "Oh god, what an awful thing this is. I just don't know what to do. Well. I guess there aren't really rules for something like this." He wrings his hands and then reaches out to squeeze mine.

Felix leans in to shake his hand. "Mr. Nicholson, I'm Detective Sergeant Felix McKinnon. Perhaps we can speak in your office?"

"Yes, of course. Susan told me you were coming. I do need to do a press conference with the mayor soon, but I think it isn't until ten. That's long enough, isn't it?"

Felix nods. "Yes, that's plenty of time. We only need a quick chat for now and then we'll get out of your way."

"Okay, well, please, come in here. You'd remember my office, Gemma—it's still the same really. I'm not one for change."

We follow him through the school office. A wild-eyed woman is fielding calls at the desk. "No, no," she is saying. "He is not available to speak at present. No, we don't know anything about that."

"Journalists," Nicholson tells us. "They've been calling since early this morning. We have nothing to tell them but they keep ringing."

"It's big news," says Felix. "It's cruel, but they are just doing their job."

"I suppose you're right. God, I just can't believe this."

True to his word, Nicholson's office is as I remember it. A faded photo of the school in the eighties hangs on the left wall. Two decades' worth of school sports days, concerts and theater shows pepper the back wall. I see a photo of Rosalind leading a kind of dance rehearsal. She is off to the side of the stage, arms outstretched, her smile wide and her eyes sparkling.

"Please take a seat." Nicholson gestures at two uncomfortable-looking chairs and walks around his desk to sit facing us. "My goodness. Do you want a drink? Coffee or tea?"

I almost laugh. Everyone we've interviewed so far has had impeccable manners.

Felix takes the lead. It's unspoken but I can tell he thinks that my history with Nicholson might complicate things. "We're fine," he says. "Now, Mr. Nicholson, we need to talk to you about Rosalind Ryan."

He slumps back into his chair. "Yes, of course. Where to start? Rosalind is…ah, *was* an exceptional young woman."

His chin trembles and for a moment I think he will cry. A memory crashes into my vision: Rosalind singing in assembly and Nicholson staring at her in wonder. I remember Jacinta White leaning across me to laugh with Janet about it. I feel the itch of my winter stockings and the weight of my long braid. I remember feeling uncomfortable about the way his eyes were fixed on her, not wanting to think badly of the man who had been so good to me after Mum died.

"Let's just start with some basics, okay?" Felix pulls out his notebook and Nicholson visibly pulls himself together. He takes a deep breath and places his palms on his thighs.

"Okay." His voice sounds very far away.

"How long has Rosalind been a teacher here?" begins Felix.

"Four years. And of course she was a student here too." He pauses and smiles weakly at me. "She was always very bright. Very good at English. She loved anything to do with words. A natural on the stage too."

The receptionist is continuing to fend off calls outside the door. The sharp sound of the ringing phone is constant. I am starting to get a headache.

Nicholson continues, "She had another teaching job before this one, somewhere in Sydney. She had some bad luck there, an issue with the principal. He made some outrageous accusations and really knocked her confidence. Anyway, she decided to come back home. Which was wonderful from my perspective. I was thrilled when she inquired about teaching here. She always was a great kid." He shifts his weight and his chair creaks loudly. "I knew she would be an amazing teacher."

Felix asks, "What kind of accusations did the principal make?"

Nicholson clutches at his hands again. "I'm not entirely sure. I think he felt that she was too close to her students. He totally misinterpreted her style. She was quite upset about it because she was just trying to be a good teacher. She really cared about her students. And they adored her. I've actually never seen anything like it."

Felix looks at me and writes something down on his notepad.

"Mr. Nicholson," I say slowly, the words both familiar and strange, "tell us about this year. This was Rosalind's fourth year teaching here, wasn't it? She must have been close to the other teachers. To you."

I watch him carefully. He plucks a tissue from a box on the desk and dabs at his eyes. They are watery when he looks back up.

"We are all close. It really is the nicest bunch of people. I just don't know what I'm going to say to any of them. Millie Janz, one of the teachers, called yesterday and I could barely speak to her. I'm not sure what to do. Rose is completely irreplaceable. A wonderful girl. And for her to be *murdered*." He sobs briefly and then bites his knuckle, trying to stop. "Sorry, sorry." Then to me, "You remember what she was like, Gemma. You two, the English stars."

Felix's shoulder jerks slightly in my direction but I keep my gaze straight ahead. "Mr. Nicholson, I'm sorry, but just a few more questions and then we'll be able to finish. Was Rosalind particularly close to any of the other teachers?"

"Really, we are all close. Rose was shy in some ways but very passionate about certain things. She kept to herself but she was well liked. And as I said, some of the students would do anything for her." He pauses. "I really don't know how some of them will cope with this."

"Was she seeing one of the teachers?"

Nicholson's eyes narrow. "What, like dating?" He shakes his head. "No, no, nothing like that. I discourage all staff from any romantic relationships."

"Things happen though, don't they? Are you sure you would know if she was seeing someone? Maybe she would want to keep that kind of thing quiet."

Nicholson's lips form a tight line. "Maybe, but I'm sure I'd know. It would be hard to hide something like that. Plus, most of the male staff are married or in serious relationships anyway."

"That doesn't necessarily rule out an affair, though, does it?"

Nicholson twists uncomfortably in his seat. "Well, I suppose not," he says finally. "But she was just really into being a teacher. She loved the kids. I don't think she was in a relationship with anyone on the staff."

"Okay. What about the students then?"

Nicholson looks puzzled. "What about them?"

"Well, Rose was a beautiful woman and still young. She could have passed for a girl in her early twenties. Maybe some of the older students were attracted to her. Perhaps she was flattered. She could have crossed a line and things got out of hand."

Nicholson sighs heavily. Suddenly he looks much older. "Sorry, but no. Really, just no. I won't have that kind of talk about her. Her students cared about her very much. That could easily be misinterpreted, but I know what she was like. Maybe some of the younger boys had crushes on her. But just normal harmless stuff. She was a private person and kept to herself but she was very principled. She had nothing to hide."

He abruptly lurches to the side and grabs some tissues, dropping his head behind the desk. I look away as he makes little retching sounds.

Felix stands and goes to him, patting him roughly on the back. "Can I call someone for you?"

Nicholson sits up, looking dazed. His face is puffy and perspiration begins to trail down his forehead. "No, I need to get ready to...talk to everyone. I'm sorry, this is just very hard."

I nod and Felix keeps patting his back.

"We will need to gather a lot of information," I tell Nicholson. "Interview teachers, students and admin staff. We don't know exactly what we're looking for yet so we need to cover everything."

Nicholson moves his head up and down slowly. His eyes are fixed on the desk.

"I'll get you some water," says Felix, leaving the room.

I stare at my old principal. I remember being in this office after Mum died. Probably sitting in this exact chair while Nicholson talked to Dad and me about the support available and the strategies that would be adopted to make sure things could stay as normal as possible at school. Nicholson has always had kind eyes. They look at me now—two dark brown smudges.

"Did you go on Friday night, Mr. Nicholson?" I ask.

His breathing is slowly returning to normal. "Ah, no. I didn't, no."

Felix reappears and places a large glass of water in front of him, catching our conversation. "You didn't go to the opening night of the school play?"

Nicholson fidgets and takes a gulp of water. "No, I didn't."

"Why not? It would have been one of the biggest events of the year for the school, surely?" Felix's voice is light but I can tell he is homing in on what he thinks is an anomaly. "Did you have other plans?"

Nicholson looks back and forth between us, his eyes slightly desperate. "No, but you see it was all a bit political."

"Political?"

"Well, maybe not political, that makes it sound too serious. But it was a bit awkward."

"Tell us what you mean," I say.

"Well, you see it was Rosalind's idea. To have the play. She was so passionate about putting on a production and last year we couldn't make it work—there were issues with funding and the head drama teacher had taken ill, so it never happened." He pauses and looks at me. "You remember, Gemma—the plays were always a winter highlight. Good for the students but also good for the whole community. I wanted to put on a show

82

too, but being principal you have to make sacrifices. Recently sport has kind of won out over the arts."

"Right, so this year Rosalind pushed to have the play?"

"Yes, it was very important to her. The head drama teacher had left and Rose was at me about it as soon as the year started and I said I was sure it would be fine. But then a major camp was scheduled for the year elevens in July, which clashed with the auditions. And some of the other teachers felt like the play created too much competition between the kids. It became controversial."

"Okay. So Rosalind was angry?"

Nicholson looks up as if to disagree and then slumps back again. "More frustrated, I think. She mentioned bureaucracy more than once and I know she was disappointed in me for not trying harder to make it happen."

"Was anyone angry with her about it?"

Nicholson looks confused. "Like annoyed? Well, maybe a bit. But not enough to do something like this. No way."

"Were you angry at her?" I ask.

Nicholson doesn't move. Outside the door the phone rings again. "No. I was frustrated *for* her. I wanted her to have her play and I was glad she finally got to put it on."

"So why didn't you go to the opening night?" Felix presses.

"I felt it would be best if I didn't make an overt show of support. I had planned to go this Friday. It was going to run for seven nights, you see."

"I heard it was very good," I say.

Nicholson nods. "Yes, yes. I knew it would be. She had a wonderful ability. So much insight. So talented. A great actress too, I think."

"Too talented to be teaching students at Smithson High?"

Nicholson looks at Felix, an unreadable expression on his face. He checks his watch and as he stands I notice his hands are shaking. "Well, that is a hard thing to measure, isn't it? All I know is that she was determined. She rallied those kids, wrote that play, checked with the education department to see if she could have the year twelves use their analysis of modernizing the script to count toward their final marks. She did all that."

We stand and step aside so that Nicholson can show us out. "I think she was happy here. Especially lately. She was thrilled with the play. Proud of the students. She was happy."

Felix smiles tightly at him. "Yes, well. Thank you for your time. We may need to speak with you again but for now we're done."

"Thank you. Now listen, you do what you need to do, but please be careful with everyone. We are hurting very badly. We loved her, you know."

Something about the way he says this is unsettling and Felix gives me a pointed look as we walk out past the frazzled receptionist into the white-hot sunlight and smack bang into a ghost.

My future is a slippery elusive thing that I have spent half my life trying not to think about too much. When Mum died it felt like everything stopped. I was surprised every time I woke up to a new day. It seemed unfathomable that out there in the world people were falling in love, having babies, studying, laughing. I struggled to think. To see. To breathe. Then somehow, one day, it was better. I started to make plans again and experienced moments of clarity where my dreams seemed possible. I met Jacob and my passion returned. I loved hard and fiercely. And then he died and I was catapulted all the way back into the relentless pain of breathing through every minute. I think, before he died, I had allowed myself to picture a future again. Just a vague one, with cloudy edges, but I'd glimpsed a life beyond school. I'd imagined uni, travel. Maybe even us getting a little place. But after he was gone there was no light in my black hole. Nothing made sense. The guilt was suffocating. I only kept going out of sheer determination to avoid drowning in my own thoughts because that was the one thing I dreaded more than trying to live a normal life. Sometimes I'm not actually sure that I ever came out of my hole. Not really.

But once I became a cop I was able to pull myself through the days a little more easily. See a direct line from A to B and feel clearer about how I was going to get there. The basic principles of right and wrong seemed solid and I grabbed on to them with everything I had.

And then I fell pregnant with Ben and that awful idea of the future loomed again. The idea of a baby terrified me. The concept of being parent to a child or a teenager was beyond comprehension. And the sudden introduction of Scott's feelings into my life was even more difficult to navigate. I'm just not great when it comes to other people. That's probably what makes me a good cop and is probably why I made detective so quickly. "Like a robot that just so happens to eat," Jonesy used to say affectionately.

Of course, Ben changed things in all the ways that everyone said he would. But I remained wary. I held him close at night and blinked away the thoughts that had me dying at gunpoint and leaving him all alone. I would fetch him in the morning and worry that I would have a heart attack after Scott went to work, or that I would slip in the shower and crack my head open. I comforted myself with the thought that Ben was probably better off with just Scott anyway. That my confusion confused things. That my ability to be the kind of mother he really needed was horrifically limited.

So I kind of just put one foot in front of the other and bathed him and fed him and held him, but I was still cautious about the future. I never let myself picture him in primary school or as a teenager. I didn't make plans too far ahead. I lived in the moment and I placated myself with the notion that mindfulness is what half the world is seeking at any given time. I had just managed to find a version of it that had been born out of necessity rather than aspiration.

And then Felix arrived in Smithson and everything went out the window. I was giddy. Blindsided. I was a new mother and a young detective and all I could think about was him being inside me. I felt raw. I developed insomnia. Anxiety. But at the same time I'd never felt so happy. It was like having Jacob back again. The blood seemed to flow more smoothly around my body. For the first time in years I willed time to move faster. Our connection was so instant, so overwhelming, that everyone else in my world faded. I wanted his opinion on everything. I thought about him constantly and felt the deep guilt of someone who wished for a different life. At night I would turn over and over in bed beside Scott until, finally, I would give up and go to the couch in the lounge, where I would stare through U.S. talk shows and wonder how it had come to this. Why did I have to meet Felix after Ben was born? Why did Scott want to be with me? Why didn't Jacob just come find me that day? Why didn't he think I was worth living for?

Within days we were brushing past each other, his hand touching mine as he handed me some papers, my arm glancing off his as I passed him at the printer. Less than a month later we were kissing in my car and making plans to do more. I could not get enough. I felt alive, charged with an invisible energy source.

The truth is, I never really got over Jacob. I've never quite managed to understand how it all went so wrong. How he could have left me like that. I loved him so much and after he died I had no anchor. Until Felix came along I felt like I hadn't really spoken to anyone properly for years. Felix makes me want the future: to pull it toward me, grab hold of it, breathe into it. I know it will be messy and complicated and difficult, but the way I feel about him means I can't see another way.

These thoughts invariably swarm around my mind. It's exhausting but it's better now than it was. Better than last summer, when I struggled to eat and found being around Felix akin to having a nonfatal heart attack. I can wait for our future. We are in this together, figuring it out as we go. Patiently yearning. But Jacob is always in my head. He's always just below the surface.

And that's why I almost faint when I walk out of Nicholson's office, into the sunlight, and straight into him.

Chapter Twelve

Monday, December 14, 9:52 a.m.

My head spins. My throat feels like it has disappeared and I make a strange choking sound. *Jacob,* my brain chants over and over as I stare at his face. It's the same slouched posture, the same rich brown hair. I'm conscious of Felix beside me and I feel suddenly confused about where I am and what year it is.

"Gemma?" The boy's voice is not right. It's lower, huskier. He's not Jacob. His eyes are red raw and freckles dust his cheeks. Jacob's skin had been clear.

My mind stumbles into reality. "Rodney?"

He nods.

"Rodney, what are you doing here?"

The boy shuffles his feet. He's wearing tight jeans and a loose black t-shirt that hangs like a dress on his slim frame. I realize the last time I saw Rodney he was seven years old. He shrugs and tilts his head so that his hair falls to the side, out of his eyes. "This is my school. A whole bunch of us decided to meet here this morning. We didn't know where else to go." He looks down but not before I see his jaw shudder. I notice the pulse in his neck is throbbing.

Nicholson has followed us out and is nervously surveying the scene. He mutters under his breath and then says, "Well, I guess it's good for you to be with each other." He rocks manically on his feet and looks beyond us to where a group of students are hugging one another and crying in a small circle. One of the girls tucks the hair of another girl behind her ear and then runs a thumb under her eyes to wipe tears away. A tall ginger-haired boy is rubbing slow circles on the back of another girl as she stares at the ground. I can remember that closeness. That intimacy. That comprehensive, inexplicable human connection you can have at that age. I can feel Janet holding my hand as we wove through parties, her doing my makeup, her eyes inches from mine, her tongue sticking out in concentration. I remember Sandra teaching me how to backflip, holding my stomach in and pulling me up into the right position. Waking up next to her after sleepovers, rolling toward her and tickling her back. Brushing her hair. I remember Fox guiding my fingers, teaching me how to roll cigarettes, laughing when I dropped the contents all over the ground. Sneaking up behind me and covering my eyes with his hands. Jacob kissing my feet, playing with my hair, breathing me in. Fox, Janet and Sandra comforting me after Jacob died. Touching me. Holding me. It was like we shared skin, space and everything in between. I remember needing them like air.

But after school that closeness evaporated.

Jacob is dead. Fox, I barely see. And I have no idea where Janet and Sandra are now. They moved away years ago and we don't keep in touch.

A new girl joins the group and starts to sob as the others pull her into their circle. I look away, feeling intrusive and oddly jealous. Their sense of belonging is palpable.

Next to me Rodney's head jerks. Jacob's square jawline plays through my mind. "Mum," he says.

I look over to see Donna Mason walking briskly toward us. Time has not been kind to her. Her eyes sink into her face and her wiry graying hair is pulled tight onto the top of her head. Her denim jacket is like a square across her small frame. I remember her cool stare as Jacob and I curled together on the couch at his house, watching a movie. She was always lurking in doorways, watching us. It was hard to relax when she was around. I can still picture her empty gaze at Jacob's memorial service.

"Gemma." She nods at me.

"Mrs. Mason." I nod back, feeling like a teenager.

"Detective Sergeant McKinnon," says Felix, sticking his hand out toward her.

She takes his hand and shakes it firmly. "Donna Mason," she says. She crosses her arms. "Yes, well. Awful business all this. Just awful." Her large eyes blink at each of us in turn.

Nicholson kicks his shoes at the ground awkwardly. "Donna, hello."

She looks at him and executes another little nod. Turning to Rodney, her face softens. "You can have an hour, sweetheart. I need to get to the shops but I'll pick you up on the way back."

"It's fine, Mum, I can grab a lift with Kai or Em."

"No." She shakes her head nervously, like a bird. "I'll be back here in an hour. I'll drive you." Her eyes flit to the quadrangle and then back to the group of distraught teenagers. "Meet me out front at eleven."

Rodney's body seems stiff but he shrugs before shuffling back to his friends. He quickly disappears into the writhing mass of grieving students. The boy with the ginger hair catches me looking and averts his eyes sharply. He's still stroking the back of a crying girl.

"Well, bye," says Donna, the edges of her mouth pulling up briefly into a polite smile.

"Right, well." Nicholson turns in a flustered semi-circle and then drifts back toward his office.

Felix and I are left standing alone in the bright square of sunlight next to the sobbing group.

Our eyes meet.

"Jesus," says Felix under his breath.

Chapter Thirteen

Monday, December 14, 9:27 p.m.

"Something feels seriously off. She was so polarizing. I can't get a grip on her." Felix is lying flat on his back, talking to the ceiling. I sip at my wine, the golden liquid sliding down my throat. "I mean, I don't even know what to call her! Rose? Rosalind?" He laughs. "Anyway," he says, "we need to get on to her old school. Something clearly happened there." He rolls over to face me. "What do you think?"

I shrug, still a little disoriented by his closeness. I love how desperate he always is to strip my clothes off and hold me. To push his way inside of me. My body is still smarting, raw from him holding me down. At some point my head connected with the wooden bed head and that, paired with the exquisiteness of what he has just done to me, has left me in a state that is both exhausted and energized. I don't really want to talk about Rosalind right now, but we always talk about cases we're working, and as her dead face looms in my mind again, I realize that avoiding speculation about what happened to her right now is unlikely.

Felix gets up to pour more wine and I stare at the side profile of his naked body and wonder for the millionth time how the hell this is my life.

We always meet here, at the tiny farmhouse that belongs to Scott's brother. It's about fifteen minutes outside of Smithson and I know that Scott would never come here with Ben at night. There is no reason for him to. Quaint and isolated, it's empty about ten months of the year, and Scott and I have a set of keys and do basic maintenance in exchange for the steady supply of fruit and vegies that grow in the garden. I have wondered what Felix and I would do if we didn't have a place like this to come to. I assume we'd end up pawing at each other in our cars, fogging up the windows along a quiet, out-of-the-way road somewhere.

I was worried I wouldn't be able to have sex with Felix tonight but the bleeding slowed yesterday and today it's as if nothing ever happened. Only the vague thrum of an ache reminds me that my life was temporarily heading in a very different direction.

"And what's with the principal? Was he into her or what?"

I prickle slightly. "C'mon, he's allowed to be upset. They worked together. She went to school there. They were close."

I push the faded image of Nicholson watching Rosalind on stage from my mind.

"*We* work together." He wriggles his eyebrows at me suggestively and I throw a pillow at him.

"I think Nicholson is a good guy. He really cares about the school. Cares about the kids. I just can't see it."

"People change, Gem. Maybe the unrequited love finally got to him, or maybe his wife found out, or maybe they were together and then Rose realized it was creepy because he's really old."

I throw another pillow at him. "Careful. He's only got about fifteen years on you."

He rolls his eyes.

"Plus, his wife is dead," I say primly. "Or at least I'm pretty sure she is."

He throws the pillows back onto the bed and reaches out to me. I go to him and lie down in the crook of his arm.

"At least we know that Marcus was one of Rose's visitors," he says.

"Yes." We spoke to Rosalind's brothers again today. Marcus confirmed he had called on his sister about a month ago, though he drove a hire car, a modest Toyota. Timothy and Bryce claim they haven't visited her place in years.

Felix and I still think that Timothy is suspicious; the preliminary search of his finances shows he did purchase tickets to the school play two weeks ago. When we asked him why he'd bought two tickets but gone to the play alone, he said that he hadn't got around to inviting someone else along.

"Seeing those kids today was full on," says Felix, into my ear.

"Yeah." I shuffle through their faces. Caught between child and adult, they were so beautiful and so dangerous, tripping over themselves to grow up.

"So that boy today, the one you spoke to?" His fingers tickle the back of my neck. "He's the lead in the play. The Romeo, right? What's the story there? You knew him?"

Outside a possum runs along the powerlines and cuts across the wire that leads to the house. It pauses, its tail dangling crookedly in the moonlight. I roll over and pull the sheets around me like a strapless dress. I have more wine as I weigh up what to tell Felix.

"Yeah, I knew him."

"How?"

I look at him, slightly exasperated. "Like how I know everyone. I grew up around here."

He nods slowly. I can tell he is deciding whether or not to let it go. He curls his fingers around mine, gently removing the wineglass from my grip. "Sure, but he's way younger. Plus, you looked like you'd had a stroke when we saw him. How exactly did you know him?"

"I knew his brother. Jacob."

"From school?"

"Yeah." I let the second hand on the wall clock do a full half-circle before I add, "He was my boyfriend."

The silence starts to make me feel itchy. I stretch out my feet.

"Where is lover boy now? Still in town?"

I lie back on the pillow and watch his face. I know he is mapping out a typical teenage love story, all awkward limbs, promises set to moody tracks and epic stormy partings. He's only half right.

"No, he died. When we were in school. He jumped off the tower at the lake."

Felix's smile retracts like a snail into its shell. "Fucking hell, Gem." His fingers pause for a few moments before he picks up the rhythm again.

I wish that I could stay here with him doing that forever. I blink a few times but he holds my gaze, his green eyes steady. I've never asked Felix where this will go, whatever this thing is between us, and he's never given me a real indication of what he wants it to be. I know he never wanted to come to Smithson. It was his wife's idea, to move from London and have a sea change far away from the sea. Felix had loved his life in the city. He said he felt freer, more independent there. I suspect that being with me is a nod to that freedom. A lifeline to his old world where desire dominates and impulses are heeded. I also sense that his wife was determined that the move here would reset their marriage. Felix seems stubbornly determined not to participate in any such overhaul. He works late and is desperate to spend time with me. He is an engaged father to his girls and polite to his wife. I am scared to ask him point blank how he feels about her, but right now, as I look at him, I see real love and I realize how important I am to him. How important he has become to me. I squeeze his hand softly.

"Were you there when Jacob died?"

"No. He went there alone."

I don't tell him that I've seen Jacob's broken body at least a thousand times in my mind. These days, I know death and I now know how he would have looked after he fell, so over the years the image I summon has changed from a cartoon-like puddle on the ground to a more fully formed version of the boy I loved. The scene crowds my thoughts and I try to blink it away but he's there whether my eyes are open or shut.

"He had lots of things he was dealing with, I think. He was really artistic, he could be moody sometimes, get lost in a project, so I knew a little bit of it but I'm not sure I realized quite how bad things were. Or if I did, I didn't really want to know."

"Do you think that's why you became a cop?" Felix asks.

"Partly, maybe." I can't figure out how to explain that I didn't really have another choice. I needed so badly to work in a world that made binary sense of things. A place where there was good and bad, right and wrong, and where I was in charge of making sure there was more good than bad.

"Was it when you were still in school?"

"Just after our final exams. It was actually ten years ago last week."

"Fuck, Gem." Felix fills our wineglasses and takes a long sip from his. "I'm guessing that having a boyfriend die like that is pretty hard to deal with. Especially on top of your mum."

I feel tears building. I picture Dad coming into my room, his face gray and old as he sits on my bed, softly sobbing into his hands before he manages to tell me what has happened, tells me what Jacob has done. I see the dam breaking around us, crashing into the room and carrying us away. Dad and I had an unspoken agreement to never really talk about Mum, and with Jacob it was the same. We would sit side by side on the couch in solidarity, his arm around me and my head on his chest as I listened desperately to the steady beat of his heart. I was so terrified it would stop.

"It was very hard. Very surreal. No one knew what to say to me." I let out a strange little laugh. "I don't really know what I wanted them to say to me."

I don't tell Felix that it was even harder because I'd already lost Jacob. That he'd already chosen to be with her over me.

I think suddenly about the note, remembering how I traced the words with my fingers before folding the crisp paper and smoothing down the edges. I wonder where Jacob put it. I always assumed he destroyed it, threw it away. I could so easily get lost in layers of memories. Jacob, Rosalind. The small lonely version of myself from back then who had no idea how to deal with the world or the people in it.

The past is seeping through my pores and my skin starts to crawl with it. I shake my head and say brightly, "Anyway, that's how I know Rodney. It was just the two of them. I'm not sure why there was such a big age gap between them but I got the sense that maybe Donna had miscarriages. She was very intense. Their dad left when Rodney was a baby and she raised the two boys by herself after that. I'm not sure she liked me that much."

Felix has more wine. "He seemed like an odd kid. Rodney."

A flash of protest courses through my body.

"Do you think so? I always thought he was really sweet."

"C'mon, Gem. That was ten years ago. He's almost an adult now."

"I guess." I want Rodney's face to get out of my head. And Jacob's. Both their faces. So similar. I want to stop thinking about them.

Blocking the soft lamplight with my body, I pull myself onto Felix and straddle him. I hold his face as I watch the vivid green of his irises pool with black. I rub my chest against his.

It has the desired effect.

"Come here," he says gruffly, grabbing my hips and pulling me down onto him.

Chapter Fourteen

three weeks earlier

"I was going to ask you to marry me on New Year's Eve."

I froze. The egg I'd just cracked leaked clear glue into the bowl. I forced my hands together slightly and the shell broke even more, collapsing into a sticky mess.

"That probably seems like a strange thing to say." Scott was uncharacteristically all worked up and pacing like a lion.

I glanced at Ben; he was alternating between coloring in a rainbow with his new crayons and eating spoons of cereal. "I guess," I said.

"We used to talk about it. I thought you wanted to get married."

I shrugged. I got a fork and started to whisk the eggs. The yellow mixed with the translucent gray. It looked like mucus. I coughed, aware of Scott's eyes on me. I felt ill and impatient, like I'd forgotten to do something important. "Do you want some eggs?" I said, wanting the conversation to go away.

"I can't believe you're trying to change the subject of marriage with fucking scrambled eggs."

"Language," I warned automatically.

"Oh, Gem. Don't start me on parenting. Your head is barely ever in the present. You're so vague it's like you're sleepwalking half the time."

I shoved the bowl across the bench and the sharp sound clanged through the room. I flicked on the gas and stared into the blue flame.

"Well, isn't it lucky we decided to raise Ben together then. The flakiness of me is counterbalanced by the reliability and general perfection of you."

I almost forgot to put in the milk. I poured some in and it immediately looked like those geography maps in high school that show the different layers of land mass.

"Gemma, you're a good mother. C'mon, that's not what I meant. Please don't turn this into something that it isn't."

I pushed my hair behind my ears. Heat rose above the empty pan and formed an invisible wall between us. I sloshed in the egg mixture and it sizzled; the sound was calming. "You were the one who started trying to talk to me about marriage at seven in the morning. You were the one who commented on my ability to be present. Not ideal when you're about to walk out the door," I said.

"Okay, okay." His hands were up high around his face in surrender. "Gem, I just…Look, we can talk about this later, but I just feel like…" He trailed off, looking lost.

A stab of guilt hit me. Scott was so sure of his life before he met me. A planner. The guy who followed instructions. He keeps the manuals for the dishwasher and the microwave and remembers where they are. He does long division manually. He's punctual. He knows what happens next.

"I guess I just feel like we need to *do* something. It's one month away from a new year. I don't want another year of drifting. I want to feel like we're going somewhere. Together." His hands fluttered uselessly at his sides. "I want you to be my wife."

"Isn't Ben enough?" It was all I had to divert the focus away from me.

We both glanced at our son. He looked up and smiled at us, a heart-breaking smile, as he tapped the end of his spoon on the table and flicked milk onto his face.

"Ben is everything to me. You know that. But this is about you and me. Gemma, I'd want to marry you even if Ben wasn't here. Don't you get that?"

The eggs stuck to the bottom of the pan. All the moisture had disappeared. I turned the gas off and prodded at the yellow mass unenthusiastically.

"I'm not sure what I want."

Scott flicked his eyes at the clock on the wall. I was making him late.

"So if I ask you, will you say no?"

"Scott!"

"Fuck, Gem! I'm trying here, okay? I really don't know what you want from me. I really don't. I want to make things work with us." He raked his hand through his hair and looked at his watch. "And now I've got to go. We'll talk later, okay?"

He kissed me on the cheek. A press of lips I barely felt. He wrapped Ben in a large hug and planted kisses up and down the side of his face until Ben screamed with laughter.

"Bye-bye, baby man." Scott looked at me. "See ya."

I tipped the pile of overcooked eggs onto my plate as he walked out.

"I just want you to leave me alone," I said to the closed door.

Chapter Fifteen

Monday, December 14, 11:03 p.m.

I pull into the driveway behind Scott's car. I flick the lights off as I look at the house. I don't want to go inside.

It's dark but the moonlight catches on the white skin of the gum trees, making them glow. It's incredibly still: nothing moves. I breathe deeply but I'm not sure if I'm trying to calm down from seeing Felix or readying myself to see Scott. I can still feel Felix's hands all over me. I bite my lip. He's a drug; I have some and immediately want more. I close my eyes and will time to rewind so I can have a few more hours alone with him. I have never wanted time to go slower than when we are together.

A dog barks sharply and I jump so suddenly that the seatbelt catches and pins me in place. I click it open. The bedroom light is still on inside. Hopefully Scott won't want to talk; my eyes are grainy with sleep. I'm all talked out. Rosalind's death has set something off inside me. I feel reckless. Wild. Like things could suddenly just come tumbling out. I told Felix a lot tonight, more than I've ever really told anyone. And I almost told him more. All of those bricks that I've carefully stacked and built into a sturdy wall feel like they are coming loose. The floodgates of my mind have been prized open and thoughts are swirling out unchecked. It's wearing me down.

I grab my bag and get out of the car. There's a rustle in the bushes near the letterbox and I startle again. I walk briskly to the front veranda. The pull of sleep is so strong.

In a beat I freeze. There is something on the porch, a dark mass in the shadowy corner. I quickly run the options of what it might be through my mind but nothing fits. It's in my nature to assume the worst, and I think of Ben asleep in his cot only meters away: uncovered because of the heat, the fan doing lazy laps above his head, shifting the warm air around his little body. I peer over the bricks and decide that whatever it is isn't moving. I can't hear anything. Stepping carefully, I round the corner and make my way toward the mysterious shape. I'm about two meters away when my brain catches up with my eyes, and I realize I'm looking at a large bouquet of long-stemmed red roses, tucked inside the softest, blackest blanket of tissue paper.

Chapter Sixteen

Tuesday, December 15, 7:39 a.m.

"I thought they were from you for a second." Felix and I are at our favorite breakfast place, Reggie's. They do half-decent coffee, plus no one else from the station ever comes here. "Too highbrow," Keith Blight is fond of saying, though I don't think he really knows what that means. Everyone else goes across the car park to the cafeteria, which does greasy bacon and egg rolls for three dollars fifty with a bitter, watery coffee for an extra dollar.

Felix is shoveling muesli into his mouth at an alarming rate, only pausing every now and then to wash a mouthful down with coffee. I find myself getting distracted by his mouth. I notice a tiny freckle to the right of his top lip that I'm sure I've never seen before. "From me?" he says.

"Well, I only thought that for a second. Then I realized that you're not really a flowers kind of guy and that, even if you were, you would never have them delivered to my house."

"Yeah, well, no, of course not." He swallows the last of his coffee. "Jeez, Gem, it's not good."

"It was pretty freaky." After I realized what they were, I'd got a plastic bag from the car, gathered up the flowers and put them in the trunk. All I could think about were the roses that had bobbed around Rosalind's body when she was in the water. Limp from the heat, the scent of the fresh flowers formed a cloud around my face. It followed me into the house, where I quickly downed two shots of whisky, scrubbed my teeth until my gums smarted and mumbled goodnight to Scott before tumbling into a deep, dreamless sleep.

I found the note this morning, which was a blessing. If I had seen it the night before I'm not sure I would have slept nearly as soundly. A small white satiny card with the words *Beautiful things are hard to keep alive* printed neatly inside. The handwriting was deliberately simple, large inconsistent block letters printed in dark ink.

Ben clutched my legs, peering into the boot and spying the blooms.

"Ooooh, pret-ty! Mummy, look!"

"Fingers," I said, yanking him away and pushing the trunk closed.

"Are you going to tell Jonesy?" says Felix.

"Not sure. Do you think I should?"

Felix looks at me. He toys with a teaspoon, flipping it over and over between his fingers. "Well, probably. It's either someone having a pretty weird joke or it's from the person who murdered Rosalind Ryan. Either way you should get it looked at."

"I know." I am angry. This type of thing is such a distraction. I just want to get on with the investigation. If we tell Jonesy about this, then suddenly it's all about me. He might even pull me off the case.

"And this person knows where you live, Gem."

"Obviously," I say, and I can't keep the sarcasm out of my voice. "But then, this is Smithson. Lots of people know where I live. Or can easily find out."

"Well, I think you should tell him. I'm worried about you."

I sigh heavily. "Okay, how about I get one of the uniforms to look into it? Check out the florists and that kind of thing."

"And Jonesy? You'll tell him?"

"I will. Just not today, all right? I want to do the check-in and then the other teacher interviews. Maybe some of the kids. We need to keep things moving. Okay?"

"Sure." Felix waves his hand, making it clear he knows it's not up to him anyway.

I kick off the check-in at precisely 8 a.m. The uniforms look at Felix and me like baby birds all vying for attention. A short, slightly buck-toothed girl reports that Rosalind joined a gym in July but only went five times since.

"Pretty normal behavior then," remarks one of the other guys. "I basically donate money to my local gym."

"Check it out anyway," says Felix. "Maybe she was getting hassled by someone there and didn't feel comfortable going anymore."

"Her doctor wasn't very helpful," reports a man with a sunglasses tan. "She was on pretty standard meds for anxiety and depression. The same stuff that you guys found at her place." He looks around earnestly. "Apparently it's all really common."

"Keep looking. See whether you can find out if she was seeing other doctors. She might have been doctor shopping. And find out whether she was seeing a shrink." I push my hair out of my eyes. "Same goes for church. Find out whether she ever went. She might have confided in someone she trusted."

"I interviewed an old boyfriend," volunteers another. "Seems like he's the only guy she's ever really gone out with seriously but I think he's clear. Lives interstate. Reckons he's bisexual. An actor type. That's how they met."

"What was their relationship like? Did he say why they broke up?" It seems important to know what Rosalind was like unchecked, what she was like in love.

The uniform blushes lightly. "He said that she was fun. Beautiful. Said that going out with her was kind of strange because people were always looking at her. He said they had a good time together but that she had an undercurrent of sadness."

"What does that mean?" Felix looks impatient and I can tell he wants to get going. He finds the station room stifling sometimes. He says it makes his bones itch.

"I asked him, but I'm not exactly sure. The guy was a bit weird. Very dramatic. He used lots of quotes from plays and movies. He said that Rosalind was a lovely girl but that he thought she felt trapped or something. He reckons she was lonely and that she had a weird relationship with her family."

I think about Rosalind's little cottage with the movie posters and the art on its walls, so dramatic compared to the plain reality of her existence, and I swallow past a lump in my throat.

"Okay, everyone, good. The ex might be worth another chat. See if she ever fought with her brothers or father in front of him. Find out if she felt scared of them. Listen out for any gossip about her relationships with teachers, students, local guys." I stand up. "We don't have anything concrete yet so let's make today a big one. See you all back here later."

They leave and we're alone. The quiet that follows their pulsing energy is uncomfortable and obvious.

"Should we get going too?" Felix asks.

"Yeah, just hang on a sec. I'll meet you at the car."

Felix walks over to his desk and I go into the female locker room to find Karly, one of the uniforms, still there. "Karly."

"Detective." Her broad face is flushed as she stands up from tying her laces.

"Karly, I want your help with something."

"Of course."

"I want you to see if you can help me work out where some flowers were bought from."

Chapter Seventeen

Tuesday, December 15, 10:07 a.m.

Sam Blackstone can't believe it.

Trudy Fisher can't believe it.

Millie Janz can't believe it.

Neither can Paula Desmond, Troy Shooter or Izzy Mealor.

The teachers have pulled their office chairs into a circle and are sitting together, crying and staring at the floor, as we enter the staffroom. Just like the year twelves yesterday, I think, but less tanned and without the trendy haircuts.

They can't believe that Rosalind is dead and that she was murdered. They saw her on Friday! It just can't be true. They all got along well. Rosalind was quiet but friendly. A sweet girl. Sometimes she picked wildflowers and put them in an old jar on the communal table near the kettle to brighten up the staffroom. She didn't talk much about her family or friends but she always had a smile for everyone.

We begin the individual interviews. The others wait their turn in the boardroom, muffled crying occasionally breaking through the wall.

"She was so young," sobs Millie Janz into her hands. "My daughter is only a few years younger than her."

"Were you at the play on Friday night?"

Sam Blackstone wasn't but he had really wanted to go. "My girlfriend was singing at a jazz club so I had to be there instead. We would have gone this weekend."

"I went," Trudy Fisher, the art teacher, tells us. "It was a modern masterpiece. Honestly. No private school could have done it better. Everything was perfect. She did an amazing job." She ducks her head forward conspiratorially. "I wasn't sure she would, you know. She was sort of a quiet achiever, always keeping to herself."

"I was against it at first," says Troy Shooter. "I was a bit sick of all the arts stuff getting through when we couldn't even get new nets for the soccer field." His muscles bulge under his shirt and he rubs at his eyes like a sleepy child. "But Rose was pretty convincing when she wanted to be. She definitely knew how to get her way! And my wife wanted to go, she loves Shakespeare, so we went along and I have to say it was topnotch. Really professional." Troy starts to cry. "She was a great girl," he tells us, tears spilling from his eyes.

"It was beautiful," says Millie. "Just beautiful. I would have gone to see it another five times. I thought it was fabulous."

"I didn't go." Paula Desmond looks like she has been crying for hours. "I wanted to stay out of the whole thing." She pauses and then whispers, "It sounds awful to say now, but I just didn't really like the way she'd gone about it. I mean, we all want things, but she just wouldn't take no for an answer. She really pushed it with John. You know, the principal. Have you spoken to him yet?" Her eyes widen. "He's absolutely devastated. She was his favorite."

Playground sounds sing through the windows and merge with the buzz of the ancient fridge. Nicholson has obviously decided that maintaining a normal routine is the best way to go. Substitute teachers have been called in to run the younger classes.

I look around the small staffroom. The ceiling seems unusually low but it's familiar in the way that generic office spaces are. I remember standing outside the front door off the quad, waiting for my teachers to come out. Peeking past the dividing wall, wondering what secrets lay beyond. Now it's clear that we wouldn't have discovered anything of note. Cheap-looking orange carpet fades in and out of the thoroughfares. A noticeboard heavy with news hangs crookedly on the main wall. A photocopier is beeping an error message softly from the corner of the room. Mismatched mugs hang on hooks above the sink. There's a large bowl of shiny red apples on the bench. A *Romeo and Juliet* poster is tacked onto the fridge.

"So would you say you were friends as well as colleagues?" Felix asks.

"Oh yes," says Millie.

"We were very close," says Sam. "That's why this is so hard."

"Like sisters we were," sobs Trudy.

"Wouldn't stay here if we weren't," mumbles Troy. "Life's too short."

"It's such a great bunch of people," declares Paula. "I've always thought we are so lucky. I was only saying so to my husband the other month how lucky we are. And now this!"

I get her a glass of water and she cries into it, sipping between sobs.

"How do you find working for John Nicholson?" Felix asks.

Paula blinks. "He's a good man. A great principal."

"He's very involved," Trudy tells us. "Always in here for a chat."

"Was he close with Ms. Ryan?"

Sam's eyes narrow. "Sure. We all were. It's a real team culture."

Troy nods. "They both love art and stuff like that so they have a lot in common. Sometimes they would go to plays and things." He looks back and forth between us. "Like the theater or other school plays, I guess. You know, to check out the competition."

Izzy Mealor shrugs and won't meet our eyes. "He's good as bosses go. Seems like a nice guy." She flicks her hair out of her eyes and chews at a fingernail. "They seemed friendly but not in an odd way."

"I've known John for years," Millie tells us, leaning forward as she clutches at her handbag. "Years. He's a wonderful man. It was very hard for him when Jessica died." Her eyes are huge behind her thick glasses. Tears teeter on their edges and threaten to spill over. "He cared about Rosalind a lot. I think he had a soft spot for her. Because she used to be a student here."

"So there was never any trouble that you can think of?"

Trudy shakes her head. "Not really. Normal teaching stuff here and there; it can be a stressful job sometimes. And there was the Valentine's Day thing."

Felix and I look at each other. "What was that about?"

"Oh, it was silly, really. One of the boys sent her flowers on Valentine's Day. A bit awkward, obviously, but no harm done."

"Do you know who sent them?" asks Felix.

"I'm not sure. I don't think anyone wanted to make a big deal about it, but the kids would talk about it. One of the girls in my class said it was Kai Bracks, but I don't know. Could have been any of them—they all adored her."

"I think she was a bit of a mystery." Izzy looks at us solemnly, her stare a haunting crystal gray. Her dyed red hair spikes sharply away from her forehead. "I mean, I'm newer than the others, this is only my first year, but I just couldn't seem to get beneath the day-to-day stuff with her."

"So you wouldn't say you were friends then?"

Izzy shrugs and her complicated-looking silver necklace jangles.

"I *liked* her, I guess. I mean we all *liked* her." She uncrosses and then recrosses her legs. "And this is just so awful. Obviously." She furrows her brow. "It's just that I never felt like I knew her. I mean, she was very attractive," Izzy continues thoughtfully. "It was almost off-putting. And I feel like she played that up sometimes, especially with the men. Even with the students." Her eyes flit to her lap. "But once you got past that it just seemed like there wasn't much there at all."

"Well," says Felix, after Izzy gathers her things and leaves. He leans back in his chair, which creaks loudly under his weight.

"Careful," I say, "these chairs are worse than the ones in our office."

I feel exhausted. Dazed from all of this chat about Rosalind. We've been playing round robin in the staffroom for almost three hours but I can't shake the feeling that we are getting no closer to finding out anything more about Rose.

"We're hardly getting a clear picture of her, are we?" says Felix. "It seems like she was as much a puzzle when she was alive as she is dead."

"Yes. That's pretty much what I remember from school too," I say, feeling the surge of anxiety from that era twist inside me. I had wanted her approval so much.

"Mostly everyone seems to like her but it's in a removed sort of way. It sounds like she was quite manipulative sometimes."

I feel mildly defensive about Rosalind even though he is right. "She was very attractive. I'm not sure that necessarily means she was manipulative."

Felix looks at me, obviously deep in thought about something.

"Let's head back," I say. "We need to review the interviews that the uniforms have done, touch base with the family and then do afternoon check-in." I get up and stretch out my stiff back. "We also need to speak with Kai Bracks. See if he really did send her those flowers."

Felix doesn't move. He is staring at the bowl of ruby-red apples.

"You coming?" I ask.

"Yeah. I'm coming. I'm just trying to think. There's something not right here, Gem, but I reckon we can't see it."

"Yeah, I know." I sigh. "Maybe we're looking for something that isn't there. It could be a random attack."

"Maybe," he acquiesces.

I continue, "Though there are some things about her situation that seem jarring. Like, why did she come back to Smithson? She had a teaching job in the city. Why didn't she just get another job in a nearby school? It's not like there was a partner dragging her back here."

"I agree," says Felix. "And she's not particularly close to her family. So why come back? I keep thinking about her being pregnant. Maybe she... oh fuck, I don't know." Suddenly he grabs my hand and kisses it. We lock eyes and my heart jerks into a higher gear.

"C'mon," he says, "let's get out of here." He pulls me up and runs his hands down the length of my body as I scramble to get my bag and quell the fire that races through me.

Chapter Eighteen

Tuesday, December 15, 6:56 p.m.

I dial Anna on the way to Dad's after work.

"Good timing," she says, "I got the tox report about an hour ago. All right, so…" Anna breathes into the phone. "She was pissed, but that was it. Traces of marijuana too, but that would've been from weeks ago. Seems like your teacher friend dabbled sometimes."

"How drunk was she?"

"On her way. Blood alcohol of .08. She would have been either overly excited or starting to get a little melancholy, depending on what kind of drunk she was and what her tolerance was like."

I picture Rose swaying as she stood in the middle of a trampoline at a house party in our final year, her eyes slanting slightly. I remember her jumping suddenly and then falling backward with her hands across her chest. She lay there for a few minutes in the middle of the noisy party just staring at the sky. I watched her for ages.

"I don't think she was the overly excitable type. But I didn't really know her that well."

"Anyway, that's about it. I can confirm her pregnancy was about eleven weeks along. We can assume she would have known."

"We haven't been able to find any medical records about her pregnancy," I tell Anna.

"Well, maybe she was in denial," Anna replies. "It happens."

I swallow, glancing at Ben in the rear-view mirror. He's playing with an action man, stretching his legs into side splits, oblivious to the content of my phone call.

"Anything else?" I ask.

"I think she was in the water for a few hours," says Anna. "And I think she was killed around midnight. Maybe a little earlier."

"Straight after the play," I say.

"Yep," says Anna cheerily.

"What about the sexual assault? You mentioned some bruising and obviously there's the missing underwear. Anything else?"

"Yeah, that's tricky. I'd guess she was assaulted because her underwear was missing, but who knows? Maybe she just wasn't wearing any. Did you guys find any?"

"Nope. Not that I've been told anyway."

"There's no DNA because of the water. No clear evidence of violence either, just the bruising around her thighs, but I'm still not sure what that means. It could have been from roughish sex. There are some strange scratches that are hard to explain. But they could be from sticks in the lake."

I'm almost at Dad's. Ben lifts his head, recognizing familiar landmarks.

"Was she seeing anyone or are we looking at an immaculate conception?" asks Anna.

I laugh. "We're not sure yet. We're still looking into whether she was officially seeing anyone. There's nothing solid at the moment."

I think about the heart-shaped stone we found at her house. Was it from a lover?

"Well, enjoy your night," says Anna. "No doubt I'll see you soon. Hopefully at the bar rather than the autopsy table."

I say good-bye to Anna.

Wild roses curl up the side of Dad's brick fence next to where I park the car and I stare at them, turning them into tiny red dots, wondering, for what feels like the thousandth time, who the hell killed Rosalind Ryan.

Chapter Nineteen

Tuesday, December 15, 7:22 p.m.

"Are you looking after yourself?"

"For the most part," I say, letting my feet dangle just above the shiny white tiles. Dad recently renovated his kitchen and there is now an island bench equipped with high stools. I kick my legs back and forth like a child as I watch him make dinner. He moved into this house on Winston Grove about three years ago. It's a sweet little street: slightly elevated, so you can look out across the center of Smithson from the hill in the backyard. Dad seems happy here; he's even mentioned getting a dog. Scott and I have been renting my family home from him since he moved here. It made sense: I was pregnant and we barely had any savings. Dad was keen on the arrangement. The memories in the house were becoming too much for him but he couldn't bear for it to belong to someone else. Three years later, and Scott and I have made no progress toward buying our own place. I feel paralyzed at the thought and change the subject every time Scott or Dad mentions it. For now, Scott seems content enough to tinker in the yard and put new cupboards in the bedrooms.

"Are you drinking too much?"

"I'm drinking enough, Dad." My voice is firm and he nods, stirring cream into the pasta.

I can hear Ben's laughter from the lounge room. He is watching *The Smurfs*. Ben's laugh always makes me nervous. I worry for the day when he won't laugh easily: the day when he can't sit back and enjoy Gargamel hunting down the tiny blue people.

"How's Scott?"

I pick at some skin that has split down the side of my nail. It pulls away and a tiny trail of blood breaks out. I hold my thumb onto it, pressing hard. "He's fine. Busy."

"Mm."

Dad's new kitchen is still small but a skylight has been cut into the ceiling and the last of the sun hits the wall above his head. Dad is tall and lean and shows no sign of stooping. His hair has been completely white for over a decade. He is the most capable person I know. Dad is a fixer. I suppose "handyman" is the technical term. Mechanical, electrical, old, new: Dad can tackle pretty much anything. He's ridden the digital revolution like a pro and has added computers and smart phones to the things he can bring back to life. His hands just seem to know what to do.

After Mum died I remember lying on the lounge, staring at the wall and hearing him say to my aunt Megan that this was the first time he'd ever felt like there was something in front of him that he couldn't fix. Megan, who is teary at the best of times, had simply howled into her hanky.

"Shame he couldn't come tonight," Dad says.

I shrug. "It's good for him to go out with his mates. My job makes that hard sometimes."

Scott and I met at Riders. Back then Riders was new and the only club in town that was considered appropriate if you were over twenty-one. At twenty-five, I had outstayed my welcome at all of the bars in Smithson and wasn't quite ready to embrace the full cop stereotype of drinking at Bessie's or The Green Frog, so Riders was my standard Saturday night. As was getting stupidly drunk and passing out, either at my place or at the home of whichever lucky stranger had taken my fancy a few hours earlier. It's fair to say it wasn't the best of times, but I did have some fun. The evening I met Scott, I had bumped into a guy I'd slept with a few weeks earlier who was mad keen for a repeat episode. I'd let him kiss me and then had spent over an hour trying to lose him by disappearing to the toilet every ten minutes and hoping he'd be gone by the time I came out. This strategy wasn't working, so I had reluctantly started to let him buy me drinks. The last thing I remember is telling a nice-looking guy that I was a cop. I woke up the next morning with a hangover that seemed determined to kill me from the inside, so bad was the stabbing pain. The guy was there too, nervously offering me an energy drink and Tylenol capsules. Scott had been amazed to discover that I really was a cop and then had insisted on staying into the evening to cook me dinner, lecturing me on the importance of decent food as I sat on the cold tiles, my head pressed against the toilet seat. To this day I don't know whether we had sex that night but I suspect not. The pattern of our relationship was established and set in that first encounter. Scott was suddenly just simply *there*, looking after me, and has been ever since.

"You should go out with your friends too, Gemma. Not always people from work."

"I don't really have any, Dad. You know cops, married to the job!" I say it cheerily but it comes out flat, even though it is partly true.

"What about Catherine?"

"You mean Carol?"

"Yes, yes. From your mothers' group. Weren't you friendly with her for a bit?"

"Sure, I guess. I'm supposed to see her on the weekend. She's pretty busy with her kids. She has a new baby." I have some of the soda water that Dad has placed in front of me. "Plus I think that she feels like my job is contagious. I don't think she likes me being around her kids."

Dad is dishing up our dinner and he stops to raise an eyebrow at me. "Did she say that?"

I jump off the stool and call Ben into the kitchen. "Not really. Just a vibe I get."

Dad makes a skeptical sound as we sit down at the table.

Ben chatters his way through the meal, and Dad and I talk around him. Despite being almost sixty-five, Dad is busy. He works almost full-time and swims at least two kilometers a day. He's telling me about some mirrored cabinets he's building for a new development out past Gowran when my phone rings.

"Hey," I say, flashing an apologetic look at Dad as I walk into the lounge room. The TV is playing the credits of some cartoon I don't recognize. I flick to the news.

"Hey," says Felix. "Where are you? Home?"

"At my dad's." I pick up some of Ben's toys and place them in the wooden chest my dad made for him last Christmas.

"Well, after afternoon check-in I spent some time digging into the RYAN empire. Mainly just financials but I made a few calls as well." I can hear female voices teasing each other in the background and I know he must be at home with his daughters.

"And?"

"There's definitely some juicy stuff. George Ryan's company has majorly pissed off a whole lot of people recently. They're cutting jobs across Australia and replacing them with overseas staff. There's talk of dodgy deals, insider trading, the whole shebang."

"You think it's connected?"

There's a loud shriek down the phone and a girl's voice is accusing someone of stealing her hairbrush. A tightness forms in my chest as I picture Felix's family, the three teenage girls from the photo on his desk. Ben comes into the room and wraps his arms around my legs, probably covering them with pasta sauce. He looks up at me while I look down at him. His dark eyes sparkle in the dim light. I sigh into the phone as Felix shushes the teenage cacophony at his end.

"Sorry. Anyway, look, I don't know if it's linked or not but it's something. Maybe one of these disgruntled guys wanted to teach George a lesson?"

"Yeah. Maybe," I say.

"Anything else come your way tonight?"

"Not really. Anna got the tox report. Rose was a bit pissed and had smoked weed in the past month but that was it. I spoke to Marcus earlier too, just to let him know how we're getting on. He was polite but very vague. They want to have the funeral on Friday afternoon."

"Is Anna okay with that?" Felix asks.

"Seems so. She's already spoken to them apparently."

"She could have spoken to us." He yawns. "Well, good, I guess. You never know who that might bring out."

We agree to meet at Reggie's before morning check-in and hang up. I pick up Ben and stand in front of the mantelpiece for a few minutes, looking at photos of Mum. There's one I particularly like of us when I was about Ben's age. We're staring into the camera, our round moss-colored eyes dancing with light. We look so happy. I brush some dust off the glass and run a finger along the side of Mum's face.

Ben is heavy in my arms as I carry him back into the kitchen. Dad is wiping down the table and the kettle whistles from the bench.

"Work?"

"Yep," I reply.

"Still partnered with the older guy? Fred, right?"

"Uh-huh. Felix."

"That's good."

I watch Dad make us tea, dipping the bags in and out of the mugs and squeezing them with a teaspoon. I almost tell him about Felix. About my miscarriage. My mouth opens and I inhale as if I'm about to speak, but the moment passes and Dad places the steaming tea in front of me and suddenly the thought of telling him is unfathomable.

"Terrible business with the Ryan girl." He passes a sleepy Ben a cookie. I shift so Ben is sitting across my lap rather than clasped around me. "One of your cases, I assume."

"Sure is."

"I remember her, you know. Pretty little thing. She was in your prep class. I knew her mother. Olivia. She was something, she was."

I sit up, surprised. "How did you know her?"

Dad stares at the wall, clearly accessing old memories. A smile plays across his face. "My old man was friendly with her family, I think. I remember her playing with your aunt Megan when we were young. They must have been in the same class. Olivia was very clever but always in trouble. And very beautiful, which never helps." Dad smiles at me. "I used to worry about you so much for that very reason. Still do."

I swat his comment away. "Dad, come on. I hardly look like Olivia Ryan did."

"Well, you have always been beautiful to me, Gemma. Anyway, I remember hearing about her dying. Such a tragedy, leaving behind four children and never really meeting her baby daughter. Very sad. And now this."

"Yeah." My heart is beginning to pound as I piece something together in my mind. The photo of Mum and me. The old newspaper photo of Olivia and George. Olivia's photo on the Ryans' mantelpiece. The photos of Rosalind staring at me from the pin board at work.

"So many things just don't make any sense." Dad shakes his head as he sips his tea and watches Ben, who is licking his biscuit, turning it to mush. "I hope you figure it all out soon, sweetheart. And please be careful."

A whistle screams inside my head as I give him a smile. My thoughts are wild. I'm pulling things together and checking them over, either pushing them aside or grasping at them to make sure they fit. I force myself to stay seated. Breathe. I shift Ben's weight away from my stomach, which still feels slightly tender.

"So," I say, a little too brightly, "what else have you been up to, Dad?"

"Oh, this and that. Did some gardening on the weekend. Finally fixed Mrs. Potter's shed door."

I've long suspected that there is something between Dad and the long-widowed Mrs. Potter, but he has never said anything and I've never asked. That's just how it works between us.

"Was Ben good when he stayed with you on Friday?"

"Sure was." Dad glances at my son adoringly. Ben's mouth hangs slightly open, showcasing a dainty string of drool. "Slept like a little champion. What did you get up to, darling? Did you and Scott end up going out?"

"No. Scott had a work thing. I just got takeaway and went to bed early. Ended up being a good thing seeing as it's been crazy ever since."

Dad nods, looking at me, his eyes worried.

I swallow back the rest of my tea and place the mug hard on the table. My throat is sore like I have the beginnings of a cold. I quickly stand and pull Ben onto my hip. Dad looks up at me, blinking, as if emerging from a dream.

"Dad, thanks. This was great but we have to go."

In the car I feel breathless, my thoughts whirling as I drive. My mind steadily working through my new theory in between glancing at Ben in the rear-view mirror, catching the exact moment his eyes close into sleep.

Chapter Twenty

then

Jacob gently pushes Gemma onto her back and sits astride her, pinning her against the bed. "Your eyes are the coolest color," he tells her and she rolls them skyward in response before closing them and pushing him away. He can tell she is pleased though.

About six months ago his mother took him and Rodney to visit her sister, who lives in a small beach town south of Sydney. Jacob, who had never seen the sea before, trailed behind the others as they walked along the narrow curve of beach, kicking at the salty water and staring out into the endless blue. He cut his foot on a piece of glass, an old beer bottle worn down by the tide. Washing the sand off the glass in the shallows, he noted that it was the exact pale green of Gemma's eyes. He watched with interest as the blood from his foot reached out into the water before merging with it and disappearing completely. He felt a pang of longing, almost jealousy, at the ease with which things in nature seemed to just happen and how jarring his own existence was in comparison.

Nothing flows in his world; it's all sharp edges and impossible corners. Except for Gemma.

Jacob runs his fingers down the side of her face and she turns back to him, her eyes sparkling and her mouth angled for more kissing. She is so responsive to him, the nerves on her body come alive at his touch, her lips glow red when they kiss.

When he is with her he *is* happy, he's sure of it.

"Do you love me?" she says, playfully, so sure of the answer.

"Of course," he says, automatically leaning forward to kiss her.

And he does of course but there is a darkness too. He feels the weight of her need sometimes, tight around his neck, pulling something deep inside, and it makes him think crazy thoughts. He feels the weight of everything. He's not sure where it's come from but it is there all the time now, heavy and painful, across his chest and shoulders. Sometimes he can barely breathe.

"What was that?" she says, half scrambling into a sitting position, the blanket falling away to reveal her small creamy breasts, her soft stomach.

"What?" he says, kissing the side of her face and noting the fine blue veins pulsing in her neck.

She pauses for a moment, eyes wide, before relaxing back next to him. "Nothing, I guess. I thought I heard Dad's car."

Ned Woodstock is at work. Jacob and Gemma came straight here together after school instead of going to the shopping center with the others. They've been doing that more and more lately, spending time alone together, blocking everything else out. Being with her is like being by himself, an intense, amplified version of it. He carefully stores their moments together so that he can pull them from his memory and observe them, turning them over before putting them back in his mind.

But lately he has imagined alternate versions of their moments together. Versions where he smashes it all apart, breaking the precious glass of their bond and watching it shatter all over the floor. The pull of the drama, the desire for this intensity has been overwhelming sometimes, and he worries that he will just do it. Break Gemma's heart. A strange ripple of want runs through him whenever he thinks about her reeling away from him in horror, but it's always quickly followed by the unthinkable terror of destroying the person he loves more than anything in the world.

Just a week ago he stood on the side of the highway, on the sharp corner near the Smithson Town sign, and wondered at the possibility of stepping out onto the road. He imagined the rushing wind that would come as a truck bore down, the sheer joy in that moment of nothing. The temptation of being gone: no longer a person, no longer anything.

"Hey," says Gemma, with only lightness in her voice.

Jacob blinks, refocusing on her lying next to him. She is his soulmate, he is sure, but she doesn't understand. No one does.

"Kiss me," she says, and he does, deeply, holding her tightly, grabbing at her frantically as they move together. Everything is clear and good again. He kisses her hard when he pushes inside her and she moans softly and he wishes that he could bundle her up and protect her, keep her safe from the darkness that is within him and everything that is to come. As he shudders into her he can't help thinking that the safest place for her might be as far away from him as possible.

Chapter Twenty-one

Wednesday, December 16, 7:41 a.m.

"Felix! Felix, I've got something, I think." I sit down opposite him. He looks up, interested but tired. A clump of gel makes his hair stand up oddly and I stop myself from reaching out to smooth it down.

He waves toward the bustling kitchen and stifles a yawn. "I've ordered you a coffee already."

The newspaper on the table between us has Rosalind's Mona Lisa face on the front page. I pick it up and toss it onto the next table, face down. I'm sick of her being everywhere.

"Great, great." I feel energized by my theory. Alive. It's a little cooler today and I blow-dried my hair this morning. It falls heavy and thick around my face. I toss it back behind my shoulders, ducking my head, trying to catch Felix's eye. It's not often I like what I see when I look in the mirror but I did this morning. "So don't you want to know what I know?" I ask him.

He laughs almost in spite of himself and grabs my hand briefly. "Yes, of course I do. Sorry. I'm just tired. Shit with Maisie."

I pause. "That's okay. I understand."

Felix has described his eldest daughter as a dangerous volcano set to erupt. I can't imagine navigating the delicate layers of a teenage girl—how to manage that raw energy—but Felix always seems fairly calm when he talks about his daughters. Not that he talks about them often. Home life is a dangerous territory for us so we normally try to avoid it altogether.

Coffees are placed in front of us and I breathe in the aroma, realizing that today is the first day since Friday I have woken up feeling normal. My stomach feels settled. I'm lighter on my feet. I rub my foot along Felix's under the table.

"Don't be doing that. We've got check-in soon." He smiles at me and everything is fine again. His eyes sparkle as he leans forward and whispers, "You look especially pretty today."

I wave him away, pleased. "We've got check-in soon, remember."

He gives my foot a soft kick. "So?"

"So...I don't think that George Ryan was Rosalind's father."

Felix's eyes widen. "No way."

"It's nothing fancy, just basic biology. Rosalind had brown eyes. Really brown eyes. George has blue eyes. So did Olivia. I saw a photo of her at their house and then there was one online too."

"Just like their sons."

"Just like Rosalind's half-brothers," I agree, downing my coffee.

He looks at me, his own eyes glowing as he considers my theory.

"Okay, okay. Look, I don't know much about that kind of stuff, but surely it's just an anomaly." He glances at his watch and gestures for me to get up. "I mean, how could no one have picked up on it before?"

He pays and we walk outside, crossing the skate park that leads to the station car park. It always strikes me as ironic that a skate park was built next door to a police station and, based on how infrequently it's used, I assume the local skaters feel the same way. Despite the rapidly warming air, dew still kisses at the grass. The gray sky looks backlit with swirls of eggshell blue breaking through.

"Well, apart from the fact that I'm brilliant, I guess no one really thought about it. Especially because Olivia died when Rose was only a few days old. People were probably pretty distracted by the idea of a tiny baby being left without a mother. And because Olivia wasn't there as Rosalind grew older, maybe the comparisons between them were never really made."

"But George Ryan might have known all along."

"He might have. Who knows? Maybe he and Olivia weren't even sleeping together. That would have made it pretty obvious. But, if they were, then he may never have realized."

"Rosalind might have known. Or found out."

"Sure. Though, equally, she might never have given it much thought. You tend to assume your parents are who they say they are."

"They might have both known and been really open about it," Felix suggests.

"Maybe. Though he certainly didn't mention it the other day."

"Probably not the best time for a family history tour," he says.

My phone trills and we both look at it in my hand. A silent number.

"Going to get that?" Felix asks.

"No. It's probably just my favorite reporter again. I keep forgetting to call her back. She can leave a message."

Felix rolls his eyes at me. He doesn't get my issue with Candy.

We step inside the station and the air turns musky with sweat, disinfectant and burned toast.

I'm still focused on our genetic mystery. "George could have found out somehow last week and lost it."

"He was in surgery though, remember."

"Yeah, but his sons weren't," I remind Felix.

"What, you think they could be working together?" Felix seems unconvinced.

I sigh. "No, not really. I just think we can't rule it out."

Felix pauses and taps the archway of the door as he looks at me, thinking. "Are we sure Olivia Ryan died the way it's reported? Maybe George found out about all this a long time ago and flipped his lid and killed her once he knew the child wasn't his."

I pause too. "I think it would be pretty hard to fake an internal hemorrhage. But we should look into it. That type of scenario makes much more sense than a random psycho."

We walk down the corridor.

"*Everything* makes more sense than a random psycho. Especially if it's like the guy I went out with last night," Anna says, smiling as she falls into step with us. She makes a gun shape and tilts it at her head. Anna's bad luck with men is notorious around the station, so much so that many of the junior cops often feel bold enough to offer her the stability of an exclusive relationship, but she prefers to find losers on the net. Felix thinks she simply enjoys regaling us with outrageous stories to liven up our dull lives.

"Rough night, Anna?" I say.

"Rough *evening*," she clarifies. "There was no way I was seeing in a new day with this guy. The night shift was bad enough." She laughs good-naturedly. "But I live to date another day."

Felix laughs. I can hear the rumble of the waiting uniforms. They are still fresh and eager for this case but that will soon fade. We have one more week before the possibility that our case will become cold looms large, the hours start to feel pointless and new crimes begin to hold more appeal. Fresh cops tend to be like kids with a new toy at Christmas; cases only have so much appeal before they want to play with something else for a while. Us detectives are different. We tend to stubbornly hold on to our favorites until the clues and cast of suspects are prized out of our hands, and we're pulled kicking and screaming away, forced to pay attention to something else.

"Wait," says Anna. "Before you go in I just wanted to say that we're going to release the body to the Ryan family today. We were pretty sure we would but it's definite now. We've got all the preliminary tox in, which seems clear, so she's good to go."

Felix and I exchange glances.

"You've got all kinds of samples, don't you, Anna?"

She shrugs. "Of course."

"For example, if we need to match DNA to prove paternity, then there won't be any issues?"

"No, confirming the paternity for the fetus won't be a problem. Or should I say disproving it."

I don't correct her assumption. The two paternity puzzles dance before me, the gaps I've started filling in my mind making way for holes again. Regardless of who Rosalind's father was, it's still far more likely that her own pregnancy was a factor in her murder.

"Great." Felix puts his hand on the door handle again.

"Hey, Anna," I say, my voice slightly bratty, "what are the chances of two people with blue eyes having a child with dark brown eyes?"

She looks at me curiously. "Almost zero."

"C'mon, let's go," I say smoothly to Felix, who sticks his tongue out at me.

I don't often dream about Jacob anymore, but for about three years after he died I had a recurring dream almost every other night in which he was running away from me in the dark, his bare feet pounding on the hard ground as he ducked past branches and pushed through long grass. I didn't know why I was chasing him but I knew that he was going to die, and panic was high in my throat, my heart pulsing like a drumbeat as we broke out of the dense bush and onto a moonlit sand dune.

"Jacob!" I screamed over and over, but he ran away from me, faster than he had ever run before, our feet catching on the cold sand.

I could feel death calling for him and I was crying messily, when he suddenly stopped and turned around. I came to a halt too. A ghostly glow bounced off his face and he looked straight through me with a sad smile. *A good-bye smile*, I thought a moment too late. A loud clock tick echoed around us, signaling that it was all over, and in unbearable slow motion, he fell backward with total abandon. It seemed impossible that no one would catch him. But he was gone and I was left alone on the sand dune. There was no sound: it was like I was in the center of a windowless dome.

Sobbing, and with silence blaring in my ears, the dream version of myself went to where Jacob had been standing, and it was then I realized I was teetering on the sharp edge of a huge cliff. I looked down at the broken star of his body. He stared blankly back at me from the middle of a rock as the arms of the navy blue ocean curled angrily around the edges of his cold, hard grave.

Chapter Twenty-two

Wednesday, December 16, 10:11 a.m.

"It must be very difficult."

George Ryan nods in reply. He looks better today. Some of the color has come back into his face. He's wearing charcoal suit pants and a crisp white shirt. I spy an ostentatious watch on his wrist. He moves slowly, his blue eyes cloudy. This is a look I know well. Often, when people lose a loved one, this flatness appears in their stare. It's not so bad when they are talking or actively performing a task, but as soon as they stop, their eyes wander back to the grief and the marble sets in. I know I have this look too. It's a sad thing when your default gaze broadcasts to the world that you're thinking about death.

George places two mugs of tea on the coffee table and settles heavily into the armchair. A slight groan escapes his lips.

"How are you feeling?"

He shrugs. "Oh well, it's hard to say really. If you mean from the operation, then I'm not sure. Physical pain has somewhat taken a backseat."

I sip at the tea and nod.

"There's not really an instruction manual for something like this," he says, his eyes fixed to a section of the wall.

"No, there isn't. That's very similar to what John Nicholson said, actually."

He looks up blankly. Then, "The principal at the school?" He straightens and his voice thickens, carrying a sudden hardness.

I watch him carefully. I can picture him in a business environment; there is a sense of quiet power about him. "Yes."

"Well. He's right, I suppose." George adds, "That man's been bothering us about having a memorial at the school on Friday."

"Yes, I heard that," I say.

A flash of anger flickers in his eyes and he grunts.

I find myself coming to Nicholson's defense. "Well, it might be good for people to have the chance to say good-bye. Especially her students."

Neither of us speaks for a few moments as thoughts run through my mind. He overreacted just now, but the difficulty with a murder case is that everyone's oddness is likely to be legitimate. Virtually everyone we speak to is feeling some sense of loss. Plus, they are scared; their normal lives have been pulled apart by the blunt reminder of mortality. Navigating the difference between weird but normal grief as opposed to truly suspicious behavior is key for any detective worth their stripes.

"Do you mind if I ask what your surgery was for?"

He relaxes back into his chair and his eyes soften again. "I have prostate cancer."

"I'm very sorry to hear that," I say.

He waves my comment away. "It's manageable so far and I've kept it all very low-key. I don't want to make a big fuss. So far I seem to be hanging on remarkably well."

"When did you go into hospital?"

He gives me a look that makes it clear he knows I'm confirming his alibi but he answers easily. "I went in at about seven on Friday morning. Marcus picked me up from the hospital on Saturday morning on the way back from the airport. I think around nine."

"Your other sons couldn't pick you up?"

He grimaces. "My other sons don't get up early. Plus, I was at Our Lady, so Marcus was coming past anyway."

His voice rolls across the vast room, up the walls and along the ceiling. It's a classic sales voice and I remind myself that this man is used to being in control. He isn't familiar with situations that you can't pay your way out of. Like a murdered daughter. Or even, perhaps, an adulterous wife.

"Do your sons always stay here when they visit?"

"Usually. When Timothy was still with Alice they sometimes stayed with him, but he's here now anyway."

"Are you happy to have him living here?"

George looks at me without talking for almost a minute and I have to force myself not to squirm. "Well, the house is big enough that I barely notice. It's fine for now."

"Mr. Ryan, I have to ask you about your sons."

"Yes," he says, a defensive note creeping into his voice.

"We've confirmed that Marcus flew into Gowran on Saturday morning but we're finding it difficult to confirm that Bryce was home all evening and that Timothy was at the school before he returned here. I assume you have security tapes in the house?"

His eyes are steel but after a moment he waves his hand. "Yes, just outside. You'll be able to see cars coming and going from the garage. And the street in front of the house. You can look at the files whenever you want."

"Thank you, Mr. Ryan," I say. "I'll have them all collected this afternoon." Then, changing tack, I ask, "How is your business these days?"

"Well, I'm getting a bit old to manage things but I believe it is ticking along nicely."

I look him in the eye. "We've heard that there are a few issues. You seem to have a few enemies."

He lightly snorts air out of his nostrils. "No one special. I have found in business, detective, that if you don't have someone upset with you then you're not doing it right." He folds his hands together and firms his jaw.

"So all the turmoil about Aussie jobs and the salaries of your senior executives doesn't concern you?"

He sighs and says mildly, "It concerns me, yes. But it has nothing to do with Rose."

"How do you know?" I press.

"Because it's all a political beat-up. And the reports are misleading, so we're focusing on setting the record straight."

"Have you received threats?"

He shakes his head. "No, nothing directly. I've never really been threatened about the company. There was a bomb threat made here to the house once but that was years ago now."

"Tell me about Rosalind," I say, changing the subject again.

His hands flutter briefly away from his lap before settling back into place. "What else would you like to know?"

"Well, how did you feel about having a daughter finally, after three sons?"

He looks surprised but says, "Rosalind's birth was not a happy time, unfortunately. As you know, Olivia died very shortly after Rose was born and I'm afraid a new baby was a very hard thing to have to deal with."

"Understandable," I murmur.

"Yes. It was very hard. It was Christmas Day, which added to the strain. This has never been a happy time of the year for our family. Rosalind was quite a good baby but the boys were young and scared without their mother and there simply weren't enough hours in the day. I made sure I had help."

"From family?"

He laughs. "No. Not from family, though Olivia's mother tried her best to help. Mad as a cut snake, that woman. I wouldn't let her anywhere near the children. No, I had paid help mostly. Fortunately, I had the means."

"What was your wife like?"

He sips at his tea thoughtfully and then looks up at me as if he is trying to decide how much to reveal. "Olivia was a very complicated woman."

"And very beautiful," I say, indicating the photo of Olivia on the mantelpiece.

He nods, looking at it too. "Indeed she was. Incredible-looking. Like Vivien Leigh, I used to think. But she did know it. I loved her to death but she was very difficult." He smiles. "My very own Scarlett O'Hara."

"Difficult how?"

He sighs heavily. "Difficult in all the ways a woman can be difficult. She was very selfish. Very demanding. She would occasionally have episodes. Quite bad episodes. We had been having a lot of trouble before she died. Pregnancy seemed to make things worse. Hormones, I suppose. I was keen to keep that side of her away from the boys."

I nod. "It's challenging looking after children when you are dealing with all the things that adults have to work out."

"Yes. Being an adult is something that I don't think you ever really get used to." He gives a brief ironic laugh. "You must have children yourself to say that." He releases another heavy sigh. "But this is not about Olivia, is it?"

"No, it's not. But sometimes this kind of background information is helpful. Do you think Rosalind was impacted by not having a mother?"

"Impossible to say. She never knew another life. She was very quiet and sort of self-contained. Smart and opinionated at times but not overly affectionate. I remarried for a while and she seemed to like having Lila around, but that didn't work out in the end."

"I didn't know you had remarried," I say.

"Yes, to Lila Wilcox. She's a good woman but we were terribly unsuited." He clenches his fists as if trying to get his blood flowing. "To be honest, their closeness bothered me sometimes. I felt a bit excluded, though I recognized it was probably good for Rose to have another woman around. Seems ridiculous now. I don't know if they were in touch. Lila lives in China." He looks around the room absently. "I should tell her what's happened, I suppose."

I make a note to call Lila Wilcox myself.

"Mr. Ryan, I know this is hard, but what was your relationship with Rosalind like?"

George Ryan glances outside to the shimmering pool. He looks regal sitting in profile, his shirt tailored, his hair groomed. I recall seeing a similar scene online a few days ago in a local news article that profiled his business. I keep catching the startling blue of Olivia's frozen stare in my peripheral vision.

"I loved Rose, but I think that, as hard as I tried, it was difficult to separate losing Olivia from gaining her. I suppose she might have sensed that sometimes." He finishes his tea and the cup slips as he places it on the saucer. The clatter of china needles up my spine. "But I always looked after her. I loved her. I'm just not sure I really knew what to do with a daughter."

His formality feels jarring. I sense he is telling the truth but there is a coolness that has me on guard.

"Do you think Rosalind liked living in Smithson? I mean, I assume she must have, to come back."

"Well, yes, I suppose she did." The furrow on his brow deepens as he says, "In many ways, Rosalind wasn't very ambitious. But she was happy to work hard. Not like my boys, who have high expectations but want everything to fall into their laps. She always had her head in a book. She liked reading and writing and those kinds of things. She did live in the city for a few years but I don't think she really enjoyed it. I understood that, as I am not well-suited to the city lifestyle either. And there was some trouble at the school she taught at."

"Trouble?"

"Yes. Some issue with a love-struck student, which caused her a lot of grief. She didn't want to discuss it but I got the sense she was quite angry about it. She decided to move back here to teach after that."

"That must have been very stressful for her," I say. Felix and I made some calls to her old school late yesterday and are waiting to hear back. Something definitely went down there.

"She took it all in her stride. She wasn't one to dwell on things, really. Despite how she looked, she was very strong."

"We've been to her house," I say abruptly.

George seems mildly surprised. "Well, yes, I suppose you have. Of course."

"Once we have everything we need we'll let you know so that you can have her things. And you may wish to sell the house in time."

He waves his hand limply in my direction. "None of that seems to matter right now."

"You bought her the place, is that right?"

He looks at me and I feel the mood shift again. He seems to shut down and sink into himself, wary.

"Yes. I've helped all my children in different ways, depending on what they wanted." He carefully rolls up the cuff of his shirtsleeve. "Rose only wanted a little place. She was not an extravagant person. I thought it was a good idea after so long being the only girl, and the baby, that she have a bit of independence." He smiles at me, his mouth pulling sharply at both ends until it seems to fall into a small snarl. "Have you any further information on what happened that night?"

"At this stage nothing concrete, unfortunately. We're gathering a lot of information and speaking to a lot of people who knew your daughter. There's still a lot to review. We're doing everything we can."

"Is it true what they say, that if there is no suspect in the first seventy-two hours, the case isn't likely to be solved?"

I make myself look him in the eye. "We certainly prefer to have a suspect or suspects straight away, Mr. Ryan. That tends to lead to a better outcome. But every case is different and follows its own course. I can promise you we're doing everything we can to find out what happened to your daughter."

"The funeral is on Friday, you know. In the afternoon."

"Yes, I heard that," I say.

"It is unthinkable to have to plan the funeral of your child."

"I honestly can't imagine how hard it must be, Mr. Ryan."

"No." He grabs at his knees, his eyes fixed on the floor.

"Mr. Ryan, you are a wealthy man. I have to ask, will each of your children receive an equal part of your estate eventually?"

He sighs. "Yes, yes. I've arranged all of that."

"Is it something that you discuss with them?"

"My wealth is not a secret. But neither is the fact that over half of my estate is going to various charities."

"Without wanting to be presumptuous, Mr. Ryan, I assume that still leaves a significant inheritance for your children?"

"Yes. Certainly. A percentage of my estate will be split evenly between them. Assuming they sell the business, they will receive around a million dollars each." His eyes drift to the floor again as he says, "More now, I suppose."

I let the motive sit between us for a few seconds. George eyes me steadily but I notice his left hand shaking.

"Your daughter…" I say, letting the word linger a moment. I want to ask him directly if he is Rosalind's father, but if he is clueless about the possibility that she isn't his daughter, I have to consider whether he deserves to deal with deceit as well as death.

"Yes?" He looks up at me expectantly.

"She seemed quite different to your sons. Different to you. Would you say she was a bit of a black sheep?"

His eyes meet mine and then drop back to the floor. "I suppose she was. Yes." His papery face creases as he brings his hands to his cheeks. "She was very special. People were always drawn to her. I used to marvel at it when she was a child." He wipes at the jowly skin under his eyes. "I hardly knew her in a way, but the thing is, I loved her all the same."

Chapter Twenty-three

Wednesday, December 16, 9:02 p.m.

Sitting in the dark on my couch, with my laptop propped on the coffee table, I watch grainy figures pour out of the dimly lit school hall again. They link elbows, lean close and talk excitedly to one another. The heat from the night is evident in their short skirts and skimpy tops. A pixellated Rosalind emerges about ten minutes after the play ends, bouquets piled in her slender arms. Her beauty transcends the poor quality of the CCTV files that Smithson High's security company provided. She looks like a ballerina, graciously accepting enthusiastic praise. Pulling my gaze away from the computer screen, I briefly place my half-finished beer bottle on each eye. Blood surges, and it feels like tiny bugs are crawling through the capillaries in my eyelids. I blink a few times, gearing up for another viewing. So far, I haven't been able to identify Timothy Ryan, though he could be one of about fifteen blurry men.

I interviewed Kai Bracks today. A vacant, clammy kid who looked up at me stupidly from underneath heavy-lidded eyes. He seemed to have trouble focusing on any one thing; his gaze swayed around the room as he considered my questions.

He said he'd heard about the flowers that had been sent to Rosalind Ryan for Valentine's Day—everyone heard about it—but he didn't know anything about them. No, he definitely wasn't the one that sent them. No, he didn't know who had. Sure, he'd liked Ms. Ryan, she was nice. Yes, he thought she was pretty, just like everyone thought she was pretty.

We had nothing. The flowers were bought so long ago and it had been vague at the time, all hearsay and gossip. And Rosalind wasn't around to question.

Kai's movements on Friday night are also unhelpfully sketchy: he was at the play, he had a backstage role, and then he went to the after party but claims to have gone home in between to pick up some booze. His parents were at a friend's place so no one can vouch for this, though some other kids do remember him at the party. Of course there's absolutely nothing to prove that he went anywhere near the lake either. A loose thread or a dead end? I can't tell at this point.

After I updated Felix on my conversation with George Ryan, we finally heard back from the former principal of the secondary school in Sydney that Rosalind taught at. Felix decided to fly down there straight away to interview him and some of her old colleagues. Apparently, though nothing formal was ever reported, there was definitely a sense that Rosalind was trouble. A male student had confided to a teacher that he thought something was going on with his classmate and Rosalind. The teacher had passed this rumor on to the principal and the whole thing had blown up, culminating in Rosalind leaving the school at the end of the year.

Felix called me from Sydney airport while waiting for the flight back to Gowran.

"What did she actually do?" I asked him.

"That's the thing," he said, and I could hear airport noises in the background, "it's all speculation. Rosalind never admitted to anything. But apart from the principal, I get the sense they all thought that the student was obsessed with her. Kept trying to trap her in situations where they were alone together. Just besotted, basically. It all seems pretty odd."

"What, don't you think a young boy can behave like that?"

"Of course I think it's possible, but I just think it's odd. Despite the fact that the boy seemed out of line, it's clear that the principal was happy to see Rose go. He definitely didn't like her. Plus, I guess no principal ever wants any kind of scandal on their watch."

"Was this kid ever formally interviewed so he could tell his side of the story? Where is he now?"

Felix sighed, and the sound was filled with the paradox of Rosalind. "Yeah. He spoke to the principal off the record. With his parents present. He said it was Rosalind's fault. That she was giving him signs that made him act crazy. The school suggested he see a counselor but he refused and that was it. It was almost the end of the school year and he was already eighteen, so legally the whole thing was tenuous anyway. A case of he said, she said. It sounds like, in the end, everyone just wanted the whole thing shoved back under the carpet. But the principal was keen to get her out of there and encouraged her to leave, which she obviously did. The kid is overseas now, studying somewhere. He's never come back since the whole scandal apparently."

"It doesn't really help us, though, does it? I mean, sure, there's a bit of tension about the play and talk of some teenage crushes, but mostly everyone seems to like her," I said.

"Yeah, I guess so. They just don't really seem to *know* her, that's half the problem. On the other hand, the principal I spoke to today thought she was bad news. Even her being dead sparked very little sympathy." Felix paused. "She was lucky she could just run on back home to Smithson and hit good old Nicholson up for a job."

"Very lucky," I agreed. "He certainly didn't seem fussed about any of this when we spoke to him, though perhaps he didn't realize how bad it was." I stretched out my legs, wincing at the stiffness of my muscles. "I spoke to Kai Bracks this afternoon," I told him.

"And?"

I filled Felix in on my interview.

"Well, even if he did send her the flowers it's hardly conclusive," said Felix.

"I know. Though at least it would be a lead. It would be *something*," I responded.

"True." Felix yawned. I could hear more airport announcements in the background.

"Anyway, I'm just watching this footage for the hundredth time," I told him as I rubbed at my eyes and looked at the frozen screen.

"Still no sign of Timothy?"

"I don't think so," I said. "But the tape is pretty shitty and it misses the ramp entrance to the hall, so even if he's not on the tape it isn't a done deal."

Felix was called to board the plane and we agreed to meet early in the morning before check-in.

Now I refocus on the computer screen, clicking on the video file to play it from the start. The one camera that provided semi-clear footage of the audience from last Friday is positioned under the eaves of a classroom opposite the entrance to the school hall and partially blocked by a droopy ghost gum. We can assume that most of those who attended the play were captured on this tape, unless a ticket-holder entered from a backstage door or along the disabled ramp around the side.

Just before the 7 p.m. timestamp, people begin to cluster around the entrance of the Smithson Secondary College auditorium, talking and fiddling with their phones. The bulk of the crowd enters the auditorium just before 7:30. Between 7:32 and 7:39 a few stragglers rush in, with one latecomer running across the screen at 7:52, head down, apologetic, as he makes his excuses to the ushers. After this, the only movement on the screen is from the two student ushers standing either side of the closed doors, playing on their phones and chatting occasionally. One of them disappears at around 8:15 and reappears six minutes later. A bathroom break or, if I'm more of a cynic, a sneaky cigarette.

The interval begins at 8:40 and a smaller number of people emerge from the hall this time. A few light up cigarettes and shift off camera before reappearing a few minutes later popping breath mints. A middle-aged woman appears to have an argument with her husband. They exchange angry gestures before he storms off and she spins on her heel to re-enter the auditorium. He makes a dash inside just after the doors are closed at 9 p.m., carrying what looks to be a woman's jacket. Rosalind doesn't appear on the tape in the interval and I assume she is backstage with the cast. That corresponds with what several of the student actors and crew told the uniforms in their interviews.

At 10:03 p.m. the ushers pull open the doors and I watch the now-familiar footage of the audience surging out into the night, noticeably excited. I recognize some of them in the hazy way that you can summon up identities from an old photo. A sharp profile tugs at a latent memory. A distinctive mannerism takes me back to a long-forgotten conversation. I recognize a man we questioned over a domestic violence incident last year. The crowd thins out fairly quickly, with about half leaving between 10:11 and 10:19. Those remaining are clearly waiting to greet the cast members. They bob up and down on the spot, craning their necks toward the dressing-rooms. Several are students who we saw at the school the other morning. I've already checked them off against the copy of the yearbook I asked the school receptionist to find for me.

Another camera, positioned on the front gate, has provided us with lopsided, out-of-focus footage of over thirty cars exiting the car park between 10:20 and 10:29 p.m., but Nicholson reminded us that most people attending the play would have parked in the streets adjacent to the school, so the cars captured on the tape are only a small sample of the attendees' vehicles. The resolution is so bad that I'll need the tech guys to work the files before they will be any use to us anyway.

After the crowd subsides, small circles of people remain, chatting animatedly and making wild gestures. I pause the file and do a quick count: there are about sixty people visible on screen, a few of them smoking, some holding flowers to give to the cast. Rosalind is visible about ten minutes after the play ends and disappears about ten minutes later. There's no indication as to where she went; all we know is that she can't be identified on the footage from the car park.

The cast start to arrive just before Rosalind disappears. They come from the left of the screen. Maggie Archer, the student who played the Juliet character, appears first. I went to her house today, as we hadn't been able to contact her by phone, but her mother informed me that she has gone to stay with her aunt in Melbourne for a few days; I called the aunt's house but there was no answer and no voicemail. On the video, Maggie is greeted with applause and does a little curtsy before joining a small group of blonde women who smother her with cuddles; her mother and sisters, I assume. Rodney Mason appears too, along with some other cast members, and there is more clapping. Kai Bracks and the other backstage crew are there, all dressed in black. I spot Donna Mason standing off to the side talking to Troy Shooter, the PE teacher. He makes his way over to Rosalind, and they embrace briefly and have a short conversation before she disappears from view, and he is sucked back into the excited tangle of people. There is a moment on the tape where Rodney seems to look at Rosalind. I pause the video but it's impossible to tell if his eyes are fixed on her. Other cast members talk animatedly to their families, most still sporting the elaborate hairstyles of their characters. Kai jumps onto one of the low benches near the canteen and appears to be acting out a scene from the play to the amusement of a small crowd of students, before he grabs one of the boys good-naturedly around the neck and leads him off camera.

Groups of kids kiss their parents good-bye and leave—the majority, we now know, heading to Jamie Klein's after party. Their adrenaline rush from performing is obvious, mixing with the anticipation of the big party still to come. Everyone we've interviewed about Jamie's party so far has been somewhat vague. It was clearly quite a party. As one year twelve student eloquently put it: "I really can't remember much but it was completely awesome." Jamie's parents weren't present that night, being in Sydney for the weekend. They'd been led to believe that their daughter was hosting a modest sleepover. Jamie's furious dad, Brad, is now ensuring that his sheepish daughter gives us whatever information she can about her unsupervised celebration.

On my screen the remaining theatergoers slowly drift away and when the timestamp clicks over to 10:47 p.m. there is no one left. I click back to the last few seconds of Rosalind and pause on the image of her mid-step. According to Anna, she was killed anytime from 11 p.m. onward.

"What happened next?" I whisper to my laptop.

Yawning, I stretch my neck, turning it one way and then another. My hair is heavy with the day's grime and I am aware of the slow thump of a headache.

I called the school receptionist earlier today and asked her to pull the data for all tickets sold online for the play's opening night. Felix and I are working our way through a master list of those who attended that evening, but with just under three hundred tickets sold in total, and over half of those purchased at the school office and paid for in cash, any audit is unlikely to help us get a clear view of all attendees. Plus, the school doesn't have an electronic system, so there's no way of knowing whether people who purchased a ticket actually attended the play that night. There are still so many gaps. And the reality is, the person who attacked Rose may not have gone to the play or have any connection to the school anyway. It is beyond frustrating that there were so many people at the play last Friday night but no one saw anything.

Karly hasn't been able to turn up anything on the flowers I received. Because of the play, the three florists in Smithson all reported a spike in sales on Friday and there were five weddings on the weekend, two of which had placed large orders of long-stemmed red roses. Over half the florists' sales are cash transactions and we don't know when the flowers were purchased. We've sent the card off for analysis but unless the author is a known offender any prints or DNA are not going to get us very far.

Snapping my computer shut, I get up and go check on Ben. He looks like he's fallen asleep midway through a conversation: mouth wide open, one arm flung high above his head and the other out to the side. He is perfect. I brush my fingers across his forehead and wipe away the tiny beads of sweat, tracing his lips.

Massaging my neck, I grab another beer from the fridge and stand in the cool air as I twist the top off and take a swig. Scott watches me from the kitchen table where he is doing e-mails and probably reading up about the cricket. A bowl of Weet-Bix sits next to an empty beer bottle on the table beside him.

He sees me looking at it and shrugs sheepishly. "Got hungry." He stretches his arms into the air. "So how's it going?"

"Okay. We're not really getting anywhere."

"Is this on the dead teacher case?"

"Yep. It's pretty much all we're working on at the moment. Everyone's pretty spooked. We really need a solve."

"Well, you can only do what you can, I guess." Scott says this as if I'm trying to work out why the paper wasn't delivered. He looks back at his laptop. The light skims the contours of his face and I think how tired he looks. Scott is so content for life to happen around him. He feels no urgency, is in no rush to pull his way through things or force his way into them. Unlike me, who races through life so quickly I get whiplash. I often think that when you haven't been touched by death you have no need to feel alive, no desperation to keep breathing. Scott greets every day with the relaxed attitude of someone who assumes there are thousands more of its kind to come.

I shut the fridge door and the heat instantly regroups around my body. "We kind of have to do whatever it takes," I say stiffly. "There *is* a murderer out there."

His eyes meet mine. "I get it, Gem. But this is not your fault. All I mean is that you'll do your best but you're not magic."

"I'm not saying I'm magic. I'm saying this is pretty fucking important."

"Seeing it's almost Christmas I just hope that you'll be able to spend some time with Ben. That's important too."

I drink the beer so I don't have to speak. His gaze holds steady on mine, challenging.

"I've got more work to do," I say and spin on my heel, returning to my search for clues hidden in the grainy footage from Rosalind's opening night.

Chapter Twenty-four

Thursday, December 17, 12:56 p.m.

I can tell Jonesy is nervous. He pulls at his tie and adjusts his ill-fitting jacket. A thin stream of sweat trickles from his temple, journeying along craggy skin and arriving at his chin. He's shaved, and the result is an array of fresh red welts that look like they will burst into song at any moment.

"Right." He beckons Felix and me close. "This won't take long. Get 'em in and get 'em out is the plan."

"Yes, sir," I say. Felix nods.

"I'm going to stick to the basics. I won't mention the pregnancy. Nor the paternity query, obviously." A sharp look at me as though it's my fault that Rosalind's father turned out not to be George Ryan. "This is just a general appeal for information and also a means to provide some calm."

He clears his throat noisily and then breaks into a hearty cough, thumping his chest aggressively. Felix and I exchange a look. I'm not sure that calm will be what Jonesy inspires, but after five days and no solve, he has no choice but to speak publicly.

"Right then."

Someone calls for quiet and a tech checks the mic. Jonesy ambles up to the lectern, his back straight, still clearing his throat. We hold our press conferences outside next to the undercover walkway between the police station and the car park. Jonesy always has the lectern positioned next to the main entrance, with the Australian coat of arms and the recently renovated front desk clearly visible for the TV cameras to capture.

"Makes us look professional and not like some hick backwater effort,"

I heard him telling our media manager—poor, downtrodden Cynthia—who I suspect is still trying to figure out exactly what the internet is.

I also suspect that Jonesy thinks there is some kind of power in making all of the reporters stand outside. It doesn't allow them to get too comfortable.

Felix and I follow Jonesy onto the small stage and stand behind his left shoulder.

"Thank you, folks. I'm going to keep this fairly brief."

I spot Candy Fyfe in the crowd, her dark skin glowing against a soft pink dress with cute capped sleeves. Candy's grandfather was a local Aboriginal elder, one of the original custodians of the land that Smithson now lays claim to. Her grandmother was from a posh English family and their union was allegedly quite the scandal in the 1950s. Candy opens her notebook, pen poised, eyes fixed on Jonesy, and then suddenly on me. She arches a slender brow and I hold her stare before looking away. My shoes are badly scuffed, worn at the front. Under my pants I'm wearing mismatched socks, and I feel a surge of anger at Candy and her silent expectations. I know she feels let down by my inability to bond with her, one woman to another, but I just don't buy into the gender roles battle. I simply push on and try to do a good job. I'm not interested in spending my time advocating for my rights: I want to earn them. In contrast, Candy is due to give her third keynote speech at the upcoming "Country Women in Conversation," an event designed to support the advancement of women in business. I threw my invitation in the bin.

Jonesy begins his speech. "A sudden death is always a tragedy. Especially that of someone as young and important to our community as high school teacher Rosalind Ryan. But we are confident that we will be able to come to a resolution quickly and put whoever is responsible into custody."

A reporter puts up her hand but Jonesy shakes his head. "I'll take a few questions shortly, but first I want to be clear that we here at Smithson police station are doing everything we can to ensure justice for Ms. Ryan and her family. We have our best officers dedicated to the case and they are being supported with extra staff from around the region. We are also in contact with our state counterparts to ensure the best methods and technology available to us are utilized."

Jonesy looks at the crowd, eyeballing people randomly, daring them to suggest otherwise. His bulky presence is powerful, but many Smithsonians are forced to endure the incongruity of having a forbidding station chief on the TV who is also regularly spotted shopping at the butcher in his two-sizes-too-small tracksuit pants.

"Of course, these cases are not always solved as quickly as we would like. But we are making good progress, piecing together Ms. Ryan's movements and the details of her death to ensure we find the person or persons responsible. We're committed to building a comprehensive case so that charges can be laid and a conviction attained." He claps his hands as if he is about to tuck into a meal. "Right. Questions?"

The young reporter who had been shushed earlier speaks first. "Mr. Jones, should people living in Smithson be scared? I mean, there's a killer on the loose, right?"

Jonesy looks at the reporter as if he'd like to immediately prove her correct.

"Nothing so far suggests that anyone need be fearful of something else like this happening. We advise everyone to simply take normal precautions. Don't walk alone at night, tell people where you're going—things like that." He waves flies away and shields his eyes as he looks out at the gathered media. "Yes?"

A young bearded man speaks up. "Mr. Jones, Dan Robuck from the *Gowran Tribune*. From what you are saying, it sounds like the police don't think the attack on Ms. Ryan was a random crime."

"At this stage we do not believe it was random. We are investigating several individuals in relation to the attack, confirming their whereabouts and matching this with the CCTV footage we have secured and crime scene evidence."

This is somewhat of a stretch based on the pathetic amount of information we have, but it causes a ripple through the audience, and they start jotting down notes and whispering to each other, no doubt mentally penning headlines that implicate the Ryan family or assume a sordid love triangle.

It is certainly a livelier press conference than most of the ones we conduct, even attracting journalists from the metro networks. Rosalind's murder is any aspiring reporter's wet dream, and none of them want to miss the opportunity to splash another head shot of her across the front page, even if the new information revealed is as weak as milky tea.

Candy stands up and her cameraman whirls around to catch her asking her question before spinning back to Jonesy for his answer.

"Mr. Jones, Candy Fyfe from Country TV and the *Smithson Times*." She smiles, faking self-consciousness at her ubiquity. "Many people are speculating Ms. Ryan was involved in several questionable relationships that may have led to her murder. Do you have a comment on that?"

"All I would say to that, Ms. Fyfe, is that my team is focused on finding the killer rather than scrutinizing Ms. Ryan's lifestyle. No one deserves to be attacked like she was. Full stop."

Jonesy's comment has all but confirmed the suggestion that Rosalind had a juicy personal life. I shudder to think of the outrageous rumors circulating around Smithson, whispered in shops and debated at dinner tables.

"I'm not suggesting she was at fault, Mr. Jones, but surely you are looking into Ms. Ryan's personal affairs?"

"Ms. Fyfe, I can assure you that we are conducting this investigation exactly as you would expect. We're looking into everything. But we are leaving our judgment out of it. I'd encourage you all to do the same."

"Of course." Candy remains standing and her cameraman whips back and forth as if he is covering a tennis match. "One final question if I may. Do you feel comfortable with Detective Gemma Woodstock leading the case, seeing as she knew the victim so well?"

Surprised, I feel my face flush as all eyes turn to me. Felix mutters something under his breath. Jonesy turns and gives me a reassuring wink, his jaw clenching.

"Detective Woodstock is one of our most capable officers. Like many people who grew up around here, she has personal connections that are sometimes going to cross over into her work but she's a professional. We all are."

"Thank you, sir." Candy sits down, a slow smile spreading across her face as she leans forward to make more notes.

Another reporter rises and questions Jonesy on the Smithson Regional Center solve rate in comparison to the city statistics. Jonesy rattles off a bunch of numbers and talks about challenging political times and the need for additional funding.

Cynthia points at her watch, indicating that it's time to wrap things up.

"Right, we're done," barks Jonesy obediently. "What would help us would be getting your readers, watchers, tweeters, whatever, to think about anything they have seen recently that seems unusual. A conversation with someone that isn't quite right. Something they may have stumbled across that, in light of Ms. Ryan's death, might be worth talking to us about."

Jonesy's voice lifts a little as he gears up for his finale. "We must remember that a woman is dead. Her life has been tragically cut short. That's what we're focused on and we would appreciate any support that Smithson residents and those living in surrounding areas can provide. Thank you."

He walks away from the lectern. Felix and I follow.

"Pack of arseholes," Jonesy says under his breath as we step back into the station.

In the background, a huddle of kookaburras on the powerline begin to laugh as if they have just heard the funniest joke in the world.

Chapter Twenty-five

Thursday, December 17, 7:33 p.m.

I'm at the pub near the train line. Anna is late and I'm almost at the bottom of my first glass of wine. I curl my hand around its stem and look down the bar. A couple of old guys throw glances my way. A young family is seated at one of the tables. Two little girls are eating chips with their sauce. I kick my legs out and hit against the wooden paneling that lines the bar. Artie, the owner, looks up at me, face ready with a scowl, and then sees it's me causing the ruckus and smiles instead.

"Another, sweetheart?"

"I should wait for my friend."

He sips at a frothy beer. He probably thinks it's Felix I'm waiting for. We come here sometimes. "Well, if you change your mind, just ding the bell."

"Will do, Artie."

The muscles across my neck feel like a block of cement. I flip open my notebook and read over my scrawls. If someone found my notebook, it would be hard for them to guess whether it belongs to a good guy or a bad guy, so bizarre are my ramblings.

I map through some of the strands of information we have so far. Rosalind's parentage: could that be the key to this whole thing? Did George Ryan somehow discover his wife's betrayal and fly into a rage? Did he throw money at the problem and arrange to have her removed when he had the air-tight alibi of a night in hospital? Or perhaps hot-headed Timothy found out and, knowing that his father is increasingly unwell, objected to his half-sister getting an equal share of the inheritance and felt he needed to rush things along? This possibility does seem quite dramatic when his share is so substantial anyway, but people have done a lot worse for less than the $300,000 or so extra that Timothy stood to receive.

Although his argument with Rosalind and their lack of contact since remain suspicious, we haven't found anything to implicate Timothy. On the night of the play he made no calls, but two phone towers have him moving between them in a manner that would make a trip from the school to his father's house plausible. His credit card wasn't used that evening and the security footage that George gave us shows his car turning into the garage just before 10:55 p.m. Timothy says that Bryce was in his room with the door shut when he got home but they didn't actually see each other. Timothy says he can't remember how he entered the school hall; says he probably just walked in the door like everyone else. But the fact that I can't identify him on the CCTV bothers me. And why did he end up going to the play alone? I don't buy his excuse that he forgot to ask someone to come along. Intuitively, I can't shake the feeling that Timothy is bad news, but I need to work out whether he's just a jerk or a dangerous killer.

And maybe this wasn't a family matter at all, despite what George Ryan said. Our forensic finance guys have turned up more issues with several RYAN developments around town and there are rumblings of possible court proceedings driven by a mob of angry investors. While I find it hard to believe that someone with a business grudge would do something like this to Rosalind, I suppose it's not impossible.

Regardless, everything I know and remember about Rosalind tells me that this is a crime of passion. Or maybe revenge.

Without realizing it, I've drawn a looping circle across the notebook page in the shape of Sonny Lake.

I snap back to the present as Anna appears in front of me.

"Sorry, Gem. Crazy day at the office, you know how it is." Anna slides onto the stool next to me and grabs my hand, giving it a quick squeeze. "You okay?"

"Yeah. I had a wine while I was waiting." I gesture to my empty glass.

"Damn right you did. Can't sit in this awful place without a drink." Anna looks around. "Hey!" she calls out. "Hello?"

"There's a bell, I think…"

Ding, ding, ding. Anna taps on the bell like it's a hammer.

Artie stumbles out from the back room as if he's been woken up in the middle of the night. He blinks at Anna and then looks at me. "Ah. Your girlfriend turned up. More wine?"

"You got it, buddy. Bring us wine!" Anna pulls her hair from its tie and fluffs it around her face. "Cripes, what a day."

Anna is not conventionally pretty but has an elfin quality about her that I'm sure makes men think she'll be a lot more passive than she is. She is small, with delicate fingers and petite feet, but her movements are big and she is loud, consistently two volume measures higher than everyone else.

Artie delivers our wine, and for a moment, Anna and I could be any two young women out for a nice drink on a Thursday night. Not two young women who have been exposed to the worst of humanity, who have dug past the horror to find the even more horrifying. I once asked Anna how she sleeps, and she laughed and said, "Like the dead, with one eye open."

A buzzer goes off and we both jump to find our respective devices. Anna tugs at her lips with her teeth as she calls in to get her message, her brow furrowed.

"Everything okay?"

"Yeah. Car accident near Ford. I might have to head there later but Jonesy thinks the team in Paxton will get it." She swallows a large mouthful of wine. "Can't get wasted though, just in case."

"I have to be home early-ish anyway. I'll be up with Ben before six."

"I always forget you have a kid, Gem. It's such a spin-out."

I laugh. "It is weird."

"So this Ryan case is big. Like the Robbie thing."

"Yup."

"It's good that Jonesy put you guys on it. You and Felix make a good team."

There's a lift in her statement, maybe a question, but I let it pass.

"Did you track down the kid from her old school?" Anna asks. "The one you told me about?"

"Sort of. He's in India, traveling and teaching, but we got his e-mail address from his mother. He wrote back to us but it's tricky. He's clearly not keen to revisit the whole thing. He does maintain that she encouraged him but there's no evidence. Possibly it was all wishful thinking on his part. I think that's going to be as good as we get. Should we order some chips?"

"Definitely." She dings the bell again. "I heard the press conference was rough today."

"It was. Jonesy did a good job though."

"Candy Cane went for the jugular?"

"She always does," I say.

My mouth contracts in pleasure from the salty chips and we munch together contentedly. It feels strange to be out with someone other than Felix. With a jolt, I realize he's become my only real friend.

"You know how I asked you about the eye color genes the other day?"

Her eyes light up. "Yeah. You think someone else was the Ryan girl's dad?"

"I do."

"This case is a tricky one, isn't it?" says Anna.

"Well, she always was a bit of a mystery. Really hard to figure out."

Anna looks at me and an almost imperceptible expression flashes across her face. "I thought you didn't know her very well, Gem?"

"Oh, I didn't really," I say lightly. "I barely had anything to do with her. But she was always kind of interesting."

"Yeah, well, you just have to take one look at her to guess that." Anna tosses her hair over her shoulder and keeps her eyes on me. "Anyway, as long as you're okay to work on it."

"Of course. Even if I knew her well, I've learned how to shut off. You know, never let the personal get in the way."

"Yeah," says Anna, throwing back the last of her wine. "It sucks. Our job seems to make sure that nothing personal gets in the way. Or in my bed." She leans close to me and grins. "Wanna hear about the latest Prince Charming?"

I relax. I don't want to talk about Rosalind Ryan anymore. "Definitely."

I laugh at Anna's dating stories, which are ripped straight from cheesy American cable, feeling a happy buzz.

"Did you really catch him going through your wallet?"

"Yes! Gem, I swear. The guys I meet online make the ones at the station seem like gentlemen. Even I think it's funny."

"You'll be disappointed when you meet a normal guy."

"Probably." She says it so glumly, sticking out her bottom lip, that I can't help giggling. "You're lucky all that's behind you, Gem," she continues. "Safely married. Knowing what you're going home to every night."

"I'm not married."

"Oh, you know what I mean." She waves my de facto arrangement away. "You're as good as married."

"Yeah. I guess."

Anna senses dangerous territory and drops the volume. "Gemma? Sorry. I was being flippant. Ignore me! I don't know what I'm talking about."

My armpits dampen. A flutter in my abdomen. "It's fine. It's just, I don't know. Things are hard at the moment."

Anna looks at me, concerned. She reaches out a hand and I let her slide her fingers around mine. "With the case?"

I want to tell her about Felix. Say it out loud and see if I can get it to make sense, but I don't know which words to use or how to explain it. "I had a miscarriage," I say instead.

"Oh, Gemma."

"Yeah."

"Are you okay?" Anna asks.

"I think so."

"What did the doctor say?"

I twist in my seat, wishing this conversation was over. "Um, nothing really. Just that it was one of those things."

"When did it happen?"

I look at her steadily. "A few weeks ago."

"Okay. Wow. But you're all fine? No fever? Pain?"

"Honestly, Anna, I'm fine. I was only a few weeks along. I didn't need to go to hospital or anything."

"Okay. If you're sure."

We sit for a minute in silence. I regret bringing this up but it feels good to have made the pregnancy real. Good for it not to have existed completely in my mind.

"Was it planned?"

"Not really." I let my mind briefly wander to the daydream I've kept at bay for the past few days. I picture myself holding a brand-new baby. Handing the child to a speechless Felix. Him wrapping his arm around me as he kisses first me and then the child, breathing it in. I shake the image away, my cheekbones pulsing. "No. Not planned. Maybe that's what is making it confusing. I wasn't really sure what I was going to do."

"How does Scott feel about it?"

It feels like my organs are expanding inside my body. "Oh, you know," I say. "Not much he can do, I guess."

"It's tough being with a cop. You're so strong, Gem, he probably thinks you don't need him."

"Maybe, I guess."

"Seriously! You should see the guys' faces when I'm on a date and I tell them what I do. Massive buzzkill. Scott must be pretty cool, looking after Ben and putting up with the Smithson police force."

I flash a smile at Anna and tip my head in what might be a nod.

Anna eyes me and then eats a couple of chips in quick succession. "Well. Life, huh? I mean I'd hate to lose you from the team, but of course it makes sense that you might have another baby someday. It's perfectly normal. But we lose an awesome detective and get stuck with a bunch of fat guys who can have as many babies as they like without giving up anything! Fucking biology."

I can't help laughing. "It does seem ironic that most of the guys in the force are carrying more extra weight than a pregnant woman."

"Yes, well, I'm sorry about what happened, Gem. Really sorry. Planned or not, it's a big thing. It's rough on top of everything else you're dealing with."

I nod. "Yeah. Thanks. It will all turn out okay, though, I'm sure." My admission suddenly feels awkward. I wish I could tuck it back into my handbag.

We talk a little about Anna's upcoming holiday to New Zealand, the food that keeps going missing from the staff fridge, how under-resourced we are, but our easy flow has been broken.

"Well, should we get the bill?" I say, before Anna has to.

It's almost eleven but I don't want to go home. Anna hugs me briefly but fiercely before she slips into her bright red Fiat and drives off. I exit the car park and head toward Main Street. The sleeping shops give nothing away while streetlamps cast sloppy puddles on the paths. Brush-tailed possums shriek from the rooftops. I pause the car in the middle of a U-turn and look up the stretch of empty road, watching stray leaves skitter low to the ground, the possums still carrying on. But there's nowhere else to go, so I put my foot down and head for home, catching a glimpse of the old shot tower peeking out from above the trees as I drive past the lake.

Chapter Twenty-six

Friday, December 18, 7:37 a.m.

Reggie Hope swipes at her brow with a tea towel as she pours the frothed milk carefully into a glass, making sure to flick her wrist up right at the end to create a perfect leaf shape. *That is one fine coffee*, she thinks as she weaves around the tables to present it to the shy man sitting in the window seat.

The café is bustling and noisy this morning despite the heat. Luckily, coffee is popular all year round. "Caffeine is one of the most socially acceptable addictions of our time," her son is fond of telling her. Jackson is always saying interesting things like that now that he is at university in the city. Reggie rinses out the silver jug and pours in some fresh milk as she pictures his face. He has grown into such a man now with his neat beard and fancy shirts. He was even wearing a pink one the last time she saw him! Wendy, one of the casuals, assured her this was all the rage these days. Reggie can hardly link this tall dark stranger to the little boy in the Batman pajamas who used to cry out for her in the night. She shakes her head. Time is indeed a strange thing.

The bell above the door jingles. Every time someone steps into the café, a blast of oven-like heat hits her face. Reggie doesn't mind the heat usually but this current onslaught is starting to become a little tedious. Molly isn't sleeping well and has been in a mood for weeks. The days feel long and by around midday Reggie's head feels heavy, as if she's one of those kitsch toy dogs people put on their car dashboards with the bobbing necks. Hopefully the weather will settle down by Christmas. Reggie's entire family is coming from Malaysia to stay for almost two weeks and she can already imagine the arguments without the heat-induced claustrophobia. Sunny pleasant days with her family are barely manageable. Forty-degree days with her nosy sister, her sister's kids and their elderly mother might just tip her over the edge.

The door opens again and the heat pours in. It's that girl detective: Woodstock. She's in the news sometimes. Reggie knew she would be coming when she saw the man that Woodstock always meets tucked away in the far corner. Reggie watches as she quickly scans the room and then makes her way over to the table where the man is. She is very boyish. No hips to speak of and sort of bouncy, like she's about to break into a run. She sits down opposite the man and he smiles up at her broadly. They have been coming here for almost a year now, heads bent close as they talk and laugh in the early hours before the eyes of the town are on them. Woodstock orders skinny lattes when he's here but if she gets here first she has them with regular milk and adds some sugar.

Reggie laughs to herself under her breath: people are odd creatures. You see all sorts of things working in a place like this. She pushes the long black and the cappuccino onto the serving shelf and dings the little bell again. She refills the front display and wipes down the bench. She needs to get more muffins into the oven. And Matt is still not here. He's a sweet kid but a little hopeless. The young ones these days just don't quite have the work ethic she had at their age.

She glances over at the couple again. The man is looking at the woman detective and nodding as she talks. He grabs her wrist briefly and she looks around and then pulls it away. *He is an attractive man*, Reggie thinks. *Tall and strong with that nice dark hair and those striking green eyes.* Even from here she can see his wedding ring, but she is not the type to judge. Who knows what goes on in other people's lives? Plus, they are good customers. In this climate it would be foolish to turn up your nose at any kind of business. Since the Carling plant opened, cafés have popped up everywhere, putting a dent in her weekday profit. And half the Carling people fly home to Sydney or Melbourne for the weekend anyway, spending their money anywhere but Smithson. She remembers Wayne Carson at the bank telling her that the plant would see them all rich and retiring early, but Reggie feels like it's made everything more confusing. Life was simple when it was just her place and Café Cha Cha around the corner. Just good old friendly competition back then. Now it's a haze of loyalty cards and two-for-one deals and imported coffee beans. Reggie sighs. *Retiring early, my arse.*

The detective girl looks very serious this morning, even more than usual. She toys with a thin silver chain around her neck as she speaks. Maybe they are talking about the murdered teacher, Rosalind Ryan. Wendy told her recently that the man is a detective too, and he and the girl work together. Like on the TV cop shows. No wonder they are in love: those partners always get close when they are working cases. Reggie has been watching the stories on the news about the Ryan woman. She came into the café once or twice. A real dreamer. She was with a young boy the last time Reggie saw her—perhaps a little brother? He looked about Jackson's age. They talked in low voices and took turns writing things down in a notebook. They smiled a lot. Maybe he was her boyfriend, Reggie thinks. He seemed pretty smitten. Poor fella. She had very pretty eyes, the Ryan woman. Like toffee.

Reggie shuts her eyes briefly, trying to imagine how terrified the Ryan woman must have felt out there in the middle of the night. Alone and dying.

Reggie's daughter Molly was set to attend Smithson High, but St. Mary's is closer and, in the end, it was where all the kids from the primary school had decided to go. Reggie is glad that she doesn't have to deal with Molly having a dead teacher right now. Her moods are hard enough to navigate as it is.

Reggie taps out the used coffee from the portafilter and washes it with a blast of hot water before snapping it back into place. She thinks briefly about Molly dying like the Ryan woman did and then forces the terrible thought right out of her head. Probably the poor woman was caught up in something sinister to be killed like that. Maybe she had a bad ex-boyfriend or there were issues with drugs. Nothing that Molly would ever be involved in. Reggie flicks on the bean grinder and mops at her brow again, pinging the bell so that Matt, who has finally arrived, knows to come and collect the fresh batch of coffees.

Chapter Twenty-seven

Friday, December 18, 8:04 a.m.

"The memorial today should be interesting. All those kids everywhere. The Ryans. Nicholson. The other teachers. Agatha Christie would have a field day."

Felix is in a good mood. I nod and play with the froth on my coffee and try to change the subject.

"The Ryans are just having a small ceremony this afternoon. Only family. George Ryan told me they want to keep it very private."

"What do you make of him?"

I think about George's pale eyes blurring with sadness and the hardness that emerges in his jaw when he feels threatened. "I really don't know. He makes me feel uncomfortable and I don't think his relationship with Rosalind was an easy one. But perhaps he did just struggle with raising a daughter on his own."

"Still think you're on the money with your paternity theory?"

"Of course. It's science. I'm just not quite sure yet whether he knows or not. I suspect he might, but a lot of men raise children who aren't theirs and lead perfectly normal lives."

"And some don't."

"Sure. Some don't." The memorial ceremony looms in my mind again and I keep talking to avoid thinking about it. "Assuming he does know Rosalind isn't his, it would help if we could work out when he found out. If it's a recent revelation, then I suppose there's a chance it could be linked to what's going on now. If he's always known, then I would say it is completely irrelevant."

Felix looks at me skeptically. "What, you think that he somehow suddenly found out last week and lost his mind and killed her?"

I sigh. "It's pretty unlikely, isn't it? I don't know. But maybe there is a link somehow. Maybe one of the brothers found out?"

"That's going to be pretty hard to nail down. I think we're going to have to show our cards and ask."

"Yeah, probably." I look out the window. The heat is invisible from in here but I know it's there. A sparrow plays in the drips from the air-con, shaking out its feathers and doing little skips on the spot. "Or maybe it was Rosalind who found out. Maybe she was researching her family history and stumbled across something that made her confront her father."

"Let's get the tech guys on to it. Maybe her school computer will show something like that if it's recent."

"She might have used a public one."

Felix shrugs. "Well, we'll see what we can find." He glances at his watch and then looks up at me. "But right now we need to get our arses to the school."

Our eyes stay locked and I reach out my foot and curl it around the bottom of his leg. He smiles and I fix my stare onto his lips.

"I wish we could spend the day alone together instead," he says.

"I know," I breathe, trying to put a lid on my emotions.

Reggie smiles at us from the counter. Such a carefree, breezy lady, she is always so friendly to us. She probably assumes we're married. I look at Felix and wonder what my life would be like if he were my husband. Wonder what it would be like waking up next to him every morning, the sun spilling in on our cushiony bed, followed by orange juice and boiled eggs on toast as we lazily read the papers, him reading interesting facts aloud to me in his crisp accent. Then getting up to work on cases together. But Ben refuses to be part of this sun-dappled scene and I push away the inevitability of one day having to choose.

It's almost 8:30 a.m. as we drive the short distance to Smithson Secondary College. The turn-off to the freeway is already clogged with trucks; I can feel their beat pulsing through the road beneath us. I can't tell Felix that the thought of being at the memorial is making the back of my eyes burn and my throat catch. I feel sick. Jacob's service is still so fresh; I can feel the exact lurch that pulled through my chest, can feel the rub of the shoes I was wearing. I can still see Donna Mason's wretched, broken face. All the girls from my class crying. Nicholson tall and awkward, wringing his hands. Rosalind, calm and serene, her eyes as cold as winter soil.

The school buzzes with quiet talking. The sun beats down and hooks sharply on a bunch of red balloons that have been tied to a gate, sending a white bolt into my eyes.

"This way," says Felix, leading us past a dotted line of fluorescent bunting.

"They must be holding it on the oval," I say. *Just like Jacob's.* I stumble slightly and Felix grabs my arm and it takes all of my willpower not to grab on to him and bury my face in his chest.

We fall into step with the growing crowd. A parade of hats bobs along on either side of us: baseball caps, straw sunhats, kids in bucket hats covered with *Peppa Pig* and *Thomas the Tank Engine* motifs. It seems like the whole town is here. I suppose this has suddenly become the biggest pre-Christmas event in Smithson. It's certainly going to be the main topic of conversation over the turkey this year.

John Nicholson rushes past, clutching a wad of papers. He squints into the sun and deep lines fan out from his eyes. A short woman with cropped blonde hair struggles to keep pace with him.

"He's hired a PR lady," says Felix, stooping to talk into my ear as the crowd pushes us together. "I recognize her. She has a little agency next door to the jewelry store shooting that I worked on in Paxton last month."

I watch the blonde woman talking seriously to Nicholson, who seems to be struggling to pay attention.

Felix shoots me a quick smile. I smile back but all I can hear is screaming. The same sound that I always imagine Jacob made as he fell.

The oval comes into view. Patchy, green faded to yellow, it looks much like it did when I was here. Every second person is holding a red helium balloon or a rose. Most people are wearing at least one item of red clothing.

I spot Kai Bracks in a bright red singlet, standing with a group of students. I half close my eyes and the scene looks awash with blood. Wet heat trickles down my sides. I quickly open my eyes wide again, blinking furiously.

"Hey, I might go grab some water."

"Okay. Sure. I'll be, ah, somewhere around here!" Felix gestures to the writhing mass, indicating that he'll do his best to avoid being swept away.

"Yep, I'll find you, don't worry."

I duck out of the crowd and cut across the quad. Memory tells me there are some taps in between the art rooms and the library. I spot them, and as I bend down to drink the tinny liquid I feel a wave of nostalgia so strong I fight back the urge to retch.

I quickly stand, heaving as I thump a balled fist softly on my chest, breathing in and out, trying to push the feeling away. My thoughts are going haywire. I see Jacob everywhere. See myself. Small and mousy. A stubborn chin hiding so much pain. Hair always falling over one eye. Scuffed shoes. Nails bitten down to the quick. Eyes burning with sadness. It was near here that he told me. Near here that he pulled me into the clearing which is now the car park at the top of the lake. Dusk on the Friday three weeks before he jumped. We'd been spending so much time apart. After years of being so entwined, so *together*, he'd seemed distant and cold, but we were almost past the madness. I only had one exam to go. I was feeling calm, confident. We were almost there. Almost free.

"Jacob!" I laughed, *laughed*, thinking he'd wanted to kiss me. That he'd missed me. I tried to pull away but he was strong. Hot. A beat went by and then I felt worried. "What is it? Jacob, what's wrong?"

"Look…god. Look, I just don't feel sure anymore, Gem." His teeth pulled at his lip. Fingers raking through his hair. Everything tilted then, just for a moment. A mild sepia lens clicked across my vision. His face suddenly didn't seem familiar at all.

"What do you mean?" I said, even though I didn't want him to explain it.

"I just…fuck. I don't know. It feels different or something. Between us."

He grabbed my hands. Slick and wet, our fingers slid around. I wanted never to let go.

"I mean, you're my best friend, Gem. That will probably never change. But I—I just...oh, I don't know."

The words tumbled out of his mouth and piled around my feet. I couldn't move. I could barely breathe. I looked at his shoes. I loved his faded Converse sneakers. I'd been there when he bought them. I'd been there for all of it. My heart roared in my ears. I could hear a football being kicked on the oval. Laughter.

"Talk to me, Jacob. Please. Come on. I don't understand. Is it the exams?"

He bit at his lip again. "I don't think it is. I wish it was."

I felt a wave come. It built up inside of me and broke into hot panic across my body.

"Jacob, c'mon, this is crazy. It's us. We're special, you always say it. Everybody knows it." I stamped my foot in the dust. I felt dangerous. Insane. I wanted to scream, hit him. Run laps around the oval. Anything to make him stop talking, to stop ruining everything. I thought of Mum, her arms around me, smelling of grapefruit shampoo and Nivea face cream, kissing my cheek. My face started to crumple. My cheeks were wet and I wiped the tears away. I could taste sunscreen. Taste hell.

Jacob looked crushed, empty after the birth of his horrible truth.

"Jacob, why? Why are you saying this?"

He stared at the ground. At his hands. Anywhere but me. "Gem, please don't make this harder than it needs to be. I just don't want to lie to you. We're not like that, right? We always tell each other stuff."

He wiped perspiration from his forehead into his hair, making it stick up high. He was so ridiculous. So beautiful. Little black dots trailed along his wrists; he sometimes drew on his hands in class.

"I don't know what's going on," he said. "Maybe it *is* all the pressure of finishing school, but I just feel different. Like I want things to be different."

A dragonfly buzzed past so close that I could see the shimmery green on its tiny body. Its crazy eyes.

"You like someone else?"

He shifted and kicked at the ground. "No. No, not really. But I do wonder what it would be like to be with someone else sometimes. Don't you?"

I shook my head, even though it wasn't true. I didn't tell him about the dreams I had. Will Cobbler. Jason Gordon. Fox. Her.

"No," I whispered. "I just want you."

"Okay, look. Look. Maybe we just finish the exams and then have a bit of a break over summer. Then we'll see. Maybe we just need a bit of a break." He nodded at me, willing me to agree. "Both of us."

"I don't want that."

He became impatient, looking beyond the clearing back toward the oval. It was done now and he wanted to go. It wasn't intense anymore, just tedious. I was annoying him.

"How long have you felt like this?"

"Just, I don't know. A little while. But it's not specific or anything. You know? It's just confusing, my head's a mess. I think this is normal. We're young. I just need some time, Gem. I don't want to drag you into my shit. Okay?"

I pulled at my bracelet. The one he'd given to me. Pulled it around and around my wrist in a slow circle.

"Okay."

"I'll call you later, all right?"

I was dismissed. He hugged me and walked off. I stood there perfectly still, imagining that I was a tree. A really old tree. So old that my roots were buried deep in the ground, snaking down to the earth's core. Burning their tips.

After a while, I made my way down to the lake. I sat on the biggest rock and threw sticks into the water, crying as each one broke the surface, the world it reflected turning into a big, blurry mess.

Chapter Twenty-eight

Friday, December 18, 9:27 a.m.

I slip back next to Felix and look straight ahead so he can't see the wildness in my eyes. "All good?" I ask.

"Yep. Just watching—you know, seeing if anything seems off."

The sun is strong and I hold my hands over my eyes. We're to the left of the makeshift stage, about twenty meters from the front. I'm already thirsty again.

I imagine that the stage is normally used for award ceremonies and school sports days. One of the teachers we interviewed the other day— Troy Shooter, the PE teacher—is wrestling with a heavy-looking lectern. A bunch of red helium balloons has been tied to a power cord on the left side of the stage. A few chairs, the same kind as in the staffroom, are dotted unevenly across the other side.

"Family's here." Felix nods his head to the left.

I see Rose's brothers and George Ryan standing in a small half-circle. Bryce's girlfriend, Amelia Posen, stands with them. George's chin is set high as if he has made a deal with God that he will get through this torturous day with dignity. The blonde PR woman ushers them into the front row and they sit awkwardly, like characters from a movie that have wandered onto the wrong set. Even from a distance I can see the blue-black sheen in their hair.

"Nothing like her," I whisper.

"Huh?"

"She really didn't look anything like them."

Felix glances back at the Ryans. "No, she really didn't. It's that blonde hair. She really did have amazing hair."

"Like Rapunzel."

"Yep." He stifles a yawn. "Fuck, I'm tired. I wish I could hold your hand right now. And more."

I smile at him and suddenly my mouth is twisting into a sob. "Later," I manage.

He nods at the stage and straightens.

A rumpled-looking John Nicholson taps awkwardly at the microphone and then mouths something to the blonde lady, who is looking on encouragingly. The shushing waves over the crowd until the only sounds that can be heard are cicadas and the ragged crying of an overtired baby.

"Thank you all for coming here today." He swallows heavily. "Rosalind Ryan was…" There is a pause and his hands grip the sides of the lectern, his eyes moving up to the sky as if in prayer and then slowly moving back to the crowd. "Rosalind Ryan was a gifted teacher, a wonderful student and an amazing person. You all know that. That's why we're all here."

A group of girls near us, faces wet with tears, clutch each other's hands. One suddenly breaks into loud crying as the others rub her back, murmuring in her ear.

Nicholson acknowledges the crying with a sympathetic grimace. "Today is about celebrating her wonderful life and the incredible passion she had for Smithson and her students. Rosalind was so proud of you all and proud of what she achieved here." Nicholson's voice cracks and he steps back from the microphone, but I can still hear the guttural sob that escapes his mouth. He thrusts his hands deep into his pockets and appears to breathe in strength, steadying himself before he talks again. "What happened last week was a tragedy. Something we will never really understand. Rosalind would not want us to dwell on that though. There are so many things to celebrate about her short life that it makes no sense to speculate beyond that. That is the job of the police, and I know that they are doing everything they can to achieve justice for Rosalind and her family."

Nicholson gives a not-so-subtle nod in our direction and hundreds of eyes turn on us. I feel a mild flush creep across my cheeks and I lean away from Felix slightly.

"People deal with something like this in very different ways. And that is completely fine. There is no right or wrong way to feel. Today a few students are going to perform for us in celebration of Ms. Ryan, or simply tell us something special about her so that we can share our memories and remember how much she meant to us all."

Nicholson clears his throat loudly. "Rosalind's family are also here with us today."

He turns to where the Ryans are seated. George Ryan seems to nod at Nicholson but his jaw remains set. The brothers are erect and steely. A low murmur rustles from the audience. I look to Nicholson again, who is shifting his weight back and forth.

"Thank you for being here today. Your Rosalind meant a great deal to us. We can't begin to imagine your pain. Please know she will never be forgotten at Smithson."

"Yes. Thank you." George's gravelly voice booms without a microphone and cuts through the singing cicadas.

Nicholson continues, "First, two of our students are going to share a reading for Ms. Ryan. And then we will have a song from Camille Hollback, one of our talented year ten students. And then the year twelves have a special announcement to make in Ms. Ryan's honor." He bobs his head as he steps backward and makes his way off the stage.

I lean forward so I can see the front rows. Behind the family and a little to the left are the teachers. I recognize most of them from our staffroom interviews the other day. The PE teacher's broad shoulders form a large square in between two petite women. I recognize Izzy with her bright red hair and the older lady who grabbed manically at her hanky when we asked about Rosalind.

Then I spot Candy Fyfe in a sleeveless red shirt talking intimately to a TV camera. She flicks her head dramatically and gazes steadily into the lens for a few moments before gesturing for her cameraman to focus on the stage.

"He's pretty upset, don't you think?" Felix is watching Nicholson.

"He's allowed to be, isn't he?"

Two girls clutching single red roses make their way onto the stage, holding hands. Nicholson nods at them encouragingly. The students look like otherworldly elves, with long feathery haircuts and large almond-shaped eyes. They exchange looks and smile grimly, as if summoning the strength to do whatever is coming.

"Ms. Ryan was the most incredible teacher." The first girl speaks in a hushed whisper. The second girl grips her hand a little tighter. "She was so passionate and wanted us to love books and reading as much as she did. She really helped us to learn. *Really* learn."

"She really did. Every day in one of her classes was like an adventure. She wanted us to know new worlds without having to go anywhere. She taught us that anything is possible."

The first girl starts to cry. The second girl continues, "We want to say thank you to Ms. Ryan. We will never forget you."

The first girl nods through her tears and manages to speak. "This is a scene from one of our favorite texts. Ms. Ryan always said that it shows how great love stories can change the way you look at the world."

"It's from *The Velveteen Rabbit*," says the second girl.

They draw deep breaths in unison, then take it in turns to read the characters.

"What is REAL?" asked the Rabbit one day, when they were lying side by side near the nursery fender, before Nana came to tidy the room. "Does it mean having things that buzz inside you and a stick-out handle?"

"Real isn't how you are made," said the Skin Horse. "It's a thing that happens to you. When a child loves you for a long, long time, not just to play with, but REALLY loves you, then you become Real."

"Does it hurt?" asked the Rabbit.

"Sometimes," said the Skin Horse, for he was always truthful. "When you are Real you don't mind being hurt."

"Does it happen all at once, like being wound up," he asked, "or bit by bit?"

*"It doesn't happen all at once," said the Skin Horse. "You become.
It takes a long time. That's why it doesn't happen often to people who
break easily, or have sharp edges, or who have to be carefully kept.
Generally, by the time you are Real, most of your hair has been loved
off, and your eyes drop out and you get loose in the joints and very
shabby. But these things don't matter at all, because once you are Real
you can't be ugly, except to people who don't understand."*

My eyes sting with tears. Felix's Adam's apple bobs up and down. The
sound of sobbing fills the air.

The two girls nod at the audience then step down from the stage.

The world tips as I spot Rodney Mason. Ghosts immediately ripple
around me. He is standing to the side of the stage; he already looks older
than Jacob ever did. Donna Mason stands next to him, a shoulder shorter,
her puckered face and upturned chin challenging the crowd. I wonder if
she too is thinking about Jacob's memorial all those years ago. The sobbing students. The guilty teachers. The relentless rain. The crippling shock.
The nothingness that lay ahead. Donna's face looks like it froze that day
and never thawed out again.

Another girl is on the stage now, white fingers gripping a microphone,
her long blonde hair pulled away from her face in a messy ponytail.

"I'm going to sing a song that is very special to me. I wrote it last year and
Ms. Ryan helped me to practice it when I was auditioning for drama school.
I will never forget her patience and support. I dedicate this song to her."

The girl looks across the crowd and into the fiery sun. She slowly shuts
her eyes, her chest moving up and down for a few beats before she begins
to sing. Low and husky, her voice wraps around the crowd, intoxicating.
Electricity zaps through the air. The song is a haunting bluesy poem. The
girl never opens her eyes. Felix glances at me and raises his eyebrows,
impressed. He can feel the current too. I can feel Rosalind around me: her
sensual, addictive presence. I always knew why Jacob fell for her. She was
magnetic. She was so beautiful, so *special*. In her presence it was hard to
think beyond her face and velvet stare. Everything else simply faded away.

The final note of the song blurs into the hum of cicadas. The girl opens her eyes as if waking. She looks skyward and mouths something to the clouds before whispering, "Thank you," into the microphone.

John Nicholson is weeping now, tears rolling unchecked down his face. The PR woman watches him anxiously. I can tell she wants him to temper the public display of emotion.

Breaking away from a huddle of teenagers, Rodney and Maggie Archer walk onto the stage. I spot Kai among the huddle, his head down, as he wipes his wrist across his nose. We finally interviewed Maggie yesterday morning, when she returned from Melbourne. She gave polite, slightly bored answers to our questions and kept repeating the words "tragic" and "awful." She recounted the opening night evening in helpful detail, including her walking to the after party with a large group of friends, but I found her overall tone deeply unsettling.

Maggie appears overwhelmed by the crowd, ducking her head and shuffling her feet. I am still high from the song, the melody having entered my bloodstream. It's disorienting. I feel incredibly hot; waves of white crash over my vision and there's no sound. I grip my chair, trying not to faint.

A few seconds pass before the scene shudders back into full color and I can hear voices again. I look at Felix, who is oblivious to my little episode. I catch the end of Maggie's speech.

"It's what she would want, so we hope to see as many of you on the second of January as possible. Plus, all of the profits will go toward supporting the ongoing arts program here at Smithson."

Rodney kicks his foot at the ground. "Being together right now is important. Stories, music and art will help us all to heal. Please do this one final thing for her. For Ms. Ryan."

A flip rises in his voice and I remember him as a child, alone and broken, mourning a dead brother. He lifts his eyes and looks over at the Ryans before quickly looking back at the ground. Maggie walks away from the microphone, a soft smile on her face as she greets some classmates. Rodney realizes he's standing on the stage alone and shuffles backward awkwardly, his eyes still downcast. Donna's scowl deepens as she watches her son leave the stage. The Ryans haven't moved. I think what stunning statues they would make.

I will my brain to work, to emerge from this endless carousel of Rosalind, escape the red haze of the past. I turn slowly to Felix. He is real and stable. He is here. He meets my eyes.

"I reckon that kid knows something," he says, leaning close to me.

"Maybe," I say, watching Rodney hugging his friends, his eyes closed.

"Well, anyway," Felix says, "looks like we're going to the theater."

Chapter Twenty-nine

Friday, December 18, 1:48 p.m.

"Yes?" My voice is snappy as I answer the phone, reaching around the back of my neck to knead the muscles. I'm tired, broken by the memorial service. My face is tight from a light sunburn and memories play Tetris in my mind as I pore over the police reports, trying to find anything of note. Felix was supposed to meet me back here at 1:30 p.m. but he hasn't shown up yet. We're getting nowhere on Rosalind's case and the collective frustration is becoming more tangible by the minute.

"Woodstock, call for you." Kenny Prosie is on the switch, his whining voice curiously managing to be both distinctive and generic. Kenny's dad is one of the old boys here and, because of this, Kenny thinks that working the switch is beneath him. In fact, Kenny thinks that pretty much any task he is asked to do is beneath him.

"Who is it?"

"Some posh English bird. Says she wants to speak to the lead detective on the Ryan case. Lila someone."

Rosalind's stepmother. I left her several messages after I spoke to George Ryan on Wednesday. "Put her through, Kenny," I say.

"Yes, sir," says Kenny sarcastically.

There's a click and then a pause. A soft clipped "hello" comes down the line.

"Detective Woodstock. Is this Lila Wilcox?"

"Ah, yes. Hello. Sorry for my tardiness. I didn't get your messages until today. I've been traveling."

Her voice is precise, like that of a newsreader. I picture a long lean throat, coiffed hair. I flick my headset on, quickly google her and confirm that I am right. A handsome-looking woman with piercing coal eyes and ivory skin stares out at me.

"I'm glad you called me back. I want to talk to you about Rosalind."

"Rose," she corrects me quickly. There is a sharp intake of breath.

"I'm very sorry about what happened. She was your stepdaughter?" I'm still scrolling down pages of search findings on Lila Wilcox. From what I can tell she is a very high-profile person in HR.

"Yes. I married George in ninety-four. We divorced seven years later."

Rosalind was about fourteen when they split. A fairly impressionable age to lose a mother figure. I should know. "What was your relationship with Rose like?" I ask her, remembering that George said they were close.

"Well, she was a Ryan," starts Lila, and then seems to interrupt her own train of thought. I can tell she is shaking her head. "No, look, really, she was a delight. A bit prickly at first but then she completely won me over. I certainly ended up being closer to her than the others. I am devastated about this. I'm in shock, I suppose, but I haven't seen her in over ten years. So it all seems very distant. My life is over here now."

"Where is here?"

"Shanghai. I moved here in 2004."

"And you and Rose didn't stay in touch?"

"We did a little. Especially at first. We would talk on the phone. Write sometimes. I felt guilty for leaving her, I suppose. Such a bright child."

"But then?"

"Then, well…" Her voice trails off and I can only hear soft breathing. "Then I guess I got busy and she grew up. She moved out. I invited her to come and stay with me but Rose was not much into travel. She was very much a homebody. Even as a teenager."

I think about her neat little place. Felix was right: it could have belonged to a grandmother.

"Why did you feel guilty about leaving her? She was always going to stay with her father, I assume?" I emphasize the word "father" to see if it sparks any response.

"Oh well, I don't know. A young girl alone with just boys. Especially those boys. I suppose Marcus was okay. The others could be a bit predatory—just the age they were at, I think, but I still worried for her. Her father was useless." There's a flash of malice in Lila's words, a bitterness.

"Useless in what way?"

Lila sighs. "Look, nothing that bad, nothing that is really notable. In fact, it's so textbook it's embarrassing."

"Textbook?" I venture.

"Oh, you know, pretty young childless woman falls for handsome, rich widower with lots of children. I was basically Maria in *The Sound of Music*. Or at least George wanted me to be."

"But that didn't suit you?"

"No! And I told him before we were married that I was very serious about my career. I think he just hoped my maternal instincts would kick in."

"But they didn't." There's a fierceness about Lila. I imagine her and a younger George Ryan fighting. I'm sure it would have been something to witness.

"Not really. Perhaps a little with Rose. Like I said, she did win me over, but I'm not made for motherhood." Lila pauses and her prim voice cracks slightly. "She did get under my skin though. She was quite a magnetic child, quite unusual. I found myself wanting to look after her. I worried about her but I don't quite know why. I think it really bothered George, actually."

"When did you last speak to Rose?"

She clears her throat delicately and there's a tissue involved; I can hear it rustling. "That's really why I called you back. We spoke last week. We used to speak every few months or so. She seemed uncharacteristically chatty. Happy. We talked about her play—she called me just before the final rehearsal. From the school, I think. She was incredibly excited about it."

"Was that all?"

"No, no. She also told me that she'd met someone."

"Like a boyfriend?"

"Yes, yes, a boyfriend. Someone who she said she was very serious about. But she seemed nervous. She wouldn't actually tell me anything about him."

"You asked?"

"Of course I asked! She and I are close when we do talk, but she doesn't usually share things like that with me. I was happy for her. She sounded very keen on him, but when I asked her his name, what he did—you know, the normal things—she was very cagey." Lila lets out a little sob. "The poor man must be beside himself, whoever he is. I suppose you have spoken to him?"

I tap my fingers on my desk. Someone has put the cricket on and there is a rumble from the crowd as a wicket is taken. I still can't see Felix anywhere. "We've been in contact with all of her friends and family," I tell Lila neutrally. "Did Rose say anything else?"

"Just that they were going to move in together in the new year. She said they had it all worked out."

Chapter Thirty

then

Letters shook across the page. I tried to reread the words, tried to take them in, but it was as if they had turned into numbers. It was my last exam. The summer stretched out in front of me, bleak and empty. Someone had forgotten to wake the sun. Jacob had called me just like he said he would and we'd spoken like we always had, about school, his job, my dad and *The X-Files*, but there was a fault line now, a dangerous shaft that we tiptoed around, in case it gave way and we found ourselves falling. Something was wrong with him but I didn't know what and I didn't know how to ask. I was too busy with my own grief.

Dad wanted to take me out for dinner later that night, to celebrate his little girl finally finishing school. "You did it," he'd said earlier that morning, but I knew he'd really meant, *You made it*, because once you have met grief so bluntly you expect it to appear at random, snatching away the things that you have carefully rebuilt, the things that keep you alive. Dad's fear of my dying had loomed over us ever since Mum had gone, hidden in every innocent "Be careful" or "Call me if you need to."

Dad knew that something wasn't quite right between Jacob and me but I'd brushed it away, blaming the exams and our shift into adulthood. He left it alone, glad not to have to navigate the choppy waters of emotion.

I only had twenty minutes left. I looked at the lines of writing—so many words. I couldn't remember what I'd written but I had to trust that my brain knew the answers, that my hands had directed the pen to write down the right words. The questions pulsed at me from the exam paper.

How real do you think Romeo and Juliet's love is? Explain your answer in the context of the era in which they lived.

Tears welled in my eyes and I tipped my head backward slightly to stop them brimming over. I looked around the room. Everyone else was bent over their desks, writing furiously. Kevin Whitby dropped his pen and it rattled noisily onto the floor. One of the adjudicators curled her lip, annoyed, before marching over to pick it up. Rosalind's long hair spilled past her shoulder a few rows in front of me. A small shaft of sunlight from a ceiling window hit her hair and it gleamed more golden than usual. *Just finish this*, I thought, *just finish*.

Ignoring the endless, tedious summer in front of me, I started to write again, making the case that the love between Shakespeare's two young characters was indeed real, so real that it transcended the reality that had previously seemed so solid to them both, right up to the day before they met. *It's real*, I wrote, *because it quickly becomes everything, and the thought of it being taken away makes them feel like they would be left with nothing at all.*

Chapter Thirty-one

Friday, December 18, 3:46 p.m.

At check-in I'm recounting my conversation with Lila Wilcox when Jonesy appears. The air in the station is hot and musky, the twin fans gallantly pushing it back and forth above our heads. My shirt feels damp across my back. Felix still isn't here; he texted me to say that he is following up something to do with Rosalind's finances and will fill me in later.

"So who is this mystery man, Woodstock?"

"I don't know, sir."

Jonesy snorts. "You must have some ideas, surely?"

Felix bursts in. He waves for me to keep talking and takes a seat in the back.

I look Jonesy in the eye. "Well, there're the teachers. In particular, the principal, Nicholson. Then there're the students." I glance at Felix, who raises an eyebrow at me, before I say reluctantly, "There was an alleged issue with a student at her previous school, so there could be a pattern with our victim and younger men. She would have had a lot of interaction with the lead in the play, Rodney Mason. And Kai Bracks, the backstage manager—also in year twelve—is rumored to have had a crush on her earlier this year. Someone sent her some flowers on Valentine's Day and a lot of people think it was him." I pause, picturing the roses on my front porch. "And one of her neighbors mentioned a man in a fancy car paying her a visit a few weeks ago but nothing has come of that so far. Or maybe it's some random, normal guy she met somewhere." I sip at my cold coffee. "Or she could have been lying to Lila about being in a relationship, seeing as Lila is overseas and would never know any better. If she was seeing someone, he hasn't come forward, which in itself would be incredibly sus-picious. In saying that, her phone records certainly don't give a clue to her seeing someone. She barely called anyone or received any calls. The only suspicion comes from a couple of calls from a prepaid phone that we can't lock down. So maybe Rosalind wanted to make her life sound more excit-ing and fabricated a romance."

Jonesy coughs and it reminds me of sandpaper. "She did seem to live in her head a bit. Ditzy, isn't that what you call it? Okay, so this is all just maybes. Anything solid yet? Where are we at?"

I stand and move toward the large pin boards. Multiple Rosalinds stare at me.

I look Jonesy in the eye. "We're not really anywhere yet, sir. It could still be a random attack, of course, which would certainly explain why nothing is adding up."

"Is that what you think?"

"No. It doesn't explain why she was at the lake. I still think it was per-sonal." I pause and then say, "The pregnancy is a possible motive."

"You think the father wanted the baby dead?"

"Maybe. Or it could simply point to the kind of serious relationship that Rosalind described to Lila Wilcox. Perhaps it turned abusive. They might have fought about something. Maybe things were going well between them but then she told him about the pregnancy and he got scared."

Jonesy grunts. "She could have got knocked up by a stranger. Someone she just met."

"She could have," I allow, "but I don't think so. That definitely seems unlikely based on what we know about her character and the fact that she was so many weeks along. It suggests she was considering keeping the baby."

"What was her character?"

I sigh, puffing air into my cheeks. "To be honest, sir, it's difficult to define. Trying to nail down her personality is hard. A lot of people liked her and an equal number didn't. She didn't seem to be particularly close to anyone."

"What about the trouble at her other school?" Jonesy presses.

I nod. "The incident at her old school seems to be an anomaly but could indicate a tendency to manipulate. She definitely made some waves when she pushed to have the school play. There's no gambling, no serious drug issues, no public outbursts or criminal record. Really, there's nothing." I glance at her photos on the board. "Plus, if she *was* seeing someone, why keep it a secret? Why keep it from her family and friends? She probably told Lila because she was a safe option living thousands of kilometers away. But it does indicate that Rosalind *wanted* to talk about this guy. It makes me think that the relationship, assuming there was one, must have been problematic in some way. Maybe it was scandalous. Maybe he was married. There must have been something that made her want to keep it under wraps."

Jonesy huffs. "Well, we need definites, not maybes, so it sounds like you still have a lot of work to do. I want you to keep looking into the kids. We've all known cases where crushes have gotten out of hand. And try to track down the man the neighbor said she saw. With the posh car. And see if you can get any more information from Rosalind's old school. There might be a link there." He wipes sweat from his eyebrows. "But remember: no bloody overtime. I'm getting whipped from all angles."

Chapter Thirty-two

Saturday, December 19, 5:42 a.m.

Tucked neatly next to the shock of Rosalind's murder are thoughts of Christmas. It's only a week away, or so the screaming ads on the radio tell me. The shops rumble with quiet panic. Smithsonians are into Christmas in a big way. The tatty plastic on the decorations in the main streets rustles uncomfortably in the heat. At this hour, there is barely a soul about, just the occasional dog walker or jogger. I wonder if people are still doing laps of the lake or whether they are sticking to the roads since Rose was found there. It's funny how paranoia seeps into the air. How it can curl around doors and into thoughts. Fasten locks and quicken steps.

In contrast to the soft dawn, the bakery on Hopkins Street is defiantly lit up like a Christmas tree. Inside, I see Nick Gould yanking empty wire trays from the display shelves. Nick was in my year, just like Rosalind. His claim to fame was being able to eat four large pizzas in a single sitting. My friend Janet had given him a blow job after one such display of manliness at a house party and she swore that his come had tasted like tomato and basil.

Huge trucks block the entrance of the Woolworths car park. A cigarette flicks from the front window of the vehicle nearest to me and lands dangerously close to a discarded newspaper. The glowing ember is followed by an impressive wad of phlegm. *Jill's Turkeys* runs in a repetitive ribbon along the belly of the truck and I think about the giant empty carcasses, headless and hanging, bobbing along silently in rows as if making small talk about the weather.

Jerking my car into a park, I grab the shopping bags and hope this won't take too long.

"Gemma!"

"Hey, Sydney." I never fail to see someone I know when I'm doing the shopping, but I hoped that my extra-early start might give me a better chance of avoiding unwanted chat.

"Nasty business with the teacher."

I nod. Sydney owns the only indoor playground in Smithson. Her favorite color is pink and she has fitted out the center accordingly. I never take Ben there: it's like being inside a giant stomach. Today Sydney looks flushed and blotchy. Her hair is pulled back tight from her face, reminding me of a water-spitting bath toy that Ben likes to bash against the side of the tub.

"Chemical peel," she says, patting her cheeks. "It's supposed to go down by Christmas. It's good for redness." She stabs at her face with a sharp orange nail. "We're starting to get old, you know, Gemma."

I nod again, assuming I'm supposed to agree, and move more quickly toward the supermarket entrance. Sydney almost trips over in her heels trying to keep up with me.

"So do you guys know who did it yet?"

"Not yet."

"Mm. Well, hopefully you will by Christmas. Is there any truth to the serial killer talk? Do you know that the council was going to have the carols at the lake? Can you imagine? I mean, urgh." She shudders. Her voice seems to roll out of her unchecked. Her large plastic handbag slaps against her bare thigh, making a sucking sound.

"Probably not the best idea."

"No. Well. It's just awful." She grabs at a trolley, aggressively shaking it loose from the pack. Then her face brightens as if the sun has come out. "Anyway, what are you doing for Christmas? With little Joe?"

"Ben."

"Yep, right, *Ben*. I think it's Georgia that has Joe. *Anyway*. What are your plans?"

"Just hanging around with Dad probably. Scott's brother and his wife. Nothing special."

"Lovely, lovely." Her mind is clearly starting to trawl the shelves, her mental shopping list taking priority over our conversation. "Well, must fly, unfortunately. I've ten people coming for dinner tonight."

"Take care, Sydney. Tell Max I say hi."

She waves her fingers at me and disappears down an aisle, weaving her trolley with impressive skill.

My trolley has a wonky wheel, and my muscles pull and burn as I round the corners.

I hate coming to the supermarket. The rows of things stare down at me—all of these things that I don't know what to do with. I'm a terrible cook. Before I met Scott I basically lived on noodles, eggs and boiled rice. A lot of the time I would barely eat at all, coming home from work and drinking wine until I fell asleep on the couch. For a while I lived with an Italian girl, a part-time actress who moonlighted as a chef. I tried to emulate her complicated creations but just didn't have a knack for it. I still remember her laughing uncontrollably the night I tried to make crème brûlée.

I told Sydney the truth. We are spending Christmas with my dad. Scott's brother Craig and sister-in-law Laura will come too, as will Aunt Megan. Scott's parents live in the UK with his mum's elderly mother. They rarely come out to Australia; they don't have much money, and we're not that close to them anyway. Ben and his simple Christmas joy will be the only thing about the day that holds us all together. Craig and Laura have been trying to have children for almost five years. I have to look away when they give Ben his presents.

I toss packets of chips into the trolley, catching the handle before it clips me in the guts. Tonight we are going to a Christmas barbecue at Scott's friend Pete's place. It's a dress-up theme. Pete's girlfriend Fee has an inexplicably large pool of sexy elf and Santa outfits and insists on hosting this annual dress-up party. Dad is minding Ben. I don't want to go. Scott and I fought about it yesterday morning.

"You could make an effort sometimes, Gem." He said it quietly, like he was talking to someone else.

"Fine, fine. I'll come."

He kept watching TV. "You like Pete. You like Fee. You like the guys. What's the problem?"

Although these points are only partly true, I said tightly, "No problem. I already said I'm coming."

Felix and I had originally planned to meet tonight. He'd texted me last night to cancel just before Scott reminded me about the party, which I had forgotten about. The disappointment at not having time alone with Felix was so strong that for a moment I almost thought I would throw the mug I was holding at Scott. I placed it safely in the sink just to be sure.

I pick up a cereal box and look at the ingredients half-heartedly. I know I shouldn't feed Ben this shit, but the likelihood of me actually coming up with an alternative that he will eat is close to zero. I toss the sugary cereal in next to the chips.

"Gemma Woodstock, I *thought* it was you."

I freeze mid-trolley push.

"Helloooo." Candy Fyfe ducks her head in front of mine and wiggles her fingers at me. "You're here early. Case causing you some insomnia?" Syrupy with empathy, her words run along the nerve in my spine that is specifically reserved for the pitch of her voice.

"I hate shopping. I'm just getting it out of the way."

She nods as if agreeing. "Mm. You certainly don't strike me as a Christmas person. Too festive for you. Too joyous."

"Go away, Candy."

"Oh, come on. You won't answer my calls at work. Fate clearly brought me to aisle five at this ungodly hour so we could talk. Do you know," she went on, clearly not caring whether I wanted to know or not, "I had a day off last Friday! First time in, like, I don't know, two years I've had a day off and there's a freaking murder! I almost missed it. Can you believe it?"

I angle my trolley away from her and push it forward.

"I was at a wedding in the city. It was lovely, thanks for asking. I made it back on Saturday morning just in the nick of time to get to the lake. But it's been a full-on week since, trying to solve this doozy."

I roll my eyes. "I hardly think you need to worry yourself with things like that. Surely there's some little Christmassy piece you should be getting your claws stuck into instead."

"C'mon, don't be like that. Let me buy you a coffee. Have a proper chat. The press conference the other day was a complete waste of time. I want to hear from *you* where you're at on this thing. Saves me from filing yet *another* story that says you guys have no clue."

"Seriously, Candy, I'm not doing this now. We've made our statement. We're getting closer every day."

"Suit yourself." She starts to scan the shelves in an over-exaggerated way.

I walk away from her, more riled than I would ever admit.

"You know what everyone's saying, don't you?"

I keep my eyes on the butter at the end of the aisle. *Keep walking, don't let her get to you.*

Candy's voice has a melodic lilt as she throws one last barb in my direction. "Mr. Principal certainly was pretty friendly with the beautiful Ms. Ryan. That's the word on the street anyway."

I spin around in anger and then force myself to breathe away a nasty retort as I watch Candy's svelte arse sashay up the aisle.

Chapter Thirty-three

Saturday, December 19, 10:34 a.m.

"I think it's only eczema but you just never know. I always panic. I've been to the doctor with her at least four times this past month!"

Carol's laugh dances around her front room. She calls it the sunroom even though it doesn't really have the right kind of window to be a sunroom. Ben has finally calmed down and is playing sweetly on the floor with Jack, Carol's son. She is breastfeeding Olive, the baby. Somewhere deeper in the house a radio is on and I hear a familiar news riff. The baby makes a loud sucking sound as she feeds and Carol tuts at her gently.

"So hungry today, aren't you? Poor thing." Carol pushes wavy hair from her eyes and looks at me apologetically. "Do you mind grabbing the cakes from the bench, Gem? I'm kind of stuck here."

"Sure, of course."

I glance at her as I rise from the couch. She's staring lovingly at Olive, who is grabbing intently at her thumb. Carol seems happy to be trapped.

In the kitchen I pause to take in the effect of the room. The dove gray couch looks incredibly soft. A mohair blanket is folded across the top cushion. The blinds are drawn and the room is cool from the air-con. The fridge hums healthily and a row of indoor plants look well-watered. A towering pine is dotted with red bows and a large gold star is perfectly centered on top. Brightly wrapped gifts are stacked high under the tree. Clearly Jack is well-behaved enough to be trusted around this perfectly styled Christmas scene. I move over to the bench and can see happy snaps on the fridge of Carol and her husband Seth. His arms are wrapped around her and she smiles symmetrically at the camera. There are photos of Jack and Olive and other small children. Nieces, I assume; I remember Carol mentioning her sister's children. At least a dozen invitations to kids' birthdays and christenings are secured with magnets. Two wedding invites and an invitation to a love ceremony covered in silver foil are displayed in a little fan.

I always have such high hopes before my visits to Carol's that everything will suddenly click, that Carol's contentedness might rub off on me, and then, within minutes, I feel a flat disappointment. I just can't seem to slot into this world. I always end up leaving earlier than I need to.

I flip back the gauzy cloth covering the cakes and take them into the lounge room.

"These look amazing!" I say, trying to will the time along.

"Oh, well. We'll see. I like trying new recipes but I have been a little unlucky lately. Hopefully these are better than the jam tarts I took to mothers' group last week!"

She bites into her cake and a few crumbs drop onto Olive. The baby scrunches up her tiny face in protest but Carol doesn't notice.

"Do you still see the others much?" I ask.

"Oh, sometimes." Carol's voice is breezy-light for my benefit. "You know how it is, everyone is so busy with the kids but it's always nice to catch up when we can."

"How's Casey?"

"She's good, I think." Carol nods as if considering this. "Yes, she seems good."

Casey's husband suffered a stroke when their baby, Zoe, turned one. Billy now requires high-dependency care. The only place suitable near Smithson is an aged-care home about thirty minutes away. Casey visits him every day.

"I mean, I think she cries every night—I know I would—but she seems to be getting better. Making it work. Zoe's a joy."

I wonder whether I would cry every night if Scott had a stroke. I can't imagine it.

Carol shakes her head. "Anyway, did you know that Sasha is having another baby?"

"That's great."

"Yep, that makes everyone but you and Casey having two."

I nod, thinking about the blood in the shower last Saturday morning. I clutch at my stomach involuntarily and then quickly drop my hand. Carol is too busy stroking the soft hair on Olive's head in a slow half-circle to notice. A faint red rash peeks out from behind her tiny ear: the eczema. A thread pulls deep in my memory. I think I can remember my mum stroking my head like that and I shift on my chair and try to focus on eating the cake. My bones itch from all the sitting still.

"You and Scott still only want the one?" Carol says it indifferently but I know she wants the answer to be no. Everyone wants the answer to be no. One child never makes sense, apparently. Over the past year I've had a front-row seat to the instinctive desire people seem to have to right this wrong. Ben needs a sibling. I will regret only having one child in years to come. Scott deserves a football team. A daughter to dote on. I will enjoy motherhood more with two. It's easier the second time around. I'm selfish.

"Yes," I say firmly. "I think Ben is the perfect amount for me. For us."

"Well, it's just lucky you both agree," Carol trills, looking lovingly at Olive.

"Yep," I say, kicking a toy back toward Ben.

I shift my weight the way I always do when the conversation gets intimate. I don't like having to justify my choices. I don't like talking about Scott either. I never tell people much about our relationship. Especially not anyone from the mothers' group, seeing as they barely know him anyway. It's far too complicated to explain and is a conversation far better suited to have over wine than cake.

Carol pushes a finger into Olive's mouth, disconnecting her from her breast with a loud pop. Olive blinks and seems somewhat put out. Carol holds her up to burp her, stopping when she gets the required sound. "Right, here you go, sweetheart. Some tummy time."

Olive stares up at me like a helpless beetle. Her useless arms and legs flail at her sides. Ben and Jack look over and giggle at her. She smiles a big gummy smile back at them. I sigh, feeling like the whole world is conspiring against me.

"I mean, one child must be sooo nice sometimes!" Carol smiles at me and then pushes herself back against the couch, closing her eyes briefly. "The cake was good, wasn't it?"

I nod.

"Yes, I thought so too. Good, well, that's another keeper. It will be perfect for Seth's work picnic thing." She's lost momentarily in a bubble of domestic to-do lists. "So…" Abruptly, she leans forward, her eyes large. "How is the case going? I saw you on the news this week." She casts a guilty look at the children, as if they might be exposed to the darkness of my job if she talks about it.

"It's early days really. We've covered a lot of ground but there's still a lot to do."

"Do you think you'll find the guy?" Carol is gripping the side of the couch now, wanting details. She has the same look that new officers get when they want bad things to happen so they can really feel like cops.

"I hope so. But it's a tricky one."

"What do you think though? Random psycho? Jealous boyfriend?" Carol grabs a cushion and hugs it. "I heard that she was seeing one of the teachers. Maybe a married one? It all makes sense in a way. I mean, she was so beautiful."

Carol is now looking dreamily at the floor as if romanticizing the beauty of dying in some torrid love triangle.

My bones start to shift inside my skin. I have to move. I stand up and look around for my bag. "I need to head off, I'm afraid. I have to drop Ben home and get a few things done."

"Oh, that's a shame. Work things?" She straightens the plump aqua cushion and then smooths the lime one. She must put extra stuffing in them.

"Yeah, work things. I have to interview someone." I gesture to Ben. "C'mon, sweetheart, let's go."

"Wow," says Carol. "Well, good luck. We'll just be here watching boring old Disney movies."

Chapter Thirty-four

Saturday, December 19, 12:05 p.m.

"I thought the memorial yesterday was wonderful. Just lovely." Felicity Shooter gives an approving nod as she tips first one, then another teaspoon of sugar into her coffee. "Didn't you think, darling? Just lovely."

Troy Shooter nods. The past week has aged him a decade. He can feel the shock deep in his bones. He watches his wife sip at her latte. Some froth lingers on her mouth. He notices a hair shining on her upper lip and how her lipstick has bled beyond the curve of her mouth. She looks a little like Jacqui did when she used to play dress-ups.

"Yes, yes," Felicity clucks like a chicken. "Very nice."

She had woken up in a good mood this morning. "Let's go to that new hotel, the one with the balcony across the front. Paula tells me it is divine. It's been a hard couple of days—I think we deserve a treat."

Troy shrugged. It had been a long time since his point of view had been worth voicing.

They drove across town in silence with the air-con blasting, the cool wind on his cheeks like a slap in contrast with the tight heat that was trapped in his suit jacket.

"Lovely, lovely," Felicity said, looking around the sunny balcony as they were led to their table. "Look at that view. Magnificent!"

Troy cast his eyes out across the rolling valley, admiring the way the sky met the green and blurred, just like a watercolor. All of a sudden he felt like he might cry, so he quickly sat down and cleared his throat, frantically trying to land on a more positive emotion.

Now, fighting mild panic, Troy looks around at all the other diners.

Large, red-faced men are furiously cutting steaks and a table of women in the corner are laughing hysterically as they drink glasses of translucent wine. Troy feels out of place. Who are all these happy, noisy diners? Smithson has changed so much over the past few years that it's harder and harder to spot a familiar face.

"It was nice seeing all your work friends again at the service. They are all very nice people. We should have them over sometime. I bet no one else would think to do that. Millie certainly wouldn't host a dinner, would she? She's very introverted. Even that young one with the funny hair was nice. It's a dreadful color but she seemed a nice girl. Very smart. John Nicholson doesn't seem to be coping very well, though, does he? It's written all over his face. But the flowers were beautiful, just lovely. I love roses. I prefer pink rather than red, obviously, but someone told me that she loved red roses, they were her favorite, so I suppose it makes sense."

Troy looks at his wife. She is breathless from her chatter and breathing deeply. The opal necklace he gave her for their wedding anniversary last year shines at her throat. He thinks about Rosalind's throat. The papers said she was strangled. And hit with a rock. He tries to picture Rosalind properly, remember what she looked like when she was at her desk in the staffroom or walking past him in the corridor, but the only thing he can summon is the photo of her that was on the memorial handout. It didn't even look like her really: too much makeup and an odd little smile. It was as if someone who didn't know her had chosen the photo.

He keeps thinking about walking into Nicholson's office, finding Rosalind there—the angry flash of her eyes and the pained look on Nicholson's face. The room felt small and Troy stumbled on his words.

"It's okay, Troy. Come in. We're done," Nicholson said heavily.

Rosalind picked up a foot and brought it back down to the floor with force before firing another look at Nicholson and whirling out of the room. That moment felt like something that might be important, but Troy couldn't for the life of him think what to do with it.

"Probably a good thing that Christmas is coming. Gives everyone a chance to spend some time with their family and put this behind them."

Felicity nods, clearly pleased with the neatness of the timing. "Yes. Hopefully this will be sorted very soon and everyone can move on." She looks at the menu, her eyes scanning the page. "I really need to get on top of Christmas lunch. I can't believe it's next week!"

Troy uncrosses and then recrosses his legs at the ankles. His left foot prickles with pins and needles. He's been getting them a lot lately. In bed late at night when he is trying to sleep. That strange buzzing feeling that has him kicking out his legs and stretching his feet, trying to distract his own brain. *Over here! Think about this! Or what about this! Football scores, words to a song, capital cities. The exact color of Rosalind Ryan's eyes.*

"Jacqui's bringing a new boy for Christmas, did I tell you? Someone she met at uni. And of course you know that Sophie managed to convince Dave to get out of his family's lunch so they're both coming too. With the kids." Felicity clicks her tongue smugly as she waves the waitress over.

"I'm not sure how much longer I'll teach for." He didn't mean to blurt it out like that, didn't even quite realize that the thought was tickling around in his head, but as soon as the words are spoken, a sense of calm washes over him. He wants to fish. Go to the beach. Read the classics.

"Troy! I mean, well. That's just silly talk. You're only fifty-six!"

"That's not young, Felicity. I'm tired. I'm tired of teaching. I think all this has made me realize just how tired."

"Of course this is all absolutely awful, but it's a one-off. A terrible, horrible thing, but it's got nothing to do with us."

"It's changed everything."

"But why? You worked with her, I understand that. It's obviously very hard, but..." Felicity's hands curl at the edges of the table, stretched white, her blood-red nails like talons. Her lips are pulled back, revealing her canine teeth. She is monstrous, terrifying, and then just as quickly her face is back to normal.

Troy blinks, wondering whether he's losing his mind.

"She was obviously mixed up in something. Something bad. Don't let it ruin your life. Who knows what she was up to, a girl like that." Felicity slowly eases back in her chair and downs the last of her sparkling water. "Come on, Troy." The discussion is clearly over.

Troy forces himself to sit up straight. To focus. He shakes out his foot, which still buzzes as if someone is sawing at his bone. Felicity begins to work through the Christmas lunch plans. Dish by dish, ingredients are reeled off. Plans are made. There is a lot to do. Troy feels the buzzing move up his body all the way into his brain.

Chapter Thirty-five

Saturday, December 19, 1:48 p.m.

I drop Ben back at home with Scott and then call Felix on my way to the shopping center. He's with the forensic finance guys, following up several RYAN employees and associates to see how deep the anger goes and whether any threats have been made against the company or George himself.

"We haven't turned up much," Felix tells me. "There've never been any serious threats made against the company. A bomb threat was made to George's house years ago but it went nowhere; it was probably just kids."

The sun skewers my eyes. I focus on the line on the road. "Okay, well, I guess I'll speak to you later."

"Wait, wait," says Felix. "I'm warming up to my big discovery."

"What is it?"

"You know how we were waiting on her bank accounts?"

"Yeah?"

"Well, aside from the standard stuff you'd expect, she has a term deposit account with a credit union and it has over one hundred thousand dollars in it."

I think about my own measly savings account, which constantly hovers at around two thousand dollars. "Wow. What for?"

"No idea. She puts about half her pay in every month, and has been doing that since she started working. It just stacks up, I guess. She's never touched it. Not one withdrawal. She must have been saving up for something."

"Maybe," I say, thinking. "Or maybe she just doesn't know what to do with it. I mean, she owns that place and her expenses must be pretty basic."

"Apart from the wine," Felix reminds me. "And the makeup."

"Yeah," I sigh. "Well, like we said, maybe they were her splurge things."

"Who knows. I think she was just really weird. But we're going to dig further and see what else we can find. Maybe she was planning to leave?"

"An escape fund," I wonder, trying to make sense of it.

"Are you still going to speak to Maggie today?" asks Felix.

"Yep, I'm heading to the shopping center now." We agreed that I will try to speak to Maggie outside of an arranged interview this time. I'm convinced she knows more than she is telling us and I want to catch her by surprise.

"Great, I'll be with these guys all day, I suspect, so I guess I'll chat to you later." I think he's already hung up when he says quietly, "Love you."

"Same," I say, my body stirring as I pull into the pre-Christmas chaos of the Ronson Shopping Center car park.

"Hi, Maggie."

Maggie Archer blinks large mascara-coated eyes at me. Her smile is practiced polite. "Oh yes. Hello." She is placing fresh packets of earrings onto little silver display hooks. Loud music pulses in my ears. Her nametag reads *Emily*.

"Detective Woodstock," I say firmly.

Her face shows a flutter of frustration as she hangs the last few sets of jewelry. She pulls herself up tall. "What do you want to talk to me about?" she says prissily.

Up close her hair is almost white. Two sections are pulled back from either side of her face and the rest spills down either side of her chest. She's like a breath of summer. She looks just like Rosalind did in school, except that her eyes are a glass blue rather than velvet brown.

I dive straight in, ignoring her tone. "It's nice of you guys to continue with the play. I'm sure Ms. Ryan would have wanted that."

She taps her foot lightly on the floor. Her eyes dart around the shop as if she is expecting someone to approach at any moment. Her toenails are painted neon pink and keep catching my attention out of the corner of my eye. I didn't get my first pedicure until I was in my twenties, but these kids grew up on *Sex and the City*. I'm endlessly surprised at how early beauty routines start these days. An abuse victim I interviewed last month had some minor burns on her legs from waxing. She was nine.

Maggie keeps her eyes on the ground.

She's working at a clothing store, Everyday Runway, which is in the middle of the shopping center. Her sister works in the complex too. Half the kids from Smithson do, just like when I was at school. I did my fair share of burger flipping here and can still summon up the dank, greasy smell that lingered on me for years, no matter how hard I scrubbed with Mango Tingle body wash.

A chattering pack of girls enters the store and Maggie looks at me pointedly.

"Excuse me," she mutters and walks over to greet them.

I sweep my eyes across the clothes on offer. Piles of pale denim shorts with threads deliberately loose remind me of plants that have had their roots tickled just before being placed into the ground. Maggie sells one of the girls a belt and shows another one into the change rooms.

"So, look…" She struts back to me with new-found confidence. "I'm working. Can we talk another time?"

"No, not really."

Her stare wavers slightly, and she juts her tiny hip and gives me a slightly exasperated stare, as if our roles are reversed.

"I'm working too, and finding out who killed your teacher is obviously a priority."

"O-*kay*. Well, what do you want to know?"

"Let's start with going over some of the basics again. No rehearsing this time. You were Juliet in the play, correct?"

"Yeah, but it doesn't strictly follow the original. There's a fair bit of creative license. I play the Juliet character but she's called Jasmine."

"Did you audition?"

"Of course. We all did."

"Rodney Mason auditioned?"

A cloud flashes over her face. "Yes. Like I said, we all did."

"So you must have been very happy to get the lead?"

"Of course. But I worked very hard. Drama is my favorite subject. I'm hoping to get into NIDA next year. I have a small part in a play in Sydney in February and I was in a few commercials as a child." She shrugs. "It's my thing."

"Congratulations."

She scowls at me and gestures to a girl who is waiting at the till to purchase a skirt. "Hang on a tick."

She slinks off and I watch her, all honey and light as she jokes with the customer, placing a free lipstick sample in the bag and commenting on her rings.

She saunters back. "Right, sorry, you were getting to a point?"

Before I can speak her phone beeps and she pulls it out of her pocket, smiling slowly as she flicks her finger over the screen.

"Excuse me?"

"Just a sec," she says.

My teeth grind against each other as I look at her perfect face. This girl is something else. "Was Kai Bracks in love with Ms. Ryan?"

Maggie snorts. "I dunno. He probably wanted to screw her; I don't think it was love."

"What about Rodney? Did he love her?"

"Same as above."

"Are you seeing Rodney? You two seemed close at the memorial."

"Seeing him? No. We went out last summer. Very briefly. He's good-looking but actually pretty boring."

"So you're not a couple?"

"Noooo." Slowly. "That would be why I said we weren't seeing each other."

"Are you friends? Playing the leads like that must be strange if you used to be together."

She stretches her neck from side to side like a cat. Her eyes remain fixed on mine. "We're friends, sure. And professionals. But that's it. I like girls now anyway."

"You're a lesbian?"

Her phone buzzes again and she glances down at the screen. She yawns sweetly. "Sure. You can call it that if you want. I prefer not to get specific. I'm so young, anything might happen."

I fight the urge to grab her by the throat and push her into the jewelry rack.

"You must be upset about what happened to Ms. Ryan. Your reading the other day was very moving."

She seems to think about this for a moment. "I was very sad to hear what had happened. Obviously. Murder is so…*full on*. It's pretty crazy, really. And I did like her, even though she was a bit flaky. Nicholson asked me to say a few words at the thing, and Rodney really wanted to, so I agreed. I like the opportunity to get up in front of a large crowd. It was an interesting event to speak at."

My mouth drops open and I quickly close it again. "It was hardly an 'event'."

She blinks at me. "Well, what would you call it?"

I shake my head, suddenly lost for words.

"Anyway," she says. "I've told you all this already." Her lips purse and she shakes her head in a way that makes me feel old.

"Sometimes people remember things that they forgot to tell us the first time round," I snap.

A soft smile plays on her lips. "I don't remember anything new. Like I said, the play was great. So amazing. We were all on such a high. Ms. Ryan too. She was so excited about how it went. I saw her afterward holding bunches of flowers. She even had a champagne at the interval. She was smiling heaps and seemed really happy."

I try to calm my breathing. "You said you didn't speak to her after. Is that true?"

"Uh-huh. Just saw her in the crowd. There were heaps of people around, like outside the school hall and in the main room, but all of us from the play just wanted to get to the party."

"At Jamie Klein's?"

"Yep. Jamie has a great party house and her parents were away so it was a big deal."

"Most of you went, right? From the play."

Maggie waves two girls toward the change rooms and glances at her phone again. "Ah, yeah. Most of us. And some of the younger grades too. Even some kids that finished school last year. There's always a couple who don't come. Like the kids really into sport or whatever. Miles didn't come; he'd had some fight with Sal or something. And Rodney wasn't going to come because he had basketball the next day, but then it was canceled so he ended up coming. But it was massive. Maybe a hundred kids."

"When did Rodney turn up?" I press.

"I don't know. I don't, like, keep track of him. I saw him around twelve-thirty maybe, but I'd been outside so he was probably there for ages before I saw him."

"What about Kai?"

"Um…" She twirls the ends of her hair. "I think I saw him when I got there. Eleven, maybe?"

I sigh inwardly. Timelines are a nightmare to map out at the best of times without having to rely on the memories of drunk teenagers.

"Neither of them did anything to her, if that's what you're getting at."

"Really?" I'm struggling to stay calm around the tilt of her chin. "And you would know, would you?"

"Sure. They're just not *real* men. Know what I mean? There's just no way. They're kids."

I take in her waxed, tan, buxom stance, the jut of her hip, the world-weariness in her stare, and feel an unexpected tug of sadness.

"Okay. Well, where were you when you found out about what had happened to Ms. Ryan?"

She shrugs. "Mum told me. I stayed at Jamie's, heaps of us did, and she called me around lunchtime and told me. I was so hungover it totally didn't seem real. We were all really freaked out. Jamie's house is only like maybe five hundred meters from the lake so that seemed weird too. We weren't sure if the play would still happen that night or whatever. It was just really weird."

She wipes her fingers under her eyes, pushing away some dark smudges. "We stayed there talking about it for ages."

"Who else stayed there?"

She looks at me wearily. "*Heaps* of us. I don't know. Amy, Jess . . . Jamie, obviously."

"Kai?"

"Yep. Kai, Jono, Joel. A few guys were in tents out the back so I'm not sure exactly."

"Rodney?"

"Nah, I think he went home."

She suddenly springs away from me and goes to the counter to put through a sale, beaming at the customer. Then she makes her way back to me.

"Look, I have to start cleaning up. Are we—"

"Yep. We're done." I turn to go and then spin around again. "Actually, just one more thing. Was anyone upset about what happened to Ms. Ryan? Like, more upset than you thought was normal?"

"Mm." She taps her fingers against her jaw. "That's kind of hard to say, isn't it? Everyone is so different. Joel Perkins cried, which was a bit weird, but his grandma had died the day before so it was probably more about that. All the girls were upset, of course. And Rodney. When I saw him at school he was upset. He's very emotional though. Like super sensitive. Probably because of his brother."

She smiles at me prettily and I yank my eyes away from hers and talk to the small patch of skin in between them instead.

"Aren't you emotional, Maggie, being an actress? I thought you would be all about feelings."

She leans toward me conspiratorially. "I *am*. I feel things *really* hard, but I mean, I have to be honest. This thing with Ms. Ryan, it's super sad, of course, but it's also the most exciting thing that's happened around here in, like, *forever.*"

Chapter Thirty-six

Saturday, December 19, 8:45 p.m.

Fee looks like she's the lead in a low-grade porn flick. Her breasts bob dangerously as if trying to escape her fluffy Mrs. Claus costume, and I hold the drinks we brought in front of me to avoid an awkward embrace.

"Scotty!" Fee grabs Scott and mashes her chest against him instead. "Yay, you're here!" She gives me a half-hearted wave. "Hey, Gem."

"Hi, Fee. Merry Christmas." I hold out the drinks, giving us both something to focus on.

"Oh great, thanks for bringing those. Now let me think…There's an cooler out the back, it's probably best to put them in there. The fridge inside is full."

I leave Scott talking to Fee and some other girl who is dressed as a Christmas pudding. I look down at my own costume: brown boots, red stockings and a forest green velvet dress that was my mother's. I wove some ivy from the back fence into an old headband. Put on red lipstick. I look like a Christmas lunch table setting. Or maybe an enthusiastic kindergarten teacher.

I pull the drinks out from the plastic bag and settle them in the esky. The ice is already pooling, more slush than hard squares. I scoop some pieces into a large plastic cup and pour white wine over the top. I've been thinking about drinking wine all day.

After speaking to Maggie, I raced back to check-in before rushing home to get Ben ready to stay at Dad's. The uniforms have made their way through about thirty follow-up interviews with the kids who went to Jamie's party. Rodney and Kai were definitely both seen there, and a few people claim to remember Kai going to get some more booze but don't remember what time he left or when he came back. Like Maggie, a few of the girls can remember seeing Kai at around 11:30 p.m. One guy swears he saw Rodney when he got there at eleven. Several others say they spoke to him just before midnight but half of the kids were wasted by the time they turned up and the stories changed with their attempts to remember. It doesn't leave us with much to be sure about.

Another headache is rearing and a small but mighty blister is making itself known on my foot. I drink more wine and survey the yard. There are maybe twenty people here already. A modest, albeit stubborn, fire burns in one of those raised barbecue bowls to the left of the house, but most people are standing around a large kiddie pool, which is filled with more drinks and two goofy-looking blow-up Santas. The talk and laughter sounds like a hive of bees. A girl, I think her name is Jennifer, makes a shocked face and slaps Greg Samuels on the arm. "No, *no*! Greg, that's *so not true!*"

I know most of these people, but only vaguely; they are mainly Scott's friends, and when I try to piece their lives together the details blur into a word cloud of facts. Married, single, sleazy, smart, rich. Renovating, traveling, baking, studying. The energy required to make small talk with them feels impossible to summon.

"Hey, Gemma." Doug's face bobs into my view as he grabs a beer, cracking it open and taking a swig in one swift movement. He's wearing a soft furry reindeer headband and a t-shirt with Santa on a surfboard being pulled along by Rudolph.

I take another sip of my wine.

"Hi, Doug," I say.

"How are you?"

"Pretty good. How are you? How's Tyson? He was in prep this year, right?"

"Yep. He finishes this week, a year already. And little Phoebe is already two, you know. I guess what they say is true: they grow up crazy fast. I mean, you know what I'm talking about. With Ben."

I nod and try to think of something else to say. "How's the house coming along?"

"It's really great. Heaps more space and we put in a spa, which is cool. Trying to save some money now, so I'm gonna do the rest of the painting myself. That's the big summer task. I keep saying to Jules, 'That's what I'll be doing this summer,' and I don't mind because I'll be able to listen to the cricket at the same time."

"Sounds great."

I see Julia, Doug's wife, walking over to us. She grabs his hand and ducks her head into his chest. "Hi, Gemma."

"Hey."

My cup is empty so I pour some more wine and gesture to Jules. "Want some?"

She shakes her head shyly and rubs at her stomach. "Can't."

"You're pregnant?"

"Uh-huh." Doug kisses the top of her head.

"Oh, wow, that's great. Congratulations."

"Thanks." They stand there beaming at me as if they've just been awarded a Nobel Peace Prize.

"Great," I say again dumbly, tipping back more wine.

"I would have thought you'd be pregnant again by now, Gemma."

"Jules, c'mon," Doug whispers.

She ignores him. "Well, I did. Ben is what . . . two, three?"

"Two and a half."

"See? That's around the best age. Nice for them to have a sibling to look after."

"Maybe."

Julia rubs at her stomach again. "I guess you are pretty busy with work. Must be so hard doing that and then going home to a family. I can't imagine." The way she says it makes it clear that she wouldn't want to imagine.

"This murdered teacher thing seems pretty weird." Doug leans forward, his breath in my face. "I heard she was mixed up in this online devil worship group, which makes sense—she had those crazy eyes. Beautiful, but crazy all the same. Is that true?"

For a second I think he is asking me whether her eyes are beautiful and I can't think of what to say. They both stare at me. Julia's head is tilted to the side, a patient look on her face, and I guess that must be how she looks at her children. *Are you perhaps a little bit tired, darling? I think it might be time for a little nap. Now tell me about this online devil worship.*

"Oh, you mean the devil stuff? No, that's not something that we are investigating. Honestly, it hasn't come up."

"Weird. That's what I heard yesterday. But she must have been mixed up with something suss. I mean, that kind of thing doesn't happen to just anyone." Doug's face is troubled, as if he's trying to work out how something so unfortunate might happen without you directly orchestrating it. The wine laps around the edges of my thoughts. Julia and Doug look like they are peering at me down the wrong end of a telescope.

"I can't really talk about it, but we're looking into a few scenarios at the moment. There are lots of things that don't add up just yet."

I know they want to ask more questions, so I busy myself with pouring wine, hoping that one of us will think of something else to talk about.

"Hey, guys." Scott appears next to me. He is dressed as a snowflake, all in white. He flexes his stocky legs as he leans down to scratch his foot. "Fucking mosquitos. I'm getting smashed already."

I smile at him and I notice his eyes drift from my glass to the half-empty bottle of wine at my feet.

"Jules and Doug are having another baby."

He smiles at them and then says to me, "Yes, I know. I thought I told you that."

My cheeks flare in a flush. "No, definitely not. You didn't."

Julia looks concerned at the possibility that her baby didn't make the nightly news in our house. Doug waves the topic away. "No stress. It's the third one—it's going to start getting hard to keep track!"

Julia gives him a look. "I'm going to get some water."

"Hey, people." Murray Evans joins our semi-circle with Paul James and

Fox in tow. Fox looks at me so intensely that I find myself looking away and tugging at the hem of my dress. I see Fox rarely these days, but when I do it's always as if my body shuts down, so closely is he linked in my head to the time in my life when everything went wrong.

"Hey, guys! Merry Christmas." Scott slaps each of them on the back in turn and they exchange energetic handshakes.

Fox looks drunk already, but then I rarely see him sober. His eyes are wide set, giving him a slightly alien resting face. His upper body sways in a circle as his feet stay rooted to the spot. Murray slaps him on the back, grinning. Murray went to school with Scott. They share a birthday, and Murray's little boy Simon is the same age as Ben. I know Murray cares a great deal about Scott. He's always been wary of me.

Paul James gives me a quick kiss on the cheek. "You look great, Gemma. Merry Christmas."

"Thanks, Paul. You too." I feel a little light-headed.

"Toilet," I say to Scott. He's showing Murray and Doug recent pictures of Ben on his phone and barely looks up.

I close the bathroom door and lock it. Then I lean against it and look up at the ceiling, where an old fan is creaking in slow circles. I'm drunk already. I go to the toilet and feel a little better. I don't think I've eaten since the cake at Carol's this morning. My stomach is creased from the waistband of my stockings. I take them off and shove my feet into my boots without socks. I need to shave my legs but I figure no one will notice in the dark. I wipe the skin under my eyes, removing a fine black film that has formed there from the heavy eyeliner. I blot at my face with some toilet paper and check my teeth, pushing my hair behind my ears. The ivy crown I made looks limp and silly in the harsh bathroom light. I wash my hands and notice that the handwash fragrance doesn't match the description on the expensive-looking bottle and I feel a little better.

I walk back across the lawn toward Scott.

Fee sidles up to me, cradling a bottle of wine.

"So how's it all going, Gemma? With work?" She speaks carefully, as if she's holding up each word and considering it before allowing it to be spoken out loud. A sharp line of fake tan cuts across her left breast where her top has edged down. "Things like this dead teacher must be so *intense*. I can't even imagine." She leans closer and I see the pores on her nose clogged with foundation. "Do they let you see dead bodies?" She shudders. "It must be horrible."

I sip at the wine she pours for me. My velvet dress is suffocating and I pull at the high neck. Fee's eyes are wide, glinting with the possibility of gory details.

"It's my case. I do whatever I like." My hip unexpectedly gives way and I stumble on the spot. "Whoops."

Fee bleats out a laugh. "Oh. Well, that's nice."

"I go to the gym with the guy who found her in the lake," Fox speaks quietly, appearing behind my shoulder. "He's pretty messed up." I remember the same voice a lifetime ago, so gentle but always so serious.

"Hey, Fox," I say. He's so close I can feel his breath on my ear.

Fee yanks up her top and raises her eyebrows at us. "I'm just going to change the music."

Scott waves at me from across the yard. He looks rounder in this light: like a bunch of circles stacked on top of each other, his head bobbing on the top. I didn't realize he'd put on so much weight. *We've all put on weight*, I think as I look around. My thighs are sweaty and rub against each other. My underwear is damp and my skin crawls. I wonder if Fox can see the dark rings under my arms.

"Mm."

Fox laughs. "What?"

I breathe out through my lips, making them vibrate. "I don't know."

"What's up?"

"I'm drunk," I say.

Fox lights a cigarette. "I can see that."

"It was an accident."

"Whoops."

"Yeah."

"So tell me. Is it weird?" He narrows his eyes at me.

"Is what weird?"

"Trying to work out who killed her?"

I look sharply at him, and for a moment, in the half-light, it seems as though the left side of his face is missing. I look back to the party. "That's a stupid thing to say."

"Maybe. Sorry." He waves his hands as if trying to erase his words. "I guess I just remember a time when you wanted to kill her yourself. Ergo, this must be a little odd."

"That's not true," I hiss. "Don't say that."

Fox shrugs. "It was a long time ago."

He offers me a drag of his cigarette. I shake my head and he shrugs again.

"I want my own one," I say, and I see his lips curl in a smirk.

"Sure." He lights one and holds it out to me, his fingers brushing against mine as I take it from him.

I remember him coming around to my house after Jacob died. Holding my hand as we sat on the couch. I almost told him everything, but my throat froze and I couldn't think how to explain it all, the weirdness that had taken me over, what I'd done, so instead we sat there in uncomfortable silence until I told him I just wanted to go to sleep. He held me too tight, kissed me on the forehead, then on my shoulder, then on my face, but I pulled away and he left. It's never been the same between us since. I feel uneasy around him. Stressed.

I look up at him now—the same softly curling sandy hair, light tan, dark eyes. A little heavier and a bit rougher perhaps; his baby face has hardened, the hairs that form his light stubble are thick and wiry. My lips fall open as I look up at him. I want him to want me in that moment.

Fox takes a long drag of his cigarette, watching me.

I remember the smell of school lunchboxes, *Friends* episodes and Slurpees. Jacob.

Squeals break out across the yard. Fee has started a limbo game. Her breasts wobble as she bends backward, shuffling toward the broomstick that Julia and Scott are holding. It's crooked and hits her on the chest, and she laughs hysterically, falling backward onto the grass. From here it appears Scott is looking down her top. He pulls her up in a light hug and they are both laughing. The smoke is sticking to my skin. I haven't had a cigarette in years and I float a little as I inhale.

"Get me a beer?"

Fox nods. "Sure."

He comes back with a bottle of Carlton Draught. "For old times' sake. A classic."

The cold floods through me and my nerves sing. "God, I needed that."

"Come with me." He walks toward the side of the house.

"What?"

He doesn't stop.

"Okay, I'm coming. Fox, what? What is it?"

We stand where the light doesn't reach. "I don't know...Look." He grabs my hands. "I guess I've just been thinking about Jacob a lot lately. Not sure why. Maybe 'cause of this Rose Ryan stuff or maybe 'cause it's been ten years. Don't know."

He's stepping from foot to foot. I look back to the yard. Shadows from the limbo game dance across the fence. Someone has turned the music up and people are singing off-key to Mariah's Christmas anthem.

"I even went to his grave last week," says Fox.

"You did?"

"You've never been, have you?"

I swig at my beer and the bubbles fizz up into my nose. "I don't really see the point."

He laughs. "Oh, Gem. You're so tough. Tougher than all of us. I cared about you so much, did you know that? I cared about Jacob too, but you more. I still don't think what happened makes sense. That's what I've been thinking about. It never made sense, did it? Why he would do that. And then when I heard *she'd* died, I just felt like, I don't know. Like maybe it had something to do with her all along. It's like she was a witch."

A fist grips my heart. It's squeezing tighter and tighter. Any more and I might explode.

"Don't be stupid, Fox. She wasn't magic!"

He lights another cigarette and the smoke finds its way into my lungs. The longing I have for the past swells in my chest and I force it away.

"Fox, look, that was then and this is now. I don't like to focus on stuff that happened back then. It never helps."

He eyes me through the smoke. "Does anyone ever look after you, Gem?"

I roll my eyes.

"Are you happy? You're not, are you?"

And then his arms are around me and his mouth is on mine—smoke and spice and weed—and my head scrapes roughly against the jagged brick wall and I'm in high school again.

"Fox, stop!" I push him away gently and then more firmly.

"C'mon, Gem. It's okay."

"No, stop it."

We stand there locked in a direct stare for a few moments and my head whirls with black nothingness.

"Um, hi." Scott steps into the light at the end of the dark passage.

I step sideways away from Fox.

"Hey, man. You good? Gem's just a bit upset. Stressful week. We're reminiscing, you know?" Fox seems unflustered by Scott's arrival. "Right, Gem?"

I nod, smiling at Scott. His face is pale but it might just be the outside light shining on it like a spotlight.

"Yeah. Thanks, Fox. And now I need another drink. Whoa. God, it's still so hot."

I slip past them both and return to the backyard. "Hey, hi, hi," I say, as I make my way to the drinks table. The music throbs through my body. I can't find any wine so I slosh gin into a cup and cover it with dregs of lemonade.

A bunch of people are dancing near the kiddie pool, their hands raised high. Scott grabs my elbow.

"I want to dance," I tell him and pull away, not looking at his eyes. I gulp down my drink and join the dancers. I don't recognize most of them but Doug offers me a high five and my hand stings as we slap.

"Go, Gem!" he says and I smile back. Everyone is smiling at me. It feels good to dance. I wonder whether Scott is watching me, if Fox is, but I don't stop to look for either of them. I shake out my arms as a new song comes on. All the women squeal and start jumping with renewed energy. I move to the beat. I need to get my shoes off; my feet are on fire. I hop on the spot and yank off my boots. I stretch out my toes and spring back into the dancing thrum, whirling wildly. Jacob, Scott, Felix, Fox. I'm so sick of thinking about them. New songs come on and I keep moving. It's so *hot*. All the other women love that I'm dancing with them. They grab at my waist and spin me around and I'm like a gymnast, or a ballerina turning in perfect circles.

I'm too hot. I need to sit down. I peer at my watch. Is that 1 a.m. or 2 a.m.? Fuck, I have to work in the morning. Keep trying to figure out who killed perfect, precious Rose Ryan. The perfect girl who ruined everything. My hair is sticking to the back of my neck. Maybe I'll stand in the kiddie pool, stop for a minute. I step over the plastic rim. There's no ice left but the water is cold. Just like the water in the lake. *Rosalind is dead, Jacob is dead. Dead, dead, dead, but not me, I'm still here all alone.* I almost laugh because it is so insane. My chest is heaving and I can't catch my breath from the dancing. I have to sit down. I take a few steps backward and squat on the edge of the kiddie pool, which immediately gives way, and I sink back into the icy water, laughter and screams washing over me as I fall.

Chapter Thirty-seven

Sunday, December 20, 7:57 a.m.

I open my eyes and the first thing I see is a bucket on the floor next to the bed. From this angle I can't tell if it's empty but either way I definitely recall heaving into it after Scott brought me home. I hear his breathing behind me, ruffled by a slight snore. My head throbs, forcing my eyes shut again. I need to get up and get ready to go to work. I had planned to pick up Ben from Dad's so Scott doesn't have to do it later, but I won't have time now. I slowly shift my body over and watch Scott sleeping. His face is relaxed and he looks peaceful, his eyelids as smooth as a child's. His lips are parted slightly and turn up at the edges. He has become a stranger.

I get up. I wash out the already rinsed bucket and quietly place it back in the laundry. Without Ben the house seems like an empty shell: like my ears are underwater. The silence roars around me. I flick on the radio but the voices and the laughter echo through the kitchen maniacally and I am hit by a wave of sickness. I run to the toilet and vomit repeatedly, my face exploding with sweat, the stale smell of wine making me retch even more. When I think it's over, I flush the toilet and drop into a sitting position on the bathroom floor. I rest my head on the cool bowl and cry, tears running down my face. After the tears stop I wash my face and my neck, brush my teeth and twist my hair into a low messy bun. Grabbing my mobile, I step out onto the deck to call Dad. I talk in a low voice to Ben, who chatters excitedly about the cereal Dad has just given him for breakfast, then ask him to give the phone back to Granddad.

"I need to get into work, Dad. Scott will come and get Ben a little later. Is that okay?"

"Of course, of course. I love having him, you know that."

"Thanks, Dad."

"How was last night? Did you guys have fun?"

"Yep, yep—it was great."

"That's good, darling. You work so hard, it's good for you two to have some fun. You're still so young."

I nod, dangerously close to crying again. "I gotta go, Dad. Tell Ben I'll see him later."

I end the call and grab my things. I write a note for Scott saying that I spoke to Dad, that he can pick up Ben later, that I'll be home around 7 p.m. I'm glad he's not awake yet. I can't bear the thought of him looking at me. Felix keeps springing into my head. All I want is to tumble into bed with him and stay there for hours, his hands all over my body. As my frustration bubbles over I slam both hands hard onto the steering wheel. I start to cry again, a messy red-eyed affair, as I think about Fox, my dancing and all the moments from last night that I can't remember. Felix, Scott, Ben, Jacob, Rose. My mouth clenches and I try to take calming breaths. I feel weightless but it's not freeing or empowering, it's as if I have no anchor: the chain has snapped and I have drifted too far away. My reality feels like a permanent state of surreal.

I think about my dad, doting on Ben, making him breakfast and snuggling up with him on the couch, maybe doing a puzzle or reading him a book. Having Ben was the greatest gift I ever gave to my father. A new era of the Woodstock family, meaning that Mum dying was officially a generation ago. That chapter could be sealed off and relegated to the past. Toward the end of my pregnancy Dad seemed almost scared to breathe around me. His eyes would fill with tears every time he looked at me. I was terrified something bad would happen. I had almost resigned myself to the idea that I would never hold my child, that happiness would loom close and then be briskly whisked away from me.

In the end Ben was early. I started labor hard and fast three weeks before my due date on a cold June morning. Asleep on the couch in the lounge, I woke with a jolt, the TV chattering softly in the darkness. Was it a noise outside I'd heard? And there it was again, a soft groan. It took me a moment to realize that it was coming from me. The baby was coming. My baby was coming. I didn't move. Instead, I lay as still as I had ever lain before. The room flickered with the light from the TV and the large photo of Mum looked down on us from the worn wooden mantelpiece, and I clenched my throat against a wave of pain then sat up in a crouch on the floor, letting it wash over me. The wetness came too but I still didn't move. It was the last time that I would ever truly be alone again. Instinctively I knew this. I was a cat heavy with kittens, a wild animal. Almost a mother. The skin on my translucent belly moved, molded by little arms, legs. My son. The pain came again and again. There was a break, finally, and I got up and quickly cleaned the floor with a towel, soaking up the water that had kept my son safe all this time. I shuffled into the doorway of our bedroom, the floorboards ice beneath my feet. In the moonlight Scott breathed in and out, his arms wrapped around my pillow.

"Scott," I said, and I felt the pain rising again, pushing against my heart, making my voice swell. "Scott. We need to go to the hospital."

He tumbled out of bed, a tangle of limbs and adrenaline, and looked at me, eyes shining.

And in that moment all I could think was: *I'm having a baby and it isn't Jacob's and nothing about this makes sense.*

Chapter Thirty-eight

It's quiet as I walk into the station. Jonesy has been under pressure from above to stop everyone's leave from banking up and has ordered skeleton staff whenever possible, so there isn't the typical buzz of the admin crew filling the rooms. A couple of people mill about in reception, eager to report lost wallets and damaged letterboxes. It's so different from the past week of frenzied post-murder activity. The walls groan in the heat. My desk is scattered with papers and stray pens. I look over at Felix's neat desk, his pens standing like little soldiers in a homemade clay mug. A present from one of his daughters. I wonder briefly whether a child of ours would be more him or me. A girl or a boy. My head is pounding with last night's wine and shame. I yearn for a day with no people. Where I don't even need to open my mouth. I swallow thickly, still tasting the acid of the alcohol and vomit.

Anna has left a chocolate heart on my desk. *Re-gifted to you from my latest NQR date. Enjoy!* reads the Post-it attached to it. I throw it in a drawer as I try to think past the nausea. My mobile phone jumps to life, vibrating across my desk. I jump too.

"Woodstock," I say and my throat burns with the effort.

"Hi. Um, I hope it's okay to call. You said to call if there was anything else that I thought about. To do with Rosalind Ryan."

I try to pull my thoughts together. "Absolutely. We're looking for any information that might help. Who is this?"

A short nervous laugh followed by a sharp intake of breath. "Oh, sorry. It's Isabel Mealor. Izzy. I teach at Smithson. You gave me your card."

I picture the bright red hair and dramatic eyeliner. "Yes, Izzy, of course. I'm listening."

"Well, look. I'm not sure that this is related but I suppose it's playing on my mind, and after the service on Friday, well, I don't know, it just feels like I'd rather say something than not, you know?"

"Definitely. In situations like this we want to know as much as we can. Things that seem irrelevant might absolutely be important."

"Yeah. I figured. So, look, I'm not sure about this, but a few weeks ago I left my wallet at work, on my desk. I realized when I was out at a dinner I didn't have it and so I decided to go back and get it on my way home. Sometimes the cleaners are in early and I didn't want to risk it being stolen."

"When exactly was this?"

"Thursday three weeks ago. I just checked my diary to be sure."

"Okay, great, so you went back to the school. Around what time was that?"

"Maybe nine? It was creepy being there when no one was around, so I just rushed in, grabbed my wallet and went back to my car."

"Then what happened?"

"Well, I saw two people coming up from the hall, down near the Forrest Wing, where the portable classrooms are. I sort of ducked behind my car so they couldn't see me. It was Rosalind. And, um, she was with a student."

"Do you know who it was?"

"I'm not one hundred percent sure, but it was definitely a student. Tall but young. You know how you can just tell by the way they walk."

My heart thumps uncomfortably. "Okay, but you couldn't see who it was?"

"No, it was dark and I didn't want to look like I was spying on them or anything," Izzy says.

"Did anything else happen?"

"Well, it just seemed a bit odd. And then I remembered that she was doing all these rehearsals for the play after hours so I figured that one of them had just finished and that's why they were there."

I let out a breath that I didn't realize I was holding. "So do you think that's what they were doing?"

"Probably. It makes sense. But..."

"What else?"

"Well, they got into her car, which I thought was a bit strange—but I guessed that she was giving him a lift home, which seemed fair enough. But then they just sat in the car for a while in the dark. Talking, I suppose."

There is a long pause during which Izzy breathes deeply into the phone. Finally, she says, "Look, it was dark and I was wedged between two cars, trying to look at them through another car window, but the thing is, their heads were close together and I'm pretty sure I saw them kiss."

"Very interesting," Felix says when I update him on the call with Izzy.

He took the morning off to go to Melissa's dance concert. When I asked him how it was he shrugged and said, "It was a dance concert for thirteen-year-olds." He doesn't ask me about my night, doesn't seem to notice my red eyes and sallow complexion. I watch him fuss at his desk, opening drawers and closing them again, avoiding my stare. He's feeling guilty. I can tell by the way he looks to the left of my pupils when he talks. I know him so well. We understand the competing pieces of our worlds. We understand the pull of obligation rubbing against the addictive feeling of him sliding inside me. My skin is like plastic on my face and I think I might be sick again. I breathe out slowly, letting seconds become a minute.

"Maybe we can catch up after work?" I say.

"Can't," he says, "I've got to get home. We've got people coming over."

Fury flares in my chest but I push it away: getting angry won't help anything right now. A lonely piece of tinsel hanging from a lamp flutters as a fan spins slowly back and forth. The air-con started working yesterday but then packed it in again last night. Apparently Jonesy went apoplectic.

I think about Christmas next week. Felix and his wife sitting at the base of a cheerful tree, Nespressos in hand, her freshly brushed blonde hair gleaming in the dawn light, their three daughters ripping open gifts and exclaiming in delight. My head throbs harder. I close my eyes.

"Okay, well." I sit lightly on the edge of his desk. "Back to Izzy. You think it was Rodney she saw with Rosalind, don't you? But she's not certain who it was. It could have been anyone."

"Oh, come on, Gemma. I think the kid knows something, you just don't want to see it." He pushes his fingers roughly through his hair. "It makes sense that he's who Izzy saw with her that night. Rosalind seemed lonely—or maybe she was just strange—but either way she was looking for validation through the play. Through male attention. Rodney was cast as Romeo, right? It all seems to fit."

I drop my chin, trying to get him to look at me, but he is staring studiously at his screen. He is tapping his foot underneath the table; I can feel the vibrations from where I'm sitting.

"What about Kai Bracks?" I ask. "If he sent her those flowers on Valentine's Day then that seems pretty telling, don't you think?"

"Sure. I've got no doubt he had a crush on her, but we know he was at the party straight after the play and was with other people all night. He might be a creep or just an infatuated teenager, but I don't think he's our guy."

"What about Nicholson? We're still unclear on his relationship with Rosalind."

He sighs. Glances at me quickly and then shifts his eyes away. "I think Rodney just fits, that's all. It figures that an attractive young schoolboy would fall for his drop-dead gorgeous teacher. I thought we were the team that doesn't fight the obvious?"

I clear my throat, which is clenching painfully as I try to speak. "Fine. But I don't think Nicholson's off the hook. It's equally likely that an older man would be lonely and pine after a beautiful young woman. That would be validating for her too. And we still haven't ruled out the possibility of a RYAN business associate. And there's still Timothy Ryan."

"Gemma, I'm not saying this is a done deal, but it's a pretty big lead. The biggest we've had so far. It would certainly explain Rosalind being cagey about her new relationship when she spoke to Lila. And we already needed to clear up the missing hour Rodney has between the play ending and his arriving at Jamie Klein's."

"Alleged missing hour. He says he went straight there."

Felix rolls his eyes. "Yeah. On his own, which is a bit convenient. Whatever. We need to check this out."

"John Nicholson could just have easily got out of bed and waited for the play to finish," I say. "You have to agree your theory on Rosalind is no more conclusive than any theory we currently have on Nicholson. Or Timothy, for that matter." I look at Felix but his eyes are still fixed to the screen. His body is a square, just like his computer, and I can't read it. "What's with you?"

"Nothing," he says, giving me a surprised look.

"You're hurting me," I say quickly, looking at the floor. Immediately I feel guilty. We avoid laying our feelings on each other, knowing that there is enough of that heavy responsibility in our worlds already.

The room tips as he stands, his face blocking out the harsh fluorescent light. For a moment I can't see him; he is just a dark, featureless blur.

"I'm sorry. I don't mean to hurt you. This is hard, Gem. Really hard. And then there's bloody Christmas on top of it all."

"I know. I'm the same."

"So it's just hard. Harder than normal. My parents are coming to stay with us next week for a while. It will be even harder to see you. All the happy family time I'm going to have to do feels impossible." He looks up at me and then around the room, as if people are listening, even though no one is there. He puts his lips together and I think he's going to cry. His voice is so soft I can barely hear him. "I get so sick of our situation sometimes, Gem."

I talk quickly, desperate to say the right words. "I know it's hard. So hard. But we both know that. We both understand, we get it. This time of year is always difficult. I'm finding it hard too. But it will be okay."

He opens his mouth and then closes it again. "C'mon, let's go and talk to young Mr. Mason."

Chapter Thirty-nine

Sunday, December 20, 9:55 a.m.

Jacob's house is almost exactly as I remember it. Squat and dark, with thick ferns licking at the windows. The garage door is closed but an old Ford Falcon sporting learner plates is parked out the front. Rodney's birthday is in January, I find myself remembering suddenly, the fact surfacing in my mind. I remember a hot blustery night in the downstairs den, the artificial smell of hotdogs and a bunch of young boys watching ghost movies on the old TV. Jacob holding my hand as we sat on the couch in the corner, supervising Rodney's birthday sleepover, laughing at how scared they were.

A tall gum still stands to the left of the house, its branches disappearing over the roof. We're not out of the car when Donna Mason appears on the front veranda holding a broom. She reminds me of a tightly coiled spring. She walks as if she's being controlled like a puppet on strings, her movements jerky. Felix winds down his window.

She comes to the edge of the veranda. "Hello," she says softly to Felix. A tiny nod for me.

"Hello, Mrs. Mason. Sorry to intrude like this, but we'd like to speak to Rodney if he's home. About Ms. Ryan."

"He's already been interviewed," she says.

"Yes, but we have further questions," replies Felix.

A flash of defiance lights her eyes and then, just as quickly, she drops her shoulders and it's gone. Another blunt little nod. "He's out the back playing basketball."

We get out of the car to a chorus of cicadas. The dull thud of a basketball forms a bass beat. Jacob played too, his long limbs perfectly suited to the ducking, weaving and shooting for goals. I loved watching him play.

"This way." Donna props the broom against a wall and leads us through the dark house. The blinds are drawn and the hot air is thick with the smell of pine—a Christmas tree. We step out through the wire door and back into the soupy air, following Donna down the creaking wooden stairs.

"Rodney!"

He spins around. The slope of his cheekbones is so familiar I could draw them with my eyes closed. I look quickly at Donna and wonder how she manages, living with a ghost. Her arms are crossed on her sunken chest and her right foot taps up and down, and in that movement I sense the long nights, the broken dreams and the hopeless crying that I'm sure have been her life for the past decade. The basketball rolls off the side of the concrete court, coming to rest near the base of a tree. Rodney's chest heaves and perspiration shines on his face. He walks toward us and his eyes are level with Felix's. He is taller than Jacob was. Broader. He wipes the sweat from his forehead up into his hair, giving it height. He is stunning. A cloud passes over the sun and we are thrown into shadow.

"Hi." He shrugs. "What's up?" He sounds relaxed but his eyes dart between the two of us and he scratches at his neck.

"These people want to talk to you about the teacher, Rodney. It won't take long."

She looks at Felix pointedly, ignoring me completely. I must remind her of Jacob, of that terrible time. She strikes me as the kind of person who would do anything possible to keep her feelings at bay. I wonder again about the note, where Jacob put it. I look up at his old bedroom window and wonder whether the room is a shrine to him, whether there are still photos of me in there, or whether she's stripped it bare, disinfected it, destroyed it, in an attempt to clear her house of her broken, dead son.

"Okay. Here?" Rodney gestures to where we are standing.

"How about over there?" Felix points to a worn-looking outdoor setting near the back fence.

Rodney shrugs again, the universal language of the young. "Sure."

We sit. There is nothing for our hands to play with, and both Rodney and I twist our fingers in our laps, scratch at our legs, pull at our hair. Felix folds his hands together in a tight ball and leans forward. Donna stands a few meters away keeping watch, her eyes shining like marbles.

"Now, we know you spoke to the police last week, Rodney," I begin, "but we have some more questions for you, okay?"

"Okay," he says.

"We'll probably repeat a lot of stuff but it's really important that you are honest with us," I say. "You know that, right?"

He swallows and nods.

"Okay, good," I say. "So. Tell us about your relationship with Ms. Ryan, Rodney."

Rodney itches at his wrist and looks at Felix carefully. "She was nice. A good teacher."

"Just nice?" Felix asks.

Rodney's dark eyes glance my way and then back to Felix. I swat at a mosquito. Blood smears across my arm.

"I liked being in her class. She was sort of different, I guess. Like, sometimes it didn't seem like we were at school."

"What do you mean? Because it was fun?"

"Yeah, I guess. She sort of made everything seem more important or something. I dunno. Probably sounds stupid."

"Not at all. Drama is the kind of subject that needs someone with a bit of imagination, right?" Felix says.

"Yeah. Everyone wanted to be in her class. She was really good."

"So she's gone from 'nice' to 'really good' then?"

Rodney leans back heavily in the chair. "Whatever."

"Did you ever see her outside of school?" My voice, higher than Felix's, is almost lost in the sticky heat.

He blows air through his lips, reminding me of Ben. "Sometimes. You know, because of the play."

"What, like rehearsals and stuff?" I ask.

"Yeah. Sometimes we stayed back late after school. Even went in on weekends if we needed to. Everyone was really committed. We still are. We have a rehearsal later tonight for the extra show we're doing in the new year. We're, like, doing it in her honor."

"Yes, we were at the memorial. We saw you speak. It's a very nice gesture," says Felix.

"Are you close to Maggie? She seems like a nice girl." I feel an odd prickle of envy as I imagine Rodney, so like Jacob, touching Maggie's face, her tight young body; running his long fingers through her silky white hair.

"We've been in school together forever. We're friends."

"Ever been anything more?"

He rolls his eyes gently. "We sort of went out for a while last summer. It was only a short thing. We decided we're better as friends."

"Who decided?" I ask.

Donna walks over to the basketball and picks it up, dropping it noisily in a large plastic tub. Thunder rolls ominously in the distance. "Rodney's very serious about his schoolwork and his basketball," says Donna. "He doesn't have time for anything else."

Rodney continues as if she didn't speak. "Mainly I decided, but it really wasn't a big deal. We just went out a bunch of times. Movies, a few house parties. Like I said, it wasn't for very long."

"Was she upset when you guys broke up?" I keep my voice light. I want to ask whether he told her the same way Jacob had told me. I wonder whether his decision had shattered her world into a million little pieces.

"I don't think so. She hooked up with this guy Matt a week later."

"Love moves fast, huh?" Felix laughs and sends a soft glance my way. "Maybe she was trying to make you jealous. Maybe she felt like you'd moved on to bigger and better things? That maybe you wanted someone more mature?"

Rodney scowls childishly. "You'd have to ask her, but I don't think so. She kind of has a girlfriend now."

I sense Donna's eyebrows lift.

"Okay, okay," Felix says. "Tell us about the play. You're Romeo, right? That's a pretty big role."

"Yeah." Another shrug. "I like acting. I love basketball too, but I want to do drama after school, like an arts college or something, so it was good to get the lead. The play is different from the original. It's set in Australia in the seventies. Like in the city—Sydney, I guess. Jasmine is the Juliet character, from a really rich family. And she has really strict parents that she doesn't relate to. I play Ricky, who's the Romeo character. He's poor and heaps younger."

"Younger man with an older woman? Very progressive. It sounds pretty cool. Different." Felix raises an eyebrow.

"It is. Ms. Ryan wrote the whole thing. I reckon it could get picked up by a studio or something. It's way better than a high school play."

"Sounds like you thought she was pretty amazing."

His eyes drop. "Yeah, like I said, she was a great teacher."

"Did you ever see anyone get angry with her? Did she ever tell you about being scared of anyone?"

"Um, no. I mean, you know, we didn't talk that much really." He pushes his fingers through his hair again. "I mean, I know that there were issues with the school. Our principal, Mr. Nicholson, he supported the play, I think, but there were problems making it happen. Funding stuff. I saw them talking about it sometimes, kind of arguing. Rose was really upset about it."

"Rose?"

He reddens deeply as if he's been caught stealing. "In drama class we all called her that. She said that everyone is an equal on the stage."

"She was still your teacher though, right? So you weren't really equals. And you're not an adult yet," presses Felix.

"Almost."

"January fifteenth. I checked." Felix squares his shoulders and tips his head to look Rodney in the eye.

Rodney's mouth opens as if he is about to say something but then he quickly snaps it shut.

"Rodney," I say, "you are still technically a child, so if Ms. Ryan was making you do anything or spending time with you outside of school, that would be wrong. She had a responsibility to you. You understand that, right? You're not in trouble but we still need to know."

He looks down again, then says, "I already told the other cops. We didn't do anything."

"What happened to your basketball game?" says Felix.

"Huh?"

"You were going to play basketball on the Saturday morning after the opening night. Did it get canceled?"

"Ah, no. It wasn't a game. I was just going to meet some guys to train but it was hot so I decided not to go."

"So you went to Jamie's party instead," I say, realizing perhaps for the first time just how much I don't want Rodney to have anything to do with this.

"Yeah."

"Have fun?"

"It was okay. I was tired—you know, from the play—but yeah, it was okay."

"And you walked there on your own?" I say.

"Yeah. I got separated from everyone after the play. Mum had already left and I had, um, some beer in my bag, so I took the back streets and drank one on the way." He looks at Donna but she doesn't flinch.

"What time did you get there?"

"Maybe around eleven?"

"Okay," says Felix, with doubt in his voice. "And what time did you leave?"

"Dunno. Maybe two?"

"How'd you get home?" I ask.

He shoots another quick look. "I walked."

"Cut through the lake?"

A quick glance at me and then back at his hands. "No, that wouldn't make sense. I came along Drummond right to the end of our street. Came home and went to bed. I was pretty wrecked."

"Are we almost done here? As I've already said to the other officers, I can certainly confirm that Rodney was home just after two. I heard him come in. He's told you what he knows and he really needs to keep practicing."

The three of us ignore Donna as a light smatter of rain sprinkles across my bare arm. I suspect it's unlikely that Rodney will practice basketball in the rain anyway.

"Did *you* ever fight with Ms. Ryan, Rodney?" I ask. "Maybe you wanted her to do something and she wouldn't? Or maybe you disagreed about the play?"

"No." He looks at me, almost pleading. "Nothing like that." The droplets fall more heavily, splashing onto the table and joining together, forming small pools. "I don't know who killed her." His eyes are bloodshot. The exhausted stare of someone with a broken heart. Of someone who isn't sure if the future is worth striving for anymore. "Really, I have no idea. The play was great that night, it went so well. I think she was really happy." He clears his throat, which I suspect is a tactic to avoid crying. I can see the telltale shake of his lips.

He's upset, that much is clear, but I can't tell if guilt is mixed with his pain or if it's just pure, simple grief. Or fear from being caught. I look at him and hope again that he really didn't have anything to do with it. A gumnut falls from the sky and lands on his clenched hand. He yanks it back from the table and rubs at his knuckle.

We get up.

"Okay, well, thank you for your time," Felix says. "We may need to speak to you again but we'll give you a call if we do. Good luck with the rehearsals. We're looking forward to seeing it, aren't we, Woodstock?"

I nod; I want to hold out my hand to Rodney. To pull him close and tell him that I understand.

"I'll walk you out," says Donna briskly, wiping her hands on her thighs as if she is wearing an apron.

We make our way back up the wooden stairs as the rain pours down. Donna's thin hair is curling already, small ringlets forming at the base of her pathetic ponytail. I pull mine back, thick and frizzy, bunching it together in my hands. Behind us Rodney is playing basketball again. The sound of the ball hitting the wet concrete is like a hand smacking against bare skin.

Chapter Forty

Monday, December 21, 6:06 p.m.

I'm late to pick up Ben. I had sort of known that this would happen, but Scott needed to work back because the rain had messed around his building schedule and he asked me if I'd be able to get Ben tonight and, thanks to my performance at the party on Saturday, I hardly felt like I could say no. I slunk out of a meeting and raced to my car, threw it into drive, then wove impatiently through the end-of-day traffic up to Martha, the small suburb in the hills where Ben's day care is. Cloud Hill for Children is a standard plastic fortress on a half-acre block around the back of Martha's primary school. It balances the garish worn plastic with a small chicken coop and a vegetable garden, both of which look rather half-hearted, though I'm sure the children don't notice. Ben has been going there since he was three months old and seems to like it well enough. I park sloppily and jump out of the car. It's after 6 p.m. and the center is incredibly strict about the pickup cut-off time, but there haven't been any calls to my mobile so I figure they can't be too concerned yet.

I burst into the main entrance. An older woman I don't recognize is doing paperwork at the desk and looks up at me, surprised.

She calmly takes her glasses off but is wary. "Hello?"

"Hi. Sorry I'm late. I'm here to pick up Ben. Ben Harper."

There is a slight furrow in her brow. "Um, okay. Just wait here, please. I'll be back in a moment."

The center is absolutely silent. It feels exactly like our house does when Ben isn't there. Hollow. Gentle panic stirs in my gut. Maybe Ben is outside.

Madeleine Phillips, the center director, walks into the room with a warm but worried smile.

"Hi, Gemma. Haven't seen you for ages. How are you?"

"Where's Ben?" I say, my voice wavering.

"Here, why don't you take a seat."

I let her guide me to a chair and I sit, but my muscles are on alert and my eyes bore into hers. "Where is he?"

"Now, Gemma, I'm sure everything is fine, but I just checked the logbook and it seems that Ben's grandma picked him up today. Maybe you had crossed wires about who was doing what?"

"Ben's grandma?"

"Yes, that's what the sheet says. Now, I've called Grace who was on shift when he left. She's new so maybe she…well, anyway, she was here when Ben was picked up. I'm sure she'll call me back in a minute."

"But Ben doesn't have a grandma." The words linger in the room and I know that Madeleine and the other woman are looking at each other, trying to work out what to do. No one knows what to do when something like this happens. I have a strange urge to call the police and then think, *That's me.* I just want to talk to Felix. No, no, Scott—I have to tell Scott. Dad. I need Dad. My thoughts race around my head.

"Well. That does seem strange. I'll try Grace again. I'm sure there is a reasonable explanation." Madeleine shuffles some papers, finding safety in doing something with her hands.

"Maybe it says 'grandfather'?" I blurt out hopefully. Maybe Dad came to pick up Ben. Maybe I had been mixed up after all. I've been so tired, and Scott and I had spoken about it late last night. Maybe I'd dreamed it.

"Well, that does make sense, I'll just try Grace again…" She is about to get up when the phone rings and we all jump. My skin is prickling and I feel feverish.

"Grace, sweetheart, thank goodness." The way Madeleine speaks makes me realize how worried she is too and I surf another wave of panic as I try to breathe.

"Yes, Ben Harper. You wrote "grandma" in the logbook today. Who collected him?"

The second hand on the cheap-looking clock on the far wall seems to move at an otherworldly pace. There is a hissing sound in my ears and I look blankly at Madeleine's lips as they move. The phone is now in her limp hand. Suddenly Rosalind's pale dead body flashes across the scene and it takes me a second to focus on what Madeleine is saying.

"A woman who said she was Ben's grandma came to pick him up at about four-thirty. Said it was all arranged. Knew all about you."

Madeleine's eyes are huge. "She told Grace she was visiting for Christmas. Grace said Ben seemed pleased to see her. He was fine to go with her. Obviously we're supposed to have something like this in writing from you, but with Grace being new and the woman being so certain . . ."

I jump to my feet and then stand there, my eyes darting every which way, my chest heaving as I try to think what to do. "Four-thirty was almost two hours ago!" The thought of all those minutes, all that time with Ben god knows where, is not registering, despite it causing worse pain than I thought was possible. I think I will disintegrate into nothing.

Madeleine starts to cry, her hand cupped over her mouth. "Oh my god. Who is she? And why would she take Ben?"

I don't answer but instead run outside and jump into my car. There is only one thought in my head and it slams across my brain over and over.

I need to find my son.

I shove my phone onto the hands-free and stab at the screen until I can hear the ringtone through the speakers. My hands are steady on the wheel as I turn out of Cloud Hill's driveway, but the minute I hear Felix's voice my throat cracks and I can't talk.

"Gem? Gemma?"

I nod, trying to breathe, but the air catches in my mouth and I'm stuttering nothing into the phone. Trees and sky whip past; I need to slow down.

"Gemma! Hello? Are you all right?"

"It's Ben," I manage to whisper.

"Ben? What about Ben? What's happened?"

I turn sharply into Neil Road and brush tears from my eyes. "Someone's taken him."

"Shit. What? Where from? Where are you?"

My throat is raw as if I've been screaming. I clutch my neck, trying to keep my eyes on the road. *Ben*, I think, *my baby boy.* My arms begin to shudder uncontrollably.

"Gemma! Where are you?"

"In the car. Near home. Someone took him from day care. Some woman. I don't know who she is. She said she was Ben's grandma."

"Okay, just—I don't know. Fuck. I'll send out an alert now."

I gasp. A shuddering sob rattles through the car. White noise pierces my ears. Ben's face is everywhere as I grip the wheel and turn into my street.

"We'll find him, Gem. I'm coming, okay? I'll come to you. I love you."

Mum dropped dead in the middle of the fruit and vegetable section of the local Woolworths when she was thirty-eight years old. A brain aneurism. Nothing that anyone could have seen coming. I remember one of the many doctors that Dad made me see afterward saying that she was basically a human time bomb. At her funeral, the man who had been next to her at the supermarket when she collapsed, a nice-looking man in his late twenties who had been fondling avocados, sought me out. He told me that as he held my mother, him squashed against the wooden base of the avocado display with people screaming for help around them, he was certain she looked at him in a way that meant she wanted him to tell me that she loved me. That was unlikely, I knew even then, but I could tell it was important to him, so I squeezed his arm and thanked him for passing on the message. Told him that I was glad that she had someone like him with her when she died. He started sobbing and I patted his arm awkwardly as they loaded Mum into the hearse.

It is a very strange thing not having a mother. It's rudderless. My mother was neither overly affectionate nor particularly maternal, but she was mine and I had her all to myself for thirteen years. I would never know love like that again, of being a daughter to a mother, and therefore her everything, and that fact alone was a crushing physical blow. Her death left a great, miserable hole in my world and, try as he did, Dad just could not fill it. We existed in the house for the months after she was gone. Two lost souls rolling in and out of the rooms, polite and considerate of each other's grief, but not able to connect meaningfully. Not able to crack through the bleak layer that had crept over our lives the instant she left us. His sadness made me uncomfortable: it was somehow worse than my own. I had lost the person who would love me more than life itself, which was a terrible, impossible thing, but that seemed unimportant, selfish even, when compared with losing the person you had chosen above everyone else in the world to spend your life with. The fact that he could even consider replacing her was complicated. I had no such complexity. My love and grief for Mum was tragically simple.

I thought about all of this the moment I first held Ben. I missed Mum in those first few days, and one thought kept pulsing through my mind, clear above the fog: that at least she had never had to go through the pain of losing me. Holding Ben, I suddenly realized that as bad as it was for me to lose her, it would have been so much worse for her to lose me.

Chapter Forty-one

Monday, December 21, 6:37 p.m.

"What do you mean, Gem? I don't understand." Scott's voice carries the same tone of frustration that it's had since Saturday night. I can tell his forehead is creasing between his eyes and that his mouth is set. I know that look so well. Scott doesn't tend to stay angry, but when he does, his rage simmers quietly for days. I seem to have a particular skill for igniting this in him.

"Someone took Ben! From day care."

"Gem, you were supposed to get him. We spoke about it last night." A gentle wave of cheering rolls down the phone line. He's at the pub.

I slam my hand on the steering wheel. "Scott, fuck! Listen to me, listen to what I'm saying. Someone's taken Ben. Some woman. I got there just now, to Cloud Hill, and someone had already picked him up. The girl on today is new and she didn't know…The woman said she was his grandma." I start to cry. "I don't know where he is."

"What? Are you serious?" He is moving, the sound changes, he must be outside. "Where are you?"

"I'm at home. I just came straight here. I don't know what to do."

A strange sound snakes down the phone line.

"Scott, I don't know what to do."

"I'm coming, Gem. I'm coming. Oh my god."

I drop the phone into my lap. Tears feel slimy on my face, mixing with makeup and sweat. The engine hums but the air-con isn't on and the car is stale and empty. My phone rings, and I jerk sideways. The noise is like a bullet.

"Gemma, Ms. Woodstock, we're so sorry," stammers Madeleine from the day-care center. "This is just horrendous. Unbelievable. I'm, well, I don't know what to do."

"You need to tell us everything. We need to know what the woman looked like. We need to know everything you and the other girl can remember. We need details. CCTV, anything you have. We need to be able to track her down. Find Ben."

I feel the familiar kick of routine course through me. I know how to do this. Know how to deal with emergencies. I know how to catch the bad guys and make things okay again. But then Ben's face looms before me and the panic is back. I don't know how to do *this*.

Madeleine is sobbing into the phone. "Yes, yes, of course."

"I've called the police. Someone will be there to talk to you soon. Don't go anywhere. Start writing down everything you can remember." I hang up on her. I turn the engine off and get out of the car.

The house looks different. Everything has frozen in the thick heat except the relentless thrum of cicadas. The sound drives like a drill into my brain. The sky is too blue. The grass is too green. I can hear the heat. *Where is Ben?* screams my head over the buzzing. I grab at my throat again. It is throbbing so hard I want to rip it out of my neck. I circle my fingers under my eyes, pushing away tears of liquid fear. *Just get inside, get inside. Then work out what to do.*

I fumble with the keys. I can't get them into the lock.

"Fuck. Oh my god." I kick the door and then crumple onto the doormat and sob. After a few moments I draw a long shuddery breath and contemplate a life without Ben. Without Ben's pudgy little fingers. His tiny hands. Without his soft breath on my neck. Without his beautiful eyes, exactly the same pale mint as mine. Another shuddery sob bursts out of my mouth. I think about where Ben could be and what is happening to him and a part of my brain shuts down.

I finally get inside. Hot air gropes at me and I swat its fingers away. Everything is still and empty. Flat. I scan each room. I am like a wild beast searching for my child. My baby. Fear pulses through every cell. Every breath is a battle and I do deals with the God I don't believe in. *If I find Ben, I will never complain about him again. I will work less. I will be nicer to Scott. Spend more time with Dad. Stop seeing Felix. Please just let me find him.*

His room is neat but for a small pile of clothes from yesterday that I meant to put away this morning. The solemn button eyes of a teddy bear stare down at me from the shelf. *Where Is the Green Sheep?* has fallen through the bars of his cot and fans open on the floor. *Where is my baby?* I scream silently at the room. The familiar feeling of dread fills my chest. Just like the moment Dad told me about Mum. Just like when he told me about Jacob. Poor darling Dad, having to shatter my entire world, not once but twice. I can't imagine telling him that Ben is gone. I wring my hands. I can't stop moving them: it's as if they are springs at the end of my arms. I want to punch them through the walls. I want to have a different life. I want Ben back here asleep in his cot.

I hear the door and my nerves jangle.

"Gemma!"

I run into his arms. The tears flow out of me like blood from a wound. I can't talk.

"Shhh, shhh. I can't believe this. You must be…C'mon, Gem, tell me what happened."

Felix half carries me down the hallway and into the lounge. He pulls me onto the couch, his arms around me. His presence here is jarring. I feel ferociously nauseated. Over his shoulder I see our shadowy reflection in the TV screen. It could be Scott and me about to have dinner. I've never let Felix come here before. He's dropped me off a few times, walked me to the door once, and now here he is, sitting in my lounge room, because Ben is missing.

He pushes me gently backward and strokes my face, extracting tear-soaked hair from my eyes. He looks older. Faded. His loose white t-shirt ripples with gray patches that cling to his skin.

Another sob leaks from my mouth. "I don't know where he is. I went to get him and when I arrived no kids were there. I was running late, but only by five minutes, so I thought they might have him out the back, but then they were so surprised to see me I knew straight away something was wrong."

"Okay. And you said some woman picked him up?"

My eyes are stinging. "Yes, over two hours ago. Said she was his grandma." I start to cry again. "But Ben doesn't have a grandma. Where the fuck is he, Felix?"

"I've called Jonesy. He and Matthews are on their way to the center. Do you want me to drive you back there now too?"

"I want my son back. *Now*. Felix, I need him."

"We'll find him. We will. Fuck, Gem, I just knew the roses you got meant something bad. It's all linked. Someone is fucking with you." He pushes me away slightly and holds out his arms, ducking down to force me to look at him. "Do you know something? About the Ryan girl? What do you know?"

I am stunned. Rage rips through my body, propelling me onto my feet. I turn on him, rabid.

"I don't know anything! How dare you! You think this is *my* fault?"

"Okay, okay, shhh. Sorry—I'm sorry. I just don't get this, Gem. Why you? Why Ben?"

"I don't know." My vision cracks again. "I don't know why this is happening." I think about my drunken dancing at Fee's on Saturday night. Fox's kiss. All the times I've been with Felix. I think about what I did all those years ago. Ben doesn't deserve this. Doesn't deserve any of it.

Felix takes my hand and pulls me down to him again. I am buried in the crook of his elbow. I feel upside down. Inside out. As solid as cotton wool.

Footsteps sound in the hall. It's Scott. I lift my head just as he bursts into the room.

Chapter Forty-two

March (three years earlier)

"You're so selfish!"

I rolled my eyes.

"Seriously, Gemma, I want to help you. To be here for you. I freaking *love* you, but you do my head in, you really do," Scott said.

The baby was pressing awkwardly on my pelvis. Large and unbalanced, I'd climbed onto the bench to get the wok from the top shelf. As I'd inched it forward, there was a moment where its weight had unexpectedly been more on my hands than the shelf and I'd overcorrected and slipped, pulling my hands down to hold on to the cupboard handles, and the wok had fallen sharply on my forehead before clattering loudly onto the floor. Scott had rushed in from outside and found me crouched and dazed on the bench, sporting a dark red welt.

"I was outside, Gemma. *Outside.* Not at work, not at the shops, fucking *outside. Ask* for my help, for god's sake. What are you trying to prove?" Scott's face was boiled red.

I rolled my eyes again. The bruise on my head smarted, making me cringe. "I'm not trying to prove anything. I'm already doing exactly what you wanted and having your baby."

Scott slammed his fist down on the bench. It made a soft thud.

"Don't do that. Don't throw that at me. You want this too. I know you do. We agreed that if we weren't both all-in we wouldn't do this. Don't be so unfair."

The anger faded from Scott's face. He shook his head, looking at me with sadness. I'd gone too far.

I sighed and felt the baby squirm inside of me. My legs ached and my forehead throbbed all the way down to my swollen feet.

"I'm sorry, Scott. I just hate being like this. I feel so useless."

My long hair curled heavily down my back. It was thicker than it used to be but the ends were still split. I was stubbornly refusing to cut it. The day before, Matthews had helpfully suggested I start wearing it in pigtails.

"It won't be much longer, Gem. I know it's hard, but people do have babies all the time, you know."

I focused on a spot on the wall where the light cut into the faded beige paint, making the rest of the surface look dark and dirty. The room was smaller than I'd realized; I could have sworn it was getting smaller. The bench was too close. The walls.

"Yeah, I know they do. But I've never done it before."

Chapter Forty-three

Monday, December 21, 7:12 p.m.

Scott's chest rises and falls. I can see his heartbeat pulsing in his neck. In that moment I am scared of how much Ben means to him. His need for our son is palpable. I feel frozen to Felix. His arm is still around me but my body seems to be hovering above us all. I look down from the ceiling and can see a line between the two of us and Scott. My future and my past circle each other like salivating dogs.

"Where is he?" His words are knives thrown onto the floor.

Felix springs up from the couch and puts his arms out as if Scott is a child who needs to be calmed. He slowly brings his hands down as he takes a step forward.

"Gemma called me. I've got the entire station working on this. We'll find him."

Scott barely looks at him. "Where is he, Gem? Where is Ben?"

I rise slowly. My legs are jelly. I shake my head. "I don't know."

"Is this to do with your work, with that dead teacher?"

My vision blurs as I shake my head again. "I don't know."

He half coughs, half splutters, then rests his hands on his thighs as his head flops forward.

"I'm sorry," I whisper and reach out my arm to him.

Scott pushes past me and then stops. He grabs his hair and turns in a slow circle. We stand in the room, the three of us, our breathing merging into a rhythmic pulsing, waves crashing onto us, over and over again. Scott whimpers and I close my eyes so I don't have to see the pain in his face. The room flips in a slow circle. I'm spinning and spinning and then I can hear the sound of Ben's crying ringing in my ears and I begin to cry again. My arms just want to hold him. I ache for his tiny body. I lift my head as the scene breaks apart. Scott runs from the room into the kitchen. The back door bangs loudly against the wall and as I open my eyes I'm already running too because I realize that the sound I can hear is real and that Ben, our little boy, is in the backyard crying for us to come and get him.

Felix was a long-awaited arrival in the Smithson police department. The cop from out of town; from the other side of the world. The older guys had been making jokes about episodes of *The Bill* for weeks. Their attempts at English accents had become very tedious. But I could sort of understand their curiosity; we hadn't had a new staff member since Amy in accounts a year earlier. Jonesy had told me Felix and I would be partners, which I was fine with. Back from maternity leave, I simply wanted to put my head down and get on with it. Adding "mother" to my already precarious status of "female" wasn't doing me many favors in the office.

"You're back early," had been the standard comment during my first week, closely followed by a judgmental look that made it clear "early" really meant "too soon."

"Aren't you even feeding the poor boy?" was another favorite, the subtext being that Ben was a child to be pitied, both from lack of proper rearing, as well as his unfortunate genetic potluck.

"The thing is," Jonesy told me, pulling me aside and showering my face with soft spittle, "you might find things different now." He clapped his hands awkwardly. "You know, you might not be as tough. And that's okay." He cleared his throat as if it had the ocean in it. "Kids can make it real for people. Even the boys." He slapped me on the shoulder. "Now, I'm not much familiar with mothers on the job, but I'm guessing it's worse."

"Thank you, sir."

His eyes widened with relief at the dismissal. "You're a good girl, Gemma." Another slap.

I was running late the day Felix finally arrived. Something had gone wrong with his paperwork and his start date was pushed out, so the initial excitement of him turning up on the Monday had dissipated somewhat by the Thursday. I'd forgotten Ben's bottle and had got halfway to Cloud Hill before realizing, so had gone home, adding another twenty minutes to my already long, brand-new morning routine.

I pushed into the briefing room at the same time as I pushed my frizzy hair from my eyes. Everyone was standing in an odd little circle with Felix in the center, Jonesy slapping him on the back while the others looked on.

Matthews and Kingston sniggered as I joined the circle. Jonesy saw me and beamed, seemingly deciding my arrival was a signal to end the huddle.

"Ah, Gemma. Excellent. Felix McKinnon, this is Detective Sergeant Gemma Woodstock, your partner. She'll tell you everything you need to know. A child wonder is Gemma."

Marty Pearson smirked at me. At least five of the others rolled their eyes.

"Hi." I swatted stray hairs from my eyes and tried to smile. I became painfully aware of my fuller figure and tatty jacket.

"Gemma's just had a baby," said Jonesy helpfully.

"Great to meet you, Gemma." Emerald eyes held mine steadily. His accent was like music. I'd never heard anything quite like it.

"Yes." I couldn't think of anything else to say. A vague waft of Ben's vomit was coming from somewhere on me and I just wanted to bolt to the bathroom so I could freshen up. Or hide.

"Well, good. Coffee's that way," said Jonesy, pointing to the kitchenette before disappearing into his office.

Everyone else slowly returned to their desks, a few final smirks directed my way.

"Well," said Felix McKinnon.

"Well," I repeated.

"How about…" We both started talking at the same time.

"I know somewhere good for coffee," I said. "Perhaps we can go there now and I can tell you all about this place. Just give me a few minutes."

He nodded and I walked away from him toward the bathroom, blood in my ears, my heart pounding.

Chapter Forty-four

Monday, December 21, 9:47 p.m.

It feels very strange to be standing in my kitchen watching half the station pour over my backyard in the fading light. I watch one of the techs bag something and I almost walk out and demand to see what it is. I know what to do in this scenario, have worked a case like this several times, but I am glad not to have to move right now. My legs ache, it's a miracle I'm still standing, and every time I focus, tiny dots appear and wriggle in circles like unformed tadpoles. *Thank god, thank god, thank god.* I glance over at my son. Scott has refused to let Ben go, aside from a customary check from the ambulance worker that Jonesy insisted on.

Ben couldn't tell us anything useful. He talked about a nice lady called "Grandma" but could offer nothing further. Once he saw us he was fine. Overtired and clingy, but fine. Now he is slumped asleep on Scott's shoulder. Scott is jammed into one of our old counter chairs wedged against the kitchen table, stroking Ben's curly hair as he stares into space. They are the white chess pieces and I am the black. The red rose that was pinned to the back of Ben's jumper is now lying bagged on the table.

She is dead and I still can't escape her.

Jonesy bursts into the kitchen and lets out a deep, tired sigh. "Right, well, as far as we can tell, Ben's been brought back here via the nature reserve behind your house and let in through the unlocked back gate. We're assuming that the person who took him from the day-care center is the same person who left him in the yard."

"Description?" I say.

For the first time since we found Ben, Scott looks up at me.

"I've got one of the boys with the day-care girl now doing a sketch, but from what she said we're looking at a middle-aged woman, probably around fifty but could be younger. Long brownish red hair. Slim. Softly spoken. No obvious accent. Average height. Well-dressed. One of those suit tops that women wear sometimes. Nothing else notable."

"CCTV?"

Jonesy smirks. "Of course there's no bloody CCTV. Do you think any-one around here actually takes security seriously? They're worse than the bloody school. The only camera they have is in the staff car park round the back. Don't worry, Cloud Hill will be having a serious review of its secu-rity as a result of this."

"So there's no footage, no record, nothing. Did she sign something? Say anything else?"

Jonesy clears his throat and, for some reason, today I find the sound comforting. Ben lifts his head slightly then drops it back onto Scott's chest. I notice a small ring of sweat forming on Scott's shirt under Ben's head. Ben is always so hot when he sleeps.

"She signed the book, the standard roll thing. But it's just a scrawl. The name written is Edith Bower but I assume that's just random. Mean any-thing to you?"

I shake my head.

Jonesy looks at Scott but he shakes his head too. "No. I'm sure I don't know that name."

Jonesy grimaces. "Well, something might turn up on the road cameras. We're pulling everything we can get from this afternoon. Unfortunately, once the driver hit the bottom of the hill they could have gone anywhere." He gestures to our yard. "And there are no cameras in that bushland, we checked."

Matthews comes in from outside. "I think we're done. We've searched the yard and a large stretch of the reserve but we don't think we've found anything. We're dusting the gate and looking for footprints but it's so dry we don't expect to find much. If the suspect was wearing gloves or wiped the surfaces down, there will be nothing on the gate. It's a tough one."

"Have you spoken to the neighbors yet?" I say.

"Sure. Phil's over there now. The lady on the left saw nothing but we're working our way up the street."

I look at Ben again, his mouth slightly open as he breathes sweetly. I try not to break in half all over again.

"Thank you."

Matthews nods at me with unfamiliar kindness. "At least it all worked out. You won't be letting him out of your sight for a while, no doubt."

I am painfully aware of our shabby carpet. The cheap décor and un-mown lawn. I haven't even offered anyone a drink.

"Do you want water or—"

Jonesy cuts me off. "Now listen, we'll leave you alone to be a family." He pulls his pants high around his gut. "Woodstock, you let me know if you need some time off. We'll discuss what this means for the case tomorrow. We'll probably need to talk to both of you again. Tonight, get some sleep."

Panic rises at the thought of being taken off the case. "But, sir . . ."

"No, Woodstock, I'm not talking about this now. Rest. I mean it. We'll talk tomorrow."

I nod and slump, exhausted. There is no more fight left in me. Outside Felix is walking across the yard. He stops when he sees me, dips his head and then keeps walking. I turn back to Scott.

"I'm just glad Ben is safe and sound where he belongs," says Jonesy. "You two look after yourselves now, all right?"

"Yes, sir," I say.

Scott nods and smiles weakly at Jonesy.

The yard clears out. I close the blinds. I want to speak to Felix but it's impossible to see him tonight. I have no idea what to write in a text message or an e-mail.

Scott hasn't moved.

"Do you want something to eat? I can cook some pasta."

There is a flash in the corner of my eye as the microwave clock flips over. I think maybe Scott hasn't heard me.

"Are you hungry?"

"I think Ben should sleep in our bed tonight," he says.

"Of course. That's a good idea."

He shifts his weight, careful not to wake Ben. "I do need to eat. I shouldn't have driven before. I had four or five beers and then left as soon as you called me. I meant to stay and sober up." He jerks out a laugh. "Pretty funny that my house is crawling with cops and I drive here pissed."

I don't say anything. Words close in my throat, choking me. The clock on the wall has stopped. I squint to look at it properly and then jump when the second hand moves again.

"Can you make me a sandwich or something? I'm going to sit with Ben on the couch for a while."

"Sure." My hands shake as I pull out bread, tomatoes, cheese and lettuce. I flick the kettle on and shiver as it boils. I stare at my reflection in the kitchen window. I clench my jaw. *Fuck you*, I think. *How dare you take my baby?* I cut Scott's sandwich in half. I pour myself a milky cocoa and slosh in a shot of bourbon. I need to sleep tonight.

"Here."

"Thanks."

Ben is curled on the couch. The red cushion under his head makes his face look white. I can see the soft feathery veins that disappear into his hair. I sit next to him and hold his tiny head in my hand. So fragile.

"Gemma, I know that you are used to this kind of thing, but that world is not my world. Cops pawing through our things. Everyone judging us. I was scared today, Gem. Fucking terrified. And I didn't even let my mind go where it could have."

Scott is not looking at me. He is staring at a bearded man on the TV who's fondling the roots of a small tree, the dirt sprinkling neatly into the hole he has prepared.

"I was scared too, Scott. I couldn't think. I didn't know what to do. That's why I called Felix, so he could take over. I knew I couldn't do what I needed to do."

"Yeah."

An ad break starts and the voices are louder. Ben stirs. Scott pokes at the remote to turn the sound down.

"I think we're just really different," he says.

The bourbon is creating a soft buzz in my ears and I knock back the rest of the drink and place the mug heavily on the coffee table. I close my eyes so I don't have to respond to Scott, but as I sneak a look at his profile in the dim light I'm not sure whether he wants an answer from me or not.

Chapter Forty-five

Tuesday, December 22, 6:02 a.m.

My dream is horrifying. I am at a florist's and every time I choose a bunch of flowers and pick it up, I realize it's sitting in a bucket of blood. The florist is amused when I show her. "What do you want me to do, love? They still look pretty. Do you want to buy them or not?" I start to cry. I wipe tears away and taste copper: there is blood all over my fingertips. The florist screams with laughter.

I wake with a start to Ben's sleeping face. Slowly relaxing, I trace the soft slope of his nose with my eyes. The spray of dark lashes, the sweet smatter of lemonade freckles. He is breathtaking.

Beyond his head, Scott is asleep too, his breathing deep and even. His hand clutches Ben's arm lightly.

I slide carefully out of bed and pull on a gray hoodie. Some days I feel manipulated by my biology, tricked into the feelings I have for Ben, but today I want to feel like a mother. Want to hold him in my arms. I want him to need me. In the bathroom I swallow a couple of painkillers and brush my teeth. My skin looks puffy. Fine lines weave along my forehead. I am so plain. There is no light in me and I wonder whether there ever really was. I think about Maggie's perfectly made-up eyes and taut cheekbones and think I must look twenty years older than her rather than ten. I look like her mother. I shut the bathroom cupboard in frustration.

In the kitchen I detach my phone from the charger. Nothing from Jonesy but a text from Felix. I hold my breath as I click on it.

I'm glad Ben is safe. Hope you are okay.

I shove my phone into my pocket and wander through the house. It's quiet; only the sound of birds chirping outside breaks the stillness. I think about yesterday, about the hours when Ben was missing. The disorienting stabbing pain that seized my entire body. And then I think, just for a moment, what I would be doing right now if Ben was still missing. Would Scott and I be together, clinging to each other? Would we be arguing, blaming, hating? I look at a photo of Scott on the fridge; he's smiling as he holds up a bug-eyed fish. It's a face I know so well but I don't see it anymore. I haven't looked at him properly for so long. Felix's face floats into my vision. So familiar. The exact grain of his emerald irises. The gentle swallow he does when I begin to touch him. If Ben was gone forever, would Felix and I have a chance? Scott and I can't work without Ben, I know that. I'm not even sure that we can work with him either.

Felix was impossible to read yesterday but I know it must have been bizarre meeting Scott, especially under those circumstances. I saw him looking at the pictures on the walls, noting the fraying rug and sagging furniture. Watching Scott and me as we grabbed at Ben, crying with joy.

I open the fridge and welcome the cold on my face. How can I be thinking like this? I'm a monster. Rosalind is making me crazy, just like she always has. Icy air bites at my eyes. The nerves in my teeth jangle.

"Hi, Mummy."

"Ben!" I slam the fridge shut and rush over to hug him. His body feels small as I lift him up; his bony hip pokes into my side.

"Are you all right, darling?"

He nods. "I want toast."

Tears brim in my eyes.

Ben looks worried and rushes to say, "Please."

I smile at him. "Sure, baby, you sit here and I'll get your toast."

I shove bread in the toaster and grab some crayons and paper. Ben begins to scribble with the blue crayon. Big loopy circles. I butter his toast and place it in front of him. He wolfs it down, crusts and all.

"Morning." Scott comes into the kitchen and makes a beeline for Ben. "Hey, little man."

"Daddy!" Ben gives Scott a smile that is all sunshine. "Look, I did this."

"Amazing. I love it." Scott pulls Ben onto his lap.

I stand up and get a glass of water. I look outside. A magpie is sharpening its beak on the top of the fence. It seems crazy that less than twelve hours ago I thought I might never see my little boy again, and yet everything that I am looking at now would appear exactly the same. "I'm just going outside for a bit."

Scott shrugs at me. "Okay."

It's already warm out. I unzip my hoodie and walk across the lawn to the back gate. I'm careful: the dewy grass is slippery. The magpie eyes me before crouching and pushing off, flying to a nearby gum. I lift the hook on the gate and step into the clearing.

Our house backs onto a stretch of land that is about a kilometer long and a few hundred meters wide. It is dotted with thick trees, squat shrubs and patchy grass. It's not a thoroughfare. Unless you live nearby you wouldn't even know it was here. *Unless you'd been watching the house*, I think. Is the woman who took Ben the same person who killed Rosalind, trying to warn me off, or are the roses just a decoy for something else? Is she working with someone? Being paid by someone to spook me off the case? The Ryans have money; they could probably arrange something like this. I push away the possibility that it's an inside job, that someone wants me to give up and admit defeat. Inviting paranoia in won't help me right now.

I think about the marks on Rosalind's neck and can't imagine a woman doing that. *Careful*, I warn myself. I know better than most what women are capable of if pushed hard enough. Maybe there are two people working together—but then *why* kill her? What would they gain from her death? And how would the woman know about the gate in the fence to the backyard? Back in high school I was out here all the time, climbing trees or having picnics. Mum and I even camped in the reserve one night, but I've barely been out here in years. Placing my hands on my hips I look up at the sky. I stare into the blue, trying to let the pieces fall into place. Nothing. None of it makes sense.

I look back at the house. The gate is open and I can see Scott and Ben through the window. Scott is laughing. He kisses Ben on the top of his head. I look along the line of the fence. I remember Jacob pushing me against the slats and kissing me with Dad just meters away inside. I felt so safe out here in the dark, Jacob's strong arms wrapped around me.

I imagine the woman who took Ben standing out here last night listening to him cry, hearing us come outside to find him. Disappearing into thin air. I spin around, half expecting to see a face quickly slipping back behind a tree. I scan the bush. The sun is breaking through the far side. A butterfly slowly beats its way from one shrub to the next. Goosebumps break out across my arms and legs. Our house suddenly seems awfully exposed and vulnerable alongside this strip of peaceful, untouched nature.

Chapter Forty-six

Tuesday, December 22, 9:25 a.m.

"Woodstock, I don't remember calling you," says Jonesy.

"I know, sir, but I wanted to be here. I wanted to know if you had turned up anything yet."

"Would have called you if we did." Jonesy is gruff but there is an undertone of kindness. "How's Ben?"

Eyes make holes as they bore into me. The soft murmur of conversation niggles like a stray itch. "He's fine. He's young, he doesn't really know anything was wrong yesterday. He's very trusting. Too trusting, obviously."

"Well thank goodness he turned up. But, Woodstock, you know this changes things."

Felix walks in from the back office and my pulse skips a beat. Jonesy is still talking and I focus on his mouth but I can see the top of Felix's head bobbing behind him and then disappear as he sits down at his desk.

"Woodstock?"

"Yes, I know. But I have to finish this case, sir. It's personal now."

"That's the issue though: it's—"

"Personal in a good way. I need to do this. Work out who took Ben. Jonesy, please."

"Okay. Okay, look. Lay low for a bit. Don't touch anything to do with your boy, let Matthews handle that. You focus on the teacher. We need to keep that moving and we don't know for certain that they are linked, anyway." He beckons me closer, indicating that he wants to talk into my ear. "I'm getting calls from the press on the hour. Your mate Candy Cane is a pain in the arse. Worse than my wife wanting the deck waterproofed before Christmas."

"You know she's not my mate."

"Doesn't matter. She's right. Everyone wants this thing done by Christmas. It's just the way it is."

"We're doing what we can, sir. We've got more interviews today. More things to look into. We'll crack it."

He pulls away and does a signature slap and clasp on my upper arm. "Right, well, off you go then."

Felix gives me a cautious smile as I walk over to my desk. "How's Ben?"

"He's fine."

"Scott cool with you being here today?"

"Yes."

Felix nods and keeps typing. I feel sick. Something is not right with us: he won't look at me. "Scott is going to stay with him today in the house."

"Good idea. He should be with you guys today. Feel safe."

"So you don't think I should be here either?"

Finally, his eyes rest on me. "I didn't say that, Gem. I'm sure he's absolutely fine. I just wasn't sure you would want to be here."

"Well, I do."

"That's cool. I get it." He finishes scribbling something in his notebook and then stretches his legs. I can see the toe of his boot peek out from under his desk.

"God, I'm tired." He rubs his eyes and the creases take a moment to settle. "Okay, so, we've got twenty minutes before check-in. I pushed it out because everyone was up so late last night. So if you like I can catch you up on what I found out yesterday."

My teeth grind together. No, I don't want to get caught up. I want to kiss the soft skin under his eyes, his eyelids. "Sure," I tell him.

"Okay, so I've been tracking Rosalind's voice messages and yesterday someone left a message about a rental inquiry that she made a couple of weeks ago. So I called them back—it was a Brisbane number. Anyway, she'd applied for a rental up there, starting the twenty-fifth of January. Offered them twenty dollars a week more than the asking price."

"She was planning to move to Brisbane?"

"She was."

I think about this for a minute. "What about a job?"

"I thought about that too, so I dug around a bit and it seems that a Rosalind Ryan successfully applied to start teaching English and drama at Waterford High. In Brisbane. She used an old Hotmail account that I've got the guys looking into."

"Jesus."

"Exactly. It turns out she had made inquiries about putting her house on the market. That was the fancy car her neighbor saw in the driveway a few weeks back. A real estate agent from Gowran drove over to evaluate the house. Rosalind wasn't planning to teach at Smithson next year."

My heart begins to thump into gear. "Had she resigned? Does Nicholson know? Her family? I can't believe that no one has mentioned it. Wouldn't the school in Brisbane have done reference checks?"

"I don't know yet. I was about to call Nicholson last night when you called about Ben. Obviously we need to pay the Ryans a visit too."

"Well, we should go see Nicholson straight after check-in."

Felix flashes me a grin and, just like that, everything is normal again.

"Great minds, Gem. I just called the receptionist to tell her I'm coming."

Chapter Forty-seven

Tuesday, December 22, 11:37 a.m.

It turns out that John Nicholson isn't at the school. The harried receptionist looks at us blankly and then taps her hand to her head as if to tell herself off. "Oh dear! Yes, you rang, sorry. He was here when you called but I forgot that he was taking a half-day today. We break up tomorrow, you see, and there're hardly any classes today anyway. I think he's doing some work from home. It's all been rather strange, really—you know, since…I did mention you might come, but he's been quite vague lately."

"So he's at home then?"

"Well, yes. I think so."

"Thanks. We'll have his address, please."

"It's all right," I tell them. "I know it."

Felix is all business as he strides back to the car. I trot along behind him feeling like an annoying child. I can't read him. My head is fuzzy. Not one thought seems able to stick, and my heart aches for Ben. I flick Scott a quick message to check on him.

"Do you know the way?" Felix asks.

"Yep. His house isn't too far from mine."

We drive in silence for a few moments.

I almost explode before I blurt out, "I want to see you. Spend time with you. I just want you to be with me." I sound like a little girl and I hate it.

He doesn't take his eyes off the road but I see him swallow heavily. He breathes out slowly, making a whistling noise with his teeth. "I want that too, Gem—I just…I don't know. Like I said, my head is such a mess. It's been different between us lately. You're not working with me properly on this Ryan case. And what happened with Ben, meeting Scott, it…it was so real. I think it just fucked with me even more."

Panic returns hard and fast. I reach out my hand and place it on his leg. "Please, Scott—*please*. You know I want you. Especially after yesterday. I need you."

He gives a short, mirthless laugh. "Gem, you just called me Scott." He slams his fist lightly on the wheel. "God, this whole thing is such a mess."

"No, I didn't. Did I?" I put my head in my hands and for a moment I think I might cry but I'm too tired, too empty. I just want it all to go away. All of it except for Felix.

Houses flash by. An elderly man wearing a baseball cap is walking an overweight dog. They shuffle along in the heat, painfully slow, the man's legs like the pale trunks of saplings.

Felix tugs at his collar as if it's choking him. "Okay. Look. I want to see you too. I do. I miss you. Holding you. But won't you need to be home? You know, with all that's happened with Ben?"

My heartbeat slows and my eyes sharpen. He still wants me. I unravel my balled hands, placing them calmly on my thighs as the color returns to them. "I doubt I'll be able to pry Scott off him anyway. I'll be able to see you, don't worry."

"Well, here we are." His fingers suddenly wrap around my hand. His voice is gruff, his accent thick. "Maybe we can meet Thursday night?"

"Yes," I whisper, squeezing his hand back. We are in front of Nicholson's neat brick veneer. The house looks like it is sitting down; "squat," my father would say. There are some flowers across the front and a large wattle tree to the side. The garden looks loved. The lawn is neatly mown and is an impressive lush green. A lazy sprinkler jerks one way before snapping back to its original position, jetting out a stream of droplets onto the grass. The front door is open and the screen door is propped open too. A narrow hallway becomes a dark square inside the house; I think I can see the corner of a picture frame on the wall.

Felix removes his hand from mine and turns off the ignition just as John Nicholson steps out the door. He is so tall that his head, encased in a retro-looking terry-toweling hat, almost touches the archway. He squints into the sun, secateurs in hand, and then proceeds over to the far side of the garden. He starts to prune the overhanging strands of ivy, chopping at them stiffly.

"C'mon, let's get this done."

Nodding, I slide out of the car. The heat hits the back of my throat and my forehead instantly buds with perspiration. My feet are fire in my dark shoes. The buildings, the roads, the whole town sweats, still chanting at us: *Who killed her? Who killed her?* The question sits at eye level, demanding an answer as it hovers in the lank, sticky air.

"Mr. Nicholson!" Felix calls out.

He turns slowly, arms still outstretched. If he is surprised to see us, it doesn't show.

"Yes, hello." He takes a few steps toward us and then seems to realize that he is holding a fistful of branches. "Ah, look. Let me get rid of this and then we can talk."

He goes to the side of the house and tosses the branches out of sight, then heads to the open front door, gesturing for us to follow him. Felix and I look at each other and he holds his arm out so that I go first. The ceilings are low; it reminds me of our place. There are portrait-style photos along the length of the hall, most of them featuring a handsome-looking woman with rosy cheeks and cropped, no-nonsense blonde hair. Nicholson is in some of the shots too, smiling over her shoulder. The woman wears an endless rotation of pastel shirts.

"This way, this way," he says.

I follow him down the hallway into a bright white kitchen. It's surprisingly modern; light bounces off the stainless-steel appliances.

"Please, go outside, it's nicer out there. I'll just get us some water. It's still so hot, isn't it?"

I step out into a small square courtyard. A wrought-iron table setting is on the lawn. A large shade cloth casts an inviting-looking shadow across the yard. A row of standard roses follows the line of the fence and then merges into wilder, leafier vines that weave and dance across the palings, disappearing behind a tree heavy with lemons in the far corner.

"The roses look stunning in the spring. It's a wall of color. Keeping them going through the summer is hard work though. Especially this summer."

"It's like being back at home." Felix is staring wide-eyed at the garden.

"My wife adored gardening. Her family was English and she fancied it was in her blood. She was out here all the time. In the end it was the only thing that made her smile."

He sets a jug of ice water on the table with some glasses. His arm shakes as he places them down. I take a seat on the chair.

"She was ill?"

He smiles at me. "Oh yes. Very ill. Cancer and heart problems. She was an amazing woman, my Jessica. Very solid. Dying annoyed her very much, she hated being weak and needy. I keep the garden alive for her. She'd be furious with me if I let it go. But I've come to quite enjoy it myself. I find it meditative."

"Mr. Nicholson…"

"I know. You need to talk to me about Rosalind. I'm not stalling. I don't have guests too often so I suppose I'm babbling a bit."

"How are you holding up?"

He sends me an appreciative glance. "Oh well, not too bad. It has been a pretty difficult time. I feel such a responsibility for the students. And the teachers. It's very hard to know what to do and what to say to everyone. And I miss her." He holds his hands out with his palms up. He looks lost. "It's a very difficult thing. Impossible really."

We nod and sit in silence for a moment. I can hear the hum of bees in the air.

"People are saying you were in a relationship with Ms. Ryan."

Felix tips his head at me, surprised. I'm surprised too; I had intended to work up to the possibility that Nicholson was having an affair with Rosalind, but it suddenly seemed better to shoot the words out, to fire them like bullets and see what they hit.

Nicholson takes a large gulp of water and a deep breath. He looks back and forth between the two of us with a pained expression.

"Ah, yes. Well. I suppose I was."

I try to keep my face still but feel my eyes bug open. An odd little trickle of relief courses through me as I wonder whether this means Rodney is off the hook. "You were in a relationship with her?"

He stares past us toward the lemon tree. "Of sorts."

Felix inhales sharply. A butterfly veers close to my head and I think I can hear the beat of its tiny wings.

Felix says, "Were you having a sexual relationship with Ms. Ryan? I need you to answer."

Nicholson looks at Felix with something between pity and sadness. "No, no. The very opposite, I suppose you'd say."

I lean forward, forcing his eyes to meet mine. "Mr. Nicholson, you need to be more specific. This is a murder investigation, so it is very important for us to understand any relationship Ms. Ryan was in."

He holds my gaze. "She was my daughter."

A strange sense of calm washes over me.

Felix avoids my eyes. "Your daughter!" he says.

I feel like I am in a tunnel. Wind kisses at my face and as I look at Nicholson suddenly I can see it: the same curve of the cheekbones, the similar slant of his eyes. "Your daughter," I repeat dumbly.

"Yes." He sighs, clearly exhausted at birthing this revelation. His hand wobbles as he drinks some more water. "I'm not sure exactly how it's relevant, but what do you need to know?"

"Tell us everything."

Birds twitter from behind their leafy curtain as John Nicholson tells us the story of how he came to be Rosalind Ryan's father.

"I was married to Jessica, you see. Probably for almost three years when I met Olivia Ryan. Jessica and I were happy, but—and this is hard to explain—she didn't *need* me. She loved me, I knew that, but she was very self-sufficient, very strong. And then Olivia came along and all she did was need. She had her three sons already, but she was miserable. She wasn't happy in her marriage, she had a tendency to intense melancholy. In hindsight it's obvious that she was deeply troubled, but at the time I admit I was simply captivated."

"Where did you meet?"

He chuckles softly, remembering. "At the library, actually. She was there with her boys, who were giving her a hard time. I noticed her struggling and offered to help her carry the books to the car. We put the children in the car and then she started crying. I comforted her as best I could and instantly I knew I wanted to see her again." He toyed with his watch, unclipping it and then snapping it gently back on. "I've never felt an attraction so strong." Nicholson looks at me intensely again and I have to look away. I avoid looking at Felix, worrying that our own attraction will betray us.

"And this was when?" I ask quietly.

"About a year before Rosalind was born."

"Okay, then what happened?"

He shrugs simply. "We started seeing each other. She would call me at the school or on Sunday morning, when I told her Jessie would be at church, and we would arrange to meet. We'd go on drives, meet for coffee in Gowran. She had help with the boys and Jessica and I had no children so it was remarkably easy to find time to meet. She was unwell though. She hid it quite well, but even so, I knew. I suppose I didn't really want to admit how unwell she might be in case it meant I had to stop seeing her."

"And then she got pregnant?" Felix asks.

His eyes become cloudy. "Yes. That was not part of the plan, but she told me a few months later that she was pregnant. I asked if the child was mine and she said she thought so but she wasn't sure. We never spoke much about her marriage but she was fascinated with mine. I knew that she felt trapped, that George Ryan was a formidable man and that she loved the children, but the details of how they were when they were alone together remain a mystery to me. I don't know if they were still lovers or not. She was vague on the topic. Olivia never spoke about things she didn't want to." He clears his throat and breaks into a cough, tapping his fist against his chest. "I assumed the child was mine and I am ashamed to say that I panicked. I didn't want to hurt Jessie, or lose her, and I wasn't quite sure what to do. Olivia seemed terrified at the idea of having another baby but seemed sure that staying with George was for the best. She wasn't exactly a maternal woman but she had a fierce love for her sons."

"Did you see her during the pregnancy?" I picture a caged Olivia Ryan, heavy with her baby, trapped in her castle, yearning for her true love.

"I did, but less. She became aggressive, very difficult. We would arrange to meet and then she wouldn't show up. Or she would call me at odd times, crying uncontrollably. Jessica became suspicious and I was beside myself. I didn't know what to do. It was around this time that Jessica told me she wanted to try for a baby and it was all very hard."

My throat feels tight and I sit up straight to try to let the air in. I feel the weight of the past few weeks begin to close in on me. "When did you last speak to Olivia?" I manage to ask.

"Well, of course I had no idea that it would end up the way it did. I saw her, I think, about four days before Rose was born. She was still quite manic but she was excited about the baby. She told me she would name the child Rosalind if it was a girl. And of course she did. I read about her death in the paper just after Christmas. Almost thirty years ago now…" He trails off in wonder.

This story still feels so raw somehow, its fault lines running across Nicholson's face.

"Did George Ryan ever contact you?" I ask him. "Did you see the baby?"

"Oh no, no. You see, I didn't know what he knew and I would not have dreamed of intruding on that. I had Jessica to think about too. She'd been told that it was unlikely she could have children of her own, a cruel twist of fate. I always did wonder if that was my punishment."

"It must have been very hard for you to grieve so privately," I say, "without being able to tell anyone."

"Oh, Gemma, my dear girl, thank you for saying that. It's so hard, you see, because you feel guilty for feeling sorry for yourself when you have behaved so badly, but the truth is I loved Olivia very much and not being able to grieve for her properly remains one of my biggest regrets. She may not have been my true love but I did love her."

Felix says, "Okay, so you thought that Rosalind was your child but you stayed away. And then she suddenly turns up as a teacher?"

"Well, she was a student first, of course."

I nod, thinking of all the times I'd caught him watching her. I had assumed that he was simply under her spell like everyone else.

"Yes, right. So first a student and then a teacher," I say. "And you never talked to her about any of this?"

"I never once spoke to her of it. Definitely not when she was a student; I never would have destabilized her like that. I always assumed that she knew nothing."

"What about more recently?" asks Felix. "Did anything give you the impression that she did know something?"

"No, nothing really. Nothing solid anyway. When she applied for the teaching role I was surprised. I didn't expect her to want to come back to Smithson, but she'd been an excellent student, loved the arts and had a real skill with language. I knew she would be a wonderful teacher, but I was nervous about the...proximity. Jessie had died the year before and I wasn't sure how I would cope. It seemed risky."

"Are you certain she was your daughter? Will you take a test?"

Felix's questions feel cruel but Nicholson doesn't seem to mind. I suspect he's asked himself the same questions more times than he cares to remember.

He seems relieved to have got his secret out. "Yes. I'm certain. I'll take a test if you need me to. I think she looked a little like me and we have similar inclinations. Similar interests. It gave me great joy to watch her teach and watch her put on her plays. She was very talented."

I say, "You didn't suddenly feel the need to tell her about all of this? You didn't perhaps tell her and then argue? She didn't get upset? It would have been a huge shock for her if she really didn't know anything."

"No. I never spoke a word of it to her. At times I felt like she knew. I know she felt close to me, but I suppose she saw me as a mentor figure. I was careful, or thought I was. I knew how it might be misconstrued."

"Do you think George Ryan knows?" Felix asks.

Nicholson shifts in his seat. "That I don't know. I don't think that Olivia would ever have said anything. She seemed to be quite scared of him and terrified of him finding out about us. But he may have suspected that Rose was not his child, depending on the nature of their relationship at the time. She looks nothing like the other children."

"Could she have been someone else's child?" I say.

He shrugs forlornly. "It's possible. But I think it's unlikely. Olivia was unpredictable and confused, but we spent a lot of time together. I honestly don't see how she could have been seeing anyone else."

"Why didn't you see the play on opening night, Mr. Nicholson?" I ask.

He looks up at us and his face is heavy with guilt. "Nothing sinister, I can assure you. I wasn't feeling very well. And I was a little upset, I admit. I had just found out that Rose was moving away. She had applied for a teaching position in Brisbane and was moving there after Christmas. She had come to tell me earlier that day; she needed me to provide a reference, which obviously was not a problem. I was happy for her, but it hit me quite hard. I suppose I had got used to having her around. Of course, now she is gone anyway." He looks off into the wild tangle of his garden. "I know I should have told you this before, but I didn't want to talk about her leaving and there didn't seem any point in the end."

"Yes, you should have told us. You should have told us everything," I say, but softly.

He nods, but his eyes remain on the garden.

"Did you fight about it? Her leaving?" Felix presses.

"No, no, not at all. I wanted to understand why she was moving away, but she said she just wanted a change. She'd done her time at Smithson, so I could hardly argue with her. She wanted to be in a more creative school—the battle for funding had rather worn her down, I think. We talked about the new school a little and I was sure to give her my blessing. But after she left my office I felt unwell so I came home."

I ask, "You were home here alone all that evening?"

"Yes. Like I told you last week, I was here watching a movie. I fed the cat next door at about seven. My neighbors are away. I had a cup of tea at about ten and then went to bed."

"And then the next day you heard about what had happened?" says Felix.

"Yes. Colin, our security guard, called me. He had taken the call from your station and then he alerted me. It is the standard procedure. Not that it is very standard, of course."

"Did you believe her explanation about the job?" I ask.

Nicholson looks slightly pained. "I'm not sure. It was quite a surprise but I figured she did just want a change. She had been at Smithson for years. It did seem a little sudden and I wondered if something had happened, but she didn't say anything like that. She seemed happy, I think. I've thought about that a lot, whether she was happy, and I think she was. I hope she was."

"By all accounts the play was a great success," I say. "Everyone we've spoken to said she seemed thrilled."

"Oh, I'm sure," Nicholson says. "It really was amazing from what I'd seen in rehearsals. I'm glad the kids are going to give it another run."

"You will go?" Felix asks.

"Yes, of course. I don't know much about anything else right now, but I will definitely go and see her play."

"Why have you told us all of this?" I ask. "You didn't have to. We'd probably never have known."

His eyes settle on me, watery dark pools. "Well, I obviously don't want anyone thinking there was anything untoward between us. But also, her being gone has changed everything. I like talking about her, I suppose, and maybe I feel like it's finally time to claim her as my daughter. I was so proud of her, you know."

My phone buzzes in my pocket. A text from Scott: *What time will you be home?*

I look at Felix, indicating I need to get going.

"All right, let's get this test sorted then," he says, pulling a kit from his bag.

He takes the sample. John Nicholson looks completely spent as if he's just come down with a virus.

"Well, thank you, Mr. Nicholson," says Felix. "We've taken up enough of your time."

He shrugs at Felix. "Time is not of huge concern to me anymore."

We make our way back through the house, following his long strides. I can see where his shirt rubs on a sharp vertebra.

I say, "We might have some more questions for you. And we'll be in touch about the DNA test."

"Yes. That's fine."

We pause in the doorway. The clock on the wall near my head ticks loudly in my ear.

"Do you know who might have done this to her?" Felix asks him directly.

"I've wondered, of course, but I can't think about it too much. I can't stand to think about her alone there all night in the water. Maybe she did have an argument with someone. She was very passionate sometimes. I think it was most likely a stranger. Some horrible man. I really don't know."

"Well, thank you," I say.

He waves at us and pulls the screen door shut.

In the car I feel broken. The years of Nicholson's grief and longing ache across my body. They mingle with my own sadness and swirl through my guts.

The police radio buzzes to life as we turn out of the street. An accident on Holmesglen Road. A psych patient at the hospital has threatened someone with a knife. A child has been rescued from a parked car at the supermarket and her parents can't be located.

"Well, you were right," says Felix. "About the paternity."

"Yeah. I was."

"Some story," he says.

"You think it's bogus?"

The sky, full of wispy clouds, flashes past as we head back to the station.

"No, I don't. I think he's genuine. Olivia Ryan may have been playing him, of course, so I want to see these test results to be sure, but I think he's convinced."

"You think he's in the clear?"

"My gut says yes, but then he has no alibi and he does have motive. He was upset about her moving away. Maybe he wanted her to stay. Maybe the thought of losing her all over again was too much. Might have made him pretty desperate."

I think of Nicholson's face as he talked about his long-lost daughter, so close all this time yet so far away. "Yes. I guess it might."

Chapter Forty-eight

Wednesday, December 23, 10:04 a.m.

Curtis Smythe eyes the mangy-looking boy at the Slurpee machine. He always watches the kids, especially the boys, or before he knows it they'll be nicking this and that, and suddenly he's clean out of stock. Some punk even got away with the cardboard display stand for the chips last summer. Curtis was out the front helping an old duck with her bags and the little prick walked straight out the back with it, an "up yours" to the security camera included free of charge. The cops, when they finally came, were as useless as tits on a bull. They took a few photos and some measurements, but Curtis knew he'd never see that stand again. He keeps the back door locked now and has installed an extra camera. You just can't be too careful. Still, Curtis is a businessman, has a shop to run, so he's learned to keep an open mind and try to assume the best in people. One bloke's dollar is as good as the next bloke's. Sure, it takes all sorts, but Curtis figures that as long as they do right by him he doesn't mind what they do in their own time.

It's true what they say, though, that the hot weather brings out the crazies. Just two nights ago he was driving home and saw a woman vacuuming her car in the car park near the turn-off to Fyson, using one of those dinky little handheld numbers that move the air around. The woman was all business with the vacuum, her long brown hair swinging around her face as she leaned over to do the floor. Maybe she'd borrowed the car and spilled something in the backseat, Curtis reasoned. Easy enough to do.

She should have come to his shop and had the car cleaned up properly, only take a few minutes. Curtis runs a better car mechanic service than the branded chains that are starting to pop up in the surrounding towns. He could have thrown in a cut and polish for a good price, spruced up the red paint really nice. Given her a bonus tank of fuel and a takeaway coffee and she'd have been all set. The plates on her car looked funny too; he could've sworn they were painted over.

But Curtis kept driving. There was no need for him to get involved. He had stopped asking questions a long time ago. It's just like his granny used to say: the world is a better place when everyone minds their own goddamn business.

Curtis notices a gap on the shelf where a packet of batteries used to be. He clenches his fists and looks furiously around the store. No point calling the shit-for-brains cops again. No doubt they're all caught up trying to sort out the mess with that poor lady teacher. From what the papers are saying they don't seem to be getting anywhere at all.

Curtis eyes a young bloke with a rose tattoo growing out of his singlet top. The bloke jerks his chin up at Curtis in greeting before disappearing down the back of the shop, out of sight. Curtis straightens the newspapers on the front desk before following him. Rosalind Ryan smiles up at him from the front page. Curtis grimaces. Just clean bad luck something like that happening to a nice girl like her.

Chapter Forty-nine

Thursday, December 24, 8:47 p.m.

"I've missed you." Felix gently cups my face with his hands, kissing me.

I don't believe you, my skin cells scream under his touch. *Stop it*, I tell myself. *Don't imagine problems.* But his touch feels forced and I'm trying too hard and I can't seem to relax. *Stop thinking*, I think. I need to get drunk, I want us to get drunk together and lie in each other's arms until tomorrow, but it's impossible because it's Christmas Eve and I need to be home to see Ben. As it is, we're missing the station Christmas party. It was easy to get out of; barely anyone expects parents with little kids to attend, and me even less so, seeing as last year I had the unfortunate luck of walking into the tearoom just as one of the junior officers was attempting to twist his cock into a knot. Plus, of course, everyone thinks that because of the kidnapping I'll need to be with Ben.

Felix grabs my face again and I think with a start just how easy it would be to blow everything up. To grab my phone and snap a photo of us and send it to Scott, to Felix's wife, to the entire station. I tuck my hands under the sheets just to make sure they can't suddenly break away and do it before I can stop myself, to make sure that I don't shatter our entire worlds with a few quick clicks and swipes.

It feels like every minute of today has been wrung out and squeezed like a lemon, that every last second was labored. It is often like this when I know I am seeing Felix. My body prickles. I become aware of millimeters of skin that I have neglected or never noticed at all.

The first half of the day moved slowly: an unsatisfying check-in, then a tedious review of some security footage from a private residence near the school that ended up showing two kids snogging enthusiastically after the school play the night Rosalind died. Fortunately, there was some progress in the early afternoon when the hotline received a tip-off from thirty-eight-year-old Moira Foss, who lives in one of the houses that back onto Sonny Lake. Moira claims to have heard a couple arguing on the night that Rose was killed.

She was up late with her six-month-old daughter, who was teething, and stepped out onto the balcony to fetch some spit cloths that had been drying on the makeshift line, when she heard angry voices. It was around 10:30 p.m., and she didn't think much of it because couples were always fighting in the parkland under her balcony. The only thing that seemed odd after the fact was that the voices didn't sound drunk. More like whispering or hissing, which was strange because the couples she and her husband usually hear are raging and loose, flowing with intoxicated abandon.

From what Moira can recall, this was different—more mature, more controlled. "It didn't sound like kids, so I didn't think much of it," she told us. "I could only really hear a woman's voice—not what she was saying, just sort of low and angry words."

Felix and I were perched on the edge of Moira's couch amid piles of washing.

"I'm sorry I only called today, I just didn't think it was anything. And I've been sleeping a lot during the day." She gestured to the obvious disarray, just as the shrill wail of a baby bored through the thin walls.

I briefly stepped outside onto the small balcony. The drill of the cicadas thrummed into my thoughts. I could see the top of the tower through the waving gums.

"Something happened at the play that night," said Felix, coming up behind me. "She pissed someone off or did something."

"I know. I can see her standing down there fighting with someone but being careful not to call too much attention to what was happening. She had something to hide. She didn't want it yelled out for everyone to hear."

"But why come to the lake?" he wondered. "Why be alone with someone who's going to put you in danger?"

"I don't think she was scared at first," I replied. "Maybe it was someone she trusted. I don't think she knew she was in trouble until it was too late. It wasn't planned. The rock was an opportunistic weapon."

The baby started to cry inside the house and I remembered Ben's needy wails at that age and wondered whether I could look after such a tiny creature like that now. Give myself up to its primal need. I looked at the tower again, the wailing baby gathering volume behind me, and pictured Jacob throwing himself from the top, crying as he fell.

We finish our glasses of wine. Jazz crackles through the speakers. Felix peels off my clothes. He's inside me. Everything is suddenly clear. His hands are on my face, then my breasts, then pulling at my legs. He can't get enough of me and I want to give him whatever he needs. For a few minutes nothing matters except us and then he shudders on top of me as he comes and my breathing slows and I realize that I'm cold. The air-con is set too low and there's a dripping sound coming from somewhere, *drip, drip, drip*, and suddenly I can't bear it anymore. My son was *missing* only a few days ago. Christ. What is wrong with me?

"This doesn't feel right." I'm like a toddler picking at a scab. A child pushing at a loose tooth.

Felix half sits. His body blocks the lamplight and the soft curling hairs on his chest look darker than normal in the shadow. I get up and wrap a towel around myself. Goosebumps have erupted all over me and I can feel each one. Craig and Laura are at the farmhouse for Christmas so Felix and I are at a hotel around the back of a pub that is popular with backpackers, about half an hour out of Smithson. It's risky, but being Christmas Eve we assume that everyone we know will be home with their families.

"I thought it felt great." He laughs, and the lightness of his tone hits my wall and is swallowed up instantly. "I'm sorry, Gem." He leans back against the plump pillows, his face serious. "I don't know what you want me to say."

"I almost kissed someone the other night," I say, remembering Fox's lips on mine. "I went to a party and I almost kissed someone. Someone I used to know."

His right eyebrow lifts. "Okay." He places his hands behind his head as if he might launch into sit-ups. "Do you want to talk about it?"

My legs feel funny. I start to pace, trying to shake the itch away. "No, I don't want to talk about it. But I wanted to tell you, I felt like I should tell you." My face starts to fall and then I actually think the words, can see them being written down, *No, no more crying over this*, and manage to halt the tears mid-spill.

"Well, I'm kind of used to the idea of you being with other guys. You *are* basically married."

"Hang on. You're saying you wouldn't mind if I was with someone else?" I sound middle-aged and worn out, like I'm yelling for my naughty children at the park. I lower my voice. "So my being with someone else would be totally fine?"

"Gem, c'mon. Come sit down." He glances at his watch. "I have to go soon and I already want you again."

I want that too but I also want him to answer the fucking question. "Well?"

He sighs. "Look. It's not fine, but I guess...I don't know, I guess it's like how I know you're still with Scott sometimes and I deal with it. So I guess I'd put it in the same place I put that stuff."

"I haven't slept with Scott since May."

Felix is surprised, I can tell: it spreads quickly up his face followed closely by a gentle guilt.

"Do you still sleep with Mary?" I demand.

"Gemma," he says warily.

"Well, do you?"

"Gemma," he says again, with a sharpness that pushes me back, away from him. Then he shakes his head and speaks more softly. "I just don't see how it will help to lay our lives out side by side. To compare every little thing. We both know it's difficult. The past few days especially. We make it work the best we can. Do you know what I mean?"

I know what he means and I understand that I can choose to let this go, put it down and shove it away to the back of the shelf. I can pull him into me, get lost in the smell and feel of him and let this pass around us. "I guess I just assumed that your relationship wasn't like that. How often are you with her?" The words tumble from my mouth and mingle with the images I have of them together. I wonder whether he acts the same way with her as he does with me. Whether he presses her down, heavy and strong, and whether he looks at her with the same wonder when he pushes inside her.

"Gemma, please. I won't do this with you. It's stupid." He gets up and pulls on his clothes. Rubs his eyes. When he looks at me again his gaze is weary.

I'm making him so old, I think.

"We need to go home. You need to see Ben. Put out a stocking for Santa. Whatever."

"I know what I need to do. Don't patronize me."

His hands rise in the air. "Gemma! I'm not. I'm just saying normal things. Don't make it out like I'm attacking you." His accent hits rare high notes and cuts at the air.

"Okay, fine. Let's just go." I dress quickly, remembering my watch and bracelet on the tiny writing desk. I pick up my bag. I comb my hair with my hands and pull it into a ponytail. I swallow past the ache that has set in my throat.

The air-con whirs from its place on the wall, the sound needling my brain.

"Hey." He takes my hand, holds it briefly to his heart and looks at me with a pained expression. There's nothing left to say and not enough time to say it anyway. We're certainly not going to solve our future tonight. We leave the room and he holds my hand even as we walk down the stairs to the small brown lobby. Brown walls, brown carpet.

"Okay. Well," he says, dropping my hand. "Merry Christmas."

"Bye."

He steps away from me and I immediately want to be back in the room. I want to take back what I said. I want him to touch me again. Like a piece of driftwood, I float out of the hotel, careful to ease the door shut rather than let it bang, and step out into the blustery car park. The air is hot and dry. Dead dry leaves scatter across the asphalt and disappear under cars. Felix follows me a few moments later and through my windscreen I watch him walk the short way to his car. He fumbles in his pockets for his keys. I start my car and crank the fan up to full power. Just as I am about to flick on the lights I notice a girl watching Felix from a parked car at the petrol station, parallel to the hotel, about fifty meters away. Her face is almost yellow in the streetlight. She stares at Felix intensely, her mouth open. Suddenly she looks over in my direction and I flick the headlights on, shielding myself from view. She must be one of the students from Smithson, their made-up, young faces blurring into a hazy MTV montage.

I am halfway home when I realize that the girl is someone I see almost every day, smiling serenely from the wooden frame on Felix's desk: his eldest daughter, Maisie.

Chapter Fifty

then

"Is it true? Did you and Jacob break up?" Janet shoved a plastic cup into my hand and sticky red liquid sloshed over my fingers. Janet's eyeliner was too dark. Her eyes looked piggy in her broad face.

I shrugged, trying to hide the pain I felt. "We're on a break," I said, sipping at the cup, the sharp tang of vodka hitting the top of my throat.

Janet's eyes bulged. "Wow! No way! So it's true? I thought you two were the forever couple... Come on, let's go outside, it's way too noisy in here." Janet pulled on my hand.

I followed her through the dark wood-paneled kitchen. There were people everywhere. Kids from Smithson. Kids from the surrounding schools. All high on freedom and booze. High on the future. There was a glass panel between myself and the others. I wondered if they could see it too. A guy pushed past me and his sombrero scraped across my face. "Sorry!" He laughed and a wave of beer fumes made me wrinkle my nose.

"Ugh. Everyone has gone mad." Janet was laughing. She looked at me and her face dropped. "So what happened with Jacob?"

What happened? What happened? That was all I had wondered since Jacob pulled me aside at school the week before and smashed my world apart.

"I don't know. It's like the exams just made us a bit crazy or something. I mean, we're basically adults now so I guess it makes sense that we spend a bit of time apart. You know?"

Janet looked at me dumbly. I wanted to slap her fleshy cheeks. Slap the stupid away.

"You're so cool about it," she said.

I shrugged. I needed to eat: it had been days. The vodka had gone straight to my head and I imagined it sitting behind my eyes, shooting out silver sparks. I had to sit down. I pulled Janet into the porch swing. She lit a cigarette and smoked it awkwardly. I spied Fox watching us from the back of the garden, the gray tails of his cigarette disappearing into the night.

"I always thought you and Jacob would be forever, I guess. It didn't seem like a high school thing. It seemed more... real or something."

It was. It is! I wanted to scream at her. "Well, we'll see. I don't know that it's *over*, over. Like I said, we're on a break."

Janet bit her lip. She sucked hard on her cigarette and then coughed out a burst of smoke. I pushed at the ground with my toe and rocked us forward gently. My heart sank into my gut and my voice sounded strange when I finally spoke.

"What is it, Janet?"

A glass smashed onto the floor inside, the noise tinkling down my spine.

"Well..." Janet swallowed. She stuck her foot out, pausing our swinging seat. "It's just that Lauren told me that Jacob hooked up with Rose Ryan at Mark's thing last night. But maybe it's not true. Or maybe it's just like a dumb, nothing thing."

Squeals of laughter exploded from somewhere and a dance song started up in the house. The beat pulsed through the deck as the blood rushed through my body. Janet rested her head on my shoulder and in that moment I missed my mother so intensely I thought I might faint.

Jacob and Rosalind twisted into my thoughts. It didn't seem possible, but at the same time it made perfect sense. How dare he? How dare she? She was everything I'd ever wanted to be and he was everything I wanted. I couldn't get the two of them touching out of my mind.

"Do you want more?" asked Janet.

"Ah, yeah," I said. "Sure."

She got up and left me alone on the swing. Laughter poured out of the house again and I looked at the dirty cigarette smudge on the ground, watching as a few tiny spots glowed fire for a few beats before fading to black.

Chapter Fifty-one

Thursday, December 24, 9:52 p.m.

I don't know what to do about Maisie and have no idea whether she'll say something to Felix, but equally I'm feeling stressed about being home late. I promised Scott I'd be home by 9:30.

"C'mon, c'mon." I tap on the wheel as I drive. My heart races and my thoughts flit madly between Maisie, Felix and Ben, and John Nicholson's confession. Did he fly into a rage at the thought of losing his daughter again? Did Rose confess something to him? Perhaps she told him she was pregnant? Or who the father of her child was? A child that he thought was his grandkid. Or am I simply refusing to consider that Rodney might be guilty, just like Felix says?

My hands clutch at the steering wheel as I turn into our street. I feel high, light-headed, as if someone else is driving the car.

The weight of the disappointment I cause weighs heavily on me as I step inside. Ben, up unusually late, hears my footsteps and squeals, the sound growing louder as he races down the hallway. Scott appears behind him, a tall dark shape. I keep my eyes on Ben.

"Mummy!"

"Darling! Were you waiting for me? I'm sorry. Are you excited about Christmas tomorrow?" I bend down and Ben's tiny arms wrap around me and I close my eyes and hold on tight.

"Santa, Santa, Santa!"

I laugh. "Yes, Santa! We should put out some biscuits and milk for Santa."

My voice sounds hollow, as if I'm on stage trying to remember my lines. Trying to remember how to move around my family, what props to pick up, what furniture to navigate. How to feel about them. I remember back to Christmases from my childhood, hazy montages of helping Mum wrap gifts, and Dad putting out red wine for Santa. Mum taking photos of me as I opened gifts, always so careful not to rip the paper.

"Okay," I say brightly. "Well, come on then. Let's see what we've got." Ben pads along happily after me into the kitchen. Scott doesn't follow us but I can still feel his eyes on me. The smell of pine is everywhere, sickly sweet. It mixes with the heat. I flick on the light and see a plate of biscuits, a carrot and a glass of milk already laid out on the bench.

Chapter Fifty-two

Friday, December 25, 6:27 a.m.

As we sleep, Smithson is surrounded by fire. The relentless heat has finally boiled over and sloshes across the landscape in a burning rage. It leaps across the thirsty bush, taking out houses and dancing gleefully around waterholes.

The fires roll on through the darkness.

A small town about two hundred kilometers north is consumed just after 5 a.m. Three people dead. Many more injured.

The fires breathe closer still.

My dreams are red and navy.

Blood and flames mix together and melt into blackness.

I wake to the sound of Ben banging on the rails of his cot just as a text shudders onto my phone. I glance at Scott who, already awake, looks first at me then at my phone before hauling himself out of bed. Rubbing sleep from my eyes, I quickly read the message from Jonesy: *body found at West-ley Reserve. 20 yrs. male. thinking suicide but he's ex-Smithson High so we're checking it out just wanted you to hear it from me but don't come in. Enjoy xmas with Ben. Keep an eye on the fires.*

I picture John Nicholson's tired watery eyes. At least this didn't happen at the school. Or at the tower.

I text back: *Are you sure you don't need me? Keep me updated.*

I know Jonesy won't reply. I can hear Scott taking Ben into the lounge. He squeals when he sees the pile of presents. I get up and swap my frayed singlet for an oversized t-shirt.

Heat lurks in the house like a white film. In the bathroom I splash some water over my face and wipe the cold wetness down my arms and legs but my skin still feels puffy, like my bones have grown larger during the night. The smell of pine is like a cake baking. I think back to the Christmas after Mum died and the one after Jacob had jumped. With Jacob it was worse: it hadn't even been three weeks by then and the hole he had left in my world was just becoming clear. I recall Dad and me half-heartedly going through the familiar yet jarring motions of Christmas, with Aunt Megan fussing around, convinced that if I just ate a decent amount of turkey and ham, then things would be all right. I remember how even though she put carols on, all I could hear was the sound of rushing, like water crashing through a tunnel.

"Mummy, look! Presents!"

I take Ben in my arms. "Merry Christmas, baby."

"Merry Christmas." Scott's voice is gruff and he looks at the floor. "Do you want a coffee?"

"Yes, thank you."

Ben and I count his presents while we wait for Scott. He claps as I say each number. I wonder about Felix, what his Christmas morning is like. Has Maisie said something about seeing us? Does he even know she was there last night? He can probably explain pretty much anything away with work. *I was just investigating a case, darling. Following up a lead.* But the explanation falls flat even in my head. She would know if she saw us together: our energy crackles around us like a thunder cloud. Maybe Scott heard the buzz of our connection when he arrived at the house the other day. Saw the sparks. I think about what might happen if Maisie tells her mother, and I realize how careless we've been. So sloppy. He makes me so needy, so thoughtless. My giddiness has led to snatched moments, me clawing at windows of light in the darkness. The foolish assumption that the universe will protect us.

Ben's head looms into my vision. I've stopped counting and he's impatient, wanting to open his presents.

"Here." Scott hands me a mug overfilled with milky coffee.

"Thanks."

"See about the fires?"

I remember Jonesy's message. "No."

"They're pretty bad. Like the ones back in the eighties, they're saying in the paper."

"Presents, presents!" Ben looks like he might burst.

"Was that work before?" Scott tips his head toward my phone.

I nod. "Yep."

"Do you have to go in?"

"No." I take a slurp of the coffee. "There's a body, but they think it's a suicide. Jonesy's got it."

Scott nods. "He's a good guy."

"Yes."

I watch Scott smile at Ben and want to avoid cracking the careful Christmas morning equilibrium we have created. We are alkaline levels in a pool, both trying to keep the waters safe. Neutral enough that we can bob past each other without turning toxic.

"Okay!" My voice is a bright fuchsia pink. "Presents?"

"Presents for the lucky little boy first, I think. Right, Ben, here you go." Scott hands him a gift and Ben tears into it with the wanton abandon that only a child on Christmas Day can exhibit. His face is pure joy, his red cheeks flushed. My heart is tender and pulpy.

"Mumma, look! Trains!"

I nod and smile at the little imp that is my son.

"Here. This is for you." Scott looks past me as he holds out the gift.

"Thank you." My voice is a shadow. "Here." I reach around to where I've wedged a small envelope between two bottles of wine under the tree. "It's just a gift voucher."

He waves my excuse away as he opens the envelope and gives me a curt nod.

I slide my fingers underneath the folded flaps of the blood-red wrapping paper. A small set of wind chimes is folded inside the box.

"I remember how you liked the sound of them at the place we went to just after your birthday. I bought them ages ago."

"Show me, Mummy, show me!" Ben yells into my face.

I pull out the chimes and let them touch. They make a tinkling noise that lulls Ben into a long stare. "Thank you," I say again.

The chiming swirls around the room until Scott claps his hands and jumps up, grabbing one of Ben's new toy trains. "Hey, Benny boy, show me how this one goes! C'mon, come over here."

Ben goes to Scott, still red-faced with excitement, and they begin playing a complicated game of trains. Their chatter fills the room and I think I should get up and take a photo. A proper Christmas morning photo. But I just keep watching them instead. I wonder, for a moment, if I am even real. I look down at the perfectly round silver chimes in my hand, smooth and cool, and clutch my fingers tightly around them, squeezing for as long as I can, until my skin turns white and I can't tell whether it hurts or not.

Chapter Fifty-three

then

Jacob loped along, sipping at a giant Slurpee and wearing a cap I'd never seen before. I grabbed my bag, leaving my half-eaten sandwich, and followed him, carefully keeping a solid distance between us. I watched his familiar walk and the way his dark hair poked out of his cap into the back of his collar. He seemed bigger, taller, as if he'd grown since we'd been apart. He passed the food court and pulled his hat off, zipping it into his backpack. I noticed an intricate design drawn in black ink starting on the back of his hand and sprawling up his arm. For a moment I wondered if he had got a tattoo, it was so good, but I guessed he had drawn it himself. He headed toward the cinema and I knew he was meeting her. He ran his fingers through his hair. It looked different. Styled. I felt a low pulse in my heart. I missed touching him so much. Ducking into the music store opposite the cinema complex, I watched as he stood next to a large indoor fern, his fingers racing madly across his mobile phone.

After a few minutes he stepped away from the plant, looking up. Rose was above him, backlit, a dazzling smile on her face. Jacob made a cute little gesture, fluttering his hands on his chest before beckoning her to come down. She shook her head, teasing, before eventually stepping back from the glass wall barrier and making her way down the stairs to where he waited for her.

She was dressed oddly, in an old-fashioned peasant blouse that exposed her shoulders and a long skirt that wrapped around her legs. She was womanly next to Jacob's all-American teenager, his faded gray t-shirt and loose jeans that dropped away from his slim waist. His face was still soft

285

with little-boy wonder: his body caught between child and man. They were nothing alike, their intimacy jarring, until she bounced into him childishly at the last minute, her blonde hair flicking up at the ends. He slid an arm around her waist and she ducked her head into the space between his head and shoulder. I felt like I was spying on myself. *That's supposed to be me.*

I kept watching from behind a CD display and then her eyes were on mine. We stared at each other, her face nestled against Jacob's body for a few moments, and then her mouth spread into a slow, knowing smile. I couldn't pull my eyes away and kept watching until they disappeared into the plush redness of the cinema, the sound of a freight train smashing through my brain.

Chapter Fifty-four

Friday, December 25, 12:36 p.m.

"I'd like us to say grace, please." Aunt Megan is at the head of the table, looking at us earnestly. She rattles through several things that we should be thankful for, then asks that my mother look down on us and especially on Ben.

"Amen," we mumble.

"Don't want gravy," says Ben loudly. "It's yuck."

Everyone laughs and then we all look at Ben expectantly for more light relief. I'm feeling funny about not telling Dad and the others that Ben was kidnapped, but Scott and I both agreed that it's for the best. We don't want to bring everyone down to our reality. Luckily Dad didn't answer the phone when I called him the other day and by the time he called me back Ben was fine, so I was able to fob him off.

"Bad day for fires out there." Craig fiddles with his phone and Megan casts him a disapproving look. Laura elbows him in the ribs. "What? Sorry. I'm worried about my mate's farm."

We busy ourselves with bursting the expensive-looking bonbons that Laura and Craig bought from David Jones in Sydney. Every time one pops, Ben laughs hysterically and gleefully collects a small pile of useless objects from its guts.

"So, Gemma," says Craig, "I imagine things are pretty intense at work at the moment. That poor dead woman has been in the news every night for the past fortnight."

"Yeah." I stab at a piece of turkey and roll it in cranberry sauce. "It's been a pretty tough one."

"Her dad is some kind of mover and shaker, right?" Craig opens his mouth wide to shovel in a large forkful of meat.

"Yeah, he has a large property business. It's pretty big time and he grew it from scratch. Apparently he's quite the salesman."

"I don't reckon you can ever trust people that rich," says Craig.

Ben suddenly bites through his tongue and starts screaming, watery blood leaking onto his lip. I dab a serviette on his mouth and duck my head apologetically at Craig, hoping he'll take it as a sign to talk about something else.

"You must have known her in school," he continues. "I was saying that to Laura the other day, that you must have known her."

"Yes, well, it's very tragic." Dad's voice is unusually brisk. "But Gem's got a day off from it today."

Craig's eyebrows shoot up. "Sure, of course."

Ben's cries cease and he bounces back to his chair to resume eating. We chew in time to some jaunty carols that Megan has put on but the volume is down low and the sound turns my stomach.

"More wine?" I stand quickly and bump my knee hard on the table.

Dad smiles at me. "Yes, love—just a little, thanks."

Laura nods.

"Do you think that's a good idea?" says Scott.

I look at Scott. Everyone looks at Scott.

"Whatever," he says, breaking his eyes away from mine. His knife scrapes the plate as he cuts through turkey.

"Great," I say, picking up my glass. "I'll open that fancy bottle of chardonnay you got from the Jacksons."

In the kitchen I breathe past anger and pour wine into my glass. As I drink, I close my eyes and wish it was the evening. I look down at my dress, bought years ago for a wedding. The hem caught on something at some point and it hangs unevenly just below my knees. It's tight across my middle.

I check my phone. A Merry Christmas text from Anna, one from Carol with a photo of her kids in Santa hats. A missed call from Fox and several safety alerts about the fires. Nothing from Felix. I toss it back onto the bench and look outside. The exhausted trees barely ruffle in the wind.

I return to the dining room. Empty bonbons lie in a glittering heap at the end of the table.

I pour wine for everyone.

"I want JUICE!" Ben screams.

"Shhh. Okay, buddy, calm down," says Scott. "I'll get you some juice, just sit tight."

Ben's face is red and he clenches his fists. Laura moves around the table and tries to pull him into her lap. When he wriggles away she tries not to look hurt and starts clearing the plates.

"Fires are pretty bad," says Craig, looking at his phone again. "Wiped out half of Felton by the sounds of it. No one seems to think they will reach Smithson though."

"Lord have mercy on those poor people," mutters Megan.

Scott reappears with Ben's juice.

Ben takes one look at the juice and starts crying. "Not *that* juice!"

"Oh, come on, Ben, I'm sure it's yummy juice," Laura says.

"No. It's. NOT!" Ben throws himself on the floor.

Laura laughs awkwardly. "Well, I guess not."

She returns to her chair and keeps her eyes on her food.

Craig continues to commentate. "Parts of Jackson have gone too, up near the river. Full on."

Dad clears his throat. "I know it's hot but perhaps we can put on the sprinkler and play some cricket. There's some shade in the yard."

He looks so hopeful, so desperate for us to break the claustrophobia of the table, that I find myself meeting Scott's eyes. We call a silent truce.

"Sure, Ned," he says.

"Great idea, Dad." He clutches me in a brief hug as I walk past. "I'll grab the cricket set."

After an hour of hot, sweaty, half-hearted cricket, we trundle back inside for more wine.

Craig is itching to put on the TV. "Might just flick on the news to see the fires…"

Megan mutters under her breath and disappears into the kitchen. I open another bottle of wine and busy myself with filling glasses. Angry flames light up the screen as a slightly panicked reporter describes the devastation.

"Bloody hell," says Craig. "They're everywhere."

Laura serves bowls of cold pudding with brandy cream.

I check my phone again. Still nothing from Felix. I picture him reflected in a hazy Christmas bauble, surrounded by his blonde daughters, their hair neatly braided, as his wife serves a traditional Christmas dinner that she cooked entirely herself. Or maybe Maisie has tattled, and he and his wife are locked in a furious stand-off, all the doubts that ever existed between them being dissected like a turkey, with "Jingle Bells" playing in the background.

Scott interrupts my thoughts by depositing a squirming Ben onto my lap. I face him into my chest, away from the raging fires, and hum softly into his ear. His body is heavy with pre-sleep. Dad pats me on the shoulder and kisses Ben on the forehead before settling into the armchair. Laura and Craig sit side by side on the couch. Scott is shoving discarded wrapping paper into a large garbage bag. Aunt Megan sits primly in Mum's old armchair near the stereo, which is still doggedly playing Christmas tunes. Rosalind would have turned twenty-nine today, I think as my eyelids drop, and the flames on TV turn into a writhing mass of scarlet rose petals.

Chapter Fifty-five

Saturday, December 26, 9:30 a.m.

The office hums with post-holiday chat. Extra people have come in because of the fires. An emergency crew is using one of our meeting rooms as a base. Everyone knows someone who lost a house in the Christmas blaze. Overnight, the wind coaxed the fires west and now they are burning wildly across acres of Australian nothingness. Smithson has let out its breath. Safe for now.

The headline in the paper screams A CHRISTMAS MIRACLE and photos show the ring of fire around the town. I flip over the front page and Rosalind's face looks out at me. STILL NO JUSTICE FOR SMITHSON'S ANGEL reads Candy's headline. I click onto the Smithson Today website and scroll through the articles. After a few minutes I push my chair away from my desk. I feel hopelessly restless and desperate to know whether Maisie has said anything. Where the fuck is Felix?

"Woodstock, need you in here." Jonesy walks past my desk without stopping.

I enter his office and sit down. He paces in front of me.

"Gemma, we're losing the uniforms. Because of the fires."

I sink into the couch. This case is slipping out of my grasp. "All of them?"

"I'd say so. There's bullshit coming at the department left, right and center. We just can't justify keeping them when so many places need the manpower."

"Does McKinnon know?"

"Yep, spoke to him last night."

"Why didn't you speak to me?" My eyes burn into his.

He holds my stare. "I wanted you to have a day with your family. Have a break from all this. Fair enough?"

"I guess." I'm trying to contain the heat flaring inside me.

"Right, well. The guys you have now will work the day out and then I'd say that will be it. So do your check-in this afternoon and then you'll need to pare it back and work out how you want to run it."

"And then?"

"And then I don't know. We get a solve ideally."

I stand up and turn to leave, feeling oddly empty. "Is that everything?"

"Almost. What's this I hear about you getting flowers, Woodstock?"

I freeze. "Flowers?"

"Yes. Flowers. Big fat bunch of red roses, in fact. Delivered to your house at the beginning of the Ryan murder investigation." Jonesy's nostrils flare and I can see bristly hairs hiding inside them like spiders under the eaves. "I'm sure you remember—unless of course you get sent flowers all the time."

"We don't know it's linked to the case."

"I didn't even know about them at all!" He glares at me. "Not good enough, Woodstock, and you know it."

"Did McKinnon tell you?"

"Who told me is the least of your problems. *You* should have told me. I want you on this thing, Woodstock, but you're making it very hard."

"I'm sorry, sir. I should have told you."

"Yes, you should have. We'll speak later. For now, just keep yourself out of trouble. That's an order."

"Yes, sir."

He walks away, thrusting a pudgy hand through his oily hair.

I go back to my desk and blindly check e-mails and make notes. My fingers curl and I imagine slamming my fists on the keyboard until it breaks and the keys rattle to the floor like teeth. I look over at Felix's desk, but he is still nowhere to be seen.

Still fuming, I catch up on the Christmas Day suicide. It doesn't appear to be related in any way to Rosalind's case. The twenty-year-old video store attendant had been a student at Smithson Secondary College but had never been taught by Rosalind, and nothing suggests they were acquainted. He had a fight with his girlfriend on Christmas Eve morning and made the decision to go off his meds shortly thereafter. That poor girl: she will rake over that argument in her mind for the rest of her life.

At midday I get a call about an incident at the Ryans'. A man covered in blood is allegedly screaming at the house from the front yard. I rush down a couple of bites of my sandwich and then call Felix, leaving him a message as I jump in the car.

By the time I get to the Ryans', two cops are already there. They have a bloodied Bryce sitting on the front steps, looking forlorn. I get out of the car, squinting as light pings off the collection of cars in the driveway.

Timothy is standing on the front veranda talking to a uniform. He's looking across at the small crowd that has gathered on the other side of the street. I spy the manager of the local bank, and a property developer, whose name I can't remember; he writes about investments in Candy's paper. Smithson's finest dragged out of their Christmas hangovers by this unexpected spectacle.

I push my sunglasses on and amble up to the front of the house. "Hi, boys."

They look at me petulantly.

"What's going on?"

"Nothing," says Timothy. "Just a misunderstanding."

Bryce nods in agreement.

"Looks like a bit more than that to me. You've created quite the scene."

Timothy grimaces. "It was just a stupid fight. No big deal."

"What were you fighting about?" I ask.

"Nothing. We were mucking around."

"Well, why don't we take a little trip down to the station and unpack it all a bit?" says one of the older cops, and I try to hide a smile as Timothy scowls.

"Where is your father?" I ask, following them to the police car.

"He's back in the hospital," says Bryce ominously, spitting on his hand and wiping blood from his cheek.

Chapter Fifty-six

then

I found the old fountain pen in my mother's writing desk. I used to love watching her write, the curve of the words like a lullaby. It always seemed that no matter what letters appeared, they would be more beautiful if written with that pen. I didn't know when I'd decided to send Jacob the note. It might have been when I saw them together at the shopping center. It might have been after that. All I really knew for sure was that it had been twenty lonely days without Jacob and I was losing my mind. We were still speaking but our private world had split down the middle, and my side had been cast into a dark, bleak winter. I was lost without my other half. I wasn't sleeping, I wasn't eating. I was frozen in place and unable to see in front of me. The grief was weighing me down. Jacob hadn't mentioned Rosalind and I'd choked on the accusation every time I'd tried to ask him. And then I'd seen them together and an overwhelming urgency had taken over. Action seemed like the only option. I'd felt so drawn to her, and she had gone and taken my future away from me. It was so unfair: she had everything already. Jacob was all I had. And I had trusted him so much and now he was wrapped in her spell too.

In my room, I laid a sheet of crisp cream paper next to the piece of foolscap I'd ripped from my notebook. I wrote out the text, agonizing over each word until I felt it read right. After that, I just needed to copy it onto the writing paper and sign it. My hand hovered over the page. My fingers gripped the thick pen so hard that they ached. The first few words were shaky but then I found my rhythm, recalling the necessary tilt of the nib, the right pressure. The flick of my wrist to round out a word. The letters turned into a hateful, beautiful cloud. The fountain pen transformed my prose into art, carrying light and shade. I signed Rosalind's name with a flourish and leaned back, looking at the page. It was beautiful. The evil words I had signed her name to would be hard for Jacob to ignore.

> *...I'm sorry to say that you mean nothing to me. It was all a game. I just wanted to pretend I could like someone like you, just for a moment. A little bit like an experiment, a bit like a dare. I wanted to see if I could make you like me. And it worked. But now it's gone too far. I'm embarrassed by being seen with you. I don't want to see you anymore, don't want you to touch me...*

I felt alive for the first time in weeks. My breath came out in little puffs and my body was on edge, as if I was playing hide-and-seek and it was my turn to be found. A noise in the other room fired a nerve ending all the way from the base of my neck to the tip of my spine. Probably just Dad waking up. I dabbed at Rosalind's signature, making sure it was dry, before I folded the letter perfectly in half. In a few hours Jacob would hold this letter and begin to doubt her. Start to feel like he couldn't trust her. Understand that she was not what she seemed. But I didn't want him to speak to her after he read it.

I wanted him to think that this letter was the end between them.

To realize that he had made a mistake.

To see what we had all along.

I needed to keep them apart. I didn't want her to beg him for a second chance. Deny that she sent it.

I bit my lip, the final stage of my plan forming in my mind.

Chapter Fifty-seven

Saturday, December 26, 4:09 p.m.

I call Our Lady Private Hospital to talk to George Ryan but I'm told he's not able to speak with me at the moment. "Only family," the nurse snaps into the phone.

Felix is nowhere to be found. I recall Jonesy dressing me down and rage pulses through me again in waves. I'm exhausted and desperate to take my mind off Felix's betrayal.

Timothy and Bryce Ryan were released without charge following the incident at the house. Neither was willing to press charges but clearly something has come between them. I wonder if it has to do with Rosalind.

It's 1:15 p.m. in Shanghai when I call Lila Wilcox. I can hear the grime and color of the exotic city pulsing down the line as she answers. It sounds a lot further than half a world away. "Ms. Wilcox? Detective Woodstock."

"Oh." She falters. "You have news?"

"No, I'm sorry, I don't. We're still working through a lot of information."

"I see." Relief comes in the form of a long breath and then, as if realizing that not knowing is worse, her breathing quickens again. "Well, how can I help?"

"Lila, I want to ask some questions about when you were married to George Ryan."

"Of course."

I arrange the photos of the Ryans on my monitor as I talk to her. "Was George ever violent?"

"No. Arrogant. Dominant, perhaps, and moody sometimes, but not violent."

"He never hit you? Never lashed out at the boys?"

"Not that I ever saw. He was very strict with them—too strict, I thought—but not inappropriate. He never touched me."

"What about Rosalind?"

She hesitates.

"Ms. Wilcox," I say, "this is important. I don't want to have to bring you back here. It's a long flight."

"No. Look, it's nothing. He never touched her either. I wouldn't have stood for it. But there was something off with the way he was with her."

"Off?"

She speaks quickly. "Nothing like that. Really. More like he was nervous around her. Don't get me wrong. He spoiled her. Gave her things. Loved her. But he seemed uncomfortable with her."

"Maybe at that age he felt it wasn't right to be too close?"

"Maybe. I never understood it. It was almost like he was scared of her." Lila laughs. It's a nice sound. "Silly, really. I tried to discuss it with him but he said I was imagining things. I don't know. Perhaps I was. She didn't mind. She was so self-sufficient."

"What about the boys? Did they ever touch her? Were they ever violent?"

"No. Not that I saw."

I look at my screen again. I'm deep down rabbit holes but the rabbits are everywhere except where I'm looking.

A horn blares. She's crossing a road.

"There was something," she says hesitantly.

"Yes?"

"I'm not sure if it's anything really. After all, they were just children."

"What happened?" I say.

"Okay, well, I could tell something was going on. This would have been around two years before I left. Rosalind was perhaps twelve."

"And what was going on?"

"Well, it started with some silly inappropriate comments. Sneaking around. Normal kid stuff."

"Then what happened?"

"They were taking pictures."

"Of what?"

"Of Rose."

"What kind of pictures?"

"You know. *Those* kind of pictures. There was a vent in the ceiling of her room, and Tim and Bryce set up one of George's cameras in it. They took photos of her in her room. Undressing and whatever."

"Not Marcus?"

"He knew about the photos but I don't think he was really involved. He was close to Rose. Tim and Bryce were always the leaders, even though they were younger. Marcus was a sweet boy. He never wanted to cause trouble."

"Did you tell your husband?"

"No. I didn't think it was worth it. I reasoned they weren't pornographic, more opportunistic. I went crazy at them and made them destroy all the photos. Grounded them. They claimed she knew all about the photos, that it had been her idea in the first place. I told George they'd been talking back to me. He was away on business anyway."

"Did Rosalind know about this?"

"No, I don't think so. I didn't want her to know. Like I said, I think it was just kid stuff. Not good, obviously, but probably just pushing boundaries. They were always hard to manage and I didn't think it was worth making it into a bigger deal. They were just messing around. Oh god."

"Ms. Wilcox? Lila?" I say, when she doesn't answer.

Her voice shakes now. "They were just kids...You don't think that the boys are involved in what happened to her? God."

Tapping my pen against my teeth I try to imagine it. "I really don't know," I say.

Chapter Fifty-eight

Sunday, December 27, 3:02 p.m.

"It feels weird being here." Melanie Cousins shifts her gaze furtively to the left, then to the right, the small piercing high in her ear sparkling in the sun.

"Because of Ms. Ryan?" Tara Boffin shades her eyes from the glare and notices Melanie's piercing, wishing her mother would let her get one like it.

"Yeah," replies Melanie. "Mum's still beside herself about it."

"Same. Mine's obsessed. Keeps shushing everyone when the news comes on." Tara hasn't minded though; she's been devouring the news on Ms. Ryan's murder, searching for information online long after everyone has gone to bed. Some of the comments she read at the end of one report were probably the worst things she has ever read.

"Do you think the guy's still out there?"

"I guess so. They haven't caught him yet."

The girls walk over the rocks to the left of the playground. The sun has shrunk the often watery pools to nothing. Tara concentrates to keep her balance. She's larger than Melanie and less steady on her feet. The slighter girl scrambles over the rocks easily.

"Want one?" Melanie holds out a cigarette.

"Sure." Tara tries to hide her huffing.

They sit companionably together in silence, smoking.

"Do you think it hurt?" Melanie asks.

"When she died?"

"Yeah."

"I reckon. I read she was raped before he killed her." Tara shudders.

"I heard it was after, like when she was already dead."

"It's so gross," says Tara.

"Yeah."

A woman who has been walking her dog near the playground stops in the middle of the path and lifts her hand to shield her eyes and then waves at them enthusiastically.

"Who's that?" says Melanie, stubbing out her cigarette.

"Don't know. Maybe our next-door neighbor?" says Tara, also killing her cigarette and managing to burn the tip of her thumb at the same time.

"Quick, let's get away from here where she can't see."

Tara follows Melanie, who weaves expertly through the bracken down to the water's edge. "In here," says Melanie.

Tara looks at the gaping entrance to the concrete tunnel and stops short.

"C'mon!" The walls give Melanie's voice a masculine edge.

"I don't know, Mel."

Melanie's voice starts to fade away, disappearing into the dark void.

"Okay, wait. I'm coming." Tara steps tentatively into the nothingness, the slosh of shallow water underneath her shoes.

There's a flicking sound and then a yellow glow; Melanie is illuminated by the flame as she leans in to light a cigarette. "For you?" She offers the lighter to Tara, who obliges by shifting forward and letting her catch the end of the cigarette with the flame.

"What is this place?"

"An old drainpipe or something. I don't think it's used for anything. Matt and I come down here sometimes to . . . you know." Melanie raises her eyebrows.

Tara pictures Matt pinning her friend against the dark concrete wall, kissing her, and the two of them having sex in this dirty place, and thinks that as much as she'd like to have a boyfriend she wouldn't like him to bring her here. Especially not since Ms. Ryan was murdered a few meters away.

"Wow. This is cool," says Melanie.

"What?"

"This. Look."

Tara makes her way over to where Melanie is standing next to the wall, using the lighter like a torch. "I think we should get out of here. What if the water comes on or something?"

"It won't. Jeez, relax. And look at these. I've never noticed them before. Some of them are really good."

Tara takes in the artwork on the curved wall. Melanie's right, some of the pictures are impressive. Complicated patterns, dramatic graffiti and excellent likenesses to people. Brad and Angelina are wrapped around each other in an awkward embrace, their heads large on tiny bodies. There is a cartoon of the mayor that makes her giggle, his recognizable features twisted into a squinty pig-like creature.

"I like that one."

Melanie moves the lighter to where Tara is pointing, illuminating a picture of a large glowing gem. Somehow it looks lit up; the artist has used white shading and silver paint to give the gem its own light. It's abstract, but beautiful. Tara's never seen anything quite like it before.

"Yeah, that's really cool." Melanie takes out her phone to snap a picture of it.

Tara drops her cigarette in the water while Melanie's not looking. She is queasy from the smoke and feels a mild flutter of panic as she turns back toward the small circle of daylight, but her eyes keep being drawn to the glittering gemstone, as if it's a rare archeological find, noting the tiny words—*JM + Gem. Always*—at the very sharpest point of the jewel.

Chapter Fifty-nine

Monday, December 28, 10:06 a.m.

From the tearoom I see Felix pulling into the car park and I bolt out the front before he has the chance to get out of the car. Kenny sniggers as I rush past. Felix wasn't in yesterday and had been mysteriously in Paxton on Saturday "looking into things related to the case." He has been ignoring my calls, and seeing him now has tipped my simmering over to a fully fledged boil.

"Why are you ignoring me?" I hiss.

He looks up at me, squinting. "What?" He takes his time gathering his bag. Putting his keys in his pocket.

"You're ignoring me," I say, though the sight of him has numbed me somewhat.

"I had a day off, Gemma," he replies, putting sunglasses on. "I needed a break."

Anger bubbles up inside me again. "Why did you tell Jonesy about the flowers?"

"Gemma, it's a criminal investigation." I can tell by the way he's talking to me that Maisie hasn't said anything about seeing him. Seeing us. He'd be different. Frazzled. Instead, he's looking at me with calm pity. I wonder whether she just hasn't realized what she saw or whether she has decided to keep a secret from her father.

"I fucking know that. Don't be an arsehole."

He looks at me evenly. "Gemma."

White hot anger burns through my body. I can't even speak.

"Your son was taken. You're not thinking straight. I think we all need to have all of the information. You can't do this on your own."

I kick at the ground and his mouth twitches into a brief smile.

"Fuck you."

He hardens. "Gemma. Come on. I'm trying to help."

"I'm not trying to do this on my own."

"Okay, good."

"What the fuck is your problem?" I cry.

"Gemma, now is not the time."

"For what?"

"For a discussion about this."

Two junior uniforms push out of the main entrance and glance apologetically our way before scuttling to their patrol car.

"About what?"

He sighs as if I am a toddler throwing a tantrum. "About our relationship."

"Oh, is that what this is? I thought we were going to discuss the case." I whirl around and stalk back toward the office, yelling over my shoulder. "I'm going to talk to the Ryans. Timothy and Bryce have some explaining to do."

Timothy had flown back to Sydney on Saturday night for a fortieth and Bryce said he had gastro, so I wasn't able to speak to them again yesterday. Neither of them was thrilled when I arranged for two fresh-faced uniforms to pick them up from George Ryan's house bright and early this morning. Then, I deliberately kept them waiting for over an hour, scowling as they sat opposite each other on the uncomfortable chairs in the front room, before I suddenly separate them to begin the interviews.

They both maintain that their argument on Boxing Day was a silly misunderstanding.

They hadn't slept well and it led to a fight over cooking breakfast.

Timothy misinterpreted something Bryce said and he snapped.

They've been under a lot of pressure.

They want to go home.

They have their lawyers on speed dial, you know.

Their father is very ill.

They need to be with him.

"You weren't with him yesterday," I point out.

"I was sick myself," says Bryce.

"It was my best mate's birthday," says Timothy.

"Let's talk about your sister," I say.

They both pause.

"Tragic, obviously," says Bryce.

"Just a nightmare," says Timothy.

"Okay, let's go over a few things again. Where were you on Friday, December 11?"

"The school play," says Timothy cockily. "*Romeo and Juliet*. It was great. Much better than I thought it would be."

"But you didn't speak with your sister?" I ask.

"No, she was busy, everyone wanted to talk to her."

"What about you, Bryce?"

"Yep. Like I said, I got takeaway from the chicken shop, went home and watched a movie. I already told you all this."

"And you heard your brother come home?" I say.

"Yeah, like I said, I think so. Around eleven. I was on the phone to my girlfriend. She had a migraine, that's why I stayed home that night. I heard the door open so I knew Timothy was home."

"Was Bryce's door closed when you got home? How did you know he was home?"

"I could hear him talking. I assumed he was on the phone."

"Okay. Back to Rosalind. Did you always get along?" I ask Timothy.

"She was our only sister. We spoiled her."

"And what about when you were younger? Did you get along?"

"Of course," says Bryce.

"Very well. She was very easygoing," says Timothy.

"So easygoing that you took photos of her getting undressed?" I press.

Indignant splutters are followed by the clearing of throats, which turn to narrowed eyes filled with suspicion.

"I don't really remember anything like that," says Bryce. "We were just kids mucking around."

"That was all her idea!" says Timothy. "She wanted us to take photos of her. She was always asking us to do stuff like that."

"So you're saying she instigated the photos being taken?" I ask.

"She definitely wanted us to take them," says Bryce.

"I really don't see the point in going over any of this. But yes, she knew. She always loved being the center of attention," says Timothy. "She was manipulative."

"Do you think your sister was manipulative?" I ask Bryce.

He shrugs. "She got what she wanted most of the time. Is that the same thing?"

"I want to go home," says Timothy. "Are you charging us with anything?"

"I'm leaving," announces Bryce. "Dragging all this up isn't helping anyone."

Chapter Sixty

Tuesday, December 29, 6:55 a.m.

The Sonny Lake car park is empty. For the first time in days it's cool and the clouds are swollen with rain. I sit for a moment inside the quiet of the car and look out across the lake. The water is still, as if someone hit pause. I let my eyes drop a little and it could almost be an ice rink. In the early light the water is silver. I know Rosalind was already dead by the time she went into the water, but I still imagine her thrashing about, gulping for air as water fills her mouth, her dark eyes wide with fear. In my vision she is terrified, knowing she is about to die.

A motorbike revs loudly on the highway. I grab my thermos of instant coffee and walk down toward the lake. Dew shimmers on the grass. Small birds twitter and jump frenetically around the low shrubs that line the path. My limbs feel loose and long, finally free from the heat, though the smoke-choked sun is staging a comeback, peeking out from the edge of the earth like a hazy fireball. I sip at the tepid coffee and some spills down my chin.

"Dammit!" My anger flares but it's Felix I'm thinking about. *How fucking dare he?*

Wiping away the coffee, I walk past the silent playground, away from the tower and over to where the lake curls out sharply from the path. The trees, mainly gums, hang low here, dipping sporadically into the water. There is only a clumsy rail to prevent people from stepping off the path and tumbling into the water. At night, it would be easy to slip and become tangled in the greenery and be eaten by the earth. We used to come down here and covertly smoke cigarettes during lunch, planting ourselves in the gazebo at the end of the pier so that we could spot the teachers coming. A strange flutter of desire for a cigarette bubbles inside me and I almost laugh, wondering whether the craving will ever fully leave me. I make do with another sip of coffee instead. I keep walking. I know I'm going to where she was found in the water but I take my time.

A rumble of thunder rolls across the sky and I look up to see I'm being watched by several sets of solemn glass eyes: the dark windows of the houses built high along the ledge that runs the length of the parkland look down at me. If only someone had seen something that night. No one in this town can keep to themselves so it seems ironic that not one of the lakeside dwellers stepped out onto their balcony and saw Rosalind with her attacker. Only bleary-eyed Moira Foss, with her screaming baby and rows of spit towels blocking her view, heard something, but her observations hardly provided clarity.

A pretty jumble of rocks leads into the water where Connor Marsh first saw Rosalind floating just over a fortnight ago. Bouquets of flowers are arranged in a sloppy pyramid a few meters from the rocks. Damp teddy bears and soggy envelopes poke out between the heads of flowers. I squat next to the makeshift shrine. Such an insignificant spot before this. Not a place that anyone would have thought to stop at, not even to pause and look out over the lake. There are far better vantage points.

Another blast of thunder shudders and I relish the cool air lapping my face. The storm is getting closer. I wish I could summon the rain to turn me inside out and wash over me. Clean my soul.

I finish the coffee and grimace, screwing the lid on tight. I absently pass the thermos back and forth between my hands, trying to think. What would have made Rosalind come to the lake that night? Could someone have forced her to go with them? But how? Blackmail? Maybe someone had found out something that was damaging to her reputation. No one saw or heard anything that would indicate she was abducted. Was she lured to the lake with the promise of something? Money? Drugs? It doesn't fit.

Of course, despite my doubts, it could have been a random stranger, but that still wouldn't explain why she was at the lake in the first place. Plus, it just feels personal. Both Felix and I sensed that from the start. Nothing about Rosalind has ever seemed random anyway.

Maybe it was attempted rape that turned to murder. I've worked cases where the killer is frustrated that he can't perform and turns lethally violent as a result. Or did the killer get spooked while he was assaulting her? I shiver lightly, thinking about someone abusing her still-warm dead body. I wonder about her brothers. Could Timothy have been obsessed with her? Followed her here?

I pull a card out from the pile of tributes, exposing a picture of a white dove inside a ring of flowers. Damp has curled its edges. Sharp edits of Rosalind's possible final moments form a steady stream of film through my mind but nothing seems right. It's a random montage without a plot. A stray droplet hits me square in the eye and I blink, trying to clear the wetness. A scraping sound behind me on the path causes me to whirl around, hairs on end, still blinking through the water.

Rodney Mason swings his leg over his bike so that both feet are on the same side, slowing it to a stop.

"Hey." He looks past me to the shrine, swallowing heavily.

"Rodney. What are you doing here?"

He props his bike next to a tree. "Dunno. I guess I just wanted to come here. You know, to where it happened. Pay my respects."

I watch as he steps forward, balancing carefully on the rocks, and looks out toward the gazebo.

His eyes are closed as he says, "I never really come here, you know. 'Cause of Jake. Mum doesn't like it."

His shoes are worn and the cuffs of his jacket have holes in them. I can't tell if it's fashion or reflective of his financial circumstances. The Masons never had much money.

"Have you been here before now?"

He turns and looks at me. "Is that a trick question?"

"No."

"Okay."

He comes closer to me and I quickly stand and step back onto the path.

"I came here last week with some of the others from school." He shrugs, blinking quickly as he takes in all the flowers and toys. "Some of the girls said it would help."

"Did it help?"

"Dunno. I'm not really sure what it's supposed to help with. It's not like she can come back."

Another rumble breaks around us. Rodney looks heavenward. "It's weird without the heat today. I'd got so used to it."

"I was just thinking the same thing." I can't pull my eyes away from him. The face so like Jacob's. The color of their eyes an exact match.

"Do you still think about him?" he asks me.

Lightning sparks in the sky and is immediately followed by a release of large droplets that turn into sheets of rain. We stand rooted to the spot, looking at each other for a moment, and then I say, "Quick, this way!" and he follows me up the path, the dust turning to mud. Water pours down my face and I run into it. It feels good. My legs pump steadily underneath me. Strong. I can feel Rodney just behind me, our feet pounding in unison. I beep the car open and gesture for him to get in the passenger side. We heave ourselves in, breathless and soaked. There are still no other cars in the car park; probably no one will come here now with the rain like this. Inside the car, noise drops away as if we're inside a drum. Rodney is wiping water from his eyes with the bottom of his t-shirt, revealing his taut abdomen. Sparse dark hairs disappear into his waistband. He sees me looking.

"Let's get the air on, hey?" I fiddle with the keys, turning the car on and feeling relieved when the wind moves through the car, creating space between us. I feel like my body has reversed through time: I am eighteen, in love with Jacob, with the world in front of me. It's hard to breathe and there is a faint ringing in my ears.

"Jeez, it's really coming down out there." Rodney stares out the window. Lightning flashes in the sky and the trees are rag dolls waving for help.

"I still think about him all the time," I say.

He turns toward me, leaning his head back on the headrest, and sighs deeply. "Yeah. I do and I don't. Less often, but deeply. Like now I really feel it when I think about him. Do you know what I mean?"

"Yes. I'm sort of the same."

"You must see some pretty bad shit in your job though. I guess you get tough from all that."

I lean my head back like his and turn to him. "Sort of. It's hard to compare really. I don't know what I'd be like if I didn't do this. This is just how I am now."

He nods and twists his hands in his lap, and I remember that he did this the other day too. "Are you working right now? Is that why you're here?" he asks.

"Once you have a case everything you do is work. It's on your mind the whole time. You can't stop."

He seems to think about this for a while. "I guess that makes sense."

"Why wouldn't your mum let you come here?"

"I don't know. It's like she thought what Jake had done might be catching or something. She just didn't want me anywhere near where it happened. I don't know why we didn't move away. No money, I guess."

A lump forms in my throat. I'd all but forgotten Rodney back then. Flashes of a skinny little boy in hand-me-downs flicker in front of me. At the memorial he sat with his mother, owl-eyed and lost, surrounded by sobbing teenagers.

"I used to like it when you came to our house."

I smile. "Yeah, I liked it too. That was a long time ago. I was your age then."

"You have a kid now, right? I've seen you with him."

My heart clicks into a higher gear. "You have?"

"Sure. Just around, you know." His mouth twists into a strange smile. "Don't worry, I haven't been following you or anything."

The rain is coming down so hard I can't even see the lake. Water zig-zags across the windscreen.

"Must be nice to have a kid to look after." His hands fidget in his lap but he doesn't seem nervous. His voice is steady. His dark hair curls slightly from the rain and his lashes clump together like he's wearing mascara.

I nod, pushing the fan onto a higher speed. "Yes. I can barely remember what it was like before. Without him."

"Jake used to look after me a lot. You know, because he was so much older."

The lump in my throat is growing bigger and I take a deep breath around it. "I'm sorry, Rodney. You must have been so scared. I think I for-got how young you were. I wasn't thinking straight then."

"It's okay. Before he died he told me you broke up. I was sad about that. I reckon that's probably why he did it."

I think back to writing that note, the letters curling beautifully into Rosalind's prose.

"Yes, well, I don't know. You never really know what's in someone's head when they do something like that. And it was a long time ago."

"I talked to her about him, you know," he says.

I glance sideways at him, wondering if this whole thing is about to be resolved right here in my car. "What did you talk about?" I say, trying to keep my voice even.

The air in the car thins and the wet has started to seep through my clothes. I wish I was home in bed asleep, preferably drugged into a deep prolonged unconsciousness. On the highway blurry headlights bob through the trees. It feels like Rodney and I are completely alone, hidden from the rest of the world, which may or may not be real anyway.

"Everything really," says Rodney quietly. "She loved talking to me. She said that."

"Ms. Ryan said she loved talking to you?" I confirm.

"Yeah."

"So tell me what you talked about?" I ask.

He shrugs, seeming young again. "Everything. Jake. Her family. Me finishing school."

"Was it important for you to finish school?"

"She really wanted me to do well. She thought I had a real future in drama."

"Were you going to move to Queensland too?" I say.

His head whirls my way. "What?"

"Queensland," I repeat calmly. "Were you going to move there in the new year?"

"What? No." His eyes won't meet mine but I can't tell if he's lying.

"Ms. Ryan was planning to move there in the new year and I wondered whether you were going with her."

A faint flush dusts his cheeks. "No, no. I don't know anything about that. I've enrolled in uni. I'm going to do it by correspondence. Online."

"Doesn't that mean you can do it from anywhere?"

He gives me a somewhat defeated look. "Yeah, I guess. I want to keep working at the newsagent. You know, save some money."

"So you can get out of here? Isn't that what every teenager in Smithson wants to do? Get out of here?"

"Well, yeah. Eventually. It's hard with Mum. She's... well, her health is up and down."

"She needs you."

He shrugs. "I guess."

Rain smatters on the bonnet, slowing. I feel like I'm running out of time. "Rodney, were you here with her that night? Arranged to meet but it went bad? Did you fight?"

"No." He shakes his head furiously.

"You need to tell us. I know you were seeing her. Someone saw you together. I want to help you, Rodney."

I've thrown in Izzy's alleged sighting, hoping it will prompt him to speak. I think about getting a confession and the look on Felix's face when he finds out. I feel sick.

Rodney grabs my hand and pulls it toward his chest, wrapping his other hand around it.

"Rodney!" Sparks shoot up my arm and burn into my own chest. He pulls my hand to his mouth, mumbling into it. His breath tickles my skin and I don't want him to stop.

"I cared about her. A lot. I really did. But we didn't do anything. I never saw her outside of school. She wouldn't. I would never have hurt her. I swear." He releases the grip on my hand slightly. "Now I'm just kind of half asleep, you know? I don't really know what to do with all the time. It's like—" he wipes at his eyes "—there seems to be a lot more time now. I miss talking to her."

He looks so helpless. An inky-eyed puppy. I want to bundle him up and hold him like I hold Ben when he first wakes up in the morning. Then Rodney grips my hand again with an urgency that feels dangerous. He laces his fingers around it. I know I should pull away, tell him it's wrong, and a wave of confusion slides through me. An odd shiver of desire. I see a flash of white—a car is turning into the car park—and I yank my hand from Rodney's grip.

The rain has stopped and the world looks vibrant and sated.

"Your bike," I say.

He sees the other car and nods, opening the door and pulling his hood up over his head. Leaning into the door, he says, "I didn't hurt her. I would never have done that." He runs off toward the lake, the flat echo of the slamming door pulsing through my thoughts. He disappears between the trees and I lean back in my seat, my hands in my hair, pulling the skin on my face to either side. I choke on a sob that rises in my throat as my face collapses. I bite my lip hard and pull air into my nose and then release it slowly through my mouth. From shaky to steady. My body aches for Felix. I want to hold Ben. I want to go back in time to talk to Jacob. To stop myself from sending that note.

A man in his sixties has got out of his car and is attaching a leash to his dog's collar. The dog is a wriggling ball of fuzzy hair and is finding great joy in dancing through the brand-new puddles. The man looks at me curiously, then gives me a polite nod. He walks off, his dog jumping in mad circles as he coaxes it along the path. He probably thinks Rodney is my boyfriend and we've fought.

My car feels empty without Rodney. I want to be close to him again, together in our pain. I turn the engine on and sit there trying not to think until my heartbeat matches the thrum of the windscreen wipers and my mind is blank.

Chapter Sixty-one

I've felt like this before. Like I'm in a dark room, feeling for the edges of a door, but instead going round and round the dark square and forgetting where I've already checked. I am hollow.

Without discussing it, Felix and I have divided Rosalind's case in half, divvying up suspects and dispensing the outstanding tasks like pieces of an apple. I've got the Ryans. He has the teachers. I have Nicholson. He has the students—with the exception of Rodney.

"I spoke to Rodney Mason this morning," I announce at the informal check-in Jonesy requested. It's just me, Felix, Matthews and Kingston now. "He admitted to having feelings for Ms. Ryan."

"Feelings." Jonesy snorts, as if it's the worst condition imaginable. "Well, that sounds promising. What are you thinking, Woodstock? Were these feelings mutual?"

I recall Rodney's grip on my hand. The flatness in his stare. I think about Jacob picking me up and throwing me onto my bed, tickling me mercilessly and covering me with kisses. Laughing until my face ached. I remember somewhere deep in my soul the contented peacefulness of love-struck teenage tiredness settling deep in my limbs.

"He says they never acted on it. But they were definitely close. I think I believe him. But then there's what Izzy said she saw. I guess we can try to get permission to secure DNA and see if it's a match to the fetus."

"And if it's his?"

"Then we'll know, sir. We'll know he's lying about the relationship. That would be fairly telling." Then I quickly add, "We're also still looking at Timothy Ryan. His alibi is flimsy but there's no indication as to where else he was that night. And we can't write off John Nicholson either. We're at a bit of a dead end."

Felix's eyes narrow on me briefly.

"Well, figure it out." Jonesy looks stressed. He clears his throat unnecessarily. "Right, everyone, off you go."

I make a coffee in the kitchen. The kettle hisses against the quiet of the station. Phones bleat sporadically from the front desk. I can hear Kenny asking someone to slow down so that he can understand them, his voice cracking like a teenager's. I walk back to my desk, the hint of a headache forming at my temples. Papers ruffle gently in response to the creaking ceiling fans. The air-con still isn't fixed. Discarded coffee cups dot across the tops of messy desks. Stale smoke mingles with the smell of men and days of heat.

I stand still for a moment and look squarely at the pin board. Rosalind's face is large, surrounded by smaller photos of the crime scene and the autopsy. The coffee mixes sharply with the freshness of the apple I've just eaten but I drink past the taste. Slowly I take everything down from the board. Maps, photos, phone records, Post-its. I look at the neat little pile on the chair. I grab some fresh Post-its and map out a new timeline from scratch. I start with the Ryans arriving in Smithson in 1980. Olivia Ryan's affair with Nicholson in 1987. Rosalind's birth, Olivia's death a few days later. The RYAN business sky-rocketing. George marrying Lila in 1997. Rosalind starting to see Jacob in November 2005. Maybe earlier, I admit to myself. Jacob dying in December. Rodney is just seven years old. Rosalind moving away, studying, living in the city. Landing a job as a teacher in a large city school. The rumored relationship with the student there. Returning to Smithson in late 2011 and into her modest cottage on the highway. In 2012 she starts teaching at Smithson. Has a passion for drama and fights to produce the school play. Has a blowout with her brother at her dad's birthday in October 2015. She applies for a teaching job in Brisbane the same month. Izzy Mealor claims to have seen Rosalind and Rodney Mason kissing at the school in November. Her play opens on Friday, December 11. Rosalind Ryan is dead sometime that same evening. I am warned off the case with the roses a few days after the investigation begins. Ben is taken, another warning, one week later. John Nicholson confesses to believing Rosalind was his daughter the entire time.

I wriggle my toes, pulling each knee to my chest and stretching my stiff legs. I look up at my newly arranged board.

Could Jacob really be relevant to Rosalind's death or is that just a tempting thought because of the link between the two of them? I've told no one else about Rose dating him; it's not something that I've ever spoken about and I don't really want to start now. I imagine coming clean about what happened all those years ago and feel panic surge through me.

Who benefitted financially from Rosalind's death? Only her brothers directly. But for others, killing Rosalind might have been a way to stop secrets from spilling out. Maybe the father of her baby hadn't wanted her to keep it; hadn't wanted her telling everyone that he was the father. Was killing her a way of getting rid of the baby and keeping her quiet? Or was she involved in something bigger? Something we haven't even thought of yet?

The pieces dangle in front of me, not quite fitting together. I squint, trying to force the notes and pictures to make sense, until the only thing I can see clearly is Rosalind's face trapped in the middle, completely unfazed by the surrounding chaos.

Chapter Sixty-two

Wednesday, December 30, 11:17 a.m.

"I need to talk to you."

I try to place the voice. "Rodney? Is that you?"

"Yeah. Can we meet?"

"Hang on."

Felix eyes me from his desk. His hair looks different today. He's forgotten to put gel in it. I get up and walk the length of the station. "Okay." I duck into an empty interview room. "What's going on, Rodney?"

Rodney sounds like he's crying. Or has been. "I just want to talk to you. Can you meet me?"

"Sure. Sure. Um, do you want me to come and pick you up?"

"Um, yeah, no, that won't work. What about at the lake again?"

Discomfort bubbles inside me. "I don't think that's a good idea, Rodney. Do you want to come to the station?" I picture parading him along the beige corridor and instantly hope that he rejects my suggestion.

"No." He says the word like a bullet. "What about the pizza place by the little park near my house? It's always empty during the day. You know it?"

"Yeah. I know it."

We ring off and I walk out of the station to my car. As I pass the skate park, I stare at the base of the skate jump, marveling at the courage that must be needed to scale the peaks.

Rodney seems nervous as I slide into the booth across from him. Cherry's Pizza is clearly not popular during the day. A frail-looking man mechanically tosses pizza dough into circles behind the counter and there is only one other customer, a wizened-looking elderly woman heroically making her way through a large margherita. I don't recognize either of them. I kept a careful eye out on the way here to make sure I wasn't tailed by reporters and it appears my efforts were successful.

After a few moments, a fresh-faced girl all of thirteen appears to take our orders. Rodney asks for a milkshake, barely looking at her. I glance at the wine menu but settle for a milkshake too.

After she disappears into the kitchen, I duck my head, trying to catch his eye. "Are you okay, Rodney? Why did you want to see me?"

He twists his hands. "I don't know. I wanted to talk to you."

"What do you want to talk about?"

He looks at the fan, the door. His mind seems to be flitting around, almost like he's on something.

"Rodney?"

"I just don't have anyone to talk to. I like talking to you."

Warmth spreads in my chest before I catch myself. *Careful*, I think. "I like talking to you too," I say.

"I guess I just feel alone now. You know, doing the play again, it's like I'm *glad* we're doing it but it's so weird that she's not there."

"I can imagine."

"I don't think that anyone else really cares! They're all talking about next year and leaving Smithson and I just can't."

"You really loved her, didn't you, Rodney?"

The tendons in his jaw work hard. He looks at me with wounded eyes. "She just *understood* me. She got me."

I remember that Rodney turns eighteen in two weeks. If I collect his DNA now and file it in mid-January I won't have to get Donna Mason's permission. I can also decide whether I want to submit it at all.

"You know, Rodney," I say kindly, "there's a lot of talk about you, people saying things about the two of you. I could put a lot of it to rest with a DNA test."

"A DNA test?" he repeats.

"Yes." I stir the milky bubbles with my straw. "There's some evidence that we collected and if we could just get your DNA we could possibly remove you from the investigation."

He puffs out his cheeks. "Okay," he says, after a minute. "How long does it take?"

"Collecting your DNA is instant. We can do it right now; I have a kit in my bag. You just need to swab your mouth. The test will take a few weeks but I'm sure it will all be fine."

"Okay. I'll do it." His voice is flat and I wonder what he is thinking.

He doesn't ask what evidence I'm referring to. I don't mention the baby. Even if it was his, he may not know anything about it. I think about the baby I lost. It would have been about eight weeks along by now. The gravity of the decision I managed to dodge overwhelms me, and I paste on a smile and hand Rodney the DNA kit.

"Just push that along the inside of your cheek and that's it."

Rodney takes the kit from me and removes the swab, running it along the wall of his mouth before placing it back into the bag.

"Thanks, Rodney," I say, taking it from him, and I swear I can see all of his tiny cells scrambling around on its tip, holding all the answers.

Chapter Sixty-three

then

I folded the letter in half and placed it in the envelope. I looked at his name, written across the front like it should be sung. I slipped the envelope in the front page of my notebook and then put it into my bag. I only had an hour until daylight.

I cycled over to Jacob's house. The sparse streetlights lit my way, the ground steamed from the recent rain. I counted on Jacob being up first. He often roamed around the house till late, watching TV, before waking early. For a moment I panicked, thinking that perhaps he was staying at her house, but Donna would never let him do that, and I could see his bike propped next to the front door, his sneakers parallel with Rodney's.

I leaned my bike on the fence beside the letterbox, got the envelope out of my bag and walked toward the house. I stared at myself in the glass of the windows, which had turned to mirrors in the early-morning light.

Before I could have second thoughts, I slid the envelope underneath the front door.

Chapter Sixty-four

Wednesday, December 30, 5:18 p.m.

I pick Ben up early from my dad's. He wraps his small arms around my neck as I kiss Dad good-bye then bundle him into the car. We drive. I'm not sure where we're going but I don't feel like going home. Scott has agreed to help one of the neighbors rebuild a fence this afternoon and even though we haven't discussed Ben returning to Cloud Hill yet, instinctively it doesn't feel like an option right now. Maybe it never will be. Everything seems temporary at the moment.

I turn corners at random, following the curves of the road. The idea of stopping, of having to do anything beyond aimless driving, seems impossible.

Ben kicks the back of my seat.

"Hey, sweetheart, stop that, come on."

"Want toast."

"You can't have toast, baby. I can't cook toast in the car."

Ben replies with a swift kick to the door.

"Ben, please. Look, we'll stop and get some fruit. I know a place just up ahead."

We whip past patchwork paddocks. The sun has dipped toward the earth, shooting sideways like a laser beam. Melancholy cows watch us, their mournful stares providing a distraction for Ben, who mercifully stops kicking the seat. I pull into the roadside stall and buy a small box of strawberries and a bag of blueberries.

"Berries!" he says with a hand out.

"Hang on, hang on. We'll just go up the road a bit."

I park in the rest stop under the shade of a giant gum. A few chairs and tables pepper the edge of the car park but I coax Ben to an oasis of faded green at the tip of the curve where the mountain juts out and you can stare forever at the infinite fields. The sky is the sea, the land its sandy base. It's beautiful. I haven't thought to come here for years. Smithson is surrounded by pockets of nature's best. Valleys pool with emerald green moss, ferns carry the faces of exotic tigers, flowers the color of rare gems. The air is cleaner up here: we're above the haze that hugs the town, above all the judgment that gets stuck in my lungs and pulls me down. I pan evenly across the outlook, catching myself as I complete my scan. It's not like I'm going to be able to spot the killer from up here. Looking down at Smithson like this does make it seem more possible though. It's smaller. More manageable. I see the large square of the Carling plant, the tiny dots of houses, the sketchy roads. Sonny Lake, the shot tower. Catching the killer shouldn't be so hard, but somehow once I'm back among the Lego-like rows of houses and familiar shops, everything is closer and yet further away. Rodney's down there somewhere, I think. I wonder what he's doing. Rehearsing for the play? Or is he at the lake, staring out at the water, missing Rose? I move my eyes back to Ben, who is chomping contentedly on his blueberries, staring at the view, a wine-colored rim quickly forming around his lips.

"You had a good Christmas, Ben?"

He nods, still eating.

"That's good." I shift over next to him in the shade and kick off my shoes and socks. I pick fluff from between my toes. Move them back and forth in a slow wave before pushing them into the dry earth.

"Hey, Ben, maybe we'll go on a holiday soon. Would you like that?"

He bobs his head up and down. "Peppa Pig goes on holidays."

"Cool," I say. "Well, I think it would be nice to go on a holiday."

"With Daddy?"

A beat goes by. I was imagining Felix and I somehow escaping to a cozy cabin, or perhaps a stormy beach house, with Ben in tow. Away from the heat and the rest of the world. Ridiculous. He has three teenage daughters, and a wife for good measure. Plus, he's not even talking to me right now. Our life together is a fantasy, one that I need to put a lid on. "Sure, Daddy will come."

"I like holidays."

"Good. Maybe we'll go somewhere cold. That might be nice, huh?"

"Like snow?"

"Well, maybe not snow."

Paris, England, Vancouver. All these places that I was supposed to see but haven't. My mother used to tell me about skiing: the feeling of trusting your feet, the feeling of flying. I look at Ben and imagine his tiny body whipping down a mountain. I imagine all the things he will do, far, far away from Smithson. And suddenly there's a lump in my throat and I'm jumping back to my feet, wiping my soles on the grass.

"Look at you. You're like a little vampire." I yank some Wet Ones from my bag and dab the berry juice off Ben's mouth. He squeals and squirms away.

After the blueberries are gone and the strawberries are nothing more than green, tuft-like weeds, we go for a walk. Ben wants to pick flowers. We assemble a ragged-looking posy of wildflowers and bracken that is appealing in a home-cooked kind of way.

"Look at this!" I fasten them together with a hair tie. "They're beautiful, Ben. Should we take them home and put them in a vase?"

"I want to give them to Daddy."

I block out the sun with my hand. I can't seem to get away from it.

"That's a nice idea. He'll love them."

The cicada chorus kicks up a notch. Shrill, the noise bores into the air as I help Ben into the car and start down the mountain, along the familiar curves, back into Smithson.

Chapter Sixty-five

Thursday, December 31, 8:24 a.m.

Candy's article details everything: from the time of Ben's kidnapping to him being found in our backyard a few hours later. The kidnapper is described as a middle-aged woman who claimed to be Ben's grandmother. There's even a quote from Madeleine at the day-care center and a reference to a piece of evidence linked strongly to the Rosalind Ryan murder case.

Propelled into Jonesy's office by a force beyond my control, I'm in such a rage I can't even feel my face.

"What the fuck is this?" I throw the paper onto his desk.

He looks up at me and I can tell he's already seen it.

I read from the paper, "'The question that we should really be asking ourselves is whether or not Detective Woodstock should keep working on this case. It seems impossible for her to remain impartial now that there is such a clear threat to her family.' I mean, what is this? Do we have a leak?"

Jonesy pushes his chair away from his desk and stands up. He looks tired and old. A stain on his shirt sneaks out from behind his jacket.

My phone is going ballistic in my pocket. I don't even want to look at it. Scott, my dad, Aunt Megan. Everyone will be wanting something from me. Blaming me. How could I let this happen to my son?

"Do you need to get that?" Jonesy says, jerking his head toward my buzzing pocket.

"No. What I need to be doing is getting on with my job. But that seems kind of fucking impossible right now, doesn't it?"

I spin on my heel and storm out, leaving an open-mouthed Jonesy in my wake.

I spend the next few hours brooding around the station like a thunder cloud. My fists clench involuntarily and I manage to drop a full cup of takeaway coffee on my shoes. I want to kill Candy, watch her eyes bug out of her head as I strangle her, but somehow I refrain from calling her office. Honestly, I'm mainly afraid of what I might say.

Scott is looking after Ben today. He's not working again until mid-January. Everyone else from the worksite has gone away for summer. It's only us who have nowhere to go. I don't call him; I just can't deal with it right now.

In the end I'm sick of my own company and I call Dad back, pacing manically in front of the park bench behind the station, listening as he wonders how this could have happened and how I could have kept it from him. His voice is rough-edged, the anger unfamiliar and sharp.

"Gemma, help me understand why you didn't tell me about this."

"Dad, I'm working a murder case. I know you don't really understand what that means but there is procedure. I can't tell you everything. Does that make sense?" I choke back a sob. "Plus, we didn't want to upset you."

Dad doesn't speak for a moment. At last he says, "Gemma, I understand how important your job is, but this is about our Ben—not some fact about a clue."

"He's not 'our Ben', he's mine!" I click the phone off and shove it in my pocket, which is nowhere near as satisfying as throwing it on the ground like I want to do. Instead, I try to calm down, watching as a blowfly stuck in the sticky strands of a web tries desperately to break free, its tormented buzzing loud in my ears.

Chapter Sixty-six

Thursday, December 31, 2:37 p.m.

I get into a patrol car and head to Gowran. My argument with Dad has upset me and I grip the wheel and grit through tears that I refuse to unleash. I haven't told Jonesy where I'm going, which is not the smartest idea, but I simply can't deal with having to explain myself right now. For the briefest moment I wonder what Felix is doing, but that line of thinking will get me even more worked up than I am already, so I focus on driving, staring at the reliable horizon and taking the kind of deep breaths that I was taught the one time I tried meditation. Paddocks flick past with cows huddled around the fence posts. Rows and rows of fruit trees reach up to the sun.

The drive takes about an hour, and by the time I arrive I'm feeling anxious and remember why I never went back to that meditation class.

Gowran was once a wealthy mining town and the architecture always makes me want to stand up a little bit straighter. I walk into the open-air shopping complex, slightly bemused by the exotic coffees on the menu at the country kitchen café. Little old Gowran has clearly propelled itself into the mainstream. The small space is writhing with teenagers, who all appear to be spending their hard-earned holiday cash on various forms of caffeine and cream, the excessive price tag clearly a matter of value perception.

Rosalind had several ticket stubs in her rubbish bin and bedside drawer from the Gowran cinema and, even though it's a long shot, I figure I'll ask the guys on the counter if they remember her and, if they do, are they able to recall who she came with. The fact that Rosalind went to Gowran is suspicious. It's a two-hour round trip and there is a cinema complex in Smithson that shows all the same films. But Gowran is much larger than Smithson; I think its population is almost sixty thousand. It's arguably a place someone might come if they want to hide in plain sight. I'd planned on sending one of the uniforms on this inquiry mission but there is no one left now. Really, I just wanted to get out of Smithson, and this seemed as good a red herring to follow up as any.

The staff on the cinema ticket booths look incredibly young but I assume they must be at least fifteen. I wait for a lull and then amble over to speak to them. Explaining that I'm a detective, I show them the picture of Rosalind and ask if they remember seeing her.

"Oh yeah," says a particularly angelic-looking boy with ringlets pulled into a ponytail. "The dead girl. She used to come here all the time."

A girl with a pixie cut and a square jaw smacks her gum and manages to serve a customer while talking to me. "Yeah. She did. Almost every Friday or Saturday."

"She come alone?" I ask them.

"Sometimes."

Another kid leans in front of me from behind and I whip round, holding my arms out in defense.

"Whoa." A girl with matching braids stands back, her arms up. She giggles. "That was kind of cool. But I was just trying to look at the picture." Leaning across me again, she pushes some stray hairs behind her ears. "Oh yeah, her. Always here. The boys used to go crazy trying to serve her and shit."

"Is there a manager on today?" I say.

Braids girl smiles at me. "I am the manager."

"Oh, right." I swallow my surprise. "Do you remember whether she came with anyone?"

"She was alone, I think."

"Nah, she was with a guy a bunch of times," says the boy with ringlets.

I spin back around to face him. "What did he look like?"

"Dunno really," he says. "I just remember sometimes she bought two tickets. And I saw her at the candy bar with a guy."

"Young? Old?"

"Ah, young, I think. Like your age?"

"I reckon I saw her with her dad. Some old guy," the pixie-faced girl chimes in helpfully.

I turn back to the manager, who is putting change in the tills.

"You have cameras here?"

"I think so." We both glance up to see a clapped-out camera that looks like it was made before electricity was invented.

"I'm going to need your camera footage from the past few months. I want to see anything you have with this woman on it." I hold Rosalind's photo up again and she stares out at us serenely.

"Roger that." The girl with the braids waves in a clumsy salute. "Don't know how to do it but I know it can be done. I'm on it."

"Great, thank you. Here's my card. Contact me directly if you find anything. My guys will go through anything you've got."

"Will do."

A slow electronic ticker broadcasts a loop of pixels across the top of the candy bar menu, advertising the movies on show. I imagine what it would be like to head back to the boy with the ringlets, buy a ticket to some shoot-'em-up gangster flick, grab some popcorn and disappear into the darkness for a couple of hours. I can see Rosalind here: the faux European walkways are a homage to the world of art that made so much sense to her.

Shaking my head, I wave at the ticket crew, who return it cheerily, and head back to my car. The air-con takes a while to get going so I stand outside, letting it do its thing for a few minutes. Checking my phone, there's nothing from Felix, but there's a text from Dad apologizing and an angry voicemail from Jonesy apologizing for the Candy article but also demanding to know where the fuck I am.

As I get into the car, my eyes stinging with the transition from hot to cold, I notice a couple in a parked car about twenty meters away. The woman's bright red hair catches my eye. I shrink down in my seat and watch John Nicholson and Izzy Mealor, heads bent close together. Izzy smiles at him before tilting her face so that he can kiss her on the lips.

Chapter Sixty-seven

Thursday, December 31, 5:42 p.m.

I go to the lake. It suddenly seems to have a magnetic pull, drawing me close. I walk a lap briskly and then another more slowly. I look out at the shimmering bed of glass, wishing it would part and show me the way. Footsteps tap behind me and blurry shapes form in the water but no one else is here, it's just me and the whispering lake.

Really, all I want is to speak to Felix. My body aches for him. I'm barely eating and I drift in between wakefulness and sleep with alarming ease.

I should tell him about Nicholson and Izzy, but at the same time there is a delicious addiction to the pain of weaning myself off him. Plus, I know if I contact him and say I need to talk about the case, he'll think I just want to see him. My anger at this likely assumption makes my blood boil. In the end I do call him, but it goes to voicemail, so I leave him a message saying we need to speak about Nicholson.

I head back to the station. Everyone is out preparing for the inevitable dangers that come with one year transitioning to the next. The silence needles my brain. I run comprehensive searches on Izzy Mealor but turn up nothing. I can't help thinking that her claim about witnessing Rosalind with a student is fueled by jealousy. Perhaps she thought that Nicholson had a crush on Rose and she wants to posthumously cast her in a bad light. Or is she planting a red herring to put us off course? Whatever the case, Nicholson told us that he doesn't endorse staff relationships and Izzy certainly wasn't forthcoming about her romance with him.

Perhaps they're somehow in on this together. Nicholson might have gone to the school that night and somehow lured Rosalind to the lake.

I want something to break, something to happen. This case is so still. Taunting me.

I need to eat. Rustling through my drawer, I find a crumpled instant soup packet and mix it into some boiling water in the kitchen. My face prickles with sweat as I drink the hot liquid and I push my lank hair behind my ears. Restless and out of breath, I can't seem to sit. I'm staring at the pin board when I feel a tap on my shoulder.

"Jesus!" I reel around.

Felix looks equally startled and steps away from me. "Sorry. I saw you standing there. I called you back but you weren't picking up."

I grope at my pockets for my phone but it's not there.

"Oh. Must have left it in the car. Or maybe it's on my desk…" I'm light-headed, his presence unsteadying me. He seems more solid than normal, somehow anchored to the ground as I struggle to stay upright.

"So you have something new on Nicholson?" His voice is all business.

"Yes! Yes. I do. I saw…"

"Gemma, you're bleeding." Felix immediately softens, peering at the side of my face.

"What?"

"You've got a cut on your cheek. Come in here."

He leads me to the disabled bathroom.

I touch the side of my face as I follow him. My fingers are stained red when I pull them away.

"See?" Felix points to the mirror and I see a red smudge in front of my ear. "What happened?"

"I don't know. I scratched myself, I guess. I don't remember."

"It looks pretty bad. Here." Felix wets a paper towel and dabs it at my wound, which slowly turns from orange to red to an angry brown, exposing a fine scabbing line.

"It's not that bad."

"Gemma." Felix leans against the bathroom sink and looks at me, eyes searching, wanting an answer but I don't know what for.

"What?" I say again.

He pauses and then shakes his head. "Nothing. So tell me what you have on Nicholson."

"I saw him in Gowran today. At the cinema. The one in the middle of the shopping strip."

If Felix is surprised at my being in Gowran he doesn't show it.

"He was with Izzy Mealor."

"The teacher?"

"Yes. I saw them kissing."

Felix nods slowly. "Okay. Yeah. Okay. That is something." He rakes his fingers through his hair. "So much for his views on staff relationships. Fuck, everyone in this town has something to hide."

The irony sits in the air between us but Felix seems too distracted to notice.

"Maybe it was Izzy who took Ben?" I say. "We know that the woman was probably wearing a wig." I'm charged with the possibility of a solve, and rattling around in my excitement is relief at the idea of Rodney not being a part of it. Of him simply being an innocent bystander who stepped a little too close.

Felix sighs. "I don't think so, Gem. The description of the kidnapper is much older. Izzy's younger than you."

"Oh, come on. It could be her. She could have made herself look older. We should at least consider it."

"Okay. Okay." He holds out his hands and I realize I am in a fight stance, legs apart, ready to strike. "We'll look into it."

"Good."

It's cooler in the bathroom and for the first time in days I feel like I can find a way around my thoughts. I look at Felix, take in his clear pale skin, the strong profile, his cap of hair and dark lashes.

"What's going on?" I say at the exact moment he says, "Gemma, I'm worried about you."

"Why?" I step away from him.

"I think…" He pauses, seemingly gathering his thoughts. "I think this case has messed with you. Perhaps more than you realize."

"Really?"

"Yes! C'mon, Gemma. You're all over the place. Not thinking straight. Now, I'm not saying you're not doing your job, but it's not healthy." He pushes a hand through his hair, his tired eyes on me. "I don't think this thing with us is helping."

"Oh. Right. So you're doing me a favor. Is that it? Poor little Gemma." White heat flashes in front of me as I draw myself as tall as I can. "I don't think so. I think that you've had enough of me. Simple as that. It all got a bit too real when you met my son. Saw my house. Saw Scott." My voice breaks but I keep going, vaguely aware of the other Gemma in the mirror. "What happened, Felix? It got too serious? Too fucking hard?"

"I don't know, Gem. I just…I don't know. I care about you a lot; I have from the start. But where does this end? I can't see the end. Can you?"

I'm shaking, suddenly ice cold. "I don't fucking know," I screech, surprising myself. "I want you to have the answers. Don't you get that?"

"That's not fair, Gem. We're equals in this. That's the deal."

"No." My voice has dropped dangerously low. "There is no deal. That's the problem. That's why you can walk away at any time like it's nothing. That's why you can still be sleeping with your wife and not have to explain anything to me."

"Gemma, please. We need to find a way to make this work. We need to—"

"I don't need to do anything!" I whirl at him, my fist on his chest. I still want him so much. "I lost a baby, you know. *Your* baby. Unlike you, I'm not fucking anyone else, so I know that it was yours. So don't tell me that you don't know where this ends. That we need to find a way to make this work."

His face drains of color. He blinks at me as if I am a stranger.

"Oh, Gemma." He holds me briefly, strong arms on either side of my head, the musky scent of him almost as familiar as my own smell, but then he pushes away, shaking his head. "How could you not tell me? How? You have too many secrets." He cups my chin with his hands and looks at me as if he can't believe what he's about to say. "I just can't do this anymore, Gem. I'm sorry. I'm sorry for everything."

He turns and walks out of the bathroom, the door swinging wide behind him. I look at the Gemma standing alone in the white cell, red-faced and heaving, her jaw clenching beneath a fresh crimson wound.

Chapter Sixty-eight

Friday, January 1, 8:40 a.m.

"Happy New Year, Woodstock." Matthews greets me when I walk into the station. "Weird how it feels just like last year, huh? Broken air-con and all."

"Sure does. And last year felt like the one before that." I smile at Matthews. He's made a real effort with me since Ben's kidnapping.

Late last night Matthews called to let me know that some CCTV footage had finally turned up from the day of Ben's kidnapping. It shows a red car, just like the one Grace from the day-care center had described, at the base of the mountain outside a garden supplies outlet. That stretch of road is an obvious route for the kidnapper to take, so Matthews is treating it as the strongest lead we have so far. The driver is all hair and dark glasses, but there is a blur of a small white face that suggests Ben is in the back.

The numberplates aren't visible on the tape.

"I'm sorry it's not more, Woodstock," Matthews said kindly. "I want to put this one to bed for you."

"Thank you," I said to him. "Hopefully it leads somewhere."

Now I am tired even though I was asleep just after midnight. I watched the rainbow explosion shatter the Sydney Harbor Bridge with Ben's sleeping body next to mine as I sipped at a weak vodka. I thought about Felix as I counted down into a new year, his apology ringing in my ears. Scott had gone out with Craig. When I woke just after 5 a.m. I had a text on my phone saying he was crashing at Craig's place because he couldn't get a cab.

Stroking Ben's head, I wondered whether Scott really was at Craig's. What if he was actually at some girl's place, locked in a desperate, sweaty tangle? Hours later I'm still trying to work out whether I would care either way.

As it was, I started the new year with the obligatory health kick, boiling eggs and squeezing a dash of lemon juice into a glass of water. When was the last time I went for a run? October? Before the heat. Funny how I still think a token decent meal will fix weeks of abuse. Ben was ratty, throwing his spoon on the floor and kicking his small feet on the underside of the table.

"I'm sorry," I said to Dad when I dropped him off. "He slept well. I don't know what's wrong with him."

"He's fine. Don't worry, Gem," Dad said. He's been on guard since our argument. Tiptoeing around me like I'm a ticking bomb. "We'll be fine, won't we, young man?" he said to Ben.

Ben scowled at him and then at me, and I reversed down the driveway wishing I didn't need to rely on Dad so much. Alone, I drove to the station, the eggs digesting noisily in my guts, a faint memory rolling through my mind of Mum holding out an egg to me, laughing because she had stuck little yellow pom-poms on it, along with some orange pipe-cleaner and googly eyes so that it looked like a demented chicken.

Kenny accosts me just as I'm heading to the bathroom. "Call for you, Gemma. It's one of the Ryan brothers. He says it's urgent."

Felix's eyes meet mine before he quickly looks away. I straighten my shoulders and say, "I'll take it in an interview room," and head into one. I don't turn the light on and sit with my back to the wall as the phone rings.

"Hello?"

"Yes, hello. Ms. Woodstock. Detective, I mean. Sorry. I don't really know what to call you. It's Marcus Ryan." His polite voice carries lightly down the phone line, reminding me of a flickering candle.

"Marcus, hello," I say as warmly as possible, even though my patience is nearing zero. "How can I help you?"

"Oh, well, it's my father, you see. He's...well, we're at the hospital. He's been very unwell these past few days. He wants to talk to you."

"Yes, I called him the other day but he never called me back. Do you know what he wants to speak to me about?"

"About Rose, I think. I don't know what exactly, but it's obviously important. The thing is, you need to come today. The doctors said that you should come quickly."

"I'm sorry to hear he's so ill, Marcus."

"Yes. Well. It has been a very difficult few weeks."

"He's at Our Lady?"

"Yes."

"I'll be there as soon as I can." I place the phone down and sit in the dark for a few moments, steadying my hands on the table in front of me, before walking back out into the station room.

"What's going on, Woodstock?" Jonesy's obviously been alerted to the call.

Everyone looks up and I feel small and shrunken standing in the dark doorway.

"It's George Ryan, sir. He's still in the hospital. I don't think he has long from the sounds of it. He wants to speak to me."

I carefully avoid looking at Felix but hope that he will decide to come with me.

Despite what he said last night, I think that if we can just talk, spend some time together, surely we can work out how to patch the gaps that have formed over the past few weeks. Relax into our rhythm again. We just need time.

I start to gather my things. I feel Felix's chair slide out as he stands.

"I'll come with you, Woodstock," says Jonesy, walking briskly to the door. "C'mon."

I glance briefly at a slightly bewildered Felix before following after Jonesy obediently.

"So he's really dying, is he?" says Jonesy, breaking the silence.

"That's the impression I got from his son Marcus," I reply.

"Is this likely to be a deathbed confession?"

Jonesy is driving and I'm having trouble keeping my hands still.

"I'd be very surprised if that was the case. George has the tightest alibi of everyone. McKinnon and I toyed with the possibility that he arranged to have her killed—he certainly has the money—but that never went anywhere. But he obviously wants to get something off his chest. Maybe he knows something."

"Well, it's a good thing that he trusts you. Good job there."

"Thank you."

Jonesy grunts and takes a corner too wide.

"Sir," I begin.

He talks over me. "How are you holding up?" He keeps his eyes resolutely glued to the road and I realize that this is what this impromptu joint venture is all about. A chat. Sunlight cuts across us like blades as we fly past a wall of overhanging gums.

"I'm fine."

"A pretty rough few weeks."

"Yeah."

"You've got a good little boy in Ben."

"I know."

"And your man seems solid. Decent. My mate Dan knows him. He's in construction. Says he's a good bloke."

I shift in my seat, willing the conversation away. "I guess."

"Suppose what I'm saying is that it can be hard to see the wood from the trees or whatever they say. You see what I mean?"

"Yes, sir."

"You've got a lot going on in your head, Woodstock. Kid, husband, this crazy shit." He flings his hand away from the steering wheel as if to point out the madness all around us.

"Scott's not my husband."

"Same thing these days."

Our Lady Private Hospital rises out of the landscape as we exit the corridor of trees.

"Look, I'm not sure you and McKinnon are a good pair."

"What?"

"I'm splitting you up. I want you with Matthews and McKinnon with Kingston."

My throat constricts. I'm terrified I will cry. "But, sir..."

"It's decided, Woodstock. My job is to see over the mountains. Above things. And that's what this is about. It's good to mix things up. You and Matthews will make a good match." He laughs. "He'll learn a ton from you."

I swallow furiously. "But McKinnon and I can finish the Ryan case?"

"Yes, Woodstock." Jonesy turns into the hospital car park. He doesn't move his body, only his arms. "Right now all I want is for you and McKinnon to finish the bloody Ryan case."

Chapter Sixty-nine

Friday, January 1, 9:47 a.m.

George Ryan is channeling a day-time TV patriarch. Dressed in navy satin pajamas, he is propped somewhat dramatically on a cloud of cushions. I half expect him to reveal an evil twin or a secret affair with the housecleaner. Instead, he waves us in, managing to retain his regal stature despite being horizontal.

The décor is much nicer than Smithson Central Hospital. Large framed oil paintings hang on the far wall and light spills in through a giant window. It's more like a hotel than a hospital room.

George's hands are riddled with sunspots that look dark against his pale skin. He's thinned in the past week, his eyes sitting deep in his face.

"Detective Chief Superintendent Ken Jones, Mr. Ryan," Jonesy says as we enter the room.

George leans forward and fixes his eyes on Jonesy as if confirming that this is his real name.

"Hello, Mr. Ryan," I say.

He nods at us in turn and rolls his eyes toward the chairs.

We sit.

He jabs at a button on the side of the bed and a mechanism whirrs into action, lifting him up. "I'm dying."

The slow beep of the machine counts down the seconds of silence.

"Your cancer," I venture, wanting to say something.

"Yes. Apparently I've got days if I'm lucky."

"I thought the operation was successful?"

"Apparently not. Or it was but now something else is wrong."

"I'm very sorry to hear that, sir."

"Yes. Well. I had hoped to know what happened to my daughter first."

"We're making good progress on your daughter's case, but we are still working through several scenarios," Jonesy says evenly.

George shifts uncomfortably and fixes his gaze on me.

"Mr. Ryan, you wanted to tell us something?" I ask.

"Yes. I did." He sighs heavily. "My daughter, Rose, she wasn't like other people. I know every parent thinks their child is special, but I really think she was unique."

I try to block out the fact that Rose probably wasn't his biological daughter and just listen.

"We had a good relationship, but I did feel differently about her than my sons. Maybe because she was a girl or maybe it was her personality. I'm afraid she took after my wife, Olivia. She could be quite manipulative. It was hard to connect with her sometimes, especially when she was a teenager."

"I think that's very common."

George looks at Jonesy. "Yes, I know. But Rose was different. It was like she had a fire burning inside her. I can't really explain it. There was always some kind of trouble. That boyfriend from school, some issue with a teacher at university, then that business with the student at the school she taught at in Sydney. And even with her brothers, there was always lying and . . . odd behavior. Inappropriate things. She wanted their attention and I wasn't comfortable with it. I bought her that place because I thought it was best that she lived away from them—especially the two younger ones, who were still at home. And then she ended up changing her mind and leaving Smithson almost straight after school anyway."

He laughs, as if dismissing the strangeness of the world, and shifts in his bed before giving up on finding a new position. The veins on his temples pulse softly. "Anyway, I guess it doesn't matter now."

"How did your sons feel about Rosalind?"

"I don't know, but they didn't really stay in touch with her after she left. Only Marcus did. He was always very good, calling Rose and making sure we saw her at Christmas. I kept in touch with her as well, but it was hard."

"Mr. Ryan, you said that the last time you saw your daughter was at your birthday in October. Is that true?"

"Yes."

"Was it unusual for the family to be together like that? Sounds like Rosalind didn't go out of her way to see her brothers."

"It was quite unusual. I knew it would be a tense night, but I'd asked them all to come because of my health. I figured it was likely to be my last birthday. I spoke to them about my finances and my plans. I think they were surprised at how much was going to be left to charity. And then Timothy made a big point of Rosalind not being entitled to as much of my estate because I'd already purchased the cottage for her. Of course, he didn't acknowledge that I'd also paid for him to go overseas and contributed to various things for him and his brothers. He was not in the mood to listen. I made it clear that I wasn't happy with his attitude."

"Did he threaten her?" Jonesy asks.

"Not physically, but he was very angry. Calling her names and accusing her of manipulating everyone. Marcus and I calmed him down. I knew he had a temper but I'd not really seen that side of him before. That's why I was so surprised when he told me he went to see her play, but he said he did it to make amends."

"Do you believe him?" I ask.

"I did. But then..." He shifts his weight again and winces. "Well, the boys all came in to see me last night to wish me a happy new year. Amelia, Bryce's girlfriend, came too. We had some food here in the room and then I dozed off. I've been sleeping a lot since I've been in here, from the drugs. I woke up at about eight-thirty. The door to my room was open but the lights were off. At first I thought I was alone, but then I realized that Timothy was still here with Amelia. They were standing near the door, talking. I don't know where Bryce was. They didn't notice I'd woken up and they were talking about the police interviews. Timothy said something about it all being fine. He told Amelia that she didn't need to worry. I kept my eyes closed so they would think I was still asleep, but then there was no sound so I presumed they'd gone. When I opened my eyes they were kissing."

Chapter Seventy

then

My hands were clammy and it didn't seem to matter how many times I wiped them. After I left Jacob's I rode around for a while, steering my bike in giant loops along the old dirt track in the reserve at the back of my house. The sun was only just stirring and I wondered over and over whether he'd read the note yet.

I couldn't sit still so I headed to Ronson Shopping Center and watched some kids skateboard through the outdoor food court. Pigeons looked on indignantly from the roof. I'd arranged to meet Fox here later. He wanted to go to the movies and I figured it would be better to do something to take my mind off Jacob. Plus, going to the movies was good, not quite an alibi but a normal teenage thing to do. It wouldn't arouse any suspicion.

The Ryan phone number was on a piece of notebook paper in my pocket. I told myself I'd make the call at 8:30 a.m. I doubted that Jacob would go to her house earlier than that on a weekend. I didn't know exactly how these things worked; I only remembered that when there was a bomb threat at the school we were all evacuated. I figured that the Ryans would be taken out of their house and wouldn't be able to see anyone for the rest of the day. Maybe longer. I thought that George Ryan might even suspect that Jacob had something to do with it and forbid Rosalind from seeing him. That was if Jacob even wanted to see her after reading the letter.

I wandered into the shopping center and bought a muffin from the bakery. I ate less than a quarter of it before I threw it in the bin.

It was almost time.

I headed to the payphone that was tucked behind the walkway, out of sight.

I picked up the phone, dropped the coins in the slot and dialed the number.

"Hello," a man's deep voice answered, and my knees almost gave way, but I made a fist in front of my mouth and said in the deepest, grainiest voice I could summon, "There's a bomb. In your house. You need to get out *now*."

Chapter Seventy-one

Friday, January 1, 1:02 p.m.

I haul a hungover Timothy Ryan in for questioning and do laps around him in the interview room. I have no idea whether what George Ryan told us is relevant or not, but I saw the fear in his eyes, sparked by the possibility that Timothy had crossed the darkest of lines, and his gut feeling was enough to make me give it another shot with his son.

"Timothy, you know this is a murder investigation."

"Yeah."

"Good. I was just reminding you that this is about as serious as it gets. Money can't buy anyone out of murder. And you are already on our radar. Violent tendencies, anger issues. It doesn't look very good, does it?"

He eyes me petulantly.

"Right? Okay. So. Tell me about your relationship with Amelia Posen."

He sits back, the air puffing out of him. "Amelia is my brother's girlfriend."

"Oh yes, I know that." My voice drips with sarcasm.

"Well, that's it really."

"Try again," I say.

"I don't know what you want me to say."

"I want you to tell me where you were on the evening of Friday, December 11."

"At the school play. I told you."

"Try again."

He looks at me, his chin raised, and then reaches out to pick up the glass of water I placed in front of him. His Adam's apple bobs maddeningly as he drinks every last drop before saying, "I was with Amelia."

"Where?"

"At her parents' house. She called me and said she wanted to see me. I told her I had tickets to the play. I hate all that live performance shit but I felt bad for being a dick to Rose at Dad's birthday and wanted to make it up to her. I'd gone right off at her, but it wasn't really her fault. Dad always spoiled her. He pretends to be such a hard-arse but really he's a pushover, especially when it comes to her. Drives me mad. Anyway, I knew that Amelia had plans with Bryce so I was going to go along and find someone to come with me, but then Amelia said she would fake a migraine to get out of seeing Bryce. That if I came over she'd make it worth my while. So I ditched the play and did that instead."

"How often do you see her?"

"Depends. She's in town a fair bit. Alone, mostly. And it's easier now I'm officially single."

"Nice."

He shrugs.

"Why did you lie about it?"

"I couldn't say where I'd really been—Bryce would have flipped. Though he's ended up sus anyway. And I had bought the tickets to the play already. I figured it wouldn't hurt anyone."

"You were fighting about Amelia the other morning?"

"Yep," Timothy says chirpily. "He reckons he could tell something was going on."

"The best thing to do would have been to tell the truth."

"Well, Amelia has some decisions to make," he replies. "It's not my truth to tell."

His smug expression irks me though I'm hardly in a position to judge.

"Yeah. I guess you're just an innocent bystander in all this."

"Look, it's not ideal, I know that. But their relationship is bullshit, I swear." He has the decency to look guilty.

"All right, all right." I make it clear that I'm not interested in debating his morals. "Can anyone apart from Amelia vouch for your latest alibi?"

He thinks for a moment. "I didn't see anyone else but she ordered a fair bit of takeaway at about nine. Amelia went to the door though. And I paid for some, ah, digital entertainment a bit later. You should be able to see it on my corporate credit card."

Chapter Seventy-two

Friday, January 1, 9:04 p.m.

The house is silent and I immediately feel uneasy. Ever since Ben was taken I find myself uncharacteristically gravitating toward the chatter of people and the hum of machinery. Silence equals danger.

I walk into the spotless kitchen. Ben's toys are stacked neatly in the corner. Our bedroom is clean too, and the globe above my dresser that blew in October is finally fixed. I race into Ben's room and find him sleeping soundly, his lips making a soft whistling sound. I find Scott on the back patio, sitting on the end of the sun lounge drinking a beer and looking out past the back fence.

"Hey," I say. The night air feels harsh between us, and a haze of self-consciousness wraps around me as if we have an audience. I will say the wrong thing: I already know this.

"Hey." It's as if he should be smoking. His simmering anger would suit the tangibility of a cigarette. "You're late again," he says flatly.

"Scott, I'm working a murder investigation."

"Yes. I know. Annoying that people keep dying, huh?"

"What the fuck is that supposed to mean? You think I *like* this? Think I like trawling through photos of dead abused people? That I like mixing with the darkest form of human life?"

Scott laughs, an unfamiliar nastiness in the sound. "Yes, that's exactly what I think."

"Well." I stare past the fence too, wishing I could walk out the back gate and run. Keep running. Running until I have scratches all over my body and my chest explodes. Running past the point of being able to run any further.

"Well what? You know I'm right, Gemma. And you know what? I'm done."

He buries his face in his hands. It's comical, a big teddy bear of a man with his head in his big hands, except that it's not funny because he's the father of my little boy and I don't know what this means for our future.

"What do you mean, *done*?"

"I'm done with this. With us. It's not good. You and me. It's broken and I let you break it."

I feel oddly vacant but find myself saying, "Scott, come on. You can't just dump this on me. This Ryan case, it's made me a bit crazy, I get that, but it will be over soon. One way or another. Maybe we can go away or something. Take Ben?"

He looks at me then and it's as if he's trying to see past me. I almost look behind me to see if there is someone there.

"Gemma, you just don't even see it, do you? You don't see it. There's always something. You're never different. And it fucking sucks because I love you. But you don't see that either. You're busy trying to find what you need anywhere but here. Don't you think I know that?" He hunches over as if he's about to cry but he's empty. I've made him empty.

"I love Ben," I say, because it is the only true thing I know.

"Yes." He looks at me and only the two of us can know the feeling of loving that little boy. "I know you love Ben. It's the best thing about you. I have to remind myself that you can love and Ben is the proof of that. But it's not enough, Gemma. It's not enough for me." He rolls the beer bottle between his hands. "I want more children. Maybe lots more. I want someone who wants to be with me. Someone who makes time for me. I want that person to be you." His eyes burn into mine and I lean back against the house. "But it can't be you, can it?"

I breathe in through my nose and out through my mouth. Breathe. Think.

Warm air washes over us. The hoot of an owl. Bugs smacking against the outside light. "I don't know," I say finally.

"Yeah." Scott kicks the deck as he stands up. "Well, the thing is, Gem, that just isn't good enough for me anymore."

Chapter Seventy-three

Saturday, January 2, 9:17 a.m.

Everything is on hold. When I look around the station, things pause for a moment before abruptly jerking back to life. I barely slept last night, tossing and turning for hours, until in the end I took myself into the lounge room and shuffled through Rosalind's case files again, as if they were cards in a deck. I feel inexplicably anxious about seeing Rosalind's play tonight. I'm almost convinced that she will deliver me a message from beyond the grave. Wired, I push my hair behind my ears and return to my pile of paperwork, trying to focus. The thought of waking up tomorrow and the answers still being on the loose is maddening.

Jonesy has briefed Matthews and me on our first job together, a cold case that has a fresh lead. Matthews and I are polite, careful, and I get the feeling that he will do his best to make this thing work between us. However, the gaping hole that was Felix is so big that I'm constantly worried I'm going to slip into it and won't be able to climb out.

At our late, informal check-in, Felix tells our dwindling group about confronting Nicholson regarding his relationship with Izzy. "He admitted he's seeing her, said it was a recent thing. Said he would have told us but that he didn't think she wanted anyone to know yet. He added that it's too new to be a big deal."

Felix says Nicholson claimed to have no knowledge about Izzy's reported sighting of Rosalind and Rodney at the school, and said that if it were true it would concern him greatly. He'd told her nothing about his suspected paternity.

"So this thing between them is legitimate? They seem a pretty unlikely pair, don't they?" Jonesy can't seem to fathom how a "looker" like Izzy would be attracted to Nicholson. Possibly he simply wants to know his secret.

"I think I've caused some trouble in paradise, but I believe they are genuinely a budding couple." Felix laughs and I keep my eyes on my hands. "I think the only reason Izzy didn't mention what she thought she saw to Nicholson is that she didn't want to upset him. Plus, she wasn't certain it was Rodney. She probably figures that Nicholson would have been obliged to follow it up and she knows how fond he was of Rosalind. She just doesn't know why."

"Well, it was a great lead anyway, Woodstock," says Jonesy generously. "I really thought we might be on to something with those two. I'd still keep an eye on her," he says to Felix, "seeing as she's the only one who ties Ms. Ryan and the boy together. What else?"

"Nothing new, sir," I say. "We're going to the play tonight in case something turns up. We have nothing solid on Timothy Ryan. Amelia Posen has confirmed he was at her place until around ten forty-five that night and he still claims he went straight home. As far as we can work out he's telling the truth—the home security camera shows him arriving at ten to eleven. Takeaway for two ordered and porn downloaded onto Amelia's wi-fi, purchased with Timothy's corporate credit card. It's not directly linked to him so we never ran it through the system. His blissfully ignorant brother is still claiming he thinks he heard him come in at about eleven while he was on the phone to Amelia, who did call him just after Timothy claims to have left her place. I think he's a shitty person but probably not a murderer."

"It's like *Days of Our* bloody *Lives*. Okay, well, I guess we play the waiting game. I know I don't need to tell you that we've got one more week on this thing before I'm going to need to downgrade it again. Woodstock, you're already briefed on the cold case, and McKinnon, I need you across something else from tomorrow as well."

"Yes, sir."

"Right. And you're both going tonight?"

We nod again.

"Meet me there just before eight?" Felix asks, trying to catch my eye.

"Sure," I reply, without looking at him.

Chapter Seventy-four

then

No one is home at Gemma's. Ned's car isn't in the driveway and no one answers the doorbell so Jacob cuts through the bushland at the back of the house and opens the gate to look into the yard—Gemma sits out here sometimes—but it's empty. He feels desperate. He just wants to find her. Talk to her. Touch her. Nothing has ever felt so important.

After ending things with Rosalind last night Jacob woke up with a strange sense of clarity. The fog that had wrapped itself around his head for the past few months has lifted a little but it's threatening to drop again. A brutal headache pounds through his skull as the seconds tick by. He needs to find Gemma. Needs to try to explain to her why he pushed her away. He's made such a mess. He doesn't know what is wrong with him.

He can't fit all the thoughts in his head.

His pulse races constantly.

He is so tired.

The emptiness is closing in again.

He slept in this morning, which almost never happens. His mother was already in the kitchen cleaning. Cleaning, even though Rodney was still sitting at the table eating cereal. She's always cleaning. Always scrubbing. The skin on her hands worn and gray. She asked him what he was doing today. She always wants to know what he's doing. He hasn't even told her about breaking up with Gemma. Never told her about Rosalind. He can't imagine trying to explain it all. His head is all over the place. Even as he's doing things, they don't make sense.

But Gemma makes sense.

He goes to the school, to the park, to the shopping center. She's not working at the burger shack. Not in the food court. She's nowhere. He lights a cigarette and sits against a phone booth, backpack between his legs. The smoke enters and exits his lungs, mixing with the air and disappearing into nothing. He thinks about what he wants to say to her. But he needs to hurry: the darkness is coming back.

And then he sees her. She appears right in front of him; her arms are around Fox. She's laughing. Jacob shuffles around to the other side of the booth and peers out, transfixed as they link arms. She looks happy. Happier than she has been in weeks. Fox kisses the side of her head, his arms still around her as they disappear into the cinema.

After half an hour Jacob goes home because he can't think where else to go.

"You okay, Jake?" His mother sticks her head into his room, her pale face pinched and worried. She is always worried.

"Yep."

She comes and sits primly on the end of his bed.

"The police called here before," she says. "They said there's been some trouble today. Something to do with a girl from school called Rosalind Ryan? There was some kind of threat made to her family. Something serious. They want to talk to you because they say you're her boyfriend, that you had some kind of argument yesterday?"

Jacob blinks. He can't seem to apply the required brain power to the scenario. His mind is full of Gemma.

"Jacob?"

"Mum, I..."

"Jacob, sweetheart, I just think that until you're clearer on next year, a girlfriend shouldn't be a priority. I've noticed that Gemma hasn't been here much lately, which I think is a good thing. But you don't want to get involved with someone else. You need to focus on your future." His mother's voice is firm.

"My future," he repeats.

"Yes. You'll get uni offers soon. You need to make sure that you're giving yourself the best chance at getting off to the right start. It's very important."

Jacob watches as the carpet pulses different shades of gray and the weave grows bigger and smaller like a beating heart.

"It's nothing, Mum. Really. We're just friends."

She gives him a look and then hands him a piece of paper. "I know you have nothing to do with it but here's the number of the policeman. You need to call him back."

"I will."

She leaves the room and Jacob lies back on his bed and stares at the ceiling. He spies a lone cobweb around the lightbulb. He tries to call Gemma but there is still no answer. She must be with Fox again. No one picks up at Rosalind's house either; there is just a strange clicking sound instead.

Rodney is watching TV in the rumpus room. "Hey," he says, without looking up.

"Hey," says Jacob.

"Did you get that letter?" Rodney asks.

"What letter?"

"Some invite, I think. It has fancy writing on it. I chucked it on your desk before. I found it in the kitchen this morning."

"Okay, thanks," he says. He sits with Rodney and watches TV for a few more minutes, but the fog is creeping back. He can't stay here. He gathers some things together. "I'm going out, Mum!" he yells from the back door.

Donna is hanging out washing and squints into the sun toward the house. "Okay, sweetheart. Did you make that call?"

"Yes," he tells her. "It was nothing."

"Good boy," she says to him.

Halfway to the lake he realizes he didn't get the letter that Rodney put on his desk, but he can't go back now. He heads to the tunnel. He feels safe there. His paints are in his backpack along with the gin he took from home. He feels like painting something for Gemma. He paints and drinks for almost three hours. Drinks and paints. Tears pour down his face. The darkness is back and it's settled on his chest. It's hard to breathe. He wishes that the tunnel would flood and wash everything away. He looks at the concrete in front of him. He's made a giant glittering diamond for Gemma, all white and silver, but it doesn't matter now, he's ruined everything. He can't see the way back. He sits in the dark, drinking. Rosalind had taken up all the space in his head and then suddenly it was like he couldn't even be around her. He puts his head in his hands. It feels weighed down and he's not sure he can lift it up again. Nothing makes sense anymore. It hasn't for ages.

All of a sudden he's outside. The gin and the soundlessness of the tunnel have made him float. He hovers over the ground. He can't feel anything anymore. He looks out across the lake and can't imagine coming here again tomorrow, or the next day. The thought of all that water just sitting there exactly the same.

Tormenting him.

He just wants it all to be over.

The desire for an end point is overwhelming.

He looks up to the tower and finally feels calm about what's going to happen next.

Chapter Seventy-five

Saturday, January 2, 7:44 p.m.

I stand in the fading light near the entrance to the school hall. The ushers are kitted out in outrageous seventies garb; sequins and glitter catch the light. There are clearly a lot of repeat viewers in the audience tonight, several people gushing about how good it is. I recognize faces: Nicholson, Izzy, Timothy Ryan, several teenagers, shop owners and the other teachers. Donna Mason. Candy Fyfe. My red dress skims my thighs and I pull my shawl tighter around my bare shoulders. I blink away stray flecks of mascara.

At home Ben watched me get ready in quiet wonder, mesmerized by my unusual routine.

"You look pretty, Mumma," he said solemnly as I kissed him good-bye.

"Have fun," said Scott, looking me up and down. "I might take Ben up to Craig and Laura's for a few days next week," he added, "but we'll talk before that. Work out a proper plan."

"Let's talk tomorrow," I replied, having no idea what I will say.

My phone shakes in my bag and I fumble to retrieve it from underneath my gun. I'm used to having pockets and a holster belt.

"Detective Woodstock."

"Hi, this is Cara."

"Sorry, who is it?"

"Cara. From the Gowran Cinema. We met last week."

"Yes. With the braids?"

"That's me," she says. "Sorry I'm calling late, I just finished my shift. New Year's is big for movies."

360

"No worries. You find anything on the tapes?"

"Yup. I've got our IT guy to zip up all the files and put them on a disc for you. He's loved it. Thinks he's on *CSI* or something."

"But he has her on tape?"

"Sure does. Alone a bunch of times but sometimes with a guy as well."

"Okay. I'll definitely need the files. Did you see the footage too?"

"Yep. Some of it."

"What does the guy look like?"

"Young. Like my age. Kinda hot. Great hair. Tall. And one of the guys that works here says he thinks he played basketball with him last year. Thinks his name is Rodney. Does that help?"

"Yes, it does," I say, hanging up. As an image of Rodney forms in my mind, Felix steps into a patch of moonlight a few meters away. Beaming ushers start ringing little bells and waving everyone toward the entrance.

I step into line. A text comes through from Jonesy informing me that George Ryan has just died.

Felix's elbow brushes mine as he shifts in his seat. He's wriggling like a child on a long car trip. I am consumed by the likelihood that Rodney was Rosalind's movie date but there's nothing I can do until the play is over. I placate myself with the fact that he will be on stage, right in front of me, the entire time. He can't escape. I tug at my dress and push my waved hair back to stop it getting caught in my lipstick.

Felix watches me. I can tell he is fascinated by my transformation too, but we are oil and water, our rhythm is gone.

"George Ryan died," I say.

"Just now?"

"A few hours ago."

"Guess the brothers won't be here then?"

Our conversation is curt, formal, and it takes all of my self-control to stop from grabbing his face and kissing him.

"I saw Timothy out the front but maybe he doesn't know yet. Or doesn't care. I don't think he and Bryce will be too upset by their father's death."

"Strange family," Felix offers.

The music peaks and the lights drop as the curtains lift.

"Aren't they all?" I say.

Rosalind's imaginary world is a masterpiece. Rodney and Maggie's passion is like a fragrance that wafts from the stage. Inner-city Sydney characters act as the chorus commentating on the doomed fate of the mismatched lovers. The Capulet parents are revered wine critics, judgmental and aloof. The Montague father is a wealthy white-collar criminal, the mother a high-class escort. The inner-city school is the scene for Ricky and his friends to bemoan their predictable middle-class futures. Jasmine's loft is her refuge from the obligation of her family's social position. The balcony scene is played out at a train station, the glamorous ball is the launch of a new wine. It is chaotic and perfect. Rodney is dazzling to watch. Gone is his shy, awkward stance; he is frenetic and bold against Maggie's measured calm. Her words perfectly cut-glass prose, his lines passionate and tumbling, as they hurtle toward their inevitable doom.

My nerves jangle and I'm breathless as I watch their tragic demise in a blood-filled spa bath. I'm so wound up that I push out of my seat just as the clapping begins.

I desperately need to get outside so I mumble to Felix, "Got to go to the bathroom. I'll see you later," and rush to the exit before he can reply.

Outside, I keep my hands on my hips and my eyes on the stars. I breathe, trying to pull the air into my lungs and simultaneously pull myself together, curbing the raging flood inside.

Rodney lied to me.

He said they'd never acted on their feelings. Never saw each other outside of school.

The possibility that he is the killer, that he smashed her perfect face, held his hands around her throat and watched her die, is making me crazy. Felix suspected him from the start. Maybe he was right all along.

Inside the curtain call is ending and I feel the rumble of seats lifting, excited talking, as the crowd prepares to pour outside.

I dart to the side of the hall near the boys' change rooms. I can hear whoops and yells. The cast is already in there. Sticking my head through the door, I am hit with the musky scent of young men.

"Hey!" I yell.

One of the boys who was in the chorus looks at me with his eyebrows raised.

"Get Rodney Mason for me. Now."

He hesitates and then nods.

I step outside and wait.

Rodney appears, slick with sweat and makeup. He's still high. He grins when he sees me. "Did you like it?"

"Rodney, you lied to me."

His face wobbles, unsure. "What?"

"You lied to me. You were seeing her. I know you were."

He steps toward me and for a minute I think he will hit me, and then suddenly he is running away from me into the night.

Chapter Seventy-six

Saturday, January 2, 10:09 p.m.

Ruby Callister sticks her chest out a little without being too obvious. She feels dowdy in her plain black gear compared to all of the performers, especially now that it's over and she has emerged from the darkness of backstage. She brushes away some cat hairs from the arms of her turtleneck. It has been such a difficult few weeks. Deciding to run the play again was the right thing to do but stressful as well. And without Ms. Ryan, Maggie Archer has sort of taken over, which is okay but kind of maddening. She is no Ms. Ryan, that's for sure. Ruby looks at Maggie now, accepting praise as if she's just won an Oscar. She remembers what Ms. Ryan said: "If you're going to go far in stage production, Ruby, you need to manage how you feel about the stars. That will be a big part of your success."

Ruby knows she was right. Anyway, it's all over now and she can start to focus on life after Smithson. She scans the crowd for her mum and dad. They are here somewhere, probably talking to someone they know.

As she's looking for her parents, Ruby notices a short, pretty woman in a red dress standing in the shadows near the boys' change rooms. It is one of the detectives working Ms. Ryan's case. Rodney Mason appears, still in his stage makeup and costume, and talks to her briefly. Then he takes off and the woman detective runs after him.

Weird, thinks Ruby. She spots her mum, who is waving at her with unnecessary excitement, her eyes wide. Ruby gives her a small wave back and starts to make her way over, just as another woman breaks away from the crowd and runs off in the same direction as Rodney and the detective in the red dress have gone.

Chapter Seventy-seven

Saturday, January 2, 10:11 p.m.

I can't see Rodney in the blackness in front of me as I run after him toward the lake. The air is hot and sticky but the smell of rain catches in my nostrils. Another storm is coming. The darkness pools around my body and part of me wishes it would carry me away. Drag me under until I'm just floating in space. I hold my arms out and push past it. Rodney's footsteps pound on the dirt and from the sound I think he is still on the main path a few meters ahead.

"Rodney! Stop!" My words come out in halves; I'm running too fast and the heat swallows them up.

The lake is to my left as I break around the bend and I catch a shimmer of water in the faint moonlight. I follow the steady beat of his stride, ducking thin branches that reach out across the path. Stones roll beneath my shoes and I land heavily on my left ankle, pain shooting up my leg. I run on. Rodney's shadowy form appears briefly ahead of me on a bend and cuts to the right. I know that he is going to the tower. I knew the moment we left the school. Fear rises into my mouth and the déjà vu almost breaks me in two. The same feeling that I used to get from my dream about Jacob washes through me and I see his broken body fresh in my mind's eye. Vomit surges up from my stomach and I swallow it down and keep running.

"Rodney! Please. No." I'm nearly crying. But now it's Jacob running away from me, not Rodney. The moon strobes white light as I pass through a thick patch of trees. I picture Jacob bringing a rock hard down against her skull. See Rodney's hands around her neck, catch the madness in his eyes. A sob breaks from my throat as I gulp in the warm night. "Please stop," I huff through tears.

His feet hit the wooden base of the tower, his footsteps turning into a sharp staccato as he starts up the stairs. I can't follow him there and yet my right foot is on the first step and my left is moving to the second. I lock my jaw and shut it all out. Focus on my legs, on climbing. Higher. Higher. I round the first level and glance down to where the moon reaches out across the water, making a white path across the lake. This is it, I suppose. Of course it all ends here.

I slow as I come to the top level. A sharp stitch stings my side. Rodney's breathing tells me he is in the corner behind me and I turn and step backward to face him.

"Rodney, please. Talk to me."

The shadows make it look as if parts of his face are missing. A shake of his head and he is all Jacob. He is crying, his smooth face slick with tears. "I didn't do it," he whispers.

I nod, trying to slow my breathing. "Okay. Then tell me what you know. Tell me the truth."

He gulps and nods. "I was supposed to meet her that night but when I got here she was already dead."

He's an actor, I remind myself, *I need to assume this is an elaborate lie.* "I'm listening."

He paces in a small circle. He makes a crying sound but when I look at him his face is still. He claws at his eyes.

"So you did see her that night?"

"Yes."

"You planned to meet?"

"Yes. We were going to meet after the play and then go back to her place. She was excited about it. She said she knew I'd be amazing. We were going to celebrate."

"So what happened?"

He steps back into the shadows. His voice floats out of the black. "I don't know." A small sharp sob. "She left and I got caught up. Everyone wanted to talk to me. It took me ages to get away."

"What time were you supposed to meet her?" I say.

"Just before ten-thirty."

"Where?"

"At the bench near the playground."

"What time did you get there?"

"Maybe quarter to eleven. She wasn't there." He's crying again.

"What did you do?"

"I tried to call her but she didn't answer. Then I just walked around a bit."

"Did you think she had changed her mind?"

"I didn't know. I wasn't worried at first, but then I just didn't know. She was the one who wanted to meet up."

"Were you angry at her?" I ask.

"No. Just worried. I wanted to see her."

"Okay. Then what happened?"

His voice is shaking. "I walked around the bend and came up to the tower. I like it up here. I was just thinking, I guess. And then I decided to leave, head to Jamie's or go home. I walked down near the lake and that's when I saw her. She was in the water. Right near the edge. Floating." He sobs and the sound is painful. "She was already dead. Someone had killed her. I could see blood on her head."

I watch him for a moment. "Then what did you do?"

Still crying, he wipes his eyes as he says, "I didn't want to leave her. I wasn't scared. I…it felt like nothing mattered anymore. I didn't know what to do."

My throat twists. "Did you touch her?"

"Yes," he whispers. "I held her hand. I tried to pull her hair away from her face. And I had flowers—someone gave them to me after the play and I'd kept them for her. I put them on her. She looked so beautiful."

"Rodney," I say softly, urging him to keep talking.

"After that I sort of sat with her a while and then…I just left. I left her here. I went back through to the school across the oval and went to Jamie's. I didn't know where else to go. I didn't want to be alone but I was pretty messed up. I drank a lot. I didn't say anything to anyone." His back is against the wooden panels, his head in his hands.

He is still crying and I don't think this emotion has been summoned. It's out of control, sloppy.

"I loved her so much. I don't know what to do anymore. I don't care about anything."

I take a step toward him. "Rodney, this is important. Did you take any of her things? Her clothing?"

He blinks up at me, wide-eyed. "No. I didn't, I swear. When I found her, her skirt was, like, pulled up, like someone had…done something. I tried to pull it down."

I can see the scene: Rodney finding Rosalind dead. His loving attempt at a watery grave. The flowers floating around her as she looked up at the stars. Is it too neat? It's certainly very convenient, him finding her already dead. I remember the little boy giggling into a pillow as Jacob kissed me on the couch. But then I think about the moment in the car the other morning, him stroking my hand. The sudden roughness.

I don't know him at all.

"Why didn't you tell anyone, Rodney? If she was already dead when you found her, you could have called the police."

"I knew that I would have to explain everything. About us being together. She didn't want that. She didn't want anyone knowing. I didn't want to have to explain why I was here."

I am suddenly so incredibly tired I'm worried my legs will give way. "Rodney, I need you to come with me. It's important that you tell me all this again at the station. We need to figure this all out properly. Go through everything. Do you think you can do that?"

"Will I be in trouble?"

I avoid his question. "Come on, Rodney. Let's go. You know we have to do this."

I step toward him. There is a sound behind me. A scraping sound. An animal?

The moonlight flickers as the gums wave in the breeze. Footsteps. I swing around. Or is it Rodney? I'm dizzy. Sick. Something about this place is poisoning me.

Someone else is here.

Suddenly the night explodes around me. Stars splinter across my vision. I fall hard onto the ground and feel a sharp yank on my waist. Someone is taking my bag. My gun! Panicked, I kick my legs frantically as I scramble backward into a dark corner, breathing heavily. I feel a trickle of wetness snake past my ear. Blood.

"Don't move," says a husky voice.

I feel Rodney falter to my left but I can't locate him in the darkness. He must be in the other corner.

Donna Mason steps into the moonlight. Her short hair is loose and bunches around her face. Her forehead is all lines, her stare is flat and hard. My gun shakes in her hands, a perfectly round black eye staring straight at me.

"I won't let you take him."

Rodney's breathing is ragged. "Mum?"

She ignores him.

My thoughts are flying, the pain is impossible. "Donna, I—"

She cuts me off. "You should have left it alone. She was nothing."

"Mum!" There is terror in Rodney's voice now.

I lean my head against the wooden wall, trying to keep it upright. "Donna, it's okay. Come on, let's get down from here. Talk about this properly."

"No. No more talking. I just want my son." Her jaw wobbles wildly. "We'll leave. Tonight. Get out of this place. We should have left years ago."

Instantly I know that she was the one who took Ben. She's lost her mind. "Donna, what happened? Tell me."

She shakes her head, and I see a flurry of muscles contracting all over her face. "She was trying to take my son away from me. Again!"

"Mum, *what did you do*?" Rodney sounds like a scared little boy.

"Be quiet, Rodney."

"Donna, what happened?" I press, feeling the life flow out of me. I'm trying to work out what to do but I can barely retain a single thought.

"She wouldn't leave us alone. First my Jacob, then my baby. She was pure evil."

The wind picks up. Moonlight turns to confetti, scattering everywhere.

"You found out about her and Rodney," I say.

Donna stamps her foot and I feel the thud underneath us. "She tricked him into wanting to run away with her! She was trying to take him away from me."

"Okay, okay. Just tell me what happened. I know you went to the play."

"Afterward, I saw her looking at her phone and I knew she was waiting for him to call her. *My* son. I couldn't bear it anymore. I saw her go to leave and I followed her around the side of the library and said I needed to talk to her. Told her to come with me or I would tell everyone everything. I said that Rodney had a diary, that I would show the police. That I would destroy her. That terrified her. She knew what she was doing was wrong. She was so worried about her precious reputation.

"We came to the lake right near where my Jacob died. She wouldn't listen to me. The stupid bitch wouldn't hear a word about what she did to Jacob and said she didn't know anything about sending him a letter. But I saw it with my own eyes! I read it! She broke my son's heart with that note and it made him crazy. He was fine before he got messed up with her. But she kept saying she didn't know anything about it. She said what happened wasn't her fault and that *he'd* broken *her* heart."

Donna's mouth twists into an awful sneer. "Broken *her* heart. How *dare* she."

My own heart thumps alarmingly. I look back at the gun and consider leaping at her to grab it but I'm too far away. Too weak. Rodney watches his mother as if in a trance.

"Then what happened?" I whisper.

The wind lifts the trees and specks of moonlight dance on her face.

"She said she loved Rodney. That it was real. That he wanted to be with her. That he loved her. That they wanted to have a new life away from Smithson. That once he was eighteen they could do what they liked. She was so smug, so sure of herself. I couldn't stand it."

"Donna, did you hit her?"

Donna's left hand clenches into a fist and the resolve on her face crumbles. "She tried to step around me to leave. I pushed her backward and she laughed at me and said she was going to meet Rodney, and that there was nothing I could do about it. That he was almost an adult and I had to accept it. *Her*, lecturing me on *my* son. She pushed past me and I just bent down and grabbed a rock and I...I..." Donna's voice cracks roughly. "I didn't mean to hurt her but I knew Rodney was coming and she was screaming and I hit her again and sort of grabbed her throat. I just wanted her to be quiet. To stop screaming. To go away."

Donna keeps the gun trained on me as thick lines of tears glint on her hollow cheeks. "She was going to take away everything I have. I just wanted her gone."

My eyes are starting to close. I shift a little, trying to jolt myself awake. I don't have much time. "Donna. Did you touch her after she was on the ground?"

Her jaw is clenching continuously and her arms holding the gun are shaking. "I didn't know what to do. I wanted to make it look like someone had...attacked her, so I ripped her skirt, pulled up her clothes and took her underwear. It wasn't *real*." She starts to cry again. "It didn't matter to her anymore. I just wanted it all to go away." The gun is still on me but she looks at Rodney, pleading.

"Did you put her into the water?"

"I just thought it would be better. She was already dead! I thought maybe the police would think she hit her head and drowned or was raped or something. I wasn't thinking. No one would know what happened and Rodney could forget about her. We'd be left alone."

My thoughts are still scrambled. "Donna, please, I can help you—and Rodney. But we need to go. We need to get Rodney to a safe place."

"No." She shakes her head manically. "I won't let you take my son."

I think about Ben and feel limp. I'm fading. "Come on, Donna," I whisper.

"You'll take him away from me."

"Donna, a woman is dead. You took my son. We need to make things right."

Donna's eyes flare. "I just wanted you to leave us alone. I thought that if you were scared of losing your son then you'd drop everything else. But you didn't! You're all obsessed with her. Obsessed with helping *her*. No one can see what she did! She tricked my sons. She was evil." Her voice drops. "I would never have hurt him. I was always going to bring him back to you. He's beautiful, your little boy. Just like my boys at that age." She's crying in earnest now, the gun pointing downward. Rodney is crying too, his noisy sobs mingling with hers.

I see writing everywhere. Pen nibs form words across the night, looping letters curl into my thoughts. The words are rolling up, faster and faster, like someone has left their finger on the down arrow. My eyes try to fix on what they say. I push my hands onto the ground and slowly pull myself onto my feet. The world tips sideways. "Donna, I…" I teeter on the edge of a confession, try to think of a way to explain my foolish teenage actions. But what good would that do the universe right now? "I need you to come with me," I say instead.

"No." The gun is back on me again.

"Please. There's no better way that this can end." I take an unsteady step toward her.

An anguished sob rips from her body. Her nostrils flare and her fingers tighten around the gun. Rodney screams at her to stop.

A noise explodes above us. Something falls from the sky and lands at Donna's feet. She recoils as I pounce, the last of my energy surging through me. The gun glints intermittently in the darkness. Her eyes are icy madness. Rodney is on his feet too and I see Jacob standing next to him as I jump at her again. I clasp her bony frame, pushing her to one side. A shot rings out, and then another, and I land heavily and smack my head hard against the wood of the tower.

The cries of a wild animal fill my ears. Pain charges through my soul.

I hear another voice.

More screaming.

A face of soft dark velvet leans over me and then disappears. Someone is moving me, stroking my forehead, saying things I can't seem to get a hold of. I let my head roll back and I see the moon, a giant glowing circle unmoving in the sky, and still there is the screaming, but then everything turns to red and the entire world seeps away.

Chapter Seventy-eight

I am curled in a ball on the slope of grass between the school and the oval. I want to go to the lake but I can't seem to make my legs walk there. This spot seems like a good compromise. Jacob's been dead for almost two weeks. I cannot comprehend not seeing him again. Every time I think about it, everything starts to dim as if the world is a TV screen turning off, so I spend most of the time trying not to think about it. Trying to do nothing and feel nothing. It is a bizarre existence, simply trying not to live. I stroke the grass. I wish I could fall asleep again; it's the only thing that makes the pain stop.

For a few moments I think I am drifting toward the freedom of sleep and then I hear a cracking sound.

I snap my head up, uneasy.

"Hello." Rosalind Ryan stands on the path about five meters from me. I think that she might be a hallucination. She reminds me of a deer, her large brown eyes solemn.

I try to remember the last time I saw her. Exams? With Jacob at the shops? At his memorial? Dead in the lake? In my murky, messy dreams?

"He loved you, you know." The only sound is her voice, there is nothing else.

I don't know where we are. Nothing looks familiar now.

What is this place?

I barely move as I keep watching her.

She looks older now. Sad and worn. She tugs at her lip with her teeth. Shuffles her feet.

I've never seen her look nervous before.

"I really cared about him. I want you to know that." Her hair flows down past her shoulders. Her white dress billows in the breeze.

I look at her for a moment longer before I close my eyes and roll the other way.

after

I hung in a place between light and shade. Officially, I was in a coma but I've come to think of those peaceful days as my time out. I needed to decide that I wanted to be part of the world. I had to choose life.

I woke after almost exactly four days, late at night, the glow of hospital machines welcoming me back. Scott had just left, the staff told me. He'd been in there almost the entire time. Sometimes with Ben, sometimes with my dad. He'd held my hand, stroked my head and told me that everything was going to be all right.

The largest bunch of flowers on the small shelf near my window was from Felix. The card was an apology of sorts and a final good-bye. He's transferring to a city squad in March, moving his whole family. Getting away from me. Jonesy's doing, I'm sure. I don't know what we ever really had, if anything, but he's part of my story now and I need to believe that being with him meant something. It was bigger than us, I think. Perhaps I needed him in my life so that I could see what I had right in front of me all along, and maybe it was the same for him. Or maybe he just used me. Maybe it will all become clear some day.

Six days after Donna Mason accidentally shot her own son, and two days after I returned to the world, I told Jonesy everything. How I'd set everything in motion. He listened, seated in the chair next to my hospital bed, silent but nodding occasionally, his bloodshot eyes fixed steadily on mine.

"You were a kid, Woodstock," was all he offered. "I think it's all best left alone. It was a long time ago. It changes nothing for me. You're still one of my best. You just need some time to get better. Find your feet and get back on track."

Find my feet. Get back on track, I thought. *Yes. I need to work out where my feet are and which way the track is.*

When I was floating in the darkness I dreamed of Jacob. His little-boy face. His hands on my body. His mouth on mine. He is embroidered into my being, woven into my core and pulses through my veins. Frozen between child and man, he is trapped in a place that protects him from shortcomings and the passage of time. Blocking him out has served me no purpose; I need to let him breathe into my life, swirl around from time to time, and trust that he'll know his place.

John Nicholson was Rosalind's father. And Rosalind's baby had been Rodney's. If Donna Mason is telling the truth, then she killed her own grandchild as well as Rosalind Ryan that night. I will never forget the sound she made on the tower when she thought she'd killed Rodney. It will ring in my consciousness for eternity.

Rodney is here in the hospital too. Donna shot him in the stomach but he will live.

Smithson is divided in two: half believe that Donna is covering for Rodney, the real killer, and the other half lean over steaming coffees, eyes huge, claiming that Donna killed Rosalind to protect her only son. I have not seen Donna or Rodney Mason since the shooting. I can't. They can't be part of the world that I'm trying to live in now. But I also can't seem to summon any anger for what Donna did. Her existence is devoid of light now. Rodney may never forgive her, and that seems punishment enough.

"You and I are the only ones that heard her that night," says Candy, her bright red lips moving so fast I feel dizzy. "And Rodney, of course." She acknowledges his presence with a flip of her hand. She paces at the end of my hospital bed like a puma, her dark skin offset by a tight white dress. "She was out of her mind at the thought of losing him. There is no doubt in my mind that she did it."

Candy saw me leave the school and chase Rodney, then saw Donna follow us and trailed her to the tower, watching as she picked up a rock and crouched on the stairs. Candy heard Donna attack me and take my gun. She texted for help and flicked on her audio recorder to capture everything. She threw her shoe at the critical moment and cradled my broken body afterward, holding her lightweight jacket hard against my wound to stop the bleeding as Donna howled at the moon, clinging to her bleeding son.

"I thought you were a goner," Candy tells me sunnily, but I know she was terrified.

One way or another I probably owe my life to her.

"I was scared, I have to admit." She leans closer. "And you are *never* allowed to tell anyone that my recorder didn't work. Worst moment of my career, I swear."

I can only laugh. "Same," I tell her.

We are tentative friends now, bound by the tragedy we witnessed. I admit I look forward to her visits. She still makes me roll my eyes but she also makes me laugh and that can only be a good thing.

I have an impressive scar that will be with me until the day I die. The bullet entered my flesh just below my collarbone and exited clean out the other side. I lost a lot of blood, but thanks to Candy I will be fine. I trace along the bandage with my fingers as I fall asleep, staring at the mountain of flowers I've been sent. So many roses.

Rosalind remains a mystery to me. So many contradictions. Alive now only in my memories. Anna is sure that she was as close to a psychopath as we will ever see in Smithson.

"A manipulative bitch," she says cheerily, bringing me yet more flowers to look at from my hospital bed. I suppose Anna is probably right. I can see how dangerous Rosalind was. She used people, chewed them up and spat them out, looking for something, but never finding it. She continues to float in front of me, just beyond reach. My eyes, which always sought her out at school, now roam around the corners of my brain, still fixed on her: remembering things, turning them over.

Of course, if I'm honest with myself, I used her too. The thought of us being more alike than different scares me most of all.

Three weeks after the night on the tower, I go home and relearn how to do my life. I let the basic things make me strong again. I cook dinner, I read in the sun, I play with Ben. I can't get enough of him: his tiny body, his heart-shaped face, his endless questions. Scott and I talk, cautiously at first and then with more confidence, making plans. I will return to work—it's part of who I am—but it will be different this time. We will try to do it together. I vow to keep no secrets from him. I tell him about Jacob, about Rosalind, all of it.

Felix hovers between us but I push him aside: my final secret. Only time will tell if I can keep him buried in my past.

Five weeks after the shooting I visit Jacob's grave. The sweet smell of a dying summer rolls across the hill. Bees fly low around the headstones, flitting over the recently turned earth, before settling on their chosen flowers. Rosalind is buried in the Ryan plot on the other side of the hill near the rose garden, right next to the grave of George Ryan. I try not to think about her. I need to row my boat toward calm waters. I pull tails of weeds from the concrete cracks on Jacob's headstone and smooth my fingers over the chiseled letters, laying my carefully picked bunch of wildflowers across the top.

I breathe in the fresh air and read his name over and over.

I gently run my fingers across my scar as I remember him. Remember how much he loved me.

I sit down on the soft grass next to his grave and stretch my legs out in the sun. Two little sparrows near my feet weave around each other, playing an elaborate game of chase, before jumping into the air and flying into the sky.

acknowledgments

Although I wrote alone, I have quite a few people to thank for *The Dark Lake* becoming an actual book.

To Tom, for the gift of extra hours and for wrangling our small humans so I didn't have to deal with reality quite as much as usual.

To my early readers, of which there are a few, you are all excellent people. Thank you for taking the time and for caring enough to give feedback. It was incredibly important to me. My parents, Kevin and Susan, were especially helpful early readers, which appeals to my strong sense of irony, seeing as they taught me to read (and write) in the first place. I would like to thank them also for lots of general things, as well as several of the commas that appear in this book.

To Deanne Sheldon-Collins, for giving me "proper" writing advice and a much-needed confidence boost at the halfway mark.

To my amazing agent, Lyn Tranter, for responding to my pitch e-mail in the first place, and to both her and Sarah Minns for helping me to shape my story, name it and save one of the characters from an untimely death.

To all of the wonderful people at Allen & Unwin Australia, thank you so much for your passion and enthusiasm for my book.

To Dan Lazar, who has championed *The Dark Lake* in the US from the beginning.

To the entire team at Grand Central, but specifically, Wes Miller, Deb Futter, Ben Sevier, Michael Pietsch, Brian McLendon, Beth DeGuzman, Karen Kosztolnyik, Andy Dodds, Jordan Rubenstein, Matthew Ballast and Yasmin Mathew. Thank you for being so amazing to work with and for introducing the book to the US market with such aplomb. Gemma hitting American shores so spectacularly is more than I could have ever dreamed of.

I would also like to thank the stranger on the plane who read sections of my draft during a long flight and who, when I noticed, told me that it was "quite good" and then begged me to tell her what happened next. Your unprompted interest was strangely motivating.

And, to the difficult-to-define but reliably awesome New York City, the magical place in which I wrote a decent chunk of this book and where I decided once and for all that I would finish it and get it published (so presumptuous!)—thank you for the epiphany.

Writing a book really is such a ridiculous thing to do. So ridiculous that I might just go and do it all over again.

Sarah Bailey was born in Melbourne, Australia, where she has lived all her life and resides with her two young sons. She has a degree in journalism and works in advertising. She is currently a partner at the creative agency Mr. Smith. THE DARK LAKE is her first novel.